# What the critics say about Formula One

"It's bloody good! Bob Judd has a deep knowledge and under-standing of the sport. And he has used it to tell the story of the excitement and the politics of motor racing at the highest level. I couldn't put it down."

Murray Walker. BBC TV

I thoroughly enjoyed its mixing fact and fiction and drama with reality. *Formula One* is a Dick Francis on wheels."

Jackie Stewart
*Three time World Champion*

"What a good novel. Judd's car-racing knowledge is superbly in-tegrated into this passionately told story . . . a perfect read"

Tom Keneally
*Booker Prize winning author of* Schindler's Ark

"Racing cars . . . sex . . . lovely turns of phrase, and a feel, a gloss, a surface tension that, at its best, captures what Grand Prix Racing is really about."

CAR magazine

Judd toured the world with the top motor racing teams to research this tale of drugs, murder and high octane sex. It races along to the chequered flag.

TODAY

The jet setting scenario of the Grand Prix world and exciting exotic locations . . . Bob Judd has done a great deal of research with the result that, even those who have no interest in the sport will race through the pages until the end.

MOTOR SPORT

This is a romp through the world of FI, with all the necessary death, sex, drugs and rock-and-roll – a novel in the classic Dick Francis whodunnit style with extra horsepower.

Where the book stands out is that it is not only well researched, but it is an accurate account of how Grand Prix racing works. 'I couldn't put it down.'

AUTOSPORT

Bob Judd's fast moving glossy yarn about the world of racing drivers, their sponsors, mechanics and groupies. This is a well made, fizzy, often tongue in cheek piece of work.

Hampstead & Highgate Gazette

Bob Judd

# FORMULA ONE

**Pan Books**
London, Sydney and Auckland

First published 1989 by Sidgwick & Jackson Ltd
This edition published 1990 by Pan Books Ltd
Cavaye Place, London SW10 9PG

9 8 7 6 5 4

© Bob Judd 1989

ISBN 0 330 31179 4

Printed in England by Clays Ltd, St Ives plc

To Tom Rayfield
who gave me the idea.

*"If you get a chance, take it."*
                    *Fay Vincent*

# PART ONE

# CHAPTER ONE

See the pretty car flying through the air. So tantalizing that slow and sexy roll. This is the long, silent moment they will always remember, the car airborne over the track, rolling. Bright colours in the bright blue sky. An existential moment, really. He still has a chance.

At the first impact the world returned to its normal speed and sound. Michel's car had been crawling across the surface of the earth at over 170 miles an hour when it ran wide at the exit of the Nagamichi curve and touched wheels with Takahashi's Brabham. In the blink of an eye, Michel Fabrot was thirty feet in the air.

A sharp intake of breath from the crowd. Time and breathing stopped while the car flew through the harmless sky.

Then it came back to earth with a crack and a cacophony that went on and on as the car ripped open its stomach, performing a noisy public *sepuku*, tearing itself into separate jagged pieces over the next 150 yards.

Picture yourself lying nearly horizontal with your arms and legs stretched out in front of you and 700 horsepower behind your neck. The thin shell that encases your body sprouts a spiderweb suspension so sensitive you feel as if you were blessed with four wheels instead of two hands and two feet. Through each wheel you feel the rise and fall of control, balance, and power.

Weighing less than a little Honda Civic, this elegant projectile has enough power to cruise the streets at 270 miles an hour, were it not for nearly three tons of downforce generated by the wings pushing the car down onto the track. Braking, cornering and accelerating, your body doubles and triples in weight. Centrifugal force drags your feet off the pedals.

The punters think that Formula One is about courage. They're misinformed.

Of course courage counts. You have to be brave to put your head in the lion's mouth on those pleasant summer Sunday afternoons. But courage doesn't count for much. The green verges of racetracks are littered with the ghosts of brave, forgotten men. What drives Formula One, and what counts, is power.

Michel's crash was the pop of a toy balloon compared to the power behind Formula One. Behind the million-dollar racing cars, and the multimillionaires who drive them, are the billions of the biggest corporations in the world. (What car do you drive? What petrol do you burn? What tyres? What brand do you smoke, wear, and splash on your face in the morning?) This is where money talks and bullshit walks. Win on Sunday. Sell on Monday.

On this Sunday afternoon at the Suzuka circuit in Japan, the noise of a Formula One racing car coming back to earth was loud enough to silence the hundred thousand spectators.

The car landed on all four wheels at once, so the first sound was of four racing tyres exploding on impact. Overlapped with the sound of the suspension ripping out of the carbon fibre tub, the shattering of fibreglass and bone, the ringing of alloy metal as the engine block departed off on its own lolloping path, and the smash of a man being turned to soup inside an unforgiving, lightweight tub as it bounded merrily along.

The ripping and tearing and smashing and grinding stopped. The red flags came out and the other Formula One cars out on the track pulled over and stopped, or trundled back sheepishly into the pits. The crowd was as sickened and as fascinated as I was. Such a shame, the waste of effort, money, machinery, and life. There was so much mess to clean up.

My view from the broadcast booth was as good as anybody's. Michel had flown right past me. But the sounds of the news business, the hum of the electronics and the glass cage isolate you from what's happening so it just didn't seem real.

Besides, there was a microphone in front of me and a TV camera pointed at my face. I had to say something. I did what any intelligent thirty-year-old former racing driver would have done in my place. I wept.

Here's to all the bright and hopeful boys and girls who cling to the racetrack fences, their fingers gripping the steel mesh. They dream that one day they too will be strapped into the wild beasts with wheels, put their foot down, pedal to the metal, and accelerate into the winner's circle, where the pop stars are and the private jet waits patiently on the tarmac, and the beautiful people beg to come near, to touch the brave heroes and give them wealth and fame and glory and all the soft open thighs that they can stand. And here's to all those same hopeful, tense and tight-lipped children, pushing their broken, second-hand Formula Fords back to the pits, on their way to the glorious prizes of Formula One. For they shall be scattered like the leaves at the side of the road.

Michel Fabrot was my replacement, my protégé, and my friend. He had been driving 'my' car.

When I first met Michel earlier that year he was just a kid, twenty-two or twenty-three, making a name for himself in Formula 3000, the three-litre, single-seater stepping stone to Formula One. He had the slight, agile build of a dancer. But it was his eyes you remembered. He had a small face with those huge, light-blue eyes, as wide open and astonished as a baby's. Sooner or later, every racing driver wakes up one morning, looks into the mirror and sees a narrow-eyed squint glaring back at him. It comes from staring into blind 150-mph corners with the sun in your eyes, from trying to see if the boil of fog ahead of you conceals one or two or three cars in the night, and from driving a car that breaks its gearbox for the third race in a row.

But Michel hadn't yet got that narrow-eyed, suspicious look. I pictured his mild face behind the face shield and the nomex hood as he soared through the air, thirty feet off the ground. Eyes wide open, curious, wanting to see what would happen next.

The day we met was one of those drizzling March Tuesdays at Silverstone, grey as cement. For some reason team managers and the gods conspire to make every test day grim, wet and freezing cold. The temperature was around three or four Celcius, the wind was gusting out of the north and the track had shallow pools of water here and there. A pig of a day. You couldn't drive the car on the limit because at any moment, there might be a millimetre more or less water on the track and, oh fuck, your limit disappears.

But on the other hand, if you're not right up close to the limit you can't find out much. The engineers stare gloomily into their video

5

monitors and say the figures are inconclusive, could you please do a few more laps.

I was coming into the pits, having done a few more laps. The car had slewed sideways coming out of Woodcote at 160 and I didn't know if it was a sudden gust of wind, a small puddle on the left side of the track, too much throttle too soon, or the trace of oversteer we were trying to cure. Maybe it was all of that, or none of it. I was freezing cold and tired, and when I came back into the pits and saw a little figure in a shining white driving suit holding a helmet, I couldn't help smiling. Great. Let some other sucker do the grunt work.

Ken was always bringing along some rookie to let him have a go. He'd earned a reputation for discovering tomorrow's superstars. So any test day was apt to see some hotshoe kid from the boondocks standing on tiptoe with his helmet in his hand and his girlfriend sitting alone in the empty grandstand, waiting for his first drive in a Formula One car. As promised by Ken Arundel, Britain's last private entrant. Britain's Svengali of hopeful racing car drivers.

Two things separated Michel from the parade of hopeful rookies. First there was Nicole. She wasn't sitting alone in the empty grandstand, she was standing next to him. She was taller than Michel and slim and she had dark curly hair, freckles and a mouth that belonged on a much bigger, more Latin face. Her eyes that were everywhere, taking in everything, judging nothing. She walked straight over to me as I was climbing out of the car, taking my helmet off.

"'Ello, Forray," she said staring into my eyes and seeing all the dark and hidden dragons. "I am Neecky, and these, Meeshell," she said with a nod towards the short, trusting, wide-eyed boy just behind her. "He is just three, so he still learn how to tok." Then a big smile for me, drawing me into a conspiracy with the two of them, playing jokes on the world.

The other thing that separated Michel, apart from his wonderful Nicky, was that he was, from his first lap at Silverstone, a superb driver. My seat was much too big for him, so we got him another. And as we were strapping him in and adjusting the pedals and the gearshift, I told him about the track, to beware of the gusts and the puddles, and for God's sake squeeze the power on smoothly coming out of Woodcote.

6

Ken gave Michel his standard speech about not wanting to see how fast he was, but how consistent and how smooth. "We're not looking for a lap record, we're looking for a driver who is consistent enough to give us the same lap, lap after lap, so we can measure the effect of our adjustments to the car. Is that understood?" Ken liked discovering new talent. But he didn't want to loose a £250,000 car to do it. Nicky translated, and Michel smiled, knowing that, of course, the whole point of his being there was for Ken to see how fast he was. And that the only way to be fast is to be consistent and smooth.

Michel spent a few cautious laps finding out where the pedals were and which way the track went. Then, when he had his lines through the corners, his braking and shifting points, he let fly. From the far side of the course we heard the engine note screaming and wailing, rising and falling in short bursts and long crescendos. Max Ellis, Team Arundel's head designer (whose normal expression makes a gorilla look like a talk show host), looked like he was having gas pains, his big meaty face screwed up in folds around his little green eyes. His thousands of hours of sweat and pain, his baby, was being tortured by an ignorant Frog.

Ken looked as if he were standing on a spike, lifting up one foot, and putting it down, lifting up the other foot, his big frame hunched over, his shoulders rounded, his heavy black eyebrows lowered under a mass of worry lines.

And sure enough, when Michel came out of Woodcote the dark metallic-blue car started to slew sideways. And that, we thought, was it. Get ready to pick up the squashed bits. But, incredibly, Michel held the tail of the car out for a beat, then brought it back in line as he brought the power on full and soared up the main straight. On the next lap he did it exactly the same. And the next, and the next.

In the modern racing car, with the aerodynamics pushing the body of the car down on the track, you really don't want to slide. Once you start to slide the aerodynamic wings point in a slightly different direction than the way the car is headed. So gradually, or all at once, you can lose those tons of downforce which give you your grip. Now you see it. Now you don't. Hello wall, goodbye world. But Michel was out there, treating us to the terrifying picture of a little slide "to see what cause the oversteer", as Nicky explained later.

His times were two and a half seconds a lap slower than my times. And I hadn't been trying hard. But when you realise he'd never driven a Formula One car before and the track was unfamiliar and a mess . . . Don't look behind you Forrest ol' buddy, somebody's trying to pass. Right from the start his car control, his ability to put the car exactly where he wanted it, and when he wanted it there, was phenomenal.

Ken signed him on as a test driver, when his Formula 3000 schedule permitted. And I started to look forward to seeing him and Nicky at test days. Michel was like a visitor from another planet, amused at the strange habits of us earthlings. He wasn't distant or uninvolved, but his mind ticked to a different, more exact timeclock. He claimed he was just very French. But Nicky called him "Tic-Toc", because he was so damn precise about everything.

We (Veronica and I, and Nicole and Michel) shared a few days that spring before Monte Carlo at a villa I'd rented in Grasse. It was a modern architect's idea of a French country château, a twenty-room, yellow-stone manor with stone terraces overlooking formal gardens. There were mahogany floors, gothic arches in the doorways and a staff of three in the kitchen.

Nicky called it "La Maison de la Casa House". "It has these terrible pretensions," she laughed. "But it don't know who are its parents. An ugly bastard but loveable, you know?" We all loved it. In the mornings, from our bedroom windows, we could see the blue of the sea.

At the side of the house, through the French doors, there was a long, deep swimming pool in a grove of cypresses. The pool was designed to look natural, set in smooth stones and fed by a cool rushing stream. The sun shone all week and the air was filled with sage and the scents of the Grasse perfumeries, the buzz of the cicadas and the musical cascade of the stream over the rocks. Veronica and Nicky lounged nude on the warm stones by the pool.

In this paradise, this lazy place outside of time, Michel wrote the dates of purchase on the eggs in the fridge. So he would eat them in the proper sequence.

There was no way he could have been that far off line. He'd been

8

lying fifth, a lap down on Cavelli in the Ferrari in fourth, and half a lap up on Praiano in the Danielli in sixth. So he wasn't under pressure.

And yet the most precise driver in Formula One – not the fastest, but the most precise – had made a huge and sloppy miscalculation, blundered into another driver, and killed himself.

I was thinking of that, the insanity of the accident, and of Nicky's warm smile when she saw me looking at her lying nude by the pool, a smile that she was glad of our friendship and glad to be alive, a sexy woman sunning herself. And I was thinking how glad I was that I wasn't in the car and how bad that thought made me feel. And I was thinking of my two crashes, and that I had to get down to Nicky to protect her from the fruit flies, the journalists who would be buzzing around the stink of death, and the obscene mess and ooze that was Michel inside the cockpit. All of those thoughts were chasing each other around inside my skull when I realised the camera was pointing at me and I was expected to talk.

I couldn't talk.

I couldn't believe the world was continuing. I couldn't believe that while the smoke was still rising from the catastrophe, that something so puny as a video camera could be stuck in my face. That I was expected to "comment". Even the sea draws back for another wave.

Later, when I saw the tapes, I saw the tears streaming down my face. But I didn't know it then. The lens just stayed there in my face with its little red light glowing, the mindless eye of 90 million people around the world. They were impatient. Expecting.

In the distance, in the headphones, I heard the voice of the announcer, "Forrest? Forrest Evers? Can you hear me? Forrest, how does it feel to see what would have been, maybe even should have been, your car crash like that?"

How does it feel? Jesus Christ. You stupid, ignorant, insensitive, uncaring son of a bitch. I found I could talk. I told the world's favourite racing announcer to fuck himself, and cracked the lens with the back of my hand.

I have no idea how long it took me to get down to the Arundel pits and find Nicky. WBC sent me a bill for four microphones, three computer terminals and two video cameras. They said I charged

9

out of the control booth like a mad bull. I don't remember. I probably did.

Unlike most racing drivers I'm not small. I'm too tall, too wide at the shoulders, and weigh too much. Out on the track, all that extra muscle and bone has to be hauled down the straight, slowed down, dragged around corners, and speeded up again. At thirteen stone three, and six foot one, I give up a 4 or 5 horsepower handicap to the other, smaller drivers. But if you are in a rush to get out of a crowded broadcast booth, I'm the one to follow.

The Arundel pits had the confusion of an army hospital after the bombs. There was a swirling undercurrent of Japanese marshals in yellow coveralls trying to be everywhere at once and getting in everybody's way. Pieces of the car were starting to come back to the pits: a shattered wheel with the tatters of a tyre wrapped around it like a scarf, a piece of the rear wing, a steering wheel with sticky blood stains on the bent leather rim.

Max Ellis was trying to get close enough to inspect the wreckage that was building up in the Arundel pit, but three Japanese race officials in blue sports jackets with red and gold badges sewn on their breast pockets were screaming at him in Japanese. From their gestures and their anger I guessed they were telling him that, as the designer, it was his fault. Couldn't happen to a nicer guy.

Then there was the noise. The shouting of hundreds of people crammed into the pit lane, the mindless blaring of some sing-song Japanese orchestra on the Public Address loudspeakers, all punctuated with the rasp and scream of racing cars starting up, revving to clear the plugs and switching off again.

Like vultures feeding on a corpse, three TV reporters with video cameramen in their wake had managed to get through security and were taping the bits of the car that lay on the ground.

Another TV crew was trying to interview a couple of mechanics from the Arundel pit crew. But Dave and Bill were having none of it, waving them off like flies. They knew Ken Arundel would have their hide for talking to the press without his specific permission.

Over in the second Arundel pit, Maurizio Alfonso, helmet and fireproof balaclava thrown over the side, was slowly dragging his cadaverous form out of the number two Arundel car, ignored as usual. Poor old 'Alfonse'. The race would go on, but it would go on without him. Ken would withdraw his second car. So Maurizio would doubly grieve: for Michel, and for yet another unfinished race.

A slab from Stonehenge, towering above the reporters, the officials and the crew, Ken Arundel was staring off into the distance where a crane was lifting the remains of the tub of Fabrot's car back up into the sky. Japanese officials and the TV reporters clamoured for his attention. They didn't get it. The Arundel crew started to busy themselves with packing up their jacks, tyres, tools and fire extinguishers. They knew better than to interrupt him now. One or two of them looked at me, and looked away. They weren't about to forgive and forget.

I pushed my way through the crowd to Ken Arundel. A fool rushing in. "It wasn't an accident," I said.

Through all the shouting he heard my voice. But he didn't stop staring at the end of the pit lane where the midsection of Michel's car was swinging like a pendulum at the end of the crane's steel rope. "What are you saying?"

"It happened in front of me. And I saw the slow motion replay on the monitor. The car didn't brake. And Michel doesn't make mistakes."

The crane was lowering the midsection onto a flatbed truck. I could read 'Michel brot' on the side. The missing part was broken away. Maybe some fan had it as a souvenir. Arundel slowly turned to look at me from his height of six foot seven. "Could we possibly talk about this later?"

He had the patrician habit of making an order sound like he was asking you for a favour. I nodded. "I wanted to tell you before you face the press."

He looked over the far side of the infield where they were transferring Michel's remains from an ambulance to a helicopter. "I don't suppose there's any chance Michel is alive."

"No," I said quietly. "There's no chance." He wasn't even in one piece. "Where's Nicole? How is she?" I said, changing the subject.

"I think she went into the Goodyear suite to get away from the mob. I expect I'll be tied up here for some time. Will you tell her . . . please tell her . . ." His voice trailed off, watching the helicopter rise up from the ground.

11

"I'll tell her," I said, glad to be useful in some way. In fact I was glad to be talking to him. Glad he was talking to me. He could hardly have me at the top of his list of favourite people.

One of the TV reporters was pushing his microphone in front of my face. I took hold of the microphone and bent it into his face. "Just trying to do my job," he said.

I suppose he was. I suppose if I wanted to grieve in private I should have chosen another line of work. But then I wasn't a racing driver anymore. And, I supposed, after my blow up in the broadcast booth, I wasn't in that line of work either.

The helicopter was disappearing over the horizon. Ken looked down at me again. "We'd planned to leave tomorrow. But now . . . now there'll be a few things to attend to. I don't suppose you'd be free tomorrow for breakfast – if you want to talk about this?"

"Breakfast, lunch, dinner."

"There's a quiet little Japanese breakfast room in the basement of the Imperial in Tokyo. It's quite private. About eight?"

"About eight." I started to push through the crowd to look for Nicole and he called after me.

"Tell Nicky she's to stay with us."

The Japanese officials were squabbling among themselves. Some of them were saying the bits of the car shouldn't be brought back to the Arundel pits; they should be in the closed garage at the end of the pit lane, impounded, for the scrutineers and the investigation.

Well there was bound to be an investigation. And judging by the way the Japanese ran their racetrack and built their racing machinery, it would be painstaking and scientifically exact. And they would find absolutely nothing. Not if my experience was anything to go by.

I looked back at Ken. He was still staring out over the heads of the crowd to the point on the horizon where the helicopter carrying Michel's body had disappeared.

"Mr Evers? Janice Henrion, BBC. Mr Evers? Don't you think it's time we stopped this pointless slaughter? Isn't that the reason you stopped racing, because the Arundel cars are deathtraps?"

Even in my stunned state I had to notice she had green eyes, and a sharp little face under a tangled heap of honey-blonde hair. My stomach was in knots grieving for Michel. I was trying to forget

12

how relieved I was it wasn't me in 'my' car and she was knifing me with her nasty question, and I was thinking, damn, she isn't wearing a bra.

Good old brave, stalwart, loyal Forrest Evers. Show him a pair of boobs doing their helpless little wobbles, and the would-be, could-be, should-be world champion turns to mush, wagging his tail, tongue dragging on the ground. I was supposed to find Nicky. To save her from people like this. "Look," I said, "Give me a call in the Imperial Hotel tomorrow, and maybe I can talk to you then." I ended with a cheap little smile. Goddamn me.

"Are you afraid to talk?"

Ah, thank you, ma'am. Nothing like a direct hit to change your point of view. I gave her my full attention and my most sincere boyish grin. "Why don't you interview Max Ellis? He'd love to discuss deathtraps and pointless slaughter with you. That's him discussing it with a group of journalists over there." Max was howling with rage at the far side of the pit. The three Japanese officials in blue sports jackets were still blocking his way to the twisted wreckage of his beloved car, and they had been joined by the police. I turned my back on little Miss Janice and bounded up the stairs to the row of corporate headquarters, trackside.

The door to the Goodyear Suite opened up to the calm of air conditioning, the orderly voices of the British announcers, and a mild hum of conversation of forty well-dressed Goodyear executives and their guests. Outside, on the track below, the cars were reforming on the start/finish line. The race, said the announcers, would restart in twenty-five minutes.

The Goodyear guests had had canapés and champagne and lunch before the race. Now the luncheon dishes were cleared away and freshly pressed Japanese waiters were passing among the guests with fresh glasses of chilled champagne. If any of the Goodyear's guests in their soft sports jackets and casual weekend party frocks felt any distress over the violent death by their front window, they were hiding it well. But of course it's one of the social habits of the Japanese and the English share, masking tragedy with indifference.

A few noticed me, one or two came over to greet me, most had the good taste to ignore me. My public temper tantrum can't have

13

raised my stock among those whose major task it is to see that nobody rocks the corporate boat.

Nicky was seated at a small table, staring out the window. She was wearing a bright blue and white jumpsuit, a playful designer parody on the Arundel mechanics' coveralls. Poor sad clown.

Hellen Wolverton, the wife of Goodyear's UK chairman, was sitting beside her, holding her hand. Hellen is a big, tough lady of fifty with a pretty face and big brown eyes twenty years younger. She's raised three children so she knows how to play the consoling mum. I smiled pleasantly hello and sat next to Nicky, putting my hand on the back of her neck. She turned to face me.

No doubt Hellen's ample handkerchief had wiped the make-up from Nicky's face. No doubt Nicky's face had been streaked with tears. But the face I saw now wasn't crying. It was the face of a child, simple and open. The sophistication of spending the summer with the Formula One crowd was gone. I recalled that she was only a year or two out of her convent school. She looked younger.

"Thank you for coming, Forray."

"He couldn't have felt a thing."

"I think maybe me too, I feel nothing."

"It's nature's anaesthetic. For the big wounds she gives us a little breathing space before we feel the pain."

"Yes well, perhaps. But I don't think I am ready. I always know it is possible, he could crash. He could die. But never do I imagine it will happen. Maybe the clock run back. Toc-tic, we start again." She managed a little smile. "Maybe we all go back to the Maison de la Casa House."

"Maybe." I noticed the little swarm of freckles across the bridge of her nose. "I think I've had enough for one day. Shall I see if I can cadge us a lift back to the hotel?"

"OK," she said. "But you better never tell Veronica," she said with a fragile, mock seriousness.

"I'll tell Veronica," said Hellen, joining the little joke.

"You mind if I steal the company 'copter?" I asked her. "I'll send it back."

"I'm sure it's all right, Forrest. I'll tell Dave." Dave was her husband, Sir David Wolverton. He'd been the first to say how much he regretted my leaving racing, and how much richer the

14

sport would be as soon as I returned. That was when the journalists were demanding I be banned for life. If there was anything I wanted or needed . . . he'd said. I saw him over in the far corner of the room with what could have been their Japanese management, or the men who did the shopping for Nissan, Toyota and Honda. When I was driving there would have been smiles and waves, "come on over".

He met my eyes and nodded. Yes, what ever it takes. Do it.

A small helicopter makes a horrendous roar, a roar so loud it blocks out almost all your thoughts. As I watched Suzuka racetrack grow smaller below us and we flew high enough to see the surrounding dark blue of the Pacific, my mind kept looking for the link, the connection between Fabrot's crash and mine. The only one I could think of was that I had no idea why I had crashed either. Nicky's head fell against my shoulder. She was asleep.

# CHAPTER TWO

Five hundred feet beneath us, the drivers were back in their cars on the grid.

They looked puny; toy men in toy machines.

When I was on the grid before a race, surrounded by a crush of mechanics and cars, I used to block out the weather, the people, all the faces, all the pretty legs and bums in tight shorts on the pretty girls. I would concentrate on my slow breathing in and breathing out until my mind was empty and I was as relaxed as a big cat sleeping in the sun.

Racing is a mental exercise. Unless you can concentrate like a samurai or a monk you will never be quick. Divide a second into tenths, and if you can separate and identify all ten parts you can probably have fun on a race track. Divide the each tenth into ten parts, into hundredths of a second and you might make a living driving a racing car. If you can find the time inside a thousandth of a second, you might drive in Formula One.

Unless your mind is faster than the car you drive, you will always be in the wrong place at the wrong time, braking too late for the corner, turning in too soon or too late, scrabbling to find the right line. But if your mind is quick enough, you will always have plenty of time.

Time to go right up and look into the darkness at the edge, smell the stink of death, and turn back to the world with your senses quickened to the sweetness of life and the slow passing of time.

Honshu island, with the Suzuka racetrack looking like a crumpled figure of eight, shrank below us and disappeared. We had forty minutes flight to the roof of the Imperial Hotel in Tokyo. Time for my in-flight movie, the one I kept loaded in the tape deck in the back of my mind, perpetually switched on and warmed up, ready for instant replay.

It's the sixth lap of the European Grand Prix at Brands Hatch. I am on the outside of the turn at Clearways, my left wheels rabbiting on the thin strip of concrete at the edge of the track, 145 mph and accelerating hard.

Cavelli's Ferrari is two hundred yards away in first, crossing the start/finish line. Aral is six feet away in second. A blue puff out of his exhausts tells me he's just changed from fourth to fifth. The force of turning in wants to drag my helmet and my head off my shoulders. The little vibration in my left wheels stops as the left wheels come back onto the tarmac just before the concrete strip runs out. My right foot is trying to push the accelerator through the floor. The engine just ticks the electronic cut off at 11,500 rpm and I let up for fourteen thousandths of a second to snatch fifth and mash the accelerator to the floor, still six feet behind Aral.

Aral is holding me up. If I can get a tow from him, stay close enough behind him in the aerodynamic vacuum in his wake, I can get up the extra speed to pass him before Paddock Hill Bend at the end of the main straight.

On the last lap I'd made a move to pass him on the outside, on the left at the start/finish line. I didn't have the speed to pass him then, but I wanted to set him up for this lap.

Aral clips the inside of the track under the big yellow Shell sign and seven thousandths of a second later I do the same. As I shift into sixth I check my gauges (everything is just fine), and more or less at the same time (I shift my attention rather than my eyes) I look ahead to the pit wall on the right to see if there are any messages for me.

Not that I care at this point; things are going to be very busy shortly. Aral's crew is holding out a board telling him that he is in second position, a second ahead of third. I laugh because Aral has his mirrors full of me and knows I haven't been as far back as a full second for two laps. Just to drive the point home, I move a little closer to his exhaust pipes, about two and a half feet, say, two to three thousandths of a second behind him. My crew give me a thumbs up sign. Over their heads, the big electronic board registers Cavelli's speed across the start/finish line: 196 mph.

We're creeping up to almost the same speed, although with me tucked into his slipstream Aral has to haul along both cars through the atmosphere, so we'll probably only reach around 190.

Looking in my mirrors I could see a group of cars behind us back in Clearways. But nobody right behind us. Plenty of room.

At that speed there are two time zones. Inside the cockpit it's slow time. Lift your foot off the accelerator as fast as you can to stomp on the brake, and so much of the track slips by underneath you while you lift off one pedal and onto the other, you have the feeling your foot is stuck in molasses. So much landscape whizzes by while you check your wing mirrors.

While the time inside the cockpit slows down, the rest of the world has picked up speed. It's like those science fiction movies when the skyship accelerates into hyperspace and everything turns to a blurred tunnel except the one distant point on the horizon.

The car is alive. It's in its element, nervous, hunting for another direction, for a new path of its own, away from human hands. It needs a graceful, easy touch *and* all of your strength and will. Ignore it for a microsecond and it will charge off in its own mad direction. Treat it roughly and it will tear your head off.

Two and a half feet behind a Formula One car at 190 miles an hour is not the ideal place to relax. Blink once, for example, and you've driven thirty yards with your eyes shut. And even with your eyes wide open the view is mostly the backside of Aral's engine, suspension rods, exhaust pipes, and big wide black racing tyres. All bouncing, jouncing, shaking, vibrating.

Strapped to the chassis, your body hums along at 11,500 rpm with the engine, and the car bounces and skitters from the uneven surface of the track and the boils of wind coming off the car in front.

And the air is bad, full of fumes, rubber dust and shrapnel from the grit and small stones picked up by the vacuum effect of the car in front and tossed back at you by the tyres and ducts from the undertray. Lots of incentive to look for a better neighbourhood.

About thirty yards before the start/finish line I moved left like the lap before. But Aral knew I wasn't likely to try to pass on the left. The main straight at Brands isn't really straight, but a gradually decreasing radius right-hand turn. Pass on the left on the straight, and unless you are going a lot faster than the car you're passing,

18

you can easily run out of racetrack. Still, Aral moved left to block me and I made my move to the right.

No problem. Except, of course, the road disappears. After the start/finish line there's a little rise, and just over the brow, where you can't see, the track turns, bends right, and dives downhill, a great roller coaster of a turn. If you get it right.

By the time we got to the top of the crest and it was time to start braking, I was alongside Aral. Theoretically, he was right where he should be: turning in just slightly to head straight at the Shell sign, do his braking, get into fourth, reach the edge of the track and turn in to the inside of the curve. Except that's where I would be. I was on the inside, which meant I would have to go through the corner a bit slower. But I was a nose ahead so I owned the track.

Out of the corner of my eye, Aral started to drop back, braking, doing what he should do, giving me room. I kept my foot down.

Instead of braking and turning into the corner, I drove straight on, and as Aral started to turn in, I drove straight over the nose and front wings of his car, with my back wheels mashing the pretty powder-blue and silver of the front of his car into the track. Since he is at the absolute limit of adhesion, the shock and sudden loss of downforce from his front wings mean that, for a few moments, Aral has no steering, and his car begins to spin, headed for the fencing and stack of rubber tyres. I'm already ahead of him.

I see the flag and fire marshals standing behind their barrier at the outside of the turn. Two of them in red fireproof suits are ducking down, either to get out of the way of the blue and silver racing car headed towards them at 190 or reaching for their fire extinguishers. One of the flag marshals has turned away as if to look for a friend in the crowd. Another stands his ground, looking straight at me, fascinated.

Looking at him, and thinking I don't want to hit him (even though he's behind an earth and concrete barrier and safe), I finally turn into the turn. A gesture that probably saved my life. But at this speed and with only twelve yards of track left, it's not much more than a gesture. But it keeps me from hitting the barrier head on and ramming my legs past my ears. The car turns slightly and hits the barrier a glancing blow, heading downhill. Behind me, Aral is spinning, about to follow the groove I've dug into the earth bank.

Eleven and a half seconds have passed since I first entered the straight from Clearways.

The impact has torn off both my nearside wheels and suspension. I'm a spectator now with a front row view. But the show is rapidly coming to a close. My head bounces against the earth bank and my helmet fills with dirt. The friction of the car's body holds it tight against the dirt bank and the car bangs along, scraping against the earth and then along the Armco barrier until the nose digs in and the car begins to flip end over end.

But most of the energy has been spent against the earth bank and the car flips just once before sliding on its stomach back out into the middle of the track where it stops, bringing with it a pile of dirt and dust, the ooze of oil from the ruptured oil coolers and a small spreading pond of steaming coolant.

By this time, the pack of cars which has been so far behind me coming out of Clearways are screaming downhill towards me, looking for a safe way round. The marshal who had stood his ground at the corner had been quick and cool. Seeing me pass by within a few feet with Aral spinning behind me, he hadn't waited for the impact but had reached for his yellow 'danger' flag, giving the following cars a critical second and a half warning. Like me, they had been coming into Paddock Hill Bend at over 190 miles an hour. Dodging Aral, who ended up on the outside of the curve, and me, three of the four cars touched, one of them slipping on bleeding oil. All three of them were out of the race. The fourth car, Prugno in the second Ferrari, managed to thread his way through.

Thanks to the immensely strong carbon-fibre tubs of the cars nobody was hurt. I had a punctured eardrum, a mouthful of dirt, and it was two days before either Aral or I could walk since we both felt as if we had been worked over with rubber hammers. The other drivers were all fine apart from the damage to their cars and the loss of the race.

So for an accident of that size and speed, the damage wasn't nearly as bad as it could have been. Two Formula One cars written off and three others moderately to severely damaged. Say £500,000 altogether. Plus five badly bruised and shaken drivers and one damaged reputation.

Everyone who had seen it happen, the drivers, the marshals,

the clerk of the course in the control tower, the spectators in the stands, and the millions watching the slow motion replays on TV, all agreed it was my fault. I had driven into the path of another racing car. "Why?" they all wanted to know. "Why the fuck?"

I had always been known as a calculating and careful driver. One who never took a risk if he could avoid it. The Italian fans called me *Il Dottore*, the doctor. The one who analyses everything and keeps his car on the edge of a knife. But I couldn't tell them or the reporters or the clerk of the course why. I didn't know why. The only reason I could think of was because I felt like it.

Nicky stirred and shifted away from me to lean against the helicopter's clear shell. On our left Mount Fuji dominated the landscape, posing for postcards. It seemed so clear, symmetrical and smooth. No wonder the Japanese have a genius for simplicity.

Sooner or later, everybody crashes. Something breaks, somebody else makes a mistake, your mind wanders for a hundredth of a second, there's a patch of oil on the track when your car is on the limit of adhesion; it can happen to everybody and it does. Everybody expects you to crash. But nobody expects you to crash two races in a row. Nobody expects you to try to self-destruct.

If you've seen the films, or watched the race on television, you know as much about my second crash at Hockenheim as I do. The German neurologist who treated me after the race explained it to me. "It's quite simple," he said. "Your brain carries around ten minutes to a half an hour or so of what's just happened in electromechanical impulses. Call it short-term memory. Some of those electromechanical impulses get translated into electrochemical molecules and stored for long-term memory. But if you get a hard enough knock on the head to destroy the mechanical impulses before they are translated into long-term memory, you'll never remember those ten, twenty, or thirty minutes before the bump. There's no point in worrying about it," he said. "It's just gone."

My strongest memory of the crash at Hockenheim is everybody else telling me about it.

Ken had been a gentleman after the crash at Brands. He'd said he didn't know what had caused it, but he wasn't going to let it get in the way of winning the German Grand Prix. Head down, all out, straight ahead.

21

After Hockenheim there was no talk of forgive and forget. There was no talk at all. He was too angry with his lead driver to trust himself to talk to him. I wasn't in a rush to talk to him either. He'd lost about half a million pounds of racing cars, his sponsors were on his back, and so were the other teams. The sponsors were the worst. They'd put up their money to see their names on the glamorous racing cars and, hopefully, in the winner's circle. They didn't like seeing their reputations smashed week after week. It was worse than backing a loser. And they didn't like the feeling that it could happen again in the next race.

For all Ken knew it would.

For all I knew it would.

So we prepared for the next race, the Hungarian Grand Prix, as if nothing was wrong. Even though we knew something was wrong. We checked, rechecked, rechecked and rechecked the cars.

Carringdon, who's in his tenth season of driving Formula One and the unofficial senior statesman for the drivers rang me in London one evening for "a quiet little chat".

Veronica had been saying she wasn't going to stay in another night and we were going out. Or she was going out. It was the conversation we usually had in the middle of the week when we started to get bored with each other. While Veronica was making a show of slamming doors and changing clothes, Carringdon was suggesting "perhaps I might consider a personality test with a psychiatrist". The drivers were worried. Racing inches away from another man with 700 angry horses in his hands, you have to trust him.

I didn't tell Ken, but I went to the doctor Carringdon suggested.

He started with some physical tests which told him I have exceptional eyesight and a much lower blink rate than normal. All the reaction, motor control and coordination test scores went off the top of his charts. His personality tests showed that I was highly aggressive, impatient and intolerant, with an overbearing will to succeed. He also gave me credit for some intelligence. In other words, apart from my size, I was an absolutely normal Formula One racing driver.

I sent the results to Carringdon. I didn't find them particularly reassuring, but maybe he would.

22

In some ways the Hungarian Grand Prix was the worst. It should have been the best. The Hungaroring is a beautiful new track just outside Budapest. It's a tight course, very difficult to pass in, with thirty-nine gear changes per lap, one of them from sixth at over 185 straight down to second at the hairpin. I had a good practice. The car never felt better. What we lacked on power we more than made up with the sweetness of the handling. At 107.56 mph I set a new track record and put Team Arundel on the pole.

On race day the only thing Ken said to me was "Try not to lose it. It's the last one in the box." I suppose he meant it as a joke and a kind of peace offering. But even if he didn't, the sun was shining and I felt good and I wasn't going to let anything get me down. The start was perfect. When I came around on the first lap I was thirty yards in the lead over Cavelli's Ferrari.

On the second lap when I came into the main straight in front of the grandstand I was fifty yards in front of Cavelli.

Then the track split in half. The track veered off to the left and it veered off to the right and I could not tell which one was real.

I braked, Cavelli went by me like a shot, and gradually the two tracks pulled together in focus. I pulled over and parked the car.

There was a change in the pitch of the rotor blades as the pilot began his descent through Tokyo's smog onto the roof of the Imperial. Nice, still day, no problem with crosswinds. But breathing could seriously damage your health.

I could still feel the bad feeling I had in Hungary walking back to the pits. The cars going by sounded as if they were ten miles away. Spectators called to me from behind the fence asking what happened. I couldn't turn my head to face them. A TV reporter came running up wanting to know why . . . what had broken? His voice sounded thin and tinny as if he were some lifesize toy. I couldn't face him either. I walked past him like he wasn't there. But I did have to face Ken. He was standing there, with his earphones on, and his face had that pinched and pained, caught-in-a-vice look that people who suffer from migraine sometimes have. Whatever it was I had to tell him he knew it wasn't going to be good. He was bracing himself.

"Nothing's wrong," I said, walking past him. "The car's fine. I'm sorry, I can't drive for you."

23

"You're under contract," he said to my back. "You better have your solicitors ring me." Which, I suppose, was better than having his ring mine.

I wasn't looking forward to breakfast with him in the morning.

The Goodyear folks had rung ahead and the Japanese assistant assistant managers were waiting on the roof. Ah so helpful; every assistance, every condolence. They lead us down from the roof to the lift to ride one floor down to Ken and Ruth Arundel's suite. They bowed in unison as we asked them to please just leave us alone. They all wore maroon sports jackets. The women wore grey skirts and the men wore grey trousers. Please to be helpful they said.

I suppose they really were concerned. I suppose I was turning into a sour old bastard.

Nicky was not in good shape. She looked across the reception room of the Arundel suite. Heads of state stayed here. Not of the major countries, the minor ones . . . the ones that still visited the Emperor. The room was done in soft pastels of blues and greens. Most of the upholstery was done in the overstuffed silk beloved by the wives of dictators of small countries. There was a little kitchen, a big corner bedroom overlooking the park, and a smaller bedroom at the back.

Nicky stood surveying the scene while I explained that maybe she should stay here for awhile. Maybe neutral ground would be a better place. The Arundels wanted her to stay with them. I'd get her things from her room. She walked into the big bedroom and looked out of the window facing the park. Across the crammed Hibiya-Dori, silenced by double glazing and air conditioning, the bright flowers and trees of the park were all the same smog grey. Maybe they were just paper cutouts filling in while the real flowers were in the country having a breath of fresh air. Maybe they were markers on the plots where the originals had died. Maybe . . .

Nicky screamed, beginning with a low-pitched moan and working up to the kind of high squeal that spoiled children make when they scrape their knees.

I walked over to the window and put my arm around her to comfort her. Her shoulders were so small. She turned slowly to face me and said, "You shit," snapping off the words, making

24

sure they hit between the eyes. "You stupid, weak shit. If you do not quit, if you are not afraid to drive, Michel he still would be here." She turned away from me.

"I'll get your things," I said.

The assistant assistants had given me the keys to Nicky and Michel's room. I thought that if, apart from bringing Nicky her toothbrush, I could pack Michel's things, it would be a kindness. It was something to do.

The curtains had been pulled shut in Michel and Nicky's room, and in the circumstances, it seemed less of an intrusion if I left the light off. There was enough light seeping in under the drapes to see.

The Imperial Hotel is one of the most luxurious hotels in Tokyo. By Japanese standards the room was immense. To my western eyes it was a little below average, a two-thirds scale model of a Howard Johnson's Motor Lodge.

I sat on the bed to let my eyes grow accustomed to the dim light.

Just after someone has died their clothes and everyday things still have some of their former owner's life, an almost invisible glow that makes that comb, that leather jacket slung on the back of the chair, Michel's. Nobody has told the maroon dressing gown lying on the bed that the man it held every morning won't be coming back.

I was having doubts about what I was doing here. Maybe Nicky wouldn't want me to be handling Michel's things. And if I packed all his things in his suitcases what would I do with them then? Send them to his apartment in Paris, coffin to follow? I felt an intruder in a life that didn't include me. The room smelt of Michel, the musky aftershave he always wore.

I went into the loo and took a good look at myself in the mirror. Not a pretty sight. Would you let this man drive your car? Pack your toothbrush? I have what one sportswriter called a "leather-beaten face", craggy before my time. My blue eyes are set deep beneath a heavy brow. My hair is short and curly light brown. Most of the motor magazine profiles of me mention how handsome I am. I'd like to believe it but I don't see it. I tried a grin to cheer myself up. Goddamn chimpanzee.

Michel was dead. Susan was suing for divorce. Veronica was in New York with "her" producer. Nicky despised me. I had walked out on Ken. And on my job with WBC. Well, I thought, one thing about being alone, you don't have to look your best.

There were two basins sunk into the frosty-pink imitation marble counter. Each one held a little paper-wrapped soap in a shell-shaped impression. On the left side, there was a neat clump of French shampoo, conditioner, some fancy moisturizer, hair spray, hair mousse, contraceptive foam, hand cream, sachets and a hair dryer. For some reason the orderly little still life of Nicky's private creams and oils reminded me that she loved lounging in the tub. When we were in Grasse she would call down to Michel to come join her. And Veronica and I would hear them splashing for an hour, Nicky's musical laugh pealing over the valley.

On the other side there was an electric shaver and a toothbrush, each on its separate holder. The toothpaste tube was squeezed neatly, bottom first. *Alles in ordnung.*

All the towels and soaps and little plastic vials of shampoo, conditioner and shower gel with the little Imperial Hotel labels were all in place.

The story in the bedroom was depressingly similar. Nothing seemed out of place, apart from the dent in the bedspread where I'd sat. None of the drawers were pulled out. The clothes in the closet hung in silent, regular intervals.

Pyjamas and nighties were neatly folded in the drawers. Socks and undies, too, neatly folded and segregated according to sex. I felt seedy, looking through their things, a Peeping Tom in the bedroom. What was I doing pawing through the clothes of the dead? And if there was a connection between Michel and my two crashes, it wasn't here, in this empty museum of Michel and Nicky's life together.

My room on the seventh floor was a replica of Michel and Nicky's on the eleventh. Except mine had more emptiness. Same rust-red bedspread on the double bed, same rust-red drapes. Nobody home, just me.

The red light on the phone by the bed was winking, indicating messages. The cool, clear telephone operator's voice went on for a very long time. She was very patient. I wrote down two numbers.

Veronica with her usual perfect timing had rung from New York to wish me good luck on my first day as a broadcaster. Some thirty

26

reporters had rung. Janice Henrion had a different approach. She'd left a note saying she was sorry for being insensitive. Couldn't she possibly make it up over a drink or a quiet dinner if I'd care to be alone with a stranger. Her pretty pink breasts wobbled into view. I considered it. Rejected it. Michel was freshly dead. No, I didn't want to be alone with a stranger. Or with a reporter. Ken Arundel had rung to confirm breakfast tomorrow morning. Mr Organization. And Bill Packer had called from WBC.

First I rang Nicole on the pretence that I wasn't sure what she wanted from her room.

"Oh Forray, I am so glad you call. I feel so terrible over what I say to you. Please can you forgive me?"

"Nothing to forgive. I've had the same thought. You be as nasty as you like, anytime."

"OK, I will be. Forray, really, I need nothing from my room. Maybe tomorrow I go down and pack. Just now I think I like to be alone."

"Sure. If you go down there, tonight, tomorrow, anytime, promise you'll take somebody from the hotel with you. And if you do go, see if anything is missing."

"With one of the whatyousay, assistant assistants? Why?"

"I'm worried about you."

"You are an old lady. I'm fine."

"Will you just do it for me?"

"I have to? Someone has been there?"

"Promise?"

"Promise."

Then I rang Bill Packer at WBC in New York. If I'd talked to the reporters, I'd have probably just made it worse. But I owed Packer an apology. He was head of WBC-TV Sports, and it was his idea to hire me for colour commentary on their worldwide Formula One broadcasts. Now he was probably sporting a black eye at the network. I didn't want to call him, but as my proper British father always said, a man has to stand up for his wrongs.

"Hey, great, Forrest. Glad you called. How's the weather in Tokyo?"

"Look, I'm sorry. He was my friend. If you want a public apology . . ."

"Hey, what'd you say, apology? Apology?"

Maybe an apology wasn't enough. I assumed they'd cancelled my contract. Maybe they wanted some compensation, some money for damages. "Well what else?"

"How's the connection on your end? Where have you been? I gotta tell you Forrest I've never seen a response like this. We got phone calls all over the world. They're still coming in. Fantastic. They loved it."

"Loved it?" I pictured Michel's car sailing through the air. "Loved it? Why don't they race in the Coliseum in Rome? Let the lions do the cleaning up."

"LOVED YOU, you dickhead."

# CHAPTER THREE

Maybe breakfast is officially frowned on in Japan. Maybe their breakfast explains why the Japanese have less heart disease than we of the land of bangers, bacon, egg and hash browns. And less height.

Bangers and hash browns. There in an eggshell is my country. Viva Transatlantica. Two passports and many crossings; antipodes in shoes. A proper English father and a wild and beautiful American mother.

Just like Churchill, I used to say. Until I noticed the tight little grimace that the remark provoked in the land of British racing green.

Brits in their heart of coal black hearts like to believe that after Harold got a spike in the eye, they have been racially and culturally pure. Anything offshore since 1066 is suspect.

Yanks like to believe there are no other countries.

I owe allegiance to both, warts and all. Give me bangers or give me hash browns. But not these little sour green shrivelled things that looked like leftovers from a frog autopsy.

Ken, I noticed, wasn't touching his breakfast either. A frail little porcelain cup was lost somewhere in his giant hand. As he talked, his huge dark head rotated slowly, like the turret on a tank. He could easily see over the screens of the Imperial's 'traditional' Japanese breakfast room and he was making sure we were alone. We were.

No doubt the Japanese had already had their morning meal and were running to work. You saw them in waves in the streets in the morning, running to work. Not because they were late, but because they wanted to get there early. Get a head start on the day. Or so I thought. Maybe they were running from the horrors of breakfast.

"It hardly needs saying, I'm in some difficulty." Ken lowered

29

his head and was looking with uncomfortable intensity into my eyes. I hadn't expected this to be light-hearted. But this man was of a class and a generation that did not talk of personal troubles. It was one of those things that was not done.

"I have now lost three racing cars; I have lost two drivers; I am losing my major sponsor. I may very well have to give up the team."

I could only nod. I knew this, but it was painful to hear it.

"What is very much worse," he said, "I appear to have lost two good friends."

"Two?"

"Michel and yourself." He raised a hand to stop me from protesting. "When you had your first accident, something went very wrong. And again, at Hockenheim, something went very wrong. And again in Hungary. I have no idea if you blame me, or the team, or even if you know what it is. I expect you don't know what it is. But whatever the case, you have kept it secret from me, and I find that quite painful."

Again I tried to object. I wasn't used to him talking to me like this. But he wasn't finished and didn't want me to interrupt.

"I owe you a great deal, Forrest."

I couldn't let him get away with that. "Like the two cars I destroyed."

"I very much doubt that without your talent there would have been two Formula One cars to destroy. We have been together four years now. And, professionally, I think your driving has always been better than the chassis I've been able to provide. The success we've had, and we have had immense success for a private entrant, has been, to a great degree, due to your ability as a driver.

"When we began I thought it would be fun. A childish notion for a man my age. But not a bad one. Our success, your success, has quite altered my life. I think you should know I hold you wholly responsible for the break-up of my first marriage." He smiled broadly. "For that alone I am grateful."

I wanted to change the subject. "Are you seriously thinking of withdrawing Team Arundel?"

"Well, I'd have to finance the last two races out of my own pocket. And they're very expensive races for us. I'd have to fly a new chassis to Mexico and Australia. And I don't have a new chassis. Except for the mule we've been using for testing Max's baby."

I knew all about Max's baby. Max may be one of the world's more obnoxious human beings, but he was the father of a sweetheart of an automatic transmission. Max angered me because, apart from being arrogant, offensive and pig-headed, he didn't spend enough time on engine development. He raged at me because I distracted him from working on his baby. And because I smashed his little darling to bits.

An automatic transmission in a racing car makes a lot of sense. If there are, say, forty gearchanges in a lap, and seventy-five laps to a race, and if you only take three tenths of a second to change gear, that means that in a two hour race you spend fourteen minutes with the clutch on the floor, in neutral, coasting. Formula One races have been won in a fraction of a second, so an extra fourteen minutes of power is something to think about.

People have tried racing with an automatic, but except for the seven-litre CanAm V8s of the 1970s (which had power to spare), automatics have been too big and too heavy and soaked up too much power. And drivers use the transmission to help braking, which you can't do with an automatic. Although now the brakes are so good you can stand on them and slip into whatever gear you need next. Shift directly from sixth to second, no problem.

The beauty of Max's transmission is that it weighs less than a standard transmission and that it's almost as small. The principle is two concentric cones, one inside the other and both with VSG (variable scroll geometry) blades like turbines. The pitch of the turbine blades is controlled by a computer that calculates engine speed, road speed, accelerator demand, and sets the blades at the optimum angle to keep the engine running at the peak of its power curve. Part of the secret of Max's transmission is a special viscous fluid which couples the two turbine cones. As friction heats, the fluid gets thicker and the drive, or gear ratio, more direct. So it's always in the perfect gear, the engine is always at peak power, and you never have to shift. At least that's the theory. Max was having trouble getting a formula stable enough to last a race. But he was working on it.

31

"How much progress has he made?" I asked.

"He thinks he's there. But we haven't tried it on a hot track. Or a high altitude one."

"And Mexico is both"

"Mexico is both," he smiled openly for the first time.

"So you're going to try it?"

"If I can find a driver. I don't think Maurizio is right for it, do you? You said you had a theory about Michel's accident."

"Theory is too grand a word. But I think Michel's crash and mine weren't accidents. Somebody made them happen."

"Somebody not you or Michel."

"Whoever it is, isn't after me or Michel. All three accidents happened to the same car, to the number two Arundel car. All three looked like a very big driver error. All three happened in the opening laps of the race."

"Forgive me, but how does this mean the hypothetical 'he' wasn't after you or Michel?"

"It's nothing you can hang your hat on, just a gut feeling. We were both your lead driver. And I'd suspect if you get another lead driver they'll make him crash too. Because they want to get you to stop racing. Whoever races for you. And from what you've said, they've nearly succeeded"

"You mean someone's trying to bonk us out of racing?"

"It doesn't mean that."

"What?"

"Bonk. It doesn't mean bump. It means fuck."

"Well, I suppose we are. Bonked." He started to make the wheezing sound that meant he was laughing.

"Do you have any idea," I asked, "who wants you out of racing?"

"Good lord, no." He was back to his old Lord of the Manor self, drawing himself up to loom over the table. "I mean without being self-conscious about it, I'm almost a protected species. The last private entrant. A sort of dodo, actually. Much too small game to be taken seriously by the big boys."

"Any ideas?"

"I'd have to think. Alicia, possibly. She loathed my racing. Wanted me to stay by the hearth in the castle. Tried to get my goat about it. She got it. I butted her out. I suppose she's

32

capable of something nasty. But I hardly think she'd hurt anyone physically. Psychological damage, that's the kind she likes."

"She's not that bad."

"You always like my wives better than I do," he said finally, putting down his teacup. Then, arching his huge black eyebrows in a look of self-mockery and irony, "You should marry one of them."

"You're enjoying this?"

"It does mean you're going to drive for me again, doesn't it?"

Looking out the window of my room the day was as bright as Spring, even though it was October. Fresh gusts off the Pacific had blown the smog off to Manchuria and the flowers in the park on the other side of the Hibiya-Dori were back in place fresh from their holiday in the mountains. I was used to the weather changing ten times a day in London. But the climatic changes in Tokyo were on another scale altogether. Bitter cold and dark at noon and presto, balmy sunshine. Stagnant smog, chango, fifty-five mile an hour gusts from Bali.

It made you realize you were living in a land of volcanoes, earthquakes and typhoons. And wonder if the weather accounted for the sudden and seismic shifts of mood among the Japanese.

Ken had tried, but he hadn't been able to come up with anybody who wanted him to quit badly enough to kill. There was a team manager he'd had to fire for no reason other than he didn't like the man. And a former sponsor whose oil additive didn't sell despite spending £750,000 for a season with Team Arundel. When his business went broke he'd sued Ken for fraud, saying that Ken had guaranteed him his sales would take off. He couldn't find a solicitor to take the case. And of course there was Alicia.

It was nice to think of Alicia again. Ken was right, I did like her better than he did. She was a high strung, leggy redhead, not quite forty. She kept saying she wanted a quiet life, but she only wanted the illusion. She loved the risk and glamour and travel of Formula One. What she didn't like was Ken's total immersion in it, his loving the cars and forgetting about her for days and even weeks during the season.

They really had owned a castle, a Victorian railroad magnate's granite folly by a lake in Wales. They were never there, but she loved to dream of cool, gloomy summers by the lake, long walks in the forest and coming back to a roaring fire in the great hall. I went there with them a few times on weekends in the winter and the illusion came true, despite the complete lack of summer. But after the first afternoon she was bored by castles and playing the great, isolated lady. The moment we finished Sunday lunch she was ready to go back to London.

Ken was right. She'd scratch your emotional eyes out, but she'd never hurt anyone physically. Still, she might have some good guesses about who would.

I had another thought: Max. Max and Ken had a fifty/fifty arrangement on any patents Max developed. Ken provided the finance and the rolling test lab, Max the ideas. It was possible that if Ken dissolved Team Arundel, he'd lose his claim on Max's baby. Potentially, the licensing fees on a superlight, superefficient automatic transmission were hundreds of millions of dollars, pounds, deutsch marks and yen. That had the feel of a real motive. But it also had a little flaw. Max was a bastard, but he wasn't a crazy bastard. He'd never kill anybody.

There was a message from Nicky. I rang her.

"You OK?"

"Of course not. The Arundels are very kind. They are looking after everything. Ken is dealing with the Japanese, arranging the shipping, arranging the funeral. I feel superfluous. And I am so sad."

"Me too," feeling sad with her. Feeling the loss of Michel fresh again. "Maybe we should get out of here, go for a walk in the sun, in the park."

"Maybe. If you think so. As long as I don't have to talk. I am not good company."

"I'll come to your door in five minutes."

"OK Forray."

I liked Nicky's calling me 'Forray'. It was the first time anybody ever had any luck trying to lighten that heavy, gloomy wooden name my mother had lumbered me with. (Yes, I have heard all the jokes about trees.) My dear, daft mother had named me Forrest because she thought it sounded British. It reminded her of England's green and pleasant land, she said. And Robin Hood.

My father loathed the name. It didn't sound at all British to him. He said it sounded as though I was begat in a woodshed. He tried to find a reasonable nickname for Forrest (Fort sounded too much like Fart) and he ended up calling me Sherwood to mock my mother. And if you think Forrest is bad, try out Sherwood on the next ten year old that crosses your path. Evers, of course, was a shortened version of Everard. Bishop of Norwich 1121–45, don't you know.

Walking in the park, Nicky was as silent as the trees with their leaves flickering in the sun, her head bowed. She slipped her hand in mine and we mourned silently together. A small and fragile hand, cool in my big, calloused fist.

When we turned to go back, she turned to me. "Forray, there is one thing strange. This morning when I am down in the room to start to pack . . . and I was feeling so terrible about Michel, seeing his things so quiet there. You said to see if anything was missing. His aftershave is missing."

"He wouldn't have taken it with him to the track?"

"Never."

Smashing my cars for no reason; Michel doing the same; the track splitting in half; that was one thing. But stealing Michel's aftershave . . . somebody was messing with my mind.

# CHAPTER FOUR

In the National Air and Space Museum in Washington DC there is a place in the main hall where you can stand and see the Wright Brothers' first flying machine.

It's a flimsy thing, made of sticks, wires and canvas, and it hangs like a mobile sculpture, suspended from the ceiling. It didn't fly very far on its first flight in 1903, just 120 feet. And it's even smaller than you'd expect. But it gets an exhibition hall all to itself.

Standing in the same spot, you can turn your head and see the first manned space capsule, Apollo 1. It looks like a big white conehead fridge. No doubt, as time goes on, it will look increasingly weird. As strange and antique in its way as the Kitty Hawk looks now. After all, there's only sixty years between the two machines; less than a man's life.

I was 38,000 feet over the Pacific in the nose of a 747, staring out into the night and the deep black below, travelling, with the help of a jetstream, at a ground speed of 680 miles an hour. A speed the British Parliament, fearing the repercussions of breaking the sound barrier, had outlawed after the Second World War.

The first class lounge tinkled with crystal and cutlery and murmured with tne cautious conversation of strangers sitting side by side, telling stories of who they were, what they did, where they'd been, where they were going, and how they would like to be remembered.

The stewardesses had finished pouring drinks and were beginning to serve dinner. Drinks-and-dinner-on-the-plane is the international businessman's most religious ceremony, the stewardesses wearing what the nuns of the future will wear, the businessmen's heads bent devoutly over offerings from the microwave, worshipping what the new technology brings.

No doubt, in the near future, this too will all seem hopelessly antique, a relic of a slower, more gracious time. Constant acceleration catapults us into the unknown. Never mind where we're going, let's get started.

I was grouchy because I didn't have any drinks and I wasn't going to get any and I wasn't going to get any dinner either. The everlasting battle against too much weight went on and on. Not to mention the struggle of one man alone fighting the forces of jet lag.

Jet lag is the one disease for which there is no known sympathy. But as any international businessman will tell you, it is real. Drink plenty of alcohol and eat heavily on the plane on a multi-time zone flight and you will jumble your judgement and your system for days. If you drive a racing car, jet lag can kill you.

I was repeating these helpful little homilies to myself when the stewardess came by. No nothing. Not the beef, not the chicken or the fish. No thank you. Nothing really. No I'm fine. Just a little more water please. "The Fish" were giant snow white butterfly shrimp in a white wine, butter, garlic and lemon sauce. Oh lord, I make myself sick being good.

She was blonde and the nameplate on her grey-blue nylon blouse said 'Susannah'. She'd had a million miles of Pacific pass under the soles of her feet, but her eyes were fresh and full of life, and her bouncy figure was no worse for the long journey. She gave me a pouting look, miming professional sympathy, making me think of picking her up, running her back to the empty seats in the back of the bus and raising almighty sexual hell (ya'll go ahead with your dinners, gennlemen, never mind the hoots and the hollers, we jess playin some good ole games back here like 'remember when', and 'did you ever', and 'you wanna try?'). But she was long gone before I got to the part where I mentally rebuke Forrest Evers for being so damn adolescent.

The balding businessman with the hearty voice in the seat in front of me was having The Fish. She served him six giant shrimp from a platter. She put them on his plate with silver tongs, one at a time. There were more if he wanted.

I turned to the little round window and looked out at the black. Even if there was nothing for supper there was a feast of problems to chew on. They were running around and around on an endless cassette. One of these days I really should sort out which were

37

the most important ones, make a Top of the Pops of Forrest's Real Life Disasters, soon to be showing here.

I wasn't sure I was doing the right thing, driving for Ken again.

All of the reasons I quit in the first place were as strong as they ever were. I was a menace to the other drivers. Ken couldn't afford to lose another car. And what scraps of pride and professional reputation I still had I wanted to keep. If I started seeing double or having delusions of grandeur, or whatever you call wanting to keep your foot down and go on forever, if that happened again I would have to pull over and park. Or smash like a bug against a concrete barrier.

Ken said he appreciated all that. But did I want another driver to take that risk? Did I want him to give in to the pressure and withdraw from racing? Did I want the people who killed Michel and tried to kill me go free? And if I didn't do it, how would we ever find out who was behind it and how they were doing it? Or why?

Forget about the international police, he said. It would take them a month to translate each other's telexes. Imagine a meeting of German, Hungarian, Japanese, Mexican and Australian Police. (What was Hungarian for "impaired perception"? Or Japanese for "perpetrator unknown"?) We had two more races in the next four weeks. And if it wasn't another driver and if it wasn't a special UN task force, who else did I have in mind?

So naturally I said yes.

Being bait didn't worry me. But being somebody else's pawn, letting somebody else flip the switches of my mind, that worried me. I had spent years exercising, practising, and honing my concentration, my judgement and my reaction time. Take away a hand, a foot, or even an eye, and I can still race. But interfere with my mind for a moment, and I am lost.

Who, how and why? All blanks.

How seemed the easiest to guess. Drugs, I thought. But why did they take effect five or six laps into the race? And how were they administered? I had a disgustingly controlled diet. But it was a pigout compared to what Michel ate. His diet was prepared for him by a Swiss nutritionist who sent him sealed glass containers of what looked like barn sweepings. He never ate in restaurants. Or if he did, he brought his own food and water. And aftershave couldn't have been the link. I wouldn't touch the stuff with a stick. Especially Michel's.

Maybe it wasn't drugs. Maybe there was some advanced radio control. Years ago I'd seen news footage of a raging bull turned into an imitation pussycat at the touch of a button. That had required a little chip implanted in the bull's brain. But maybe the technology had gone beyond that by now. Maybe now they had a transmitter that could access the electronic connections in my brain. Whoever 'they' were.

There was another more likely alternative that was even less reassuring. One I didn't like to think about but it would answer all the questions. Maybe there wasn't any they. Maybe I was losing just a bit of my mental edge. It wouldn't take much. Maybe nature in her gentle way was tossing me some hints. Maybe Michel made a mistake too.

Maybe I was going a touch nuts.

Ken said that the first instant I felt anything strange or wrong I was to slow down and pull into the pits. Which sounds fine, except you are always feeling something is strange or wrong. Is that left-front wheel out of line, or is the suspension loose? Or am I just imagining it? Can I take him on the inside, or didn't he notice me in his mirrors? Every driver worries about his car, the other drivers, and oil or dirt on the track. Worrying about your judgement, let alone your sanity, at the same time would be a serious disadvantage.

Still, we agreed, as soon as I felt any of the old symptoms I would slow down, and pull back into the pits and we would blame it on Max's new automatic transmission.

Max would be delighted, no doubt. He was going to be overjoyed anyway learning that I was coming back. He already blamed me for ruining the team and crashing his cars. When I walked out of the race in Hungary I passed Max in the pits and he'd said, "You better keep walking, you fukkin' coward. You come back here, Evers, and I'll kill you." It was loyalty and charm like that made Max so much fun to be around.

Max would be flying into Riverside, California, with the car. The father of the first automatic transmission in Formula One with his little darling under his wing, facing the rapist who wants to take his baby out and make her scream. But I didn't mind facing Max if it meant I could drive again.

Susan would be less easy to face. Susan wanted the Georgian house we'd rebuilt in Edwardes Square in Kensington, the contents, and the Aston Martin DB5 Volante I'd rebuilt with my bare hands. And a guaranteed income of £150,000 a year. She had suffered so much, I had been such a bastard. I could understand that couldn't I? No, she wasn't living in the house, she'd moved in with Charles until we got this whole thing sorted out. It was her lawyer's advice. Charles was her lawyer.

Their affair had crippled our halting marriage in the first place. But I was to blame because I had been away too much and hadn't paid enough attention to her. And I was to pay because I hadn't fought hard enough to keep her.

The rattle of the drinks trolley brought me back into 747-land.

Would I care for some sweets, inquired Susannah sweetly. And some coffee? And some after-dinner brandy? Wouldn't I like just a drop of a very nice twenty-five-year-old Martell. Sure, go ahead, have a drop Forrest, urged a little voice at the back of my head. You love brandy. A little drop will help you sleep. "No thanks," I told the delectable Susannah.

I am a millionaire and live like a monk.

I can hear Veronica hooting at that. "Monk? Hoot hoot." Veronica's dark eyes lit up my dark and gloomy place. She could make a Trappist sing and a Cistercian dance. She could do anything.

But she didn't do much.

She was beautiful and rich and she could draw and she could paint and she was a good actress when she wanted to be, and she wrote well enough to have some stories and poems published. And she had a good eye for figures and she loved solving problems. She could have been an actress, an artist, a writer or an executive. She was thinking about it. She was twenty-nine. Too old to be a model. Almost too old to start as an actress. One by one her options were slipping away from her. She would keep thinking about it. How, I wondered, could I see her?

My days were filling in like the bricks of a wall. Real life has to wait while I do a few things. I'll be right back after this, and this, and this.

I'd lost two days in Tokyo over the enquiry over Michel's crash. The Japanese police felt there might be some link between Michel's crash and mine. I was sure there was a link. But there was nothing I could tell them. And they found nothing.

The Japanese officials were immensely polite to Max (who had taken to calling them "slopes" and "slanteyes" and reminding them who "won the war"). Another trait the Japanese and British share; they think they are fair because they are polite to people they despise. But even the Japanese couldn't hide their disappointment when they found that Max had nothing to do with the crash. "Driver error", they concluded.

Tonight was Thursday 8th October; gain a day over the dateline, arrive LA at 10.10 in the morning on the same day. Two days before Mad Max arrives with his new baby. Maybe Veronica could fly out from New York, and we could have two days together.

Max and the car were due to arrive at Riverside on the 10th. The track was reserved for testing the car on Sunday and Monday, and we planned to ship the car to Mexico Monday night, Tuesday morning the 13th at the latest if it needed any overnight modifications to the new skin (which was flying into Riverside on the morning of the 11th).

Fly to Mexico City on Wednesday the 14th. First practice laps in Mexico on Friday, race on Sunday the 18th.

I could go to New York on Monday the 19th. I had to see Bill Packer at WBC. So if Veronica was still in New York then, maybe take her back to London with me on the 20th or 21st. I could see Susan on the 22nd or 23rd to see if maybe we could work something out that would keep the lawyers from taking everything. Except, as all thoughts about Susan seemed to be ending up, the lawyer was her lover.

Then there was a memorial service for Michel in Paris on Saturday the 24th. I should fly from there directly to Adelaide, and give myself a couple of days to get acclimatized before the first practice session on Friday the 29th. I'd call Veronica when I got to LA, see if she'd meet me in New York on the 19th. See if she'd come back with me to London.

41

As I was juggling my days I had another thought, more a question really. Written answers, please. Take all the time you need. If the jet, which is after all the grandchild of the first flying machine, if the jet allows me to complicate my life this much, what mad complications will we dream up with the grandchild of the first space capsule?

Maybe I should ring Alicia in London and see if she's free on the 22nd or 23rd. She should know who Ken's enemies are. I had to find enough time to find the person or persons unknown who were trying to get at Ken by getting me to smash myself into little red bits. But that wasn't really a problem, was it? I didn't have to do anything. All I had to do was be the bait.

And Nicole. I should call her from Los Angeles, see if she's OK. Poor kid. I'd asked her if she wanted to come with me or go to London with Ken and Ruth. But no, she wanted to go straight to Paris, to be there when Michel's body arrived. Perhaps I could spend a day with her in Paris after the memorial service.

Nicky, Susan, Veronica, Alicia, Janice. Who was Janice? I thought, half-dreaming. Tokyo, Los Angeles, Mexico City, New York, Paris, Adelaide. Around and around it goes. Where it stops, nobody knows. Michel's pale blue eyes, wide open, trusting, wanting to see what would happen next.

I must have been sleeping. I felt soft hands tucking a blanket around me. There was a perfume I couldn't place, musky, spicy. My eyes opened to the blue flickering light of the movie and saw, in close-up, a silver nameplate: "Susannah." I closed my eyes.

At less than a third of this speed, a mere 200 miles an hour on the ground, driving the Arundel Formula One, the air would be stuffed full of noise, heat, vibration, stink and danger. This was better.

# CHAPTER FIVE

The sea below did a slow change from blue to green to bronze as we crept up on Los Angeles, a city seen through a glass of smog, darkly.

A glare from a strip of beach told you where the shore was, but the sea and the land were the same colour of industrial-haze brown. A third of the city, said an article in the Pan Am magazine, is paved with streets, freeways and parking lots. From the air it looks more like half. Maybe LA had added a few percentage points on its way to a solid 100 per cent. The world's first all-freeway city, paved wall to wall.

We cruised inland over Watts before banking west again to make our approach on the New York ramp. I looked down to see if I could find it, and ah, yes, there it was, Watts Towers.

Watts Towers is a survivor: a delightful, fanciful, glittering trio of joy rising out of the poorest and blackest section of Los Angeles.

Watts Towers is everything bureaucracy hates.

The towers were built by a ninety-eight-pound Sicilian mason, Simon Rodea, in the 1930s. No one is sure why he built reinforced concrete towers on his tiny triangle of land. A religious monument, a sculpture, a hobby, a gesture of gratitude to America; there are plenty of theories. During the Second World War, the authorities suspected it was a radio tower for enemy transmissions and had him arrested. But of course there were no radios and they let him go.

If anyone knows why Simon Rodea built the towers, they're not telling. One day he just started mixing concrete and bending reinforcing rods. He told the kids in the neighbourhood he would pay a penny for every ten pieces of broken glass and crockery they found and brought to him. The local mothers got him to stop that because their kids were smashing up the family china.

But the children kept bringing him the pieces of glass and plates and saucers they scrounged from the scrap heap even though he stopped paying them.

When he'd finished the tallest tower was ninety-eight feet high and as light and white and airy as lace. It looked like something Gaudi might have dreamed up for a Barcelona playground with its web of surfaces sequined with blue, green and yellow bottle glass and not a little of the neighbours' china. After he'd finished, he lit it up with spotlights at night. Until the authorities found he'd dug a trench to the trolley line for the electricity. One day, in the early fifties (he was in his seventies), he just walked away. Moved out. Gone to Chicago, maybe.

Again no explanation.

A few years later, when it was clear he wasn't coming back, a person or persons unknown burned his little wooden house down. A few years after that the City of Los Angeles condemned the towers. They said the towers were dangerous and had to be pulled down. Some people formed a Save the Tower committee, bought the land and fought City Hall.

After a long legal battle, the City said they would conduct a test that would prove the towers were unsafe.

This was the test. A giant steel crane trundled down Graham Avenue to Simon Rodea's towers and rose up to the same height as the tallest tower. Steeplejacks attached a steel cable from the crane to the tower, and the crane started to reel in the cable. A kind of giant mechanical arm wrestling. Mine is stronger than yours.

As the crane pulled harder, the tower began to show signs of stress. One by one pieces of glass and china started to pop off the surface, fall to the ground and shatter. Cracks started to appear on the sides of the tower. Then with a tremendous bang, the crane broke.

I knew how the tower felt being "tested". I was beginning to feel the stress of being pulled at by "them". Little bits of patience and normal everyday courtesy were beginning to pop off my hide. I growled at the lovely Susannah on my way out of the plane. Just because her goodbye to me wasn't different than her goodbye to the balding businessman in front of me. Spoiled petulant boy. Biting the hand that fed me.

But gradually Simon Rodea and his towers began to cheer me up.

Going through customs, hearing the flat nasal American twang ("Hi, howarya?" "Oh honeee! Look what they've done to my beeag"), I decided to take a tip from Simon Rodea. The rest of the world was on holiday, why not me?

I had the incredible luck to have two whole days with nothing to do. The sun was shining, the sky was blue . . . well, brownish-blue. Instead of wishing I was somewhere else – home, in London, or in New York with Veronica or holding Nicky's hand in Paris – let the good times roll. Have a good day, Jose. Have a ball in LA.

First thing I did when I got my bags, was to call Rent A Wreck. I was in luck, they still had it. Yup, they'd bring it round. "Just be out front, Mr Evers. You know where out front is?"

"Only place to be."

A few years back, when they'd had the Grand Prix at Long Beach, I'd rented a real showboat from Rent A Wreck. A metallic silver-blue, four-door, 1964 Lincoln Continental convertible. It still had the same effect on me. When the kid drove it up in front of the Pan Am terminal I was grinning so wide I burst out laughing. The car went on and on and on and on and on and on. It was just immense. And wide. Yes, and tasteful silver-blue metallic leather upholstery to match.

White side-wall tyres, wire wheels, air conditioning, electronic am and fm stereo radio, individually adjustable six-way power seats, cruise control, radar automatic headlight dipper, power windows, power aerial, power brakes, power steering, automatic transmission and 425 horsepower to haul its three tons around. It handled like a pig in a mud wallow, its suspension pleading "please don't make me go around corners, please, anything but that, heeeelp". On the other hand, in the land of the freeways and a speed limit of the double nickel, it was as smooth as cream.

I asked the kid to put the top down. He undid a latch, pushed a button. There was a whirring sound and a panel behind the rear passenger seat rose up as the brilliant white canvas top reached for the sky ("hands up or I'll shoot") paused, then as if shot, folded quickly into the grave laid open by the panel. The panel shut, the rear deck was a smooth expanse of metallic powder-blue and the top never existed. The whirring stopped. End of show.

"Can you give me a lift back to the lot?"

"Sure kid."

When I left him off, outside his lot, he stood at the gate and watched me drive off, watching the history disappear.

Driving out Century Boulevard, out to the San Diego Freeway, the other drivers and their passengers gawped. A QEII among rowboats. The Lincoln was almost twenty-five years old, a certifiable antique in California. Adults over thirty-five arched their eyebrows in disapproval. Kids loved it.

Sure they did. Sheeit, man, this is the west coast of America. Restraint is no virtue. No advantage being small. None a'tall. Wonderful country this Transatlantica. From shining bronze sea to foggy grey channel the contrasts can take your breath away.

The first question everybody in LA asks you when you arrive is "Wher're ya stayin'?" It comes from the natives pigeonholing each other by geography. Hollywood – out of it. Beverly Hills – rich. Bel Air – super-rich. West Hollywood – interior decorators. The real snobs are more complicated than that, but you get the idea. Their definitions come from streets, numbers on streets, how far up the hill, etc. And their classifications are as subtle and as specific as the cubbyholes the British stuff each other into on the strength of the pronunciation of a vowel.

So, "Wher're ya stayin'?" is another way of asking who you are. LA is very big on identities, who's in, who's out, and who's catching up. And if I was going to take my identity from my geography, I had plenty of hotels to choose from.

You could think of the hotels as time zones. The Bel Air, in its lush and secluded tropical glen, redolent of the twenties when the movie money started to get really big. The Chateau Marmont for a slightly faded trip into the talky drawing room melodramas of the thirties. The Beverly Hills Hotel, for the big time wheels and deals of the forties and fifties. The Hyatt Regency on Sunset where the rock groups did heavy dope in the sixties. The immense and impersonal glass and steel of the Century Plaza from the seventies, when the big corporations took over the film business. Or the Beverly Wilshire, the hotel for the eighties, where money comes in first, second and third, and the lobby is crawling with suburban imitations of Joan Collins in town to "do a little shopping".

I pulled into the Beverly Hills Hotel, and tossed the keys to the parking attendant in the way that the nouveau biggies do in Hollywood, confident that my bags would arrive in my room before I did. He didn't bat an eye at the Lincoln. He probably drove more Ferrari Testa Rosas, Bentley Turbos, Aston Martin Volantes and Lamborghinis in a day than most motoring journalists do in a lifetime. If you were going to impress in Beverly Hills you couldn't do it with nostalgia, even if it weighed three tons.

Frankly, Charlotte, I didn't give a damn.

I gave the attendant the standard $5 tip. Also the doorman, and the head bell hop who asked for my name so that he could get my room number from the desk. From then on it would be "thank you Mr Evers, thank you Mr Evers, thank you Mr Evers", and $15 every time I walked in and out of the hotel. I wondered if there was a side entrance.

But of course the whole point of the Beverly Hills Hotel is to make an entrance, to be seen. It's a pink and green temple to showbiz. Tables in the lobby and the Polo Lounge; the bar and by the pool have telephones so you can make the big-buck deals while the voluptuous starlet by your side stares off into space, bored out of her skull.

Walk into any public room at the Beverly Hills Hotel and people look up to see if you are anybody. But they don't stare. There are so many celebrities even Cher or Robert Redford don't get a second glance. Nor does a Formula One racing driver with a growing reputation for losing control.

The hotel comes from a pre-1940s era of dark wood and soft lights, freshly squeezed orange juice, a fireplace in your room and a garden outside your bedroom door. And golden California sun streaming in through the vines on the window. My bags were in my room and so was a note from Janice Henrion. Our lady of the wee pointy wobblies. It was hand written on the hotel's notepaper. Determined lass.

*forrest*

*I keep missing you.*

*Please, please forgive me. A working girl after a story is not a pretty sight. My editor wants more on poor Michel. Hounding me to hound you.*

*That's the excuse. The truth is more complicated and less easy to explain. Except, except, I would love to see you. Just for me, off the record?*

*I've made reservations for two at Olivier at nine. Let my editor pay. He'll never know it's my pleasure and none of his business.*

*Ring me at the Regency Apartment Hotel in Hollywood, Please?* please

*janice*

It implied everything and said nothing. I remembered the stab of her questions. She carried cold steel.

It was the year that Olivier was *the* restaurant in Los Angeles. Two weeks waiting list. They would call you if they had a vacant table. If they felt you were worthy of one. So either she had high connections or she had planned this for a long time.

I rang up the Regency but she wasn't in. I left a message that I would pick her up at 8.30. "Dress up," I said.

I had just one piece of business in LA: Walter Agabasian. But doing business with Walter Agabasian was more fun than playing with almost anybody else.

Walter Agabasian was about six foot three, weighed 225 pounds, had a big moon face with a happy grin. "Big Bash", we called him.

"Funny," I'd said when I first met him, "I thought Armenians were short, dark and wore a mustache."

"Yeah," he said, grinning, "but that was before I moved to California."

That big happy grin could fool you. A few years back he had been one of the phantom racers of the freeways. He had stuffed a twin turbocharged eight-litre Cadillac engine into an innocent-looking Seville, tweaked the suspension, and gone out hunting in the early hours before dawn to see if there was anybody else fool enough to think they were the fastest cat on the freeway. Top speed was around 210 on the straights.

Bets ranged up to $50,000 for the run on the Hollywood Freeway from the Pasadena to the Ventura. They drove the California Highway Patrol nuts. Well, how would you feel if you were doodling along at 55 just before dawn, feeling kinda dozy, and all of a sudden a little innocent-looking Cadillac Seville passed you going 210 miles an hour? That was a 155 miles an hour over the legal limit. It happened. The California Highway Patrol drove into the ditch.

Bash was the best fabricator on the coast. He did special effects for Hollywood. Rigged stunts. Made the bits for Dan Gurney's suspensions when Dan was building Indy cars. If you wanted something strange and mechanical, something nobody ever asked for before, and you wanted it soon and you wanted it right, Bash was the man.

It was entirely possible that when Max and I got through testing the Arundel we'd want some changes made. And if any of those changes involved parts we didn't have, it'd be handy to have Bash ready and waiting. I was glad for an excuse to go see him. "Forrest, you crazy fucker," he said on the phone, "come on over, I've got some neat new stuff to show you."

He always had "some neat new stuff" to show you.

After a short parade of Rolls Royce, Mercedes and Italian exotica came burbling up from the parking lot, the big blue barge hogged the scene in front of the Beverly Hills Hotel.

The kid with the short red jacket who drove it up took my $5 without looking at me. "Thank you Mr Evers." His eyes were fixed on a pretty little eighteen year old in a child's dress, hanging on the suede arm of a thirty-five-year-old man who was either the next Paul Newman or an assistant bank manager. In Hollywood you never know.

Driving north, on the Golden State out of Los Angeles, out of the smog and into the dry mountains, the air was cooler, fresher. The six-lane highway wound up into the mountains like an invitation and I felt a great sense of space and freedom warming my chilly soul. Exactly the opposite of what I felt in Japan. The top was down, the sun was out, the big blue Lincoln was purring. I looked down at the speedometer: 105. I had no idea the old boat could go that fast uphill.

Walter Agabasian Enterprises is a ranch house up in the rocky hills near Saugus. It looks like its main crop is dirt because this is the desert and out here, without water, nothing grows. The house is set at the end of a long dirt road, and in the big lot in front you're apt to see Ferraris and road-going CanAm Lolas. Not to mention wingless P51 Mustangs, Empire Road Raider's Warships from the year 2020, 1941 Cadillacs, funny cars, tow trucks, transporters, buses, and mobile homes.

Detroit and Turin and Birmingham may be where they manufacture cars, but California is where the automobile is a religious object. A thing to worship. And Bash was one of the rogue bishops.

As I came over the hill his 'workshop' rose out of the dirt and rock landscape to greet me: a vast shed, formerly an aircraft hanger from an airport bulldozed aside by a shopping centre.

I pulled up in a cloud of dust and Bash came out of his corrugated cave, pushing back a welder's visor from his face. He was wearing his usual blue polo shirt, jeans, topsiders and a gold Rolex GMT Master.

"Goddamn, Forrest, it's great to see you. Where'd you find Cleopatra?"

I got out of the car and shaking his big, calloused hand, mimicking his accent. "Howarya Bash, and whaddaya mean, Cleopatra?"

"The barge," he said nodding towards the car. "This is the old boat I rigged for the Kennedy film." He was on his knees at the back of the car, peering underneath it. "Look, I'll show you." He pulled out a small platform from behind the rear bumper. It clicked into place. "See? There are four of those, one at each corner for the Secret Service guys, and you could use them for mounting the cameras for the special effects close-ups for when the bullet hit," he said happily. "What was the movie called? *The Big Kill*? We always called the car Cleopatra because it was such a damn barge. I tweaked the motor some to haul all the actors and cameras around. I always thought it would make a good camera car. Where'd you get it?"

No wonder it would do 105 up a mountainside without breathing hard. I told him it was a rental stone from Rent A Wreck and switched the subject. Bash's revelations about my car and assassinations didn't exactly relax me. But I was glad to see him and I wasn't going to let it worry me either. "Whattaya got?"

"Lotta stuff. C'mere, I'll show you."

I followed Bash into his nirvana for car freaks. Over in one corner there was a huddle of what looked like a dozen fairground bumper cars, the kind that are painted bright red and green and yellow and have a big rubber bumper all the way around and a tall aerial sticking up from the back to take electricity from an overhead wire mesh. Except these had a little shiny disc at the top of their aerials.

"They're for a sci-fi film," he said. "Watch this." He picked up what looked like a radio phone, punched some numbers, and one of the little cars went "beep beep", backed up, turned around and came whirring across the floor to Bash, where it stopped, and waited expectantly.

The sight of a car driving itself looked eerie. "Drivers are an endangered species Evers," he said. Bash pushed some buttons and the little beast whirled around and went back where it came from. "The plot revolves around who controls this box of tricks," he said, putting the control radio back on the bench.

"You mean the President sits in one of these and suddenly it takes off for Goldfinger's hideout?"

"Something like that," he said. "The story takes place in the future when the prisons look like amusement parks. 'Course on a modern car, like the new BMW, you put your foot down, and what you're doing is sending a signal to a computer."

I walked over to the other end of the shop, where he kept, under dust sheets, his collection of classic cars. "What's wrong with that?"

"Well nothing really, except there's no reason the computer couldn't have other inputs, like, 'That's too fast for this road, and I don't care if you've got your foot down to the floor.' And 'I don't give a shit if there's a truck coming, we're not going any faster'. Or, 'Sorry but I'm not programmed to go over the speed limit'. Or, 'That's the third time this week you made me go fast and I'm telling the police'." His voice, mimicking the computer, had turned falsetto.

"You mean you're not in control, the computer is."

"In the future, Forrest, you are going to have to ask a computer permission to pee."

I peeled back the dust cover from one of a dozen cars: a 1929 Minerva dualcowl phaeton, Belgium's attempt at making a Rolls Royce look ordinary.

The car was a four-door convertible like Cleopatra, but there the resemblance ended. It was higher and longer. The distance between the front windscreen and the silver-helmeted lady on top of the grill was measured in yards. There was a second windscreen for the rear passengers, tall wire wheels mounted on the front wings for spares, a wicker-covered Louis Vuitton trunk for a boot, polished silver and crystal in the liquor cabinet, walnut picnic tables that folded down, and, thrown across the soft, dove-grey and green leather rear seat, a vicuna lap rug.

There is something different about the colour of the finest classic cars that goes beyond the chemistry of paint and the shortcuts of the assembly line.

Like the perfect English lawn that can only be achieved by rolling for three hundred years, you have to begin with thirty coats of enamel, hand-rubbed between each coat, the way they used to finish the coaches before the turn of the century. Add the slow gloss of time that covers imperfections with a golden haze, and forty years of a chauffeur's daily polishing. And stir in the slow mellowing of colours and the hardening of the surface and you will have a sense of that deep, calm, bottomless sea of blue-green and the golden light of an earlier time that glowed under the surface of the Minerva's skin.

Bash saw me staring into the Minerva's sea-green depths. I could barely see myself. I looked ghostly, transparent.

"Why'd you quit?" he asked.

"I'll tell you about it. But you were going to show me something first."

A few minutes later I was standing alongside his dirt track when a screaming appeared on the dirt horizon, and out of the blue sky, in a cloud of dirt and rocks, a mad fury roared past me looking like a hurricane on wheels. Bash had a new toy. He disappeared over the next dirt ridge, but the awful noise went on. Two minutes later he was back.

"The course record," he said, unstrapping his helmet, is one minute, thirty-four seconds."

I was looking at a birdcage with wide wheels, like a dune buggy, but smaller. "God, what an awful noise. You know, Bash, I think all you really want to do is strap a rocket to your ass and set fire to the fuse."

"You gonna try it?"

"What is it?"

"My new Bashmobile. I heard they were getting 220 hp out of these little rotary outboard motors, and I thought if they only weigh 150 pounds, the power to weight ratio must be pretty good. We're thinking of producing a couple dozen of 'em for team racing on TV."

"One thirty-four, that's it, that's your record? Didn't anybody ever teach you to shift out of second gear?" I was climbing into the thing. Bash handed me his helmet.

"Yeah, that's my record. I heard you lost your nerve so I guess I won't have any trouble hanging on to it." He was grinning, goading me, knowing nerve never had anything to do with it. He'd raced sprint cars on dirt tracks. Bash had been there.

"Racing cars just frightens me to death," I said. "How 'bout a little bet to sweeten it? How about my Aston Martin against your Minerva?"

"That little green tin shit box with a rag top isn't worth the Minerva's tea set. How about a beer?"

"You're on," I said, and popped the clutch, giving him a rock and dirt shower. The little bugger spun its wheels and slid side to side before it began to scoot. Vroom, roar, there was plenty of power, but not much grip on the loose dirt. An overpowered roller skate on marbles. I set off up the hillside.

Bash had scraped off a mile and a half track up and down the hill at back of his house. Originally it had been for dirt bikes, with the terrain much too rugged for four-wheelers, but recently he'd scraped off a few of the more jagged rock piles and pronounced it open to all comers. "Anybody who's dumb enough to want to race here, can. As long as they bring their own beer and clean up their mess, and I invite them in the first place."

Some men have pool tables, some play golf, and some like to watch TV. Bash liked to strap on his helmet and charge into the rocks and the dirt. It did have its practical side. It was a good shakedown for the off-road racers he sometimes built. But as a race track it had all the subtlety of a tank proving ground.

Improving on Bash's time wasn't going to be easy. The little flea-flicker wanted to spin as much as go forward, and it's brakes were not much use. The best way to slow it down was to put it in a big four-wheel slide before a corner, point it in the direction you wanted to end up in, and stomp on the accelerator just before you got to the entrance to the corner. The other tricky bit was that Bash knew where the rocks were. I kept finding them the hard way.

On the fourth lap, when I was up on top of the ridge, I noticed something that might work. When I passed Bash I gave him a thumbs up, pedal to the medal, scramble, vrroom, roar. It was like being a rodeo rider in the open countryside. Whaahooooo, I said, lifting the front wheels in the air.

At the top of the hill the track ran straight for a quarter of a mile, then plunged down the other side of the hill to a sharp banked left turn. The track then went into a series of tight 'S's before doubling back on itself.

Sliding through the turn at the top of the hill, I kept my foot planted flat on the floor as I headed down the steep hill, the car bounding but keeping to a generally straight line. I celebrated passing the braking point for the banked turn at the bottom (the place where I should be standing on the brakes, shifting down and starting one of those crazy sideways slides,) by keeping my foot down, shifting up into fifth and heading straight for the banking. I wasn't going to slow down, I was going to take off.

Fly, baby, fly.

Straight into the corner, up the bank and into the air. Nice, even take off. The vibration stopped. I was on holiday, flying, relaxing.

I let up on the throttle to keep the rotary from overrevving and looked out over the California countryside. A gorgeous view out over the valley. The air was delicious, smelling of sage and warm earth. I eased back onto the throttle and landed hard, back on the track headed in almost the right direction, having cut out a good half mile. Total flight time: 1.7 seconds.

I lost about four seconds in the next turn, coming in too fast and all crossed up, but it didn't matter. When I passed Bash at the start finish line he looked like a stunned mullet, staring at his stopwatch. I did a 180-degree handbrake turn, headed back for him and did a second turn in front of his shoes. I had a right to show off.

"The clock broke."

"Come on, dogbreath, you owe me a beer. And if you ever beat that time I'll give you the Aston Martin."

"Forrest, no way you could've done that course in fifty-four seconds. Wha'd you do, fly?"

We sat in the shade of his front porch, looking out over the valley. It was a hot afternoon, and we were cooling our hands and our throats with ice-cold bottles of Dos Equis. I told Bash why I'd quit Formula One, and why I was going back.

Bash put his feet up on the railing, threw his head back and started to ask questions. "What was the difference between the cars?"

"Which cars?"

"Yours and Michel's and Alfonso's."

"None, really. If anything my car would have been a little better prepared than Maurizio's. And I suppose that there were one or two developments in the course of the season that would have made Michel's car faster than mine, but nothing really significant."

"Suspension and wing adjustments?"

"Nothing important that I know of. The cars didn't show any big gains in speed during the season."

"So they were virtually identical?"

"About the only difference was the decals."

"Different sponsors?"

"Sure. We all had the Wyoming decals of Empire Tobacco; they're by far the most important sponsor. And Alfonse had a deal with Fasolini Heaters, and Michel had Les Amis du Vin Français. And he and I both carried the Florelle decals for the Coleman Fibre Group."

"Florelle?"

"It's the European brand name for a new fabric. Made by one of your American chemical companies, actually. It started as a flameproof thing. Then they found it repelled water and dirt and it's lightweight, comfortable. My driving suit and my fireproof undersuit are made of it."

"You sound like a drape salesman."

"I went to a couple of their trade shows last winter. They've built a whole promotion around the car. As sponsors do." I said, neglecting to mention that I was on the cover of the Florelle Catalogue. A man has to have some secrets.

"Anything else that was different about the cars – oil, gas, tyres, electronics?"

"Maurizio had a contract with Olio Braganzi, Michel and I with Europetrol. And of course the team is sponsored by Calculus Computer Systems, as well as Coleman's. Calculus does a certain amount of our engine management development. But they're not a major player."

"And you don't know anybody who'd be willing to see a Formula One car drive into a crowd?"

That stopped me for a moment. "Nobody drove into a crowd."

"Not yet, they haven't. But you don't know why you crashed, except you just put your goddamn foot down. And you started seeing two tracks. And if Michel was way the hell off line, I'd guess that whatever is causing those crashes is not all that predictable. Let's face it, a 190 mile an hour rolling projectile is not that easy to control even when the driver knows what he's doing. So whoever is causing this has to at least consider the possibility of one of you turkeys heading off into the crowd and mowing down a few rows of spectators. They have to consider that possibility and say, 'to hell with it we'll crash the son of a bitch anyway'."

He put down his empty beer bottle, and looked at me with an intensity I hadn't seen for a while. "I think," he said, "you're right, they're not really after you. But I also think Ken isn't really the target either. There's too many other easier ways to get to him or to you. It's got to be something bigger to not give a damn about that many lives. I smell some very big bad fish out there. And I'll tell you, Forrest, they *are* out there. If you feel something coming your way and it's as big as a corporation, put down your toys and go home."

He paused, and turned away from me, taking in the view over the valley, the city a brown smear in the distance. "Look for where the big money is. The money that wouldn't give a damn if you drove into a crowd."

"I'm not looking for anything," I said putting down the empty bottle. "I'm waiting for the sharks to come to me."

He called after me as I turned Cleopatra around and barged down towards the road. "Keep your head down driving that car, Evers."

I drove back to my hotel, past the three open palms, glad to see me ("Thank you, Mr Evers"; "Good evening Mr Evers"; "Nice day, Mr Evers?") and called Veronica. She wasn't in.

"Any messages?"

"Just the usual. Say I called."

"Your name again, sir?"

I also called Ken's ex, Alicia. She was in. "God, you're not going to drive for the old turd again are you?" And, "I should think anybody that knows Ken well, loathes him. But I don't think he has mortal enemies." In the way that British ladies sometimes do she stretched 'mortal' into a long and happy life. "Still, if it means you buying me lunch, I shall have a think. I don't suppose you've just stepped out of the shower have you? I like to picture you dripping."

And I called Nicole in Paris. She sounded very far away. "I wish you could be here, Forray. It is miserable. Cold and raining. Just like London; you'd feel right at home. My family is not nice, and I wish they would go away. After the service – you are coming to the service? – after the service you must take me away for a while so I can be horrible. Now I have to be very nice to all Michel's relatives. Will you take me for a holiday?"

"Suppose I take you with me to Australia?"

"Everyone will talk and raise a big stink. OK."

Finally I called Susan. Her lawyer answered. Yes, he supposed she would be free for luncheon on the 22nd. He would check with his client. Yes that was fine. Did he mind if she came alone? No, he didn't mind, that was perfectly acceptable to him.

So after that emotional trampoline, it took a little while to recapture my holiday mood. But after I passed the three "thank yous" again and slipped back behind the wheel of the blue pleasure barge, I began to feel like a man on the prowl again. It was a balmy night, the top was still down, and who knew what the evening might bring.

I pulled up outside the Regency and parked Cleopatra on the little rise outside the front door, walked past the clerk who was talking to his boyfriend on the phone, and into the courtyard and swimming pool.

I walked right past her.

Not that I didn't see her; no man could have missed her, sitting at one of the poolside tables in a little white chiffon mini-nothing. She'd had her hair cut: it stood up straight on top of her head, but because it was fine it fell forward over her forehead. The effect of the punk-kid look was to soften her face.

"Am I so easy to ignore, Mr Evers?"

"It takes all my willpower, Miss Henrion. But you do look very different."

"Well, you did order me to dress up," she said with a pouting little girl look. She stood up. She was quite small, and very slim.

"It's nice to see you, Forrest. Is Forrest all right?"

"I've grown used to it. Would you care for a drink?"

"Oh, let's go straight to Olivier. I know I'm supposed to act blasé, but I'm excited about going to the poshest restaurant in California with the best-looking man for miles."

The false note of flattery sounded clumsy, coming from her. "Only today I was offered a part in a movie."

"Really?"

"A series, they're bringing back the talking mule."

"All right, you're not the handsomest man in California, just the sexiest. Let's go," she said, linking her hand in mine and turning her face up to me. Her blonde hair, pale skin and pink mouth . . . I started to think she looked fragile, almost translucent, when the fullness of her mouth stopped me. She had a lovely mouth.

She had to give me a little tug, to break my train of thought and set me in motion for the car. Six foot one of perfectly conditioned muscle and bone, with reflexes honed to a microsecond response, and all it takes is a little tug and good old Forrest shambles happily along after the pretty lady.

"Good lord, you're not serious. You can't go to Olivier in that!"

"You want to ride in the front or the back?"

"It looks like something out of a clown's funeral."

"In the back then."

# CHAPTER SIX

We made a game of Janice sitting in the back of Cleopatra. Miss Janice, the wealthy eccentric. Evers, the chauffeur.

"Left at the next light, Evers."

"Yes, Miss Janice."

"Slow down, Evers. No need to scrabble with the common herd."

"Indeed, Miss Janice."

We were both laughing when Olivier's doorman opened the rear door for Janice with the slightest of nods. But he lost his façade for a moment when I stepped out and tossed him the keys. Janice didn't help him when she said "Follow me, Evers."

He may have paused when he saw a wealthy, pretty lady leading her chauffeur to dinner. But he knew exactly what to do with Cleopatra the Barge. The keys never stopped moving as he took the toss from me and flipped them behind him to a car park attendant who was in the Lincoln, behind the wheel and moving before I'd shut the door. Olivier, like the other poshest of the posh LA restaurants, likes to decorate their forecourts with automobiles costing seventy-five thousand and up. Poor blue trash like Cleo was swept out of sight to the lot at the back.

Olivier knew, said their match covers and menus, that the last great urban luxury is space. And that the missing dimension in cities is time. Nothing was rushed, nothing was crowded, they were glad to see us, there was plenty of time, plenty of space. Would we like to go in or would we prefer a drink beforehand, in the garden by the pool?

Outside, the front of Olivier was a polished black granite façade reflecting the Sunset Boulevard parade. Inside the back of the restaurant was a wall of invisible, curved glass. So when you walked through the front door you saw the city of Los Angeles glittering beneath you, stretching out to the sea. It was like being on the bridge of a great skyship, coming in for a landing. The small foyer opened onto the dining room where the waiters, passing back and forth, were silhouettes against the rows of city lights in the distance. More polished black granite for the table tops, solid silver cutlery, Baccarat crystal, and five yards distance between the tables. All of the surfaces were dark and reflective. Hidden spotlights made each table a small island of light.

"Miss Henrion and guest?" asked the pretty young man in the dinner jacket inclining his head over the reservation list. That anonymous "guest" made me wonder if Janice had had a back-up boyfriend handy in case I hadn't shown up.

"Miss Henrion, and Mr Forrest Evers," I said for the record.

"Of course, Mr Evers," said the maitre d', acting grateful for this tidbit of information.

He led us into the room and there was a scattered turning of faces to greet us as the glitterati checked to see if we were of their rank or of another.

Janice in her little scrap of white chiffon could pass as either one of tomorrow's stars or today's producers. Now that I was separated from Cleopatra I looked more like the big money behind the film, the owner of several blocks of condominiums in Marina Del Rey. Or a Formula One racing driver high on the comeback trail.

I was wearing a muted blue-grey tweed sports jacket I'd had made in London and one of Blades' quieter dark blue striped shirts, and the dark blue tie of the Royal Thames Yacht Club. Confident and conservative for Hollywood, too garish for London. ("Tweed?" I could hear one of the old salty voices at the Royal Thames intoning. "My dear chap, *really*.")

It was no trick at all to get Janice to talk about herself. One of the benefits of the struggle for equality is that now women can be as boring as men about their careers.

Janice was "a real rarity", a Londoner all her life. I learned she grew up in West Kensington, not far from Edwardes Square where Susan and I had lived, so we shared some streets and shops, but no friends. She'd gone to Cambridge and joined the BBC when she came down to London. Her goal was to do some "real" investigative journalism. Not so much the sensational kind that exposed Presidents as crooks or Prime Ministers as transvestites. More the redeeming, social kind of story that had an effect on housing, say, or closed the "rip-off" tax loopholes. She was bored, she said, with covering motor racing.

Looking at her small, pale and pretty face beneath her spikey blonde hair, she looked so vulnerable I could imagine her squeezing secrets from the slick operators in the city. They would bring stories to her like gifts.

She opened her eyes wide, feigning interest as I traded her my stories of growing up in Westchester and in Suffolk. The stories of cold summers by the freezing Channel and snowy winters in America, shuttled back and forth between parents who corresponded by letter. And how angry my father had been when I left university to race in Formula Three, dragging my patched racing car across Europe behind a Morris Minor van. And how my mother insisted she have a drive in "that noisy little zapper". They were old stories; I'd told them many times. My mother and father both died in a car crash on the A30 after their re-engagement party.

My father, said the police, had been going over ninety in the rain and skidded off the road and into the trees. It was that car, his Aston Martin, that I had rebuilt, that Susan wanted now.

The wine waiter stood patiently by her elbow, while Janice scanned the wine list, her mouth pursing as she weighed the choices. She settled for a John Daniel Society Dominus 1983. This, apparently, was going to be a special night. The Daniel Society is a partnership between the proprietor of Château Petrus and two delightful sisters, daughters of the late and distinguished John Daniel. If you'd like to obtain a bottle of their wine, bring enough money to fill a large paper sack.

Janice swirled the dark wine in her mouth, closing her eyes, lifting her face as if for a kiss, tasting the first vintage ever of Dominus. I decided that one glass would do me no harm at all.

I was holding the first big sip of the Dominus in my mouth, swashing it around, thinking it had the fine aristocratic face of a Bordeaux and the big voluptuous body of a Burgundy, the lush opulence . . . when Janice interrupted. "Why do you do it?"

I thought she meant why do I make the big sucking sounds

when I taste the wine and I was about to swallow it and give her my standard boring speech about aeration when she said, "It is so obviously pointless, rushing around in circles."

"You don't like motor racing?"

She leant forward into the pool of light on the table, the front of her white chiffon just grazing the surface of the polished black granite table. The light shone through her dress. Nipples like pink thimbles. "To tell you the truth, Forrest," she said, lowering her voice, "I loathe it. I loathe your silly, macho, pointless game. I hate the mess you make, I hate the stink, hate the noise. The automobile is the worst killer on the earth and I hate making it into some kind of sexual symbol. It's dirty, nasty and corrupt."

"But other than that, you love it."

"I was supposed to be assigned to the Middle East for current affairs. Then Bill Oppegaard got something, I don't know, pleurisy, and I was flung into the pits with the mechanics and the jockeys."

"Lucky girl."

"I'm sorry. I do a good job. I just don't happen to be in love with the subject. And I can't get excited about a story about one man going around in circles a few hundredths of a second faster than another man. But I didn't bring you here to talk about my impressions of motor racing. What are you going to order?" She took hold of my hand across the table and gave me a half-worried, half-smiling look. As if the subject of motor racing was really too crude to be discussed in a rarefied place like this.

"The transmission broke," I said. The words lay in a big greasy lump in the middle of the crystal, the silver and the china.

She put down her menu, and all the pretence fell from her face. She saw at once what I was talking about. This, said the reporter in her, was the real stuff.

"We couldn't say anything because we're under contract to Darien. And besides, there's nothing you could prove. The car jumped out of gear."

"Your car?"

"My car at Brands, in Austria, and in Hungary."

"Why should that matter? Can't you just stick it back in gear? My old Mini used to jump out of gear all the time. It was a nuisance, but it wasn't dangerous."

"It matters because the car coming out of the corner is using its power to head in a certain direction. If you lose that power all of a sudden the centrifugal force pulls you out on a much wider line. Out onto the marbles."

Her eyes searched the ceiling as she looked for holes in the story. "What about Hungary? You stopped on the straight. There wasn't any danger of going off there, was there?"

"No, but on the two corners before I stopped it jumped out of fourth, and I damn near lost it. And I just said enough is enough. If they couldn't fix it before the race, they're not going to fix it now. And I wasn't going to risk killing myself and the other drivers."

"And Michel's car?"

"Michel's car was out of gear when we took the box apart."

"Do you think somebody tampered with them?"

I shrugged a noncommittal shrug, as if I didn't care.

"But you're not the only team using the Darien box."

"Maybe we mount them differently. Anyway, I have a little announcement for you. I'm going back with Team Arundel," I said taking another sip of wine. "I'll be the Team Arundel driver for the rest of the season."

"Wait a minute, you're going too fast, and it doesn't make sense. I mean I was right, wasn't I? The car is a death trap. Forrest, you can't go back into a car that almost killed you and killed Michel."

I smiled, and leant back in my chair, enjoying the view over Los Angeles. "Max has a new automatic transmission."

"Who else knows this?"

"No one outside Team Arundel. At least not yet. We'll have a little press conference at Riverside in a couple of days if our testing goes well."

Janice pushed her chair back, straightened up, walked around the table, put her arms around my neck and gave me a big wet kiss on my mouth. It gave me some insight into how Judas felt kissing Jesus, even though Judas was the kisser instead of the kissee or whatever the hell you call it. Betrayer.

There was a scattering of applause and Janice stood up, embarrassed. I smiled politely at the couple at the nearest table, a businessman on a business trip with a businesswoman on a business trip. They'd been talking loudly of "market shares," "relevant imagery," and "brand development index" in the remote awkward language of people who make their living selling mass-market products to the masses. They smiled back, then bent their heads close together to consult over who Janice and I might be.

Janice was as happy as a schoolgirl at a birthday party, laughing, giggling, ordering more wine. "Shall we have champagne? No that would be over the top. Waiter, champagne: Dom Perignon, if you please." They pleased, and Janice drank it all. But not without a nonstop stream of questions. What about poor old Alfonso? How did this new transmission work? Did we think it could be used in passenger cars? And did we plan to sue Darien for faulty transmissions? Shouldn't the other teams know about this? Or, if it was intentional, was that murder?

This was better than a birthday. Janice had come hoping to seduce one story from me, and I'd given her four. Big stories. Wonderful stories. Fat juicy stories. She was so happy. So grateful. Waiter, brandy please. You sure you won't have one, Forrest?

She leant against me in the warm night air as we waited for the attendant to bring Cleopatra around. Please, she asked, could she sit in the front this time? Her face looked up at me, Forrest, the giver of good stories, trust shining from her big green eyes. When I opened the door for her she slid all the way across the front seat, so when I got in, she put her arms around my neck and snuggled in close with her head against my chest. As I turned onto Sunset, she slid down so her head was in my lap. I looked down at the little blonde spikey head. "Mumph," she said, "Forrumph."

When I pulled up in front of the Regency she sat up, shaking her head and blinking her eyes. "Oh, wow. Whooo. Forrest. You have to take better care of me. Whooo. You have to help me home. Please? I make a wonderful cup of instant coffee."

It was a soft, warm evening, with that relaxed summer feeling that Los Angelenos take for granted and acts like a balm for my chilly northern soul. In the old days, they say, you could smell the orange groves that ranged all around Hollywood and ran for miles out past Whittier to Riverside. Now the air was perfumed with burned and unburned hydrocarbons. But as we walked through the little lobby and to the pool there was the scent of the night jasmine flowering in the borders, making a heavy, fragrant, sexy connection to the primitive centre of my brain.

Janice's suite was on the second floor, up an outdoor staircase to a balcony overlooking the pool. She groped in her little white satin bag for her key, found it, and let us in. "You wait right here," she said. "I'll just be a tick."

Several hundred ticks went by as I sat on a deep-cushioned beige couch and surveyed the awful decor. Brown shag carpet that probably began life in a low budget gorilla movie. Heavy ceramic vase lamps sculpted with tasteful red and black swirls accented with gold flecks. Blond laminated coffee and end tables. A round white plastic breakfast table with white plastic imitation wrought-iron chairs. A big black imitation wrought-iron chandelier that had little linen lampshades. They looked like upended tea mugs on giant fish hooks.

I wandered into the kitchen to look in the fridge for entertainment. One thing about America, their fridges are a proper size. Janice's certainly had plenty of space. The little phials of vitamin capsules and prescription pills, a carton of orange juice and an empty carton of milk looked lonely. Not a lot going on in there. I shut the door, temporarily blinded by the bright white refrigerator light.

"Forrest?" she was calling me from her bedroom. "Forrest, are you still out there?"

"Still here, Janice," I said, heading for the couch again.

"Forrest, can you help me please?" Her voice sounded muffled. "Please?"

When I walked into the bedroom the bedside lamp was on and Janice was standing by the bed with her arms straight in the air as if somebody with a gun had just said "stick 'em up". She was encased in a violet silk nightgown that extended from her wrists to her belly button. A little puff of honey-blonde hair between her legs didn't look like it would keep her warm.

"I'm stuck," she said through the nightie. I started to tug it down, pulling at its hem. "No. No, not that way, pull it off."

I did as I was told, slipping her silk casing over her head and tossing it on the bed. She put her arms around my neck, kissed me, let go and spun and fell face first on the enormous bed. "Please,

Forrest. Please." She was talking into her pillow and I bent over her to hear what she was saying. "Please, Forrest darling. Please use a condom." She rolled over on her back, smiled at me, closed her eyes and started to snore.

I stood up. Lying there on the green bedspread she looked like a little bird of paradise that had lost all its feathers. Just a working girl, working. I pulled down the covers under her and then pulled them back over her, tucking her in, turned out the light, and walked out.

On the way out I checked with the night clerk to see if she had a wake-up call. He put down his paperback on the switchboard and stood up, a tall, thin and gentle person, with thinning hair and a long tortoiseshell cigarette holder. "Henrion," he said in an unexpectedly deep voice that sounded like someone else was standing behind him. "Miss Henrion. That's right, 34B. Yes, she has a wake-up call for 12.30 this evening."

That would be 8.30 a.m., London time. "Thanks," I said. "Just checking."

It was midnight when I got back to my room at the Beverly Hills Hotel, so I rang Ken.

"Forrest," he said, "isn't it past your time for beddy-bye?"

"Sorry to interrupt your beauty rest, but I thought you should start cooking your hot denials."

"She bought the faulty gearbox story?"

"It hardly makes me feel proud."

"It was an act of courage."

"It was a nasty, dirty trick."

"It may save your life. If it works, our mysterious *they* will think we haven't a clue and come after you with a low moan."

"As long as I hear them coming. We don't have a clue. Shouldn't we let Max in on this?"

"Forrest, really. We must act as natural as possible. Imagine Max smiling, trying to be charming."

"You're right. The less he knows the better. You have told him I'm driving for you again? At your request."

"At my request. Yes, he knows. Maybe the trip will quiet him down."

"And you've spoken to Alfonso?"

"I've spoken to Alfonso. I explained to him that I can't afford to continue to campaign two cars, and he said he understood. As long as I understood he was contracted for the season and would have to be paid whether he drove or not. However, under the unfortunate circumstances, he said he would be willing to continue not driving for half-pay. Especially if he didn't have to go to Australia. Apparently he has an ex-wife or mistress in Australia."

"Always the gentleman. After you, Alfonse."

"The thought occurs to me, Forrest, why the papers so rarely print the truth. Nobody ever gives it to them."

His laughter was a dreadful gasping and wheezing. To stop him I said, "I'm having lunch with Alicia on the 23rd in London. Do you want to come?"

"Good God, no. You do have the most preposterous ideas, Evers. Tell me, Forrest, you are making yourself conspicuous, are you not?"

"As conspicuous," I said, stealing Janice's line, "as a clown at a funeral."

After Ken hung up I looked at my watch: 12.30, time for Miss Janice to be phoning London. I rang the switchboard and told them I wasn't to be disturbed. I'd had enough holiday for one day. There was still one more day to go.

# CHAPTER SEVEN

I woke with the sunlight streaming in my window and the little red message light on the phone winking. There was a knock at the door. A Latino bus girl, dark eyes in shadows of dark hair, wheeled in the silver trolley with my breakfast, keeping her eyes strictly on the tray and the carpet while I rang the messages operator. No damn nonsense.

I told the operator to hold on, and held my hand over the phone. "Excuse me," I said to the girl, thinking she was probably Mexican and being careful to speak clearly and slowly so she could understand the gringo's English. "Excuse me. Would you be kind enough to take the five-dollar bill on the dresser. Thank you. Tip. Thank you very much."

She looked at me suspiciously, went over to the dresser and pocketed the bill. "Thanks, dad," she said over her shoulder as she went out the door. " 'Preciate the gesture. Have a nice day."

Veronica had called. I asked if she'd left a message. There was a pause, then the woman, who sounded as if she were in her seventies, read it over the phone in a flat midwestern twang: "I miss you darling. And I love you very much. Staying in tonight for a one-woman orgy with a sandwich and the telly, thinking of you touching me here, and here, and me kissing you there and there. Ring me soon. Love Veronica."

No, the woman said, there were no other messages.

I rang Veronica in New York, and she'd gone out. Goddamn long-distance romance. In the future the telefax machines will have all the fun.

Breakfast was as I had ordered: a bowl of fresh fruit, herbal tea, toast, no butter. The bowl of fruit was a technicolor triumph of genetic engineering. Fruits for a new and larger race. Mangoes, guavas, grapefruits, oranges, peaches, melons. Pears, apples, passion fruits, lychees. The black cherries were the size of lemons. Gorgeous, delicious, wonderful. And too much sugar. Fruit carries a big sugar hit. I stopped after eight bites. At my rate of consumption, the bowl held enough for twelve large Formula One drivers.

It was just 7.15, the start of a beautiful California day. Friday 9th September, the last day of my holiday. The lobby was bustling with people checking out, TV producers and businessmen waiting to meet their 'associates' for a breakfast meeting.

I waited in line to change some yen into dollars, studying the bald spot on the back of a short blond Englishman in front of me. He stood with an aggressive slouch and I remember wondering if I'd seen him before. He was dressed California casual, yellow cashmere pullover, no shirt underneath. Maybe he had a hairy chest he wanted to display. Like me he wanted to change yen into dollars. How, I wondered, does a certain Midlands accent manage to put a sneer into every syllable.

"You absolutely sure that's the rate?" He sounded irritated, impatient.

"Fresh this morning, sir." She was bubbly, cute. Too cute to be cast as a bank clerk in a hotel.

"I wonder if you'd care to check it again. Because if that's your rate it's a bloody cheat."

"I'll check it for you in a moment, sir. Would you mind stepping aside while I wait on the gentleman behind you?"

"You're damn right I mind. I mind being waited on by cretins, and I mind wasting time while you avoid answering a simple question. Now you check that rate right now or I shall have your fat ass fired for incompetence."

It was too sunny a morning to be annoyed. "That's all right," I said, "I don't mind waiting." When he didn't turn around I started to get curious about his face. "Hotel exchange rates are always stacked against you," I said to the back of his head while the girl went off to check the figures.

He turned around. He had a little doll face, the kind that mothers call 'cute'. On a middle-aged man who'd smoked and drunk too much, his face looked like a hard pink rubber ball, yellowing at the edges. "When I want financial advice from an asshole . . ."

69

he started to say, then stopped, his head jerking back a fraction as if he recognized me. At the time I thought he was just another crass little rich man.

"Don't worry about it," I said as he walked by stuffing hundred-dollar bills into his wallet with a flash of gold and diamonds from a ring. "When it comes to assholes, size isn't everything."

He pretended he didn't hear me.

The Open Palms were so busy the first two missed me. The parking lot attendant suffered a momentary lapse of memory. "Good morning Mr uh, ah."

"Evers," I said loudly, "Forrest Evers," practising public conspicuousness. But of course the Englishman in the yellow cashmere was living proof that Hollywood is wall to wall with self-important people. ("Hi, I'm Mr Bigtime." "Glad to meet you, I'm Mr Bigtime myself." "Mr Bigtime, Mr Bigtime, and Mr Bigtime, I'd like you to meet Bobby Bigtime, he's really big time.")

If I wasn't careful, I'd pass for a native. Forrest Bigtime, boy racer. I slid in behind the wheel of the big blue, big-time nostalgia barge and headed out Sunset, towards the sea.

The day I'd planned for myself began with a two-mile run up the sand to Malibu and back. I set up a nice easy rhythm with the big rollers coming in from Shanghai crashing on the sand, and the sun throwing my long shadow into the waves. The air was still cool and clear. I'd kept in shape over the past few months. But I had to work on my endurance. Mexico City is 7,300 feet up, and the air is thin up there. With the heat, the roughness of the track, and the lack of oxygen, it was the toughest race on the calendar, physically.

As I ran, I thought of the other drivers. They would be in Mexico City now, joking around the pool at the Camino Real, riding the beautiful horses on the big haciendas outside the city, playing golf. They would be giving themselves plenty of time to become acclimatized to the thin air and the heat.

As a private entrant, Team Arundel was always coming from behind. We just didn't have the money to be on the front row. Honda had twenty technicians staring into video monitors at every practice and every race. They were reading data directly from the car when it was out on the track so they knew exactly what effect their suspension and wing settings had at every corner. And they knew if the engine had a problem, and why, and how serious it was before it happened. Ferrari had a pipeline to Fiat's endless sea of money, as well as their wind tunnel and a research and development group in Britain to work on next year's car while another group in Italy continued development on this year's Ferrari.

We had plenty of popular support in Britain. We were the good little 'un against the good big 'uns. But we didn't have the money to be truly competitive. We were a sideshow in the Formula One circus.

Max's automatic transmission had the potential to change all that. If it worked we might attract a major sponsor who could afford a competitive research budget. And we might build a big enough financial base where we could afford to buy all those extra horses we didn't have now. I wasn't complaining, but I did envy the drivers who could put their foot down on fifty to eighty extra horses costing £5,000 a hoof. My feet were starting to feel tender in the sand. My thighs and calves were starting to burn and feel heavy. I was puffing and I could just see the first of the multi-million-dollar beach shacks of the Malibu colony.

We were so close. Getting on pole in Hungary had been partly a fluke, but only partly. Ferrari were having trouble with their electrics, and Lotus' suspension was reacting strangely. And Hungaroring is a tight track where our disadvantage in power didn't cost us much in lap times. But still, we had done it. We had gotten on the pole. We could win. If we would win just once, we'd get over having to cut corners, having to make do, and "play catch-up ball" as the big-time film directors say in Malibu.

When I got to Malibu, running past the decks and the beach houses with their walls of glass facing the Pacific, pretty people in their beach clothes were lounging over their breakfast. Some of them were having a look at the sea before driving to the studio. I was sweating and gasping. A shark had taken a big bite out of my side. A barracuda had locked his teeth into my right shin. The sand felt like wet cement. And someone had lit a barbecue inside my chest. Looking at the pretty people having their leisurely coffee, I wished, not for the first time, that someone else could do my work-outs for me.

71

I stopped running and went into my routine, as taught to me by the Swiss Army Knife, Dieter Kuebel. "No gain mittout pain," I could hear his voice dripping with Sweitzerdeutsch. "If you vant energy, you must spend energy."

Nowadays any athlete who reaches the top hears plenty of theories about how to stay in peak condition. All the good ones begin with the same thought, "There are no shortcuts". Kuebel had designed a course for the Swiss army based on the theory that relaxing and extending the muscles is as important as contracting, so he combined rigorous exercises with yoga. Having been through his course in Zurich, I would strongly recommend that you not mess with the Swiss army in hand to hand combat. He'd added a few special twists for me. "You are not running up and down ze sides of ze Alps," he said, "so for you ze thigh muscles are not so important. But you must have a strong neck to keep your vision clear and you must have very strong and supple muscles in your upper body. Stamina, you must have, above all." Indeed you must.

I was doing what looks like a hindu sun worship on the beach when I heard from a distance, someone calling my name.

"Forrest. Forrest, you old fart. Heeyyyyyy, Evers!" Up on the deck of one of the beach houses a figure was waving. He kept waving and his voice had a kind of familiar authority. The boyish tousled blond hair, the big sunglasses, the aw shucks crinkly grin, the freckles; it was Arthur Warren.

"Christ, howthehellareya? Goddamn," he said drawling, growing more serious as I walked up to his deck, "I saw you hit the camera on television. Shit, I'm really sorry. Whattaryou up to?" He was leaning over his balcony, dressed in faded blue swimtrunks and a faded blue denim shirt. It didn't take any imagination to picture him on a horse.

"I'm going back to racing. I'm driving in the Mexican Grand Prix next week."

"Hey," he said, brightening up, "fabulous, ole buddy. Hey come on up and meet Beverly."

I'd met Arthur when he was playing the part of a racing driver, and I was the technical adviser and drove the racing scenes. Before we'd done half the film, he was insisting on driving all his own scenes. The director and the producer and his agent all said no way was America's biggest box-office attraction going to risk pushing his handsome face through a windscreen. "Fine," he'd said. "You let somebody else do the driving, you get somebody else to do the acting."

With half the film in the can, he had them by the short hairs. So for the second half of the shooting schedule he sat behind the wheel. (If you ever see "The Last Race" Arthur is the one wearing leather driving gloves in the driving sequences. The bare hands on the wheel are mine.)

The big stars always get their way. They are surrounded by people who tell them how bright and beautiful they are, how truly wonderful, fair, generous and wise they are. They end up making Caligula seem like a pussy cat.

Arthur had managed to avoid that. His one great self-indulgence was women. And the kind of women Arthur liked kept his feet on the ground. On the screen most women found him attractive. Up close in real life he was irresistible. He was famous, he was rich, he was handsome, he was charming, he was smart, he was fun. And above all he was a star.

So it took a rare, strong woman who could take Arthur or leave him and not care one way or the other. Naturally they were the ones Arthur fell in love with. One after the other, they kept him in line.

No doubt Beverly was one of those rare and strong ones. I couldn't tell, she barely spoke to me. But she did look gorgeous, with the morning sun making a golden halo around her dark hair as she brought me an iced herbal tea, no sugar. I said hello and she looked at me with mild indifference and walked away, leaving me with an impression of dark blue eyes, high cheekbones, a perfect nose, and slender ankles. Her waist was small enough for me to imagine fitting my big hands around her. But she was just a little too broad in the backside and average in the chest to be one of Hollywood's superstars of tomorrow. Still, she was as beautiful as Mary Aswell was when she was fifteen.

I asked Arthur if she was an actress. Turning to look at her stretching her long legs on the railing like a ballet dancer, he said no, she was a professor of philosophy at UCLA. "God bless California. What's her field? Philology, logical positivism, the existentialists?"

"You ask her."

"What if she answers? I only know the names. I don't know the rules."

We were leaning over the redwood railing staring at the Pacific. With Arthur you felt like it was the fence of the OK Corral. Arthur talked about his cars. About his new Ferrari GTO that they couldn't get to run right. It kept fouling up its plugs at the traffic lights.

"What the hell do you want an 180-mph car for driving around LA?"

"I don't. My manager said it would be a good investment. The only place I can park it without attracting a mob is in my garage. And it overheats. Do you know anybody at Ferrari who can fix that?"

"That's easy to fix." I said. "All you have to do is change the country. Drive in the Italian Alps and you won't have any problems. Why don't you sell it?"

"I can't afford to. The sucker's doubled in value in the six months since I bought it."

"It must be a bitch being a star."

"Yeah," he said grinning, "it's awful." He paused for a moment, frowning, as if he was trying to remember his lines. "So tell me, what happened? I saw the crashes on television. It didn't look like the Forrest Evers I know. I mean if you drilled one thing into me, it was 'smooth'. Drive smooooth. All the transitions, all the changes, make them flow like a river, you said. But those crashes, Forrest, you looked like a goddamn cowboy."

I told him the story, leaving out my suspicion about being drugged. I also added that the transmission was jumping out of gear. Consistency counts.

"Listen, we're only here for a couple of days. I'm going back to the ranch in Montana in the morning," he said, looking at me. "So we're having a party tonight. Nothing fancy. You know, drinks, buffet, a few friends. Why don't you come, get your mind off the goddamn racetrack. You said you're on holiday. Let the pretty ladies see a gent who's straight for a change."

He said to come at six, I got there at eight. If you're not drinking and you're going light on the eats you can only stand around with a glass of water in your hand for so long.

74

From the street, Arthur's beach house looked shabby. Unless you noticed that the streaked and faded blue paint was the same shade as his shirts. He had those blue denim shirts made by a couturier in Paris who knew how to fake the sunbleach so it looked like Arthur had been out on the high Sierra mending fences. And the skies were not cloudy all day.

A man with the build of a linebacker and short grizzled hair opened the door. "Good evening, Mr Evers. Arthur and Beverly have been expecting you. If you'll wait here. I'll find Beverly."

Inside, Arthur's home off the range was not shabby. The walls were soft pastels and the floors polished natural redwood. There were cushions thrown around, sofas made from saddle leather, green plants, and three large clowns from Picasso's blue period on the walls. (They looked like originals to me; but in Hollywood, as the saying goes, you never know.) It had the casual, haphazard look of a bachelor's flat with a lot of money thrown in through the front door. There were bedrooms, a library with stacks of scripts and cassettes, and a kitchen with a Garland range, but the glassed-in terrace at the end of the main room was the main attraction with its big glass wall overlooking the sea. Californians liked to look out of the big walls of glass, looking for new frontiers. It made for nice views and wacky lifestyles.

Beverly had a trace of a smile for me followed by a more cool appraisal. "I was afraid you weren't going to show up," she said. "Arthur's been bragging about you to everyone."

"I didn't know you spoke to strangers."

"I'm always shy at first, but eventually it goes away. I hope I wasn't rude this morning."

"Funny," I said, "you don't look like a professor of philosophy." Beverly was wearing a funky little pale yellow California playsuit about four sizes too big for her. It gaped here and there so I could see flashes of tanned and smooth woman.

She laughed. "Arthur's always exaggerating. I'm just a graduate student with another six months to go for my doctorate. Anyone who can read without moving her lips is a professor to Arthur. Actually philosophy is like driving a racing car. We both go round in circles." She rolled her eyes and smiled. "Come meet the gatecrashers."

"Hey, Forrest! Great. Where you been, turkey? Gottalotta people want to meet you." Arthur Warren was beckoning with a gin and tonic held high over his head.

"Apparently, I'm to give you up," she said looking over at Arthur. She turned back to me and squeezed my hand. "Don't go away without saying hello."

There were probably twenty-five people between me and Arthur's group out on the terrace. Beyond them, the glass wall had been opened to the deck where another dozen or so figures were holding glasses in the last light of the sunset. There was no music, but the roar and hiss of the waves falling, sliding up the sand and sliding back was a rare and soothing noise.

There was no one I knew, but the faces turned towards me as I passed, "Hi, Forrest." "Good to see you, Forrest." "Glad you're back on the track, Evers."

"Hey, Forrest. Want to do a couple of lines?"

"No thanks, I'm driving."

Some of the women were astonishing. Waiting, I supposed, to be discovered. Just like me.

Some were part of the carnival, on the edge of the glamour game. A tall, extra-blonde woman in her late forties with heavy gold jewelry, big breasts under white jersey and a face like an oiled walnut said, "Forrest we *must* get together for lunch *right away*. I have wonderful news for you. I'll have my secretary call you at your hotel to fix a date."

"Sure," I said, "ring me."

"Sally Deaver," explained Arthur. "This month's heavy casting lady. You going to make a picture?"

"Not if I can help it."

"If Sally Deaver thinks you're going to make a picture you might have to make a picture."

"I'm not going to make a movie."

"Too bad," he said, waving his arm to include all of his guests. "These are the folks who make the movies move."

"We're not making movies; we're just children," said a tall man standing next to Arthur. He had eyes sunk deep into his skull, black bushy eyebrows, and an intense, hungry look as if he hadn't eaten for days. "We're just children making messes in the sandbox – while before us there is the sea." His long forearm unfurled a

76

hand to indicate the beach and beyond. He seemed drunk. But in Hollywood you never etc.

"Frank Diminiani, my producer," said Arthur by way of explanation. "He's just seen the box office on our last picture and he thinks he may have to sell one of his countries." Arthur continued his introductions. "Phil Sapperstein, my new director."

This was a short, tubby, balding man in a Hawaiian shirt, Los Angeles Dodger baseball pants and red sneakers. Despite his clown outfit he looked as affable as a broken bottle. Then he smiled and he was OK. "Hi," he said. "When you gonna grow up and find work?"

"Blessed are the children," I said, looking at his shirt, "for they shall be film directors."

"I had a childhood once," he said. "But lost it."

"Nonsense," said the spectre, Diminiani, revealing two rows of perfect white teeth in a grin. "You're working on your fourth."

"Nicolas, my manager." Nicolas I couldn't place. He looked like one of those financial whiz kids, those twenty-eight-year-old Wall Street multimillionaires who push models into limousines in front of the Green Street Café. But there was something else about him that was disturbing. He looked as if he wasn't glad to be alive. "And Jeremy Tarsian who's a producer. And who is going to be *my* producer *aren't* you, Jeremy? Say hello, Jeremy. Forrest, Jeremy. Jeremy, Forrest."

We said hello, but his mind was elsewhere. The two producers, Jeremy and Diminiani, exchanged a series of high-speed looks. Their expressions said nothing to me, but they looked like they knew what they were not talking about.

I turned to Nicolas, Arthur's manager. "Any relation to Saint Nicolas?"

"I don't give away that much."

"You don't give anything away without taking twenty-five per cent," said Arthur, smoothing Nicolas's crumpled Comme des Garçons lapel.

Nicolas gave a thoughtful nod to acknowledge the truth of that. "You got a moment?" he asked me.

He steered me out onto the deck where I'd talked to Arthur that morning. Halfway down one side, silhouetted against the last glow of the sunset, a thickset man in a swimsuit was lighting a grill. There was a flare as the kerosene burst into flame. We walked past him to the corner. Nicolas leaned with his back against the rail, the light flickering in his face.

"This is going to sound strange, but it is absolutely straight." I waited while he looked away from me, down the beach towards Santa Monica. Then he looked at me. He was so still I wondered if he was breathing. "Arthur tells me you're going back to drive for Arundel."

I nodded. "That's right, that's what I'm going to do."

"That is not a good idea."

"Is that a threat?"

"That is the opposite of a threat. It is very good advice to a good friend of my client."

"I'll bear it in mind. You mind telling me where this advice comes from?"

"It comes from me," he said, and walked back into the house.

Well, I thought, the sharks are biting.

Later, when I got Arthur alone, I asked him if Nicolas' advice was any good.

"We have a saying out here," he said, swirling his ice in his glass. "If your manager doesn't make you ten times extra over his twenty-five per cent, fire him."

I thought about that for a moment. "How the hell can he do that?"

"That's his problem. And frankly I don't want to know how he does it. But I can tell you Nicolas gives good advice."

On my way out I felt Beverly's hand on my arm and turned to face her. She kissed me lightly on the mouth.

"Hello," I said.

"Hello. When will I see you again?"

"I like Arthur. He's a friend."

"I like him too. But he's going to Montana without me. And I have to finish my thesis. And I'm slowing down going up the last hill. I think I've OD'd on philosophy. I keep thinking all the philosophers with any guts are horrors. And the good ones are bores." She looked around the room for Arthur, saw him in the distance by the deck and turned back to me. "I don't know why I'm boring you with this except I'd like to see you. You're not an actor or a producer, or an agent or a director. In my book that puts you pretty high on the list. You are also not a philosophy student or a philosophy teacher which puts you even higher."

"Beverly I wish I could, but I'm only here for a couple more days and that's booked solid test driving out at Riverside." She looked at me as if that was no problem. So I told her the rest of the story. "Look, I have a wife suing me for divorce in London, a lady I've been living with in New York, a woman in Hollywood who's going to hate me in the morning, and a girl I care about in Paris. The last thing I want now is more pain."

"I don't hurt."

"I'll call you." It was what you said to people in Hollywood when you wanted to get away from them. When you meant maybe I'll see you in a couple of years. The holiday was over. No more riders. She gave me her number anyway. And a kiss and a look into my eyes that made me think I was seeing things when I walked out the door.

Outside, somebody was sitting in the driver's seat of my car.

He must have heard me because he turned around to look at me. He looked around nineteen or twenty, a beach kid. His arms were spread out over the back of the seat and the car door as if he owned it. They were impressive arms, lots of definition of biceps and triceps. Short blond hair, with a long wispy bit hanging down the back of his neck. One dangling gold earring. One very thick neck.

"Hi," he said with a big healthy California smile. "Just checkin' out the unit."

I stopped two steps from the car. "You mind checking it out from outside the car?"

"Sure. Hey, no offence, such a great-looking machine. I just had to sit in it, you know. See what the world was like way back then, in the days of yesteryear, a history lesson. Direct experience."

He was opening the door, moving towards me. A sudden tightening of his right deltoid under his T-shirt gave me plenty of time to see the fist coming out from his right side and pull my head back. I was just far enough back for the missed swing to throw him off balance. As his fist went by I gave him a little extra momentum with a backhand chop that sent him face first into Cleopatra's side.

"Check out the unit, ole buddy," I said, diving a short punch into his ribs. He said "*awwwww*" like he was disappointed as the air left his lungs all at once, and his face smeared blood down the side of the car as he went down onto his hands and knees. I heard car doors opening. And another door behind me.

The car doors were a Mercedes 300 up the street. Standard regulation California beige. Three men, blue jeans, T-shirts, were getting out. They didn't seem to be in any particular rush. Just getting out to admire the scenery. Maybe say hello. Something behind me made them pause.

The door behind me was the grizzled linebacker, Arthur's friendly doorman. He was sprinting towards me and he was very fast. But he wasn't quite fast enough. When I turned towards him, Sunshine drove his head into my side, knocking me over. He took the opportunity of kicking me in the back between the shoulder blades before running to his gentlemen friends in the Mercedes. By the time the linebacker got to me, the Mercedes was making sounds of slamming doors and squealing tyres.

"Jesus Christ, you all right?"

I said yes, I was fine. My hands were scraped and a knot twisting tighter between my shoulders was going to help me sit up straight for a couple of days. But I wouldn't want to trade places with the Sunshine Kid.

Cleopatra had a big dent in the passenger door and smears of blood right down to the door sill. Rent A Wreck wasn't going to like that a bit.

# CHAPTER EIGHT

A dingling. Ringing, the goddamn phone was ringing, dragging me up into the lower regions of consciousness. I had left instructions not to be disturbed. Oh fuck, it was five-fifteen a.m. It must be some disaster I thought.

It was Veronica. "Forrest, Forrest, please don't be angry. Darling. I have to talk to you. I haven't heard your voice in weeks. You sound all sleepy and warm. Oh I wish I was there in bed with you."

"It's five-fifteen in the morning."

"Oh, my darling, I know. But it's after eight here and I've got to run. I'm having breakfast with Langford Evans and I just couldn't face another day without talking to you. Maybe it wasn't a good idea, hearing your voice again. Forrest I want you so much, I'll be squirming all day thinking about you." She paused; I waited. "Don't you wish we were in bed together now? God, I love you so much; I'll bet you're hard now. Oh I just love you and miss you so much I wish I was there; I'd wrap my legs around you and squeeze you to death."

"Chomp, slurp." I said playing along with her, remembering her wet and squishy scissor grip. On the other side of that sexual smokescreen she was up to something. "Who's Langford Evans?" I asked.

"Darling I had to call you because I heard the most terrible news."

I waited. She was headed in her direction and nothing could deflect her. Stone walls she could leap in a single bound.

"Forrest tell me, tell me please, you're not going back to racing. You're not going back to driving for Ken Arundel again."

"Where'd you hear that?"

"Dan called me from London. Apparently it was on the radio this morning. On the BBC. Forrest it's not true, is it?

"Who am I to deny the BBC?"

"Goddamnit Forrest, don't get flippant. I'd always thought you were intelligent, that you had some concern for the way I felt. You mean it's true? You are going to drive in Mexico?"

"And Adelaide."

"If you live that long. Forrest, don't you understand? This is hard for me, very hard to be separated this long. And when you take a decision like this without even talking to me about it, without even mentioning it, I feel such a fool. I can't believe you'd be so inconsiderate, so totally careless of the way I feel. Why, Forrest, why didn't you tell me? Why couldn't we have talked about it? Don't you realise your life involves me?"

"I tried to call you, Veronica. Several times. You must have got the messages. I had to make a decision. This is what I do. I'm a driver."

"You're a prick. But a nice prick. Aren't you frightened? After Michel?"

Those two last questions fell like lead weights into my sleepy mind. Afraid? I couldn't be afraid. If I admitted to myself I was afraid I couldn't do this. My mind was fine. Wasn't it? Absolutely perfect in every way.

Michel? Eyes wide behind the plastic visor. Waiting to see what would happen next. His face looks like mine behind the smooth reflecting surface of the plastic visor. On the surface of the visor the clouds in the sky are passing by. Beneath, peering out, framed by the balaclava, are those eyes. His or mine?

"They're having a memorial service for Michel in Paris on Saturday the 24th. Do you want to go with me?"

"Darling I can't. That's what I called you about. I got the part. Isn't that terrific?"

Out of that black and empty place I call my heart I tried to forget Michel and the thought of losing control and dredge up some enthusiasm for Veronica's news. It would be the death of Veronica and Forrest. But it was exactly what she needed. It was her life. She deserved a break. Her personality shone out from the stage. She could be a star. Why should she drag around the world in my wake like a jet-set camp follower? She didn't even like motor racing. Why shouldn't she have a life of her own? Without me.

Maybe the play would flop and she'd be home in London for Christmas. Maybe New York would get its act together and hold the Grand Prix they'd been promising for years. At least then I'd see her once a year.

"Verónica, you goddamn star. Tell me, tell me all about it. What's the part? Who else is in it? What's the director like? Can I have free tickets?"

"Sweetheart, I can't. I've got to run."

"Breakfast with whatsisname."

"Langford Evans. The director. Oh stop worrying you old sod, he's gay and looks like Mary Poppins. Ring me tonight and I'll tell you all about it. Forrest, there's no reason for you to go back to racing. Everybody says you were super on TV. Go back to sleep. I've got to run. I love you."

"You too," I said, but she'd already hung up.

It's hard to believe the drive out to Riverside International Raceway is only seventy-five miles. It seems like two hundred. The tract houses roll by and roll by at a steady fifty-five. You go out the San Bernadino freeway past Alhambra, Rosemead, El Monte, Baldwin Park, West Covina, and on past Pomona. Once upon a time this was all orange groves. Before that it was desert. Now it's the endless repetition of assembly line houses, shopping plazas and parking lots seen through the dark filter of smog.

This is Richard Nixon's hometown country. He grew up here in Whittier. And it is where people hold tight to the TV dream of stainfree carpets and carefree days, of toothpaste romance and fishing trips with buddies carrying six-packs. They watch television an average of seven hours a day until the dream they see on the screen becomes real. This shit here, they say, this Chevvy Malibu with the broken tranny, this here worn out leatherette living room suite with the cracks and five $76.36 payments to make, this 125-horsepower outboard with the broken crank on the trailer with the flat tyre, this shit here is only temporary.

Temporary because one day they will be Rambo and take revenge. And that will be real.

I was going out the San Bernadino to meet Ken and Max and the mechanics at Ontario International Airport. To relieve the boredom, I started itemizing Ken's expenses for the day. Two first class tickets for himself and Max, London to LA, at £1,520 apiece: that's £3,040. Two club class tickets for Dave and Bill, London to LA, at £1,035 each: £2,070.

Phil and Nigel were already in Mexico City to meet Maurizio's car which we'd use as a backup. They'd flown on the Formula One charter plane direct from Tokyo to Mexico. But Ken would be paying their *per diem*, say £85 each for hotel and food: £160. Then there was the air freight for the car – two engines, two backup transmissions, one dozen racing tyres, various parts – say £3,750, London to LA. Hotel and dinner tonight for the five of us, say £350, plus two more car rentals, £100. And the rental of the transporter at £375 per day.

Without counting the cost of the engines (£45,000 each) or the chassis, or the tyres or transmissions, or my seven-figure yearly fee, or Max's percentage, or even the rental of Riverside International Raceway, Ken was paying out around £10,000 out of his own pocket for today's expenses.

Ken must have had a sweetheart of a week. He'd arranged to fly Michel's body back to Paris, attended the inquiry, arranged to send the bits and pieces of Michel's car to Hemel Hempstead and Maurizio's to Mexico City. He'd flown from Tokyo to London, got Max and the Mule prepped to go to LA, arranged for a transporter with the papers to go into Mexico, and arranged for a Mexican fixer to smooth the team's way through the Mexican customs and police. He'd booked hotels for himself, Max, and the two mechanics, found a racetrack for testing near the Mexican border, hired it, dealt with the press, and made sure Nicole was looked after. And he'd arranged for a second flight to fly the new bodyshell from London to LA as soon as it was ready on Monday. And he'd held the hands of nervous sponsors. (Although Wyoming, the cigarettes, had told him they were out for good, and they were the big money.)

And he'd tried to cheer up the depressed crew back at Hemel Hempstead. The loss of Michel and the car would have been a tremendous blow to their morale. And, after all of that, he'd had to sit next to Max for eleven hours on the plane.

Fortunately he'd had the lovely Marrianne Plummer to do the bookings and the paperwork. "There isn't anything I can't do," he'd once said, "as long as I've got Marrianne to do it." The "lovely Marrianne", "Plummy". So gorgeous, so voluptuous, so capable. Shame about the policeman for a husband.

I was a little early, so I drove past the entrance of the airport to see if there was any trace left of the Ontario Motor Speedway. If there was, I couldn't find it. Just more rows of suburban houses. Maybe it was buried, like Cheops, underneath them. I wondered if any of the housewives knew that once upon a time I'd driven through their front door at 175 miles an hour.

In 1970 the Ontario Motor Speedway was the world's newest and largest racetrack, a combination dragstrip and road racecourse, and big Indianapolis/NASCAR oval was going to fill the stands with 250,000 people. But the scale was wrong. The stands were so big and so far from the track that the cars were tiny little crawling things in the distance.

Denis Jenkinson's definition of a racing car: "When it starts up, if the public doesn't leap back, it's not a racing car." 150 yards away nobody leapt back. From 150 yards it wasn't a race, it was just traffic. The people stayed away in huge crowds and after a decade of struggle the eighth wonder of the world closed.

Beware of the old dinosaur theory. Biggest is only biggest, not best. And the tallest shaft of rice, say the Japanese, is the first to bend.

But then they would say that.

I was trying to think of another, more reassuring homily about good little 'uns as Max came boiling towards me out of the customs area at the Ontario airport. He was doing his imitation of Tyrannosaurus Rex, his little beady eyes red from the eleven-hour flight. "You fooking liar," he started to bellow when he spotted me. "You bloody fooking liar." He was waving a copy of the *Evening Standard*. Max is not really taller than me but his great width gives that impression. He looked like a Sumo wrestler squashed together with a gargoyle.

"I can't tell you how good it is to see you, Max," I said without smiling.

A giant hand came out of the sky and rested on Max's shoulder. It was Ken, whom I hadn't seen behind Max's bulk and fury. Ken's presence seemed to soothe Max for a moment. "Hello, Forrest." Ken should have been in the Diplomatic Service. He had that grand, ambassadorial presence. "Max," he said, "is concerned over a story that's been going around London. Apparently you told some reporter that the transmissions were faulty. And that that was the reason for your crashes and Michel's crash."

Max was glaring at me. His thinning, black curly hair was plastered on his scalp. His face had gone red to match his eyes. When he was a baby, I thought, he must have looked like a gorilla in his mother's arms. "You're lying to save your skin," he said in a voice loud enough to make people stop and stare. "You panicked, that's what happened."

Ken spoke down from his height. He had stepped between the two of us. "I've issued total denials, of course. And I have publicly apologized to Darien. No doubt you will do the same, Forrest. The last thing I want to do now is get into a legal battle. Where's your car, Forrest? Can you manage Max and myself? Bill and Dave have their own car, and a transporter. They'll bring our new chassis and the rest of our gear out to Riverside."

"New chassis? I thought you were bringing the Mule."

"Possibly you could give us a hand with our luggage. We'll tell you about it over dinner."

Even Max smiled when he saw Cleopatra. I made her do her top-disappearing trick and Max said, "That's not a motor car, that's a fookin' parade."

"In the back," I told him. He and Ken rode in the back together, looking like visiting royalty. The sun threw Cleopatra's shadow ahead of us on the San Bernadino freeway as we headed for our motel, the shadows of our heads rising up over Cleopatra's shadow like three towers.

We had dinner at the Hoof & Flagon, one of those American cartoons of a British pub, with brass light fixtures and pine stained to look like blackened oak. Max and Ken ordered steaks the size of tabletops. I made do with a dainty sole while my stomach wept for the big thick and tender juicy steaks.

At programmed intervals some strapping young lad or lass rolled out of the gloom to announce that "Hi, I'm Keith, I'll be your waiter for this evening", and, "Are you gentlemen all having a good time?" A busty girl wearing an apron and a prim, fixed smile inquired, "How's your fish, sir?" I had an unreasonable urge to slap her in the mouth with my fish. Just to see if she was real. Must be a lot of free-floating aggression right here in Riverside. Nothing like impersonal friendliness to set your teeth on edge.

Max was explaining his new chassis through mouthfuls of steak. Strands of it clung to his teeth. "It's not exactly new, Evers; it's more a refinement. The new transmission, because it weighs less, and because it delivers the power more smoothly, lets me save a little here and there. Also, because of its shape, I was able to set the engine a little lower. Which means the aerodynamics are a bit better."

"They're a good deal better," Ken cut in. "While you've been away from the team, Forrest, we've been busy playing in the British Aerospace wind tunnel. Lord Godleigh is an old chum of mine and he let us have the use of it at odd hours for a sixpence. All in the national interest of course. Very useful it was. Although you didn't like starting work at 3 a.m. did you, Max?"

I was grinning, leaning forward in my seat, my sole drowning in green sauce, forgotten. "In other words, the new car is quicker and handles better than the one I put on the pole in Hungary."

"On the pole and parked in the grass," said Max with disdain. His lower lip looked like a raw kidney.

"Oh, do shut up, Max." Ken put his hand on his partner's arm and smiled benignly at him. "You agreed on the plane you would try to be civil." Ken then turned his attention to me. "Forrest, we expect it's quicker, but all we know for certain is that it is new. We've just two days to test it and shake the bugs out. Not that we expect there will be bugs."

I could feel the hairs rising on the back of my spine all the way to the top of my scalp. It was the same feeling I had when I was a boy when, late one Christmas Eve, I was looking out of my bedroom window and I saw my father coming out of the barn pushing a new yellow racing bicycle across the gravel drive. For me.

Ken took a deep sip of his Zinfandel and held the glass up to a shaft of light from one of the miniature spotlights scattered across the ceiling. The wine was a deep and dark red, almost black. "Now that we have a few moments together there are one or two things I'd like to say." He looked at each of us in turn. Speech time. "I think it is true, for the first time since this team has been together, that we have a chance of winning. The odds are very much against it but we have a chance. At the same time we are under threat." Max looked puzzled. "I think it's important we understand the threat as best we can and face it equally. Which is why I think, Forrest, we must take Max into our confidence."

"You already have."

"Only so far as you have heard now."

Ken put his empty glass down and signalled for a fresh bottle. It was brought over to the table, the label shown to Ken, knowing nods exchanged between Ken and the solemn sixteen-year-old schoolboy with the little silver plate hanging around his neck. He wrapped the bottle in a white cloth, carefully cut the top of the seal off the bottle, put the bottle into a long-legged brass replica cork extractor, pulled the cork, showed the cork to Ken, Ken nodded, poured a splash into a fresh glass, Ken tasted, more knowing nods, more fresh glasses, poured the wine, and with a knowing nod, left. The old ceremony of the sommelier was alive and well and living in parody, California.

"What are you boogers on about? What threat?"

I pushed my chair back from the table. "I think someone is trying to fix it so I'll crash in Mexico City."

"Don't be daft," he said. "You don't need any help." His little piggy eyes narrowed, darting between Ken and me.

"You tell him Ken, if you want to. I'm going to have a look at the car." I stood up to leave. "And let me tell you, Max, before we get into this, you give me any shit and I'll tear your head off."

Max smiled, or had a gas pain, I couldn't tell. "Glad to see you're getting back on form, Mr Evers."

The California night was working its magic again. Soft, warm and sexy. The blue barge cruised down the side streets of Riverside, looking like the plaything of a 1960s real estate developer, out for a good time on a Saturday night.

The transporter was in the forecourt of a defunct Sunoco gas station. The gas pumps were gone, but behind the big overhead glass doors the lights were on. There was a stack of tyres, two engines mounted on stands and, standing on little skinny set up wheels, the naked chassis of the new Arundel. I rapped on the door and Dave let me in.

Dave was twenty-eight, immaculate, tense, and powerfully built.

He wore his spotless white coat and his fingernails were clean, a neurosurgeon among mechanics. He said he was glad to see me back, but his eyes looked suspicious. He'd have to see. Bill was bent over the suspension packed into the nose of the car. "Hey Forrest, lovely to see you back," he said without looking up. Off to the side, the drab fibreglass panels of the Mule's body lay on the concrete floor of the garage. The new body, with fresh paint and decals, was due on Monday.

"OK to sit in it?"

"Yeah, sure, no problem. It's all there. We're just getting organized for tomorrow, setting the suspension, putting in petrol, oil, water, checking the electrics. It'll be helpful to see the deflection in the springs with your weight on board." Dave was standing behind me. Until now this car had been his. He had been there for every one of its five hundred hours of construction. Even before that, even before it came alive under his hands, he had worked with Max on its dimensions, clearances, tolerances. It was as good as he could make it, and he was the best. He looked at me with distrust and looked away.

I stepped into the tub and with my hands on the sides of the cockpit lowered myself slowly down, twisting my shoulders to get into the close-fitting space. The seat had been moulded to the contours of my body. All of the controls, all of the dimensions inside the cockpit, had been designed to fit me as closely as a second skin. One of the world's quickest, most elegant and expensive automobiles, tailor-made for Forrest Evers; sorry, no passengers. My feet found the pedals set at exactly the right angle. For a moment I groped for the missing clutch. "Can you move the brake pedal over to the left where the clutch used to be?"

Bill looked up from the dense twist of suspension he was working on in front of me. "Sure, no problem. You want to brake with your left foot?"

"It'll be easier to overlap the throttle instead of doing it all with my right foot."

"No problem, Forrest. Same height?"

I put my hands on the wheel, looked at the gauges and closed my eyes. I could feel the mean, cramped thing I'd become draining

89

away, the strength coming back into my arms and shoulders. Goddamn, it felt good to be alive again.

When I went back outside, somebody was sitting in my car. I was going to have to stop leaving the top down. Besides, I'd seen this movie before. This time, though it was a different cast of characters. And this time, when I got closer to the car there were three of them and they got out of the car. They must have been rehearsing.

"Mr Evers?"

"You were just checking out the unit."

"Mr Evers, I wonder if you could spare a moment of your time."

They were well-groomed, tanned, and had that intense look of the true professional. No time to spare. Late twenties, early thirties, working their way up the organization. Apparently I'd gone up in somebody's estimation. This was the first team.

"Why don't you get into the car, Mr Evers?" He had the slick, dark look of a businessman. Insurance or banking. Very conservative, very polite. The man standing on my other side emphasized his partner's question with thumb pressure on the back of my elbow. The pain was making me nauseous. From ten feet away we would have looked relaxed, just talking. The third man was behind me; I couldn't tell where.

"Just slip in behind the wheel, Mr Evers. We won't inconvenience you for long. Pleasant evening for a drive in the desert."

"I don't have a driver's licence."

"Isn't that ironic," he said, "when what we'd like to ask of you is to not drive for a while." The pain increased dramatically. What had been a hot red bloom in my elbow wired a shot up my arm to my neck and into my brain, flooding my head with pain. I smashed the one who was giving the orders with the back of my hand. There was a satisfying crunching sound as I hit the bridge of his nose.

But that was it for satisfaction. The gentleman on my left hit me in the larynx with the side of his hand. At the same time the one behind me announced his presence with a sharp kick from his pointed shoe into my coccyx, that vestigial tail bone we keep tucked away. The coccyx is a very tender little bone, capable of thundering waves of pain. I screamed from the bottom of my lungs and no sound came out. I tried to break my fall by twisting onto my side, but my face hit the concrete first.

I suspect it was the man whose nose I broke who kicked me in the stomach until he grew bored with that and ground the heel of his shoe into my right hand instead, but it could have been the one I never saw. The one from behind. Before he left he kicked me sharply in the balls. I tried screaming again, but I couldn't manage it.

As they were walking away I heard one of them say, "Why the fuck don't they let him drive? Serve the cocksucker right."

Bill and Dave found me trying to stand up when they came out of the garage half an hour later.

"My God, Forrest, what the hell happened to you?" Dave was peering at my face under the street lamp. "What were you hit by, a lorry?"

"Thugs," I choked.

"Bugs?"

They stretched me out on the back seat of Cleopatra and drove me to the motel. On the way back, Bill turned around and looked at me. He winced. "Goddamnit, Forrest, can't you even wait to get into the car before you crash?"

When they got me to the motel I was starting to find my voice again and I found that I could walk through the door under my own steam. But Bill insisted on calling a doctor who came and went, leaving warnings about fractures and ruptures, a jar of liniment and a prescription for painkiller which I tossed into the wastepaper basket. I had to drive in the morning and I couldn't afford the mental fog that came with painkillers.

There is a difference between the bruises you get in a crash and the ones you collect in a beating. After a crash you get better, or you don't; a physical process that works or it doesn't. In a beating the bruises go deeper. Down to some long-forgotten link in the bottom of your brain that was forged when your father held the switches in his hand and told you as he flailed away, "Bad boy, Forrest. Bad." Basic training.

So maybe it was because I wanted someone soft and forgiving to tell me I was OK, that it was probably just a mistake and that everything was going to be fine, even though I knew I wouldn't believe any of it. Some spring of need bubbling up out of the pain. Maybe it was simpler than that. Her kiss goodbye kept coming back to me. Besides, I had an excuse. I'd said I'd call. It took me a while, but I finally found the number wadded up in the pocket of a jacket. She answered on the second ring.

"Forrest, I didn't expect to hear from you again. Your voice sounds scratchy. You catching a cold?"

"What are you doing?"

"I'm in my pyjamas. I was just reaching for Kant. Two paragraphs of Immanuel on the nature of being and my head turns to lead. Three paragraphs, and I'm sleeping. Where are you?"

"I'm out in Riverside in a motel, and I'd like you to come out."

"Mr Romance." Her voice stopped being sleepy and took on a hard edge. "Forrest, when a woman tells you she'd like to see you again it doesn't necessarily follow she wants to see you in bed. I mean doesn't that sound just a tiny bit insulting to your tiny brain? I mean fuck you."

"Who said anything about fucking. I'm going to be here for two more days before I go to Mexico and this is probably the only time I'll have to see you before I leave. We could just talk. I am better than Kant."

"In what way?"

"In the nature of being. He's dead. And I'm still alive, so far."

"What?"

"I said I'm alive."

"You don't sound it. Are you losing your voice?"

"I've been mugged."

Beverly drove out in her little VW bug. It had taken me about five minutes to climb into bed so I didn't exactly rush to the door when she knocked. Walking, standing, sitting and lying down were difficult. Breathing wasn't too bad. "It's open," I said.

She was wearing a sweatshirt and blue jeans and no make-up. Her hair was all over the place and obviously she hadn't given a thought to making herself pretty. I thought she was the most beautiful woman I had ever seen. When she saw what had happened to my face she couldn't help a little yelp of fright.

"You're a mess. Look at your throat! It's all black and blue,

92

you're face is all swollen, and good lord, what have you done to your hand?"

I knew the catalogue of damages. "It'll go away."

"Who did this?"

"I wish I knew. Somebody out there doesn't like me. Or at least they don't want me to drive. Want to see my stomach?" I pulled down the sheet to show off my purple and red and yellow collage of bruises.

Her face rumpled with disgust. "Oh Forrest that's awful; pull the sheet up."

"You said you wanted to see me." I started to roll over and pull down the sheet to show her the source of the sharp, throbbing pain, at the bottom of my spine. "Want to see the worst bruise?"

"Stop that. That's not funny. Can I get you some water or something? Fluff your pillows? I feel as if I ought to do something. Shouldn't you be in the hospital?" She started to straighten the covers of my bed and I pushed her away with my good hand.

"I'm fine. I don't need a hospital."

"Aren't you even going to admit it hurts?"

"It hurts," I admitted.

She stood back from the bed and looked at me. A cool appraisal. "Why'd you ask me to come out, really?"

"To see you."

"That's it? To see me?"

"Talk to you. There was something there, at Arthur's party," I said, shifting uneasily.

"There was something there." She gave me a little shy smile, but it didn't last. "Now I feel like I've walked into the wrong room."

"Me too. But it's a lot better now that you're here. Why don't you tell me about Beverly?"

"Most people want to know about Arthur."

"I know about Arthur. I want to know about the future Dr of Philosophy who's crazy enough to drive an hour and a half in the middle of the night in her pyjamas to see some beat-up wreck she doesn't know."

"I'm not wearing my pyjamas."

"Then what's that sticking out of the bottom of your blue jeans, knickers with long legs?"

She looked down at her ankles where a little ruffle of blue silk stuck out the bottom. "I was in a hurry. There's not a lot to tell."

"Where'd you go to college?"

"Oberlin, in Ohio. You probably never heard of it."

"I've heard of it. It's got a reputation for music. I picture a campus full of cello players. Why don't you sit down?" She sat on the little cinnamon sofa, not taking her eyes off me

"Well that's what I studied; music. Musical composition."

"Sounds innocent enough; but a long way from philosophy."

"Not really. They're both intellectual games. You know, remote and uninvolved. At least the modern stuff. Do you know the kind of modern music that goes on and on and doesn't seem to get anywhere; the kind that keeps repeating the same phrase with endless insignificant variations . . .?"

"Phillip Glass?"

"Like that. Well, the parallel between that and contemporary epistemology . . ."

I listened while she got around to the heart of her thesis, and why she felt her life was going in little circles with "endless insignificant variations". She was a lanky one, with a long neck and a high forehead. She had a habit of searching the corners of the room for the words she needed to bring her thoughts back to earth. Finally, a big yawn crept up on her and I stopped her. "Come to bed," I said.

She looked at me as if she hadn't considered the possibility before, her eyebrows arching in mock disdain. "You can't be serious. If I even sat on the bed I'd probably hurt you."

"I thought you said you didn't hurt. Anyway, I think I'm probably safe from sexual attack."

"Forrest, I've seen raw porkchops look sexier than you do."

"So come to bed. It's one-thirty and I need my beauty sleep. I've got to get up at seven."

"How could any woman resist you, Mr Romance," she said as she stood up. She pulled her sweatshirt over her head and her breasts were unexpectedly heavy, swinging as she bent forward to step out of her pyjamas and blue jeans.

There is something about the sight of a woman stepping out of her

94

clothes that seems so private that I feel privileged and protective. I pulled down the covers with my good hand. She ignored the gesture.

"This is my side," she said, climbing in on the left. She rolled over to face me. Up close her face was smooth and her eyes were clear. She had two little pockmarks on her forehead, a straight and narrow nose, and perfect, white, even teeth that must have cost her daddy a fortune. Her blue eyes were calm and sleepy. "Good night, Forrest," she said and gave me another light and long kiss like the one I had remembered from the party. "You are better than Kant," she said, turning away from me to sleep on her side.

I woke her when the light started to creep in under the curtains, taking her face in my hands, kissing her eyelids and kissing her mouth. Her eyes opened and there was a moment while she sought to find who I was and where she was. Then her blue eyes looked straight into me and said yes and her hands went behind my neck and she pulled me up onto her and I kissed her again as her long legs went around me.

"Aghhhh."

"Forrest, what's the matter?"

"My balls are sore."

"Mr Romance. How could any girl resist you?"

# CHAPTER NINE

"Forrest, what's that French veggie dish, the one with eggplants, tomatoes, zucchinis and onions all squished up?"

"Ratatouille?"

"That's the one. Look, there's purple, and red, and green, and a really tasty yellow: your stomach looks just like ratatouille. And your bottom looks like, like it's got a big splodge of, what's that ink's name, the blue-black one? Quink. Your bottom looks like Parker's Quink."

"Parker can shove his bloody Quink."

"Apparently he did."

I was not enjoying this game. I was trying to get out of bed and it was proving difficult. I finally worked out that if I rolled on my side and stuck my legs straight out there would be a kind of lever effect to raise my head and get me sitting up, using my stomach muscles as little as possible and sitting on my butt as little as possible.

"Can you pull me up?"

"Sure." Beverly bounded out of bed and pulled me into a standing position. "*Eeeeek*," she said in mock horror. "Is this the monster I slept with last night? Forrest, look at you. How could you have made love with me last night?"

"Look at you," I said. "It was painful, but somebody had to do it."

"Rat," she said, kissing my bruised neck. "Rat's short for ratatouille, although now that you're standing your stomach looks more like dog sick. Do you want a hand into the bathroom?"

I was bent over like an old man, my sore stomach pulling me forward. "No thanks I need the exercise." I was only half joking. Among the oddities in the annals of modern medicine is the fact that Formula One drivers recover from physical trauma two to three times faster than the average punter. The knot between my shoulder blades from the Sunshine Kid two days ago, for example, had almost gone, with just a bruise to mark the spot. The pain was bad from last night's beating, but if I got moving, kept the circulation going and got the swelling down, I would be all right in a few days.

"Is there anything I can do?"

"Indeed there is. If you could go out to the ice machine, get about four or five buckets of ice, dump them in the tub and fill it up with cold water, I'd be grateful."

"The old passion-cooler?"

"It'll help the swelling go down."

"It seems like a lot of trouble just to get rid of that hard on, Forrest, but if that's what it takes." Then her face softened. "Then you're going to a doctor, get some x-rays."

"Then we're going to the track. If you've got the time."

Later as I lay in the freezing tub trying to shrink the swelling and bruises of my hand, backside and stomach, Beverly was sitting nude on the edge of the tub beside me, her beauty lending grace to the harshest of all interiors, the pink-tiled American motel bathroom. Looking at her I thought that the world is full of girls with the good fortune to be pretty. They get their way. A very few women have the misfortune to be beautiful and the world has its way with them. Beauty stirs envy in women and greed in men. And by the time a beautiful woman learns to deal with the envy and greed she's rarely as beautiful as she was.

Beautiful Beverly. Greedy me.

"Can I tell you about Arthur?"

"I thought you did. I don't need confessions."

"Well it's not really a confession, but it is important to me. I want to tell you. Obviously he's attractive; I mean I was very attracted to him and all the money and the famous people. And I thought it would be a big change in my life. When I was a little girl I used to dream of living in the big house up on the hill and being fantastically rich. And the idea of living with Arthur was like that. Like living on top of the mountain where everyone is nice to you and everyone wants to please you and tells you how beautiful you are.

97

"I know it was childish, but I had this silly idea that everything would be easy. I really didn't want to make any of the choices; I thought with Arthur all the choices would be made for me. You know, go with the flow. Like a child. I really thought that it was going to be a kind of existential freedom so I went with it. It didn't take any effort, I just went along. But in the end it was just another minor variation on the same theme. Same old Beverly, only nobody tells you the truth and the handsome prince has terrible problems."

"What problems?"

"Well Arthur wouldn't sleep with me for one thing. I got the feeling he wanted me for decoration, an ornament at his table in the restaurant, you know? Someone bright enough to carry her end of the conversation and know the big words like Schopenhauer, but not to steal his thunder, you know what I mean?"

"I know. But I don't understand his not sleeping with you. Arthur's not exactly gay."

"It was strange. When we were home, alone, he said he just couldn't. He said he hadn't gotten over his divorce even though it was two years ago."

"When he was married he would have screwed a woodpile if he thought there was a lady porcupine in there."

"Well not anymore. At least not that I know about. I mean there was all the superficial flirting that's Hollywood, but I never saw him look at another woman. I thought maybe it was my fault. It's funny; I felt more used because he wouldn't sleep with me. I was like a thing he kept on a shelf. I tried, but he wouldn't let me get close to him, not emotionally, not physically."

"Most women want to feel close before they want to sleep with the gentleman."

"I wanted to be close to him."

"You're in love with him?"

"Forrest, I'm telling you I'm *not* in love with him. He wanted me to go to Montana with him and I wouldn't go. He said if I didn't go we were finished. So I left. I took a look at what the two of us had between us and I couldn't see anything, so I left." She took my battered hand out of the ice bath and held it for a moment. "I was never really in love with Arthur; I was in love with the idea of him. But that's not what I wanted to tell you.

"What I wanted to tell you was that living with Arthur didn't change me and didn't change anything. It was like an empty room. You could walk in or walk out, it didn't make much difference one way or another. It was like another one of those minor variations. I'm trying to explain to you, Forrest, why I slept with you last night; it's not something I've ever done before, slept with a man I hardly know. I guess it's not sleeping with anyone for months. But that's only part of it and maybe not even a very important part of it. And really, Arthur has nothing to do with it. I should be too old to believe in love at first sight, but the first time I saw you, that morning on the beach, I felt so much for you I couldn't speak to you. I was afraid I'd make a fool of myself."

"I'll tell Arthur that the next time I see him, that he's a minor variation."

"Well it's over and I'm in exactly the same place as when I started."

"Sitting nude on the toilet seat in a motel, holding hands with a beat-up racing driver who's lying in a bath full of ice cubes . . . You started there?"

Beverly laughed and carefully put my hand back into the water. "No," she said, standing up and stretching. "It's me who's just the same."

"Thank God for that."

"Forrest," she said, looking at the bruises on my stomach, "I didn't ask you because I thought maybe I could just kiss and run. I mean I was attracted to you, but I really didn't set out to sleep with you. But now I kind of feel responsible. You're in terrible danger, aren't you?"

"I don't know. What I do know is that I'm going to race in Mexico City on Sunday. Before then somebody is going to try and stop me. And if they don't succeed, then they will try to make me crash."

"Why?"

"Give me a hand out of the tub." She pulled me upright, and feeling as fragile as an old lady I stepped out. "I don't know why. I'm trying to find out." I put my arms around her and pulled her to me.

"*Ahhhh*," Beverly screamed. "You're freezing." Then she pulled me close to her.

Later, I was stretched out on Cleopatra's back seat wearing my driving suit, feeling the warmth of the early morning sun as we headed east out to the track.

"Beverly, if you can find a supermarket open could you pull over?"

"What do you need?"

"Ten two-pound bags of frozen peas and a cooler to put them in."

"Any special brand?"

"The little baby peas are the best."

Beverly found an A&P open 24 hours and pulled into the vast, empty parking lot. When she'd parked she turned to me lying in the back seat. "Out of the many things I don't understand Forrest, tell me this. If you can barely walk and you can't even drive this ice cream barge, how do you expect to drive a racing car?"

"Carefully."

# CHAPTER TEN

I've always hated Riverside. It's a dirt bowl; dirty, nasty and dangerous. It's also bumpy. It would help prepare us for Sunday's Grand Prix in Mexico City, but the course itself was tricky, with a couple of turns cambered the wrong way and dirt on the edge of the course. There was very little in the way of crash barriers or deep gravel to slow a car down and plenty of lethal obstructions. If you fell off the course into the dirt you could be in serious trouble. My backside was going to regret the bumps, but that couldn't be helped.

An empty racetrack is a barren place: food wrappers and styrofoam cups scattered across the dirt, the grandstands looking unfinished and abandoned, the big billboard posters blaring their brand names to no one. And on the surface of the track, at the corners, the skid marks going off the edge, where last Sunday's heroes paid for a microsecond of inattention. The archaeology of violence.

I loved it. I loved the isolation and the zero distractions. Even though I hated Riverside, an empty racetrack had the same pull for me as an empty stage has for an actor. The great names of Formula One racing had driven there: Jackie Stewart, Stirling Moss, Juan Manuel Fangio, Dan Gurney, Jimmy Clark. In another month, Riverside Raceway would be bulldozed to make way for more tract housing. I didn't care. I couldn't wait to drive Max's new car, to strap myself into the fuselage and pull the trigger.

We surveyed the desert. Earthmovers had started scraping away at the edges, eager to get on with transforming the lumpy landscape into condoland. There was a small clutter of cars and heads in the pit lane. As we pulled up, I was struck again by the gap between Team Arundel and the big teams. If this were McLaren or Ferrari or Williams, there would have been around a hundred people for the test day. Computer engineers staring into video screens, scores of mechanics and pit crew, Goodyear technicians, journalists, sponsors, friends and relations. But this was Team Arundel, on the way up if we weren't on the way out. There was Ken and Max and Bill and Dave and Bash and the driver and his lady friend helping him out of the car. And that was it. *Nada mas.*

Ken came over to greet us, staring first at Beverly and then more intently at me. "My, my, my," he said, "if a young lady did this to me I'd chuck her out."

"Beverly Wyeth," I said, "David Kenneth Debrueil Arundel-Barrington. David Kenneth . . ."

"Oh do shut up Forrest," Ken interrupted amicably. "Please do just call me Ken. All those names depress me. A catalogue of my ancestors' indiscretions. Dreary." Then he drew himself up to his full six foot seven inches and looked down his nose in a parody of himself, "And may I call you Beverly, Miss Wyeth?"

Beverly laughed, delighted. "Call me anything you like, as long as it's not Bev. I always thought Bev sounds like a brand of floor polish."

"Bright, shiny and no scuff marks." He made his wheezing sound.

"Ken owns the team," I explained, "so he thinks he has a right to make appalling jokes."

"Not as appalling as you look, old boy. Bill and Dave told me about your little contretemps. You don't look fit to drive. I'm not at all sure that you should."

"I'm fit. As long as I don't have to change gears, I can drive." As I walked over to the car, Ken walked behind talking to Beverly, charming her, working up a conspiracy between the gorgeous girl with the long legs and the poor, suffering owner.

Bash was sitting on the pit wall talking to Dave and Bill. "Hello, Bash," I said. "Glad you could make it. You've met Dave Spence and Bill Williams, our mechanics?" They nodded. No introductions necessary.

Bash had brought a camper, a small island of cool comfort between sessions on the track. A place to get out of the sun and wind and lie down. Thank God for Bash. His big face was hard with concern.

102

"Christ, who'd you run into? Dave told me about last night. You sure that hand isn't hiding some broken bones? It looks like it's been chewed on by a horse. Same horse as chewed your face."

"It doesn't feel broken. And I don't have to look at my face. You guys ready?" Out of the corner of my eye I could see Ken was introducing Beverly to Max. Poor lady.

The car had the old scratched and patched mule fibreglass body on it, so it looked like the tired old chassis I'd flogged around Oulton Park, Donnington and Silverstone. But underneath it was brand new, begging to be driven for the first time.

"Let me see your face." Max's voice was booming with the authority he always assumed. "You look bloody terrible."

"So everyone keeps telling me."

"You should have seen him when we scooped him off the pavement last night," Bill threw in happily. "We thought he'd be in hospital for weeks."

Max put his hands into his tent-sized blue jeans, glaring at me as if I'd deliberately injured myself. "I don't think you should be driving my car. In fact, I forbid it."

"Don't be ridiculous, Max. Or be ridiculous," I said. "I don't care. Either way, we've come too far to turn around and go home empty-handed."

Max pushed his face into mine. Lumps of scrambled eggs were glued to his teeth. His face was turning red. "We're not ready for this race, you fookin' idiot. And you are in no condition to drive; I don't want another crashed car. Not by you at any rate. We'd best skip Mexico and go straight for Adelaide."

Ken loomed behind Max's toad-like face. "Sorry, old man." Ken's voice was measured and reasonable. "Even if we don't put on much of a show in Mexico, we need the experience. Both with the chassis and the new transmission." Ken put his great flipper of a hand on the car. The fond owner, looking after his steed. "Skipping Mexico would just put us that much farther behind. And I doubt that the few sponsors we have left would sit still for a no-show. Assuming, of course, that you can drive, Forrest. I say, you are looking a bit lumpy."

"That's his frozen peas," Beverly said, anxious to be helpful.

Ken's nose lifted as if he'd just noticed he was standing over a blocked drain. "Frozen peas?"

"It helps keep down the swelling." They still looked doubtful, except for Beverly who was trying to keep a straight face. She'd stuffed the plastic bags under my driving suit and thought it was hilarious. My ass was freezing cold, but at least the bruising wouldn't get worse. "Let's go. I'll be all right once I get inside the car."

Normally the best way to get into a Formula One car is to put one hand on each side of the cockpit and lower yourself down into it. I couldn't put any weight on my right hand, but I wanted to look as natural as possible. I tried standing on the tub and then stretching my legs out, supporting my weight on my left hand and my right elbow. With my stomach throbbing and the shooting pain in my coccyx, I must have looked like a turtle trying to climb backwards into his shell. It took a while, but they let me have the dignity of doing it on my own.

Bill strapped me in, I started the engine and forgot about the pain. Max plugged in his portable Olivetti computer to take his readings from the Formula One equivalent of an in-flight recorder. Now he would be concentrating on the engine, reading intake manifold pressures and temperatures, oil and water temperatures at crucial points, exhaust temperatures and pressures, fuel flow. The data would be recorded for comparison later in the day. Once I'd had a run, the computer would also tell Max cornering, braking and accelerating force, suspension movements, camber changes and tyre temperatures.

The bigger, better-funded teams had telemetry so they could read the numbers on their screens in the pits while the car was out lapping around the track. Which meant they not only knew what was happening, they knew when and where it happened. Which put them two steps ahead of us, since the surface, grip and temperature of the track can change from one corner to the next and from one lap to the next.

But that's the whole point of Formula One: to create the most technologically advanced racing machinery in the world. And the new technology, as everybody knows, is very expensive.

The "Formula" of Formula One is spelled out in the Yellow

Book, the *FIA Yearbook of Automobile Sport*. Team managers carry and study it with the same devotion as acolyte priests clutching their bibles and muttering chapter and verse. (Alicia complained that Ken took his to bed on their wedding night.)

The Yellow Book tells you exactly how long ("no more than 120 cm in front of the centerline of the front wheels and no more than 60 cm behind the centerline of the rear wheels"); how wide ("no more than 215 cm"); how high ("no more than 100 cm from the ground"); and how heavy ("not less than 500 kg").

It's full of catchy phrases like "throughout its length the structural material in the cross section of each box member shall have a minimum area of 10 cm$^2$, a minimum tensile strength of 31 kg/mm and a minimum panel thickness of 1 mm on unstabilised skins or 5 cm area and 0.5 mm thickness on stabilised skins." Etc, etc, etc, and etc.

Engines are limited to 3.5 litres and have to be "normally aspirated". No turbochargers and no superchargers.

No turbos?

In 1986, when the rules allowed turbocharged engines, the money teams were building special "kamikaze" engines just for qualifying. They could spin their wheels on a dry track in any gear, including sixth.

BMW calculated that there were moments when they were getting 1,300 horsepower from their 1.5-litre qualifying engine. When Gerhard Berger saw a 5.5 bar boost on his turbo pressure gauge at Monza during qualifying in 1986, it meant he was getting five and a half times the normal atmospheric pressure of fuel and air into his combustion chambers. So theoretically his little 1.5-litre engine was pumping out power like an 8.25-litre monster. 1,300 horsepower from 1.5 litres made those qualifying engines go boom in the afternoon and sprayed the countryside with tiny bits of exotic racing engines.

With all that stress (twenty-five tons on the top of the piston on the downstroke 12,000 times a minute) even if they didn't blow up they had to be rebuilt after five or ten qualifying laps. At £70–110,000 a pop for an engine, and two or three or four or five engines just to qualify two cars, the cost of going Formula One racing was rising beyond the counting abilities of the sponsors.

So FISA banned special qualifying engines, and turbos were phased out. Whereupon the engine designers started looking for other ways of getting more power.

Engines are breathing devices. They breathe in fuel and air, light it up, and breathe out exhaust. Make their breathing easier and they'll give you more power. Make them breathe more often (higher rpm) and they'll give you even more power. Short of turbos and superchargers, nothing improves an engine's breathing like more valves. More valves open more skylights in the roof of the combustion chamber to let in more fuel mixture. And individually they weigh less, so you can make them go up and down faster.

Most racing engine designers prefer several small cylinders to a few big ones. The flame path from the spark plug has a shorter distance to travel to the cylinder walls in a twelve-cylinder engine than it does in an eight. The distance from the spark plug to the cylinder wall is only a couple of inches, but at 12,000 rpm, the fire only has some two thousandths of a second to travel across the combustion chamber before the party is over and the piston comes back up again, pushing the smoke and the unburned fuel out of the exhaust valves.

If you have twelve pistons instead of say, eight, each piston will be smaller and weigh less. So they, like smaller multiple valves, can be made to go up and down faster. Less mechanical mass, as they say in the trade, means more rpm.

But other engineers will tell you the extra cylinders aren't worth the complication, friction and weight. Or length. Formula One engines act as the rear end of the chassis and support the rear suspension and transmission. So even a little torsional deflection in the engine block will go a long way towards sloppy handling. A stiff, short engine, in other words, will outhandle a long flexible engine.

So take your pick. Four, six, eight, ten or twelve. Ferrari runs twelve cylinders (the most FISA's Formula One regulations allow); Renault and Honda, ten; Judd and Cosworth, eight.

The other route to power – higher rpm – means making all the whirling bits as light and strong and balanced as computers and modern physics know how.

Is it worth it? Should you spend £1,000 each for a dozen titanium con rods which are lighter than aluminium and stronger than steel, when you have to throw them away after every other race? The answer is yes, it's worth it. If you have the money.

Higher rpm also means polishing and finishing by hand. And then assembling the jewel-like bits and pieces with the kind of care and patience and tolerance that make a Rolex seem crude. And doing it in sonically and chemically clean conditions lest a stray speck of dust attach itself to one of the moving parts and throw it out of balance. (Things gain weight when they spin. A piston, gudgeon pin and connecting rod that weigh just over a pound in your hand, will weigh over seven tons when they are on their way up inside an engine at 12,500 rpm.)

But before you get beyond 12,500 rpm, you'll have to get over the problem of valve springs. Even when they are OTEVA-70 (the finest spring steel known to aerospace engineers), valve springs tend to float above 12,000 rpm. Floating may sound like a harmless activity for a valve on a Sunday afternoon until you realise that while a valve hangs down into the cylinder (floats), the piston is approaching with those seven tons of momentum. Should the two kiss, the valve will punch a hole in the piston and the engine shall ring with the sound of shrapnel. Hence the search for a better valve spring or a better way of shutting the valves.

Renault think they've found the answer with compressed air taking the place of springs. And they may have. But since nobody outside Renault knows how they do it, it's not a solution for everybody.

When Mercedes built Formula One Cars in the 1950's they used the pressure of the gas inside the cylinder to close their desmodromic valves that last little bit. So they may use desmodromic valves when they return to Formula One. Theoretically it should allow unlimited rpm. In real life it doesn't and the search goes on.

Over the winter Honda was rumoured to have spent £30 million building and testing twenty-five different specification engines. Some, went the rumour, had beryllium pistons, ceramic cylinder walls, plasma ignition and desmodromic valves that worked.

Meanwhile Team Arundel carried on with last year's frontier technology. Our good old Ford-Cosworth V8 was a solid design from last year, and a solid stone compared to the power of the new engines, including this year's new Ford.

Ol' Evers would just have to make it up on the "slow" parts of the track. Drive that little bit harder. Renault turns 13,000 rpm. We turn 11,500. Keep your foot down just a little bit longer, brake a little bit later, Evers, and try not to pray that the fast ones go smash on the walls. Money talks; bullshit runs to catch up.

When the engine had warmed up and Max unplugged his computer, I took off, leaving a rapidly disappearing cluster of figures looking like statues in my wake.

My right hand was too sore to use. I let it rest on the steering wheel, steering with my left. This wasn't going to be easy. But, I thought as I put my foot down, it could be fun, once I got the measure of braking with my left foot. At first I was braking too soon, and had to drive up to a corner. But once I got used to it, I found I could be much more precise, feeding in the braking gradually, with my foot still on the accelerator.

The new chassis felt lighter, easier to drive, better balanced. Max had been doing his homework. For the first few laps I just cruised, keeping to a maximum of 8,500, making sure it all worked, warming up the tyres and bedding in the brake pads. The pain was a distraction, clamouring for my attention. But it didn't get it. I had been months out of the cockpit and my mental edge was rusty. I could so easily make a mistake. I did ten easy laps, then they signalled me to pull back into the pits.

"What do you think? Can you keep it on the track?" Max was first in line, his face showing the concern of a mother hippo for her calf. He had to shout over the engine as he plugged in his computer.

"You got lucky, Max. It feels good. The turn-in is slow, but no doubt Dave can dial that out. It's going to take a little while to get used to braking with my left foot. But if your transmission isn't losing time on acceleration and top speed, I think I'm gaining around a half a second a lap just on braking."

"Booger," he said. "Just think what a real driver could do." Apparently Max was in a good mood, this being his idea of a jest.

Ken stuck his head in the cockpit and gave me his usual speech about responsibility, not wanting to prove anything, testing the car not the driver. We had done this so many times I think he did it for the ceremony. And to take his mind off the worry of 5,500 pieces of

108

racing machinery and one racing driver, any one of which could go wrong at any time.

If the automatic transmission was soaking up extra power, I couldn't feel it. I blasted out of the pits to do ten more laps, this time at eight tenths; the sort of quick but careful driving you do when you're in fifth place, a lap down on fourth and a lap up on sixth with ten laps to go for the finish.

There is a kind of freedom on the track; freedom from the rest of your life. All of the wives and tax collectors, radio jingles, bank statements and the men who come and beat you in the middle of the night, all of them disappear in the dust. The world blurs and you go round and round on the carnival ride.

Driving deep into a corner at hyperspeed; braking, balancing the car on the edge of its limit along a line so perfect that the car almost drives itself, as if it were in an invisible groove; accelerating so hard as you exit that your cheeks flatten against your teeth; surrounded by the wails of the engine and the screaming of the brakes and the tyres; that, ole buddy, is the closest you can get to stretching that tiny bit of time that's gone before you can say "now".

That little philosophical cherry chiclet popped up along the back straight because Max's automatic transmission was giving me so much more freedom and time. Since I didn't have to pump the clutch and heel and toe, the car was more settled, more relaxed.

And so was I. I had more time to find the perfect time to turn in, the perfect point to clip the inside of the corner, the perfect time to get back on the throttle and exit under full power as if the exit wasn't even there. If the transmission wasn't making me a better and faster driver, it was making me feel that way.

Except my neck. Evidently I hadn't been doing enough neck exercises to compensate for losing the workouts behind the wheel. Look at the neck of any experienced Formula One driver and you'll see straight lines down from his ears to his shoulders. The new ones wear their heads to one side, nursing the sore muscles. I was beginning to feel the pangs of a rookie neck when I saw a plume of dust streaking down the service road towards the pits. Visitors.

When I went past the pits on the next lap, Ken held out the ten-lap sign. Behind him the driver's door of a shiny little Toyota

109

was open and a small blonde head was sticking over the roof. Balls, I thought, my heart sinking. Janice. The bruise on my Adam's apple was saying enough. My stomach muscles and my backside were too painful to think about. It was time to come in. I did one more lap, and coming into the hairpin before the pits the brakes gave way.

One moment I was Forrest Evers, cruising into the last corner at 105, vaguely thinking of the pretty lady with the short, spikey blonde hair and the pretty pink wobblies, wondering if she wanted revenge or a rematch, a racing driver coming in for a landing among the slower species.

One moment I was in control, with plans for the future and scores to settle, and the next I was a passenger, out of control, brake pedal falling away to the floor, the Armco guard rails growing large. There wasn't much I could do. Two quickee jabs established that pumping the brake pedal was a waste of time.

I wanted to minimize the crash. This was the only new chassis we had. And I didn't want to go feet first into the guard rail. One possibility was simply leaning up against the Armco, putting both left wheels gradually into it and hope that the curve of the rail would conduct the car around the corner and slow it down. But I was already turning into the corner. And even if I could manage to get the car parallel to the Armco, the steel rail could easily tear the wheels off the car and we would go flippity flop, ass over petrol tank. So that wasn't worth considering and I didn't. It was an option I discarded before my foot jabbed the dead brake pedal a second time.

Over to the right there was something.

With my one good hand I took the car by the scruff of its neck and flung it into the corner, tightening the line and making it slide, trying to scrub off as much speed as possible, treating it like a dirt track racer. I was coming into the corner too fast and my line was too tight to have any hope of getting around it. But by hitting the apex early, keeping my foot on the accelerator, I ran way wide in a long curving arc and went off the track at the exit of the turn, just squeezing past the end of the Armco barrier and into the dirt. I planted my foot on the floor, sending a rooster tail of dirt and rocks behind me, blasted under the Exxon sign, machine gunning the back of it with pebbles and rocks, and, fishtailing, wildly bounded over the rough dirt to scramble back onto the track in time to head into the pit lane and into the pits.

Max couldn't wait to plug in his computer. It was his way of talking to his poor raped darling. "How are you feeling, dearest?" "Does it hurt?" "Let me take your temperature." "Oh dear, I think you have a fever in your transmission." "Poor baby, is anything broken?" His bright red scowl said he was intending to deal with me later. After he looked after his baby. The baby that wanted to kill me. Fuck him.

Ken stuck his vast face down in front of me.

"Not the prettiest of sights," I said.

"I beg your pardon."

"Your face is blocking the view."

"How are you?"

"Not bad." The adrenaline was still pumping through me, my mind racing and my bruises and sore muscles forgotten. "The brakes quit and I want to know why. The suspension could be bent from going cross-country. Did you see it?"

"We only saw you coming back onto the track. Looked like it could have been serious. You sure it was the brakes?"

"The pedal's on the floor. They just disappeared."

"Anything else?"

"The car is understeering on the fast bends, so I'm late into the corners. There's also a bit of oversteer coming out. Nothing drastic. But if we could fix it, I can take off at least another second."

"It will take at least an hour to go through it. We really ought to magnaflux the suspension, but we'll have to rely on Dave's judgement. If he suspects some cracks, we'll pack up now. We have a visitor."

"I can see her. Give me a hand. And tell Dave to do the brakes first. Tell Dave I want to know why. I want to know exactly why." Ken undid my harness and reached down with a big meaty paw for me to grab and haul me out.

As we passed Max he muttered that the transmission was running hot. And that I couldn't drive. And that I was never getting into his car again.

"That fucking car almost killed me, dogbrain. And before I get in it again I want you to tell me if it was your design fault, or

111

a manufacturing fault, or if you screwed it together wrong, or if somebody has tampered with it. You tell me, Max. You tell me." I'd said all that quietly but he must have sensed how close I was to violence. He didn't reply. He just looked at me, his mouth hanging open like a bulldog, his little eyes bright behind narrow little slits.

Act of will, brake hard, shift down, lower the rpm, smile for the nice lady. "Hello, Janice, what an unexpected pleasure," I called out, feigning gladness. I could give a hooker lessons.

Janice was walking over from her car. She was wearing a loose cotton short-sleeved shirt with leopard spots tucked into tight blue jeans. Tight blue jeans tucked into snakeskin cowboy boots. She held a notebook in her hand. Short tight stride. Janice the tough. Janice the reporter. Strictly business. "Looks like somebody beat me to you," she said, her nipples doing little loop de loops under the thin cloth as she walked. "Who do I have to thank?"

"The last time I saw you, Janice, you were asking me to help you off with your nightie."

"That was before I knew you were a liar."

"I gave you the story of Max's automatic, and my going back to drive for Ken."

"And you lied about your transmission breaking."

"Three out of four ain't bad."

"Don't give me that shit, Evers; I can run my pen right straight through you. And I will."

"You came out here to tell me that?"

"I came out here because I had a wonderful idea for a story. The death of a Formula One team. The driver who can't stay on the track even in practice."

"Hello Janice." Ken had done his trick of gliding up silently. Next to his great height Janice looked like his little girl about to stamp her foot. "To what do we owe this honour?"

"I was just telling Forrest about my new story. About the Formula One team owner whose cars keep killing his drivers and who loses his sponsors and tries to manipulate the press. Convincing demonstration of Forrest's a moment ago, don't you think? Or are you giving up on Formula One and practising for Baja?"

Ken laughed his folksy, friendly laugh. Some of her cuts went deep, but Ken would rather break his arm than let her see the pain. "Janice, I don't have any illusions about how difficult life is for us now. But we've been on the brink so long I think we've got a pretty good sense of balance. And you can predict our demise if you want to, but we are going to Mexico and to Adelaide."

"Ken." Max was covered with bits of stones and racetrack. Apparently he had been under the car. He was waving what he thought was a discreet wave for Ken to come over to him. From the distance he could have been Oliver Hardy signalling Stan to watch out for the falling piano.

"And about the Formula One designer who's being sued by a Belgian transmission company for stealing their design."

I knew about that one. The Belgians were claiming that Max was infringing on one of their patents. Max didn't think they had a case. The designs were fundamentally different, he said. Nothing to worry about. Janice's attack was making me worry about it. Would Max steal another design? A soft arm slipped through mine. "Janice Henrion, I'd like you to meet Beverly Wyeth." It was my day for introductions.

"Oh you're the new flavour of the week, are you? Did he tell you he has a wife in London and a girlfriend in New York?"

"Nice to meet you too, Janice." Beverly had been to the Bel Air school of backbiting. Wear a tough hide, and don't hit back harder than you have to. "I'm not surprised there are lots of women interested in Forrest. Sometimes they follow him for days." She let that sink in for a beat. "But sure, he told me."

"Well whatever he told you it probably wasn't the truth. You're not overly given to telling the truth are you, Forrest?" There was the smallest quaver in her voice. Little girl acting tough.

"Janice, let's talk for a minute." I took her hand and led her away, her little hand in my big one. We walked into the dry grassy fields in the middle of the track.

"What happened to you? You look terrible."

"Professional thugs. Somebody wants me not to drive."

"Oh really, Forrest. You must think I'm terribly naive. Why would anybody want to stop you driving when it's so much fun to watch you crash? You think just because I'm terribly attracted to you – "

"Janice, you're not attracted to me."

"All right, have it your way; I'm not attracted to you. And I am not going to write my story. 'Epitaph for a Loser' — what do you think of that for a title?"

"You don't have to be so shitty."

"Yes I do. I do have to be shitty. Because if I'm not somebody always takes advantage of me. I know some big interests in motor racing Forrest. And you know what, they despise you. They say your team are amateurs. They say the sport would be much better off without Team Arundel. I think it's going to be a good story." Then she smiled, stood on tiptoe and with her hands on my shoulders, kissed me. Then she walked away.

When I got back to the pits Ken and Beverly and Max were standing in a group. They'd been watching us, wondering.

"Forrest," Ken asked, "what did you do to that woman to make her so angry?"

"I didn't do anything to her."

Beverly laughed. "No wonder she's so mad."

Over Beverly's shoulder, Janice was talking to Dave.

# CHAPTER ELEVEN

Ken led the way into the cool shade of the camper, the vehicle hissing and leaning towards him as he put his great weight on the steps. Stooping as he entered, his head skimming the ceiling, he sat down at the formica table looking as awkward and oversized as an adult at a children's party, while I slowly and carefully stretched out on my back on the daybed at the back. There was a pause while he gathered his thoughts. "We don't need more attention."

"I feel I've been noticed," I said, touching the bag of Bird's Eye petits pois underneath my driving suit.

"Indeed. They've bitten." He bent forward, his hands on his knees. "They probably thought that what they did to your hand would have prevented you from driving."

"It would have if it weren't for Max's transmission."

"Exactly. And when they learn that they didn't stop you, they're bound to try again with, uh, shall we say, less restraint."

"A couple of old ladies could knock me over with feather dusters. I'm not exactly in perfect shape."

"Yes, well, I don't think you should have to face them alone."

"Good, you go next."

"Forrest. I wish you'd take this more seriously. Our team is under seige and I think we have got to protect each other, operate as one unit  Who's your new friend?"

"I don't know. Beverly's OK."

"She's the most astonishing-looking woman. But I'd feel more relaxed if I knew more about her besides her being an ex-girlfriend of Arthur Warren."

"OK, I agree that's a popular category among pretty females in California. But I think she is who she says she is. Nobody's going to fake being a graduate student in philosophy, it's too difficult. Too easy to check."

"Maybe. She could be a philosophy student and still be paid to look after you, let people know where you are. I'm suspicious of any woman who's that attractive who pretends she's attracted to you."

"You're not suspicious, you're jealous. And she didn't know where I was last night until I called her."

"Well, check. Because until the race is over in Mexico I'd like us to stick together like hairy rickshaws." Ken had gotten up and was rummaging in the fridge, his voice muffled among the cans of Coke, Pepsi, beer and water.

"Hairy what?"

"Hairy rickshaws, you know that Eastern sect you always see in airports. Bald heads, jangling bells, saffron robes, that sort of thing. They keep chanting 'hairy, hairy, hairy rickshaw'."

"Hare Krishna."

"Right. That lot." He came out of the fridge bearing his prize, a can of Gatorade. Too tall to stand up straight, he moved in a half-crouch back to the table and sat down. "Anyway I don't want you left alone for a second. I want the whole team to eat and, as much as possible, sleep together. We're much less vulnerable that way."

"Look, Ken, I know the lady well enough to think I might get to like her a whole lot. If I ever get the chance. But I don't want company in Mexico. I'm in lousy shape, I'm sore, and I just don't have the time. You know what I'm like before a race. Besides, if they come after me again what's Beverly going to do, scream?"

"If she'd been there to scream outside the Sunoco station you wouldn't be stuffing frozen peas in your trousers now, would you?"

The camper lurched as Bash and Max came on board, filling the inside with male bulk. I pictured the wheels splayed and bulging under the tonnage of the four of us.

"Well, Max, what happened to the brakes? And how long before they're fixed?"

Max shifted uneasily, his face sweating and streaked with dirt. I reached over my head to turn up the air conditioning another notch. "To answer your questions in order, Forrest: I don't know, and about two hours."

"Don't mess me around Max. I'm short of patience."

Max squeezed past Bash and held out his hand to me. Show and tell. He held a small stainless steel block that looked like it had been worn down by a grinding stone. The severed trunks of copper tubes stuck out of both ends. "The proportioning valve," Max explained. "It's so abraded it leaks. You wouldn't notice it for several laps, but the leakage there could cause a sudden drop in pressure and a sudden loss of brakes. The pipes leading to the dual braking system also appear to have been weakened."

"Why don't you know what happened?"

"When you went off the road you tore away the undertray of the car. It's perfectly possible this happened after you lost your brakes. If you look closely you can see bits of dirt and stone embedded in the metal." Max closed his fist around the scraped metal. "So there could have been a manufacturing fault; or sabotage; or there might have been an air bubble in the system."

"Just one of those crazy things," I said, remembering the brake pedal falling to the floor, useless.

"Forrest," Bash said. "Dave and Bill and I have been through every component in the system, checking and rechecking each other. Except for this it all looks a hundred per cent. But it's true, there could have been an air bubble in there."

"There wouldn't have been an air bubble in there and there wouldn't have been a faulty part if the car had been checked the way it's supposed to be checked. And if it wasn't mounted too low in the chassis it wouldn't get torn up every time the car goes off."

"I told you," said Max, his anger coming back with his confidence, "we are not ready for Mexico. We need more time to test the car."

"Forrest," Ken said, looking at Max as if our chief designer might be hiding something, "perhaps Max is right. Perhaps we should give ourselves a little more development time."

"Of course we need more development time. Everybody needs more development time," I said. "But we can't miss Mexico. How soon can you have it ready for the track again, Max?" I asked. "We better find out if there are any other bugs in there."

Max looked at his watch. "About another hour and a half, two hours." Bash took a pull from his beer and made a face like he'd just noticed there were frogs in his bottle. "You looked a little raggedy

117

out there," he said, leaning against the sink. "And I don't mean when you went off."

"It's been a while."

"Well don't push it. The sucker bites."

"I'm going to get you a nice flower-print dress. Then you can play mum. Goddamnit," I said, getting mad, "it's Sunday. Next Sunday I'll be in Mexico City bouncing around the Peralta at 170 miles an hour. How the hell am I going to get anywhere if I don't push? I appreciate your concern, Bash, but if I let up I lose control."

"I'm not worried about you losing control."

"What then?"

Bash crumpled his beer can into a little ball of foil and helped himself to another out of the camper's fridge. "I ever tell you why I left Mexico?" he asked, punctuating his question with the pop of the can opening.

"Is this a long story?"

"Could have been a lot shorter." He took a long pull from the can. "I was building racing cars in Mexico City ten, fifteen years ago. Pretty good little business. I'd been racing TransAm, team fell apart, and I thought 'fuck it', let's go to Mexico." He pronounced it Mayheeco.

"Lotta money in Mexico if you know where to look. Rich kiddies' daddies buy them Mustangs. And as soon as the rich kid gets his new Mustang he wants it to go faster than the other rich kids' Mustangs. So I was making a name building racing cars, and money building go-faster Mustangs.

"Some of the kids had a lotta money, and there was a lot you could just bolt on, intake manifolds, headers, Holly carbs. But these kids wanted what kids always want: more. Well, serious engine building, boring, stroking, balancing, bench flowing, dyno checking; that shit takes a lot of expensive equipment. So I took a silent partner. He had a lotta money, his kid had a Mustang and I thought, he's safe, he's the Chief of Police.

"One day, his kid is trying out the latest supertrick I laid on his Mustang, laying down rubber up and down the street in front of my shop, and a cop stops him. The kid tells the cop to fuck off because his daddy is the Chief of Police. The cop doesn't get the bribe he thinks he's entitled to, so he gives the kid a ticket and impounds the car. Which really pisses the kid off.

"The next day, a couple of new cops show up, they get the cop that gave the kid a ticket out his cop car, put him up against the wall next to my shop and cut him in half with machine guns." Bash paused for a moment, remembering. "I never knew a man could bleed so much. Day after that, I pack up all my shit on a flatbed truck, lock my shop and drive to California."

Beverly stuck her head in, holding a fresh bag of frozen peas. She squeezed past Bash and Max and sat down on my bunk.

"And the moral is . . .?"

"The moral, Forrest, is that Mexico is a shallow pond with some very big sharks in it. That Police Chief retired a couple of years ago with two billion dollars in Swiss banks."

I looked away disbelieving.

"Goddamnit, Evers; you think Iaccoca's rich? You think GM's chairman whatsisname, Smith, Roger Smith, is going to get a nice golden handshake when he retires from GM? Shit, those guys aren't rich. They barely got 500 million between them. Two billion is serious money."

"Buy a nice lunch," I said. "You get those figures from a Swiss banker?"

"Near enough. Look, Forrest, I'm not trying to scare you. God knows what it would take to scare you. I just want you to be careful."

"I'll carry traveller's cheques."

"What's understeer?" Beverly had been stuffing a fresh pack of frozen peas into the back of the hero racing driver's driving suit and reading a car magazine at the same time.

"Gently now," I said, feeling the fresh shock of the freezing cold plastic bag. "Understeer means that the front wheels slide more easily than the back wheels. So if you're going fast and you turn into a corner the front wheels slide and you keep going straight ahead. It's not difficult to control, you just let up on the throttle, and when the straight ahead force lets up, the front wheels get some grip, and the car turns."

"Yeah," said Bash. "We call it 'push' in America because the car tends to push forward rather than turn when you want it to."

"And the opposite is oversteer?" She'd finished with a little pat on my sore bum and had drawn her legs up, with her arms wrapped around them and her chin resting on her knees. People like to see racing cars race, go fast, crash and burn. Could she possibly be interested in the theory?

"Oversteer means that when you turn into a corner your back end hangs out and, if you're not careful, the car spins."

"Which one was it that made you crash?" asked Beverly as she checked her face in a mirror she'd taken out of her handbag.

"Neither one. I just kept my foot down and went straight ahead when I should have turned right."

Bash finished his beer and threw the crumpled can in with the others. "Sounds like understeer to me, Forrest. Like you want to turn and you can't."

Two hours later, after warming the car up again and making sure everything was right, I did ten more laps in anger, but the understeer was still there. It could be the front or rear-wing setting, tyre pressures, the damper settings, it could be the camber settings, the castor, something in the chassis, weight distribution, fuel load, the spring rates, it could be any combination or something else. Max consulted his computer while Dave and Bill discussed cures.

As problems go for a new car, this wasn't serious at all. We could deal with it. It was the unknown that took a little more time.

By the end of the day, we still hadn't solved the problem. Bash had left saying if it was him who was a target he'd find another line of employment. Beverly said she had to leave because she hadn't meant to stay and she didn't have any clothes.

"Nonsense, dear girl," said Ken, putting an avuncular arm around Beverly's shoulders, "I'll buy you new ones. Has he told you how wealthy I am? Well, let me tell you I am blessed with immense wealth and I would be delighted to share it with you if you'll only stay to dinner. I'll take it out of Forrest's pay packet."

"Don't let him fool you, Beverly. He doesn't own a great fortune, he owes one. But stay for dinner. For me."

"I'll stay for both of you. But I'll buy my own clothes. On one condition, Forrest."

"Mmmm," I said, being as noncommittal as possible.

"Take me around the track in Cleopatra. Make her howl," she said, grinning wickedly.

We all piled in. Ken, Max, Dave, Bill, Beverly, and me behind the wheel; the whole Hairy Rickshaw team. I was sore and tired, and by now I knew the track so well I could have driven it with my eyes closed. And I was in better shape than when the day began.

If anybody up in those hills was watching, they would have seen the old powder-blue pleasure barge loaded to the gunwales, lumbering down the straights, lurching over onto two wheels, screeching, and scrambling, and bellowing smoke. After two laps, the brakes had faded away to nothing and the only way I could slow the monster down was by sliding sideways before the corners like it was the little Bashmobile.

Beverly turned the radio on full to rock 'n' roll and we flew. It hurt my stomach to laugh, but I didn't care and I'll bet they heard the sound for miles.

Late that night we'd turned the lights out and the traffic made a sound like irregular waves on the beach. Beverly was rubbing the back of my neck, easing the sore tendons.

"I'd forgotten," I said, "how much fun the team used to have together. It all turned so bad when I crashed at Brands Hatch. That's it, that's the bugger — ow!" She had the strength of a stonemason in her fingers. "But I do apologize for exposing you to the sight of Max at his trough."

"You don't have to look at him."

"True, but then you run the danger of getting splashed."

"Dave and Bill's imitation of Ken was so funny. Are they always like that?"

"It's their way of letting off steam. Just before a race they'll be up all night, working flat out to get the car ready. The pressure's high. They know that the race and my life depends on their work. How many times have you heard of a racing driver crash because of a loose nut or some two-dollar part breaking?"

"I don't know, I think you're all nuts. You're like little boys all worked up about doing something dangerous while mommy is out shopping."

I rolled over to face Beverly in the half-light from the window. "Psychology now. And I thought you were just a philosopher."

"Please don't make fun of me. I loved being with you today, but I feel very frail with you. I feel like something will break if I'm not careful."

"That's just because we're new together and we haven't had time to make the rules."

"Let's keep it that way, Forrest. No rules."

My hand was on the small of her back, and I pulled her towards me. "No rules," I said and kissed her mouth, "because we'd only break them."

"Isn't that," Beverly said, kissing my chest, "what rules are for?"

The first night, when Beverly had shown up with her pyjamas sticking out of her blue jeans, making love had been awkward and halting. I was so glad this lovely woman was in bed with me, I'd kept thinking she would get up and leave. And I was so sore in so many places I could never quite forget the pain. We were both out of practice and cautious, unsure of each other and starving for each other.

Now we had more time and we were sure. We are all fumblers in the dark, guessing what our fellow fumbler is thinking and feeling. We try to tell each other but the words are never enough. Here, here is this caress and this. And take this kiss here and there. Oh, yes more. No, no, not like that. Like that? Yes, just like that.

Beverly woke up screaming. I put my arms around her and she tried to fight free, screaming even louder before she realized it was me. Moments later she was crying, out of breath, and there was a pounding at the door.

"Forrest, what's going on?" Ken's big English voice, which could make a horse jump three fields away, was waking up the motel.

"Nothing. We're fine. Go back to sleep." I tried to sound reassuring, but Ken didn't hear me. He kept pounding on the door, shouting.

"For God's sake, Forrest, are you all right?"

I got out of bed and unlocked the door. He filled the forecourt with pyjamas. The sight of me naked visibly jolted him. He stopped shouting. "Yes, well," he said. "Stop beating that poor child and go to sleep. You have a great deal of driving to do tomorrow."

I closed the door.

"Darling, I'm sorry. I didn't mean to wake anybody up. Was that Ken?"

"In yellow silk pyjamas," I said. "He looks like a St Bernard in drag."

When I got back into bed and put my arms around her, Beverly told me about her nightmare. "I'm standing on a cliff over the sea. It's a bright, sunshiny day and I'm looking out over the waves. When I turn around there's a group of men in suits, you know, business suits, and they are smiling and they want to give me something but I don't know what it is, and I take a step back and I fall off the cliff. While I'm falling I see the jagged black rocks below me."

I held her for a while saying something meant to be soothing like it's been fifteen million years since the sea has been to Riverside and that she was safe here.

"I do feel safe with you. I think it means, Forrest, that I'm falling in love and it frightens me." She kissed me, her face still wet from crying.

If there were just one thing, of all the things that I said to Beverly, that I could take back it would be what I said next. Foolish, selfish man, God forgive me. Holding her in my arms I said, "Will you come to Mexico with me?"

She thought about it for a while, weighing the difficulties, counting the emotional costs. "I have to be back next Monday," she said. "But I'd love to come with you." Then she paused, looking at the ceiling, then back at me. "On one condition: no rules."

The phone rang at a quarter to five a.m. I reached across Beverly and picked it up. Naturally it was Veronica.

"Veronica, I can't talk to you now, I'm in bed with someone."

"Darling," she said, "what a coincidence. So am I."

123

# PART TWO

# CHAPTER TWELVE

Once you enter Peralta, you are committed. No escape lanes, no runoffs; keep your foot down and hope for the best.

Peralta is a bitch, a long, banked, 180-degree turn leading into the main straight. It's one of the fastest turns in Formula One as well as one of the roughest. 170 miles an hour at the apex, bumps all the way round. She sucks you deep into her mouth, then tries to spit you out over the side.

Enter too fast and you will slide over the edge into the loose gravel and the Armco barriers. Too slow and you'll be kicking yourself all the way up the main straight as the lost seconds tick by. You have to get your entrance right because where you enter Peralta determines where you will exit – down the main straight or up into the air.

The *Gran Premio de Mexico* is held at the Autodromo, or the Estadio Hermanos Pedro & Ricardo Rodriguez, to give it the name engraved in five-foot-high letters on the start-line tower.

Pedro Rodriguez drove for Ferrari in Formula One thirty years ago. His little brother, Ricardo, was an even more talented driver. The local press predicted that it was Ricardo who would be the world champion. One sunny afternoon, when he was nineteen, Ricardo entered Peralta a little too low. In those pioneer days when safety was still a dirty word, his car went under the Armco barrier and took off his head. Brother Pedro died several years later in a German sportscar race. And their father, who had been rich enough to keep the kids in racing Ferraris from the time when they were fourteen, died without a peso. All in all, the Estadio Hermanos Pedro & Ricardo Rodriguez is not a happy place.

Especially since a municipal incinerator litters the sky with charred scraps of paper that float down like perpetual funeral confetti for Los Hermanos Rodriguez. The track also runs alongside the Mexico City Airport and the smog is so thick the planes look like shadows; I couldn't even see the end of the main straight.

Every time I came off Peralta, I hoped there would be no surprises as I put my foot down and accelerated into the bronze haze.

It was Thursday. The organizers had waived the "no practice" rules to allow us an extra day to get used to the new surface, and I was cruising up the main straight thinking I had better get Peralta right or I would end up in charred bits floating down from the sky. I was feeling angry, edgy, nervous. I realized I'd been taking it much too easy on myself at Riverside. That had been a nice Sunday drive on a Micky Mouse track compared to Hermanos Rodriguez. I'd been away too long and I hadn't pushed myself nearly hard enough. My lap times were lousy and it wasn't the car, it was me.

I'd swear the bumps were moving. I couldn't see them; they were undulations that hid in the black of the asphalt. On one lap I'd be right in the groove in Peralta, right up there at the limit, when a series of sharp jolts would knock the car loose, out of the groove and towards the marbles, the debris of rubber, oil, dirt and gravel on the high edge of the turn, and the car would want to slither off the track and lunge into the Armco.

So the next lap I'd enter Peralta a little lower, as low as I dared before the turn became too tight and threw the car out like the snap of a whip. And the same damn bumps would be there, only this time it would be worse because my line was tighter. So, the next lap I'd enter Peralta the way I did the first time, bracing myself for the three jolts that would be worse than all the others, and they never came. And when I came out of the turn my speed was down and I would be thinking that next time I would have to go through it faster. Anyway, my times were lousy; so bad I was worried about qualifying.

Like so many racecourses you have to set up a rhythm. How well you set up one corner affects the next, the next, and the next. So if you get the first one just a bit wrong, they are all wrong. There's a saying that an amateur practises until he gets it right. And a professional practises until he can't get it wrong. I was feeling like an amateur. One bit would fall into place, one corner might feel right, but then another would be too slow or too fast and the next six would be all wrong.

The long, wide straight gave me a chance to relax, if you call driving at 212 miles an hour into dense smog relaxing, but I wasn't putting it together the way I should. I felt jerky when I should feel relaxed and flowing. The electronic timers simply said I was slow.

I pulled into the pits to let Max and the mechanics fuss over the car. Since the air was so thin and hot, they'd had to change all the settings from Riverside, but I had no real complaints. Except about the driver.

Ken knew exactly what was going on. "Don't worry about it," he said when I got out of the car and headed over to the Team Arundel villa behind the pits. "The more you worry about it, the more you will tighten up. Actually," he said, holding the door open for me, "you're supposed to enjoy it. Do that, and the rest will follow."

I was enjoying the cool air-conditioned air that came pouring out as Ken held the door open. That and the idea of lying down and easing the throbbing of my coccyx. Every jolt out on the track felt like a stab all the way up my spine. It was better than it had been at Riverside, but not a lot better.

Beverly had her long legs curled underneath her. She was wearing skimpy little shorts and a skimpy little yellow T-shirt that stopped short of her soft and supple stomach. A line of fine dark hairs parted for her navel, came together and ran down to disappear under her shorts. She was reading something called *Cancionero* by Unamuno.

I'd just closed my eyes and let the lazy thought crawl across my mind that I wouldn't mind if they took all day adjusting the car, when the door banged open and the villa was suddenly full of men in yellow racing driver suits.

There were only two of them, but they had enough energy for five so I had the impression they both came through the door at the same time: Phillippe, with his ferret face and his eyes darting everywhere, leaning forward on the way to the fridge to look for a beer. Maurizio, with his lined and solemn face too big for the rest of him, looming ahead of him, as stately and dignified as possible for a man five feet no inches tall; Maurizio heading like a heat-seeking missile for Beverly.

Maurizio, the Italian, twenty-eight, three years younger, had been second and third in the points in the four years since he had started driving in Formula One. His eyes had a glaring look, as if nothing could stand in his way. But he also had the slow and dignified charm that some short people cloak themselves with as a substitute for height.

Phillippe was Brazilian. He had been the World Champion twice, and even though this season hadn't been a good one for him he had no doubts he was going to win the championship again. If not this year then next year, or the one after that. He was fantastically quick, the sort of driver that makes it look easy, as if anybody could do it. His head was in the refrigerator so his voice sounded muffled. "Whatsa matter darling, you gotta headache, you gotta lie down? You ignore the pretty lady, you don't say hello?"

He came out holding a bottle of Negro Modelo. "And how come you got no good beer, only this Mexican piss?"

At the same time Maurizio was pushing past him, his face in the cocky little smile he thought was irresistible, going straight for Beverly. Beverly with her black hair and her blue eyes looking over the top of her book. "Forrest, I allow you to introduce me to this charming lady if it is no too much trouble." He bowed slightly before Beverly. "I am Maurizio Praiano, the finest racing driver in the world."

"And the biggest pain in the ass," I said, sitting up slowly.

"Hey, how come is you who has the pain in the ass, Forrest?" Phillippe said, sitting on the end of the daybed where I'd been lying. "I hear you been beat up. Is your ass how come you drive like a truck?"

"Beverly," I said standing up, "may I introduce the Danielli Team drivers Maurizio Praiano and Phillippe Cartablanca. Watch out for your purse or they'll steal it."

"Forrest," said Maurizio, acting wounded, "is not fair. We never steal from beautiful ladies. Only from the gentlemen who drive like the tortoys."

"That's right?" he asked Beverly. "That's how you say the word, 'tortoys'? You know the reptile" (he pronounced it ray-pah-tee-lay) "with a big shell on his back and a look on his mouth like he knows he goes too slow, he's too late, his life already happen before he get there." Maurizio had turned down the corners of his mouth like an old turtle.

"Tortoise, you mean," said Beverly, charmed by him.

"Yes, what you say. My English is not so good, I think. Maybe you help me." Maurizio smiled and nodded his head, solemnly agreeing with himself.

Phillippe's eyes had been darting around the room as if he were searching for the right words. He spoke four or five languages, but his cadences were from Brazil, syncopated like bossa nova.

"You know, Forrest, I worry when I hear you are coming back." I started to object but he held up his hand to make his point. "No, really. You are very good driver, but lately I think maybe you are not so much in control. But now I am not so worried because I look at your time and I see you are slow. So the only time I have to worry about you is when I pass you. Otherwise I can forget." He put his bottle of beer down on the floor. He'd only taken a sip. "But I don't understand, Forrest. Why are you going so slow? Is this automatic transmission so bad? Is not like you."

Maurizio had been examining the cover of Beverly's book. He put it down, puzzled. Then he looked at Beverly again and his face lit up. "I think this beautiful Beverly she take all his strength."

"I think it'd take all your strength to reach high enough to kiss her, Maurizio. No, it's not Beverly. And it's not the car. I've just been away too long."

"I think I know your problem," said Maurizio. He had been looking out the window, then he turned his big head to face us. "The same was for me," he said in a low voice, "when I have the big crash at Monza and the first day I am back on the track six months later I try to prove right away I am just as quick. But I am not so fast and I feel terrible. I feel, whatsa word, awkward, like a dancer who dance with no music."

He sat down on the couch next to where Beverly was curled up. He put his hand on her bare foot and gave it a little tug along with a smile to ask her permission. He drew her foot towards him and bent forward to demonstrate. "Is like a beautiful woman, you cannot do it all at once right away. Sometimes, Forrest," he said, looking up for a moment before bending back down to his task, "you have to begin slowly. You have to kiss her toes and her ankle before you can kiss her mouth."

"Or knee," said Beverly, withdrawing her leg, tossing her head

131

and standing up. Then she leant forward and kissed him lightly on the cheek to give him back his dignity. "But you are a very nice kisser."

Maurizio nodded his head thoughtfully as if to say yes, he was a very nice kisser.

Maurizio and Ken were right. As soon as I went back out and started to relax, started to work on one turn and then another, my times started to improve. I still felt I was a long way from pushing the car to its limits, but then the race wasn't until Sunday. By four o'clock the track was closed and we were finished for the day.

Every city has its smell. The baked exhaust of Florence smells different to the spice of Siena. Mexico's was tortillas and coriander overlaid with a blanket of diesel breath.

On the way back to the hotel, Beverly was peering at the side streets and the markets, seeing splashes of reds, blues and aquamarines against the brown of poverty. "This must be what a city looks like after a war," she said. "I mean it looks like it's been broken and abandoned but the people still live here."

The official guess was that there were 18 million people living in Mexico City, but it was only a guess. People were living in packing crates on the roofs of buildings and in the alleys and on the streets.

Two years after the earthquake, there were still jagged walls sticking out of piles of rubble. Nearer to the centre, office blocks looked as if they had suffered a nuclear blast. In twenty years, Mexico City will have 28 million people and it will be the largest city in the world. Compared to Mexico City, Calcutta will look like a village green.

Ken had insisted we stay in the middle of the city at the Camino Real. "We'll be going against the traffic, old boy. Much better than the Holiday Inn with the riffraff. Well worth the bother."

"Are they all like that?" Beverly was looking out at the solid jam of traffic heading out of Mexico City. It looked as if there had been a car war thirty years ago, and the losers were still staggering home with torn wings, wheel wobble, smashed doors and dragging exhaust pipes. We were sitting in the back seat of a big, air-conditioned American Ford, headed the other way, into the heart of the city. The driver wore a chauffeur's cap and a plaid sports jacket.

"Are all what like what?" I pulled her across the shiny blue plastic seat.

"Those drivers, Maurizio and Phillippe, are they all, oh I don't know, that pushy? Or are most drivers more like you?" She snuggled up to me putting her hand behind my neck for a kiss.

"I'm very pushy," I said, pushing my thumb against her nose. "If you want to win you've got to push. You've got to push people out of the way to get there. Some drivers cover it up with charm, some don't. They're like anybody else, except they're shorter than I am."

Beverly's hand was in my lap and she gave me a squeeze. "You're the perfect size," she said.

I kissed her again.

The Camino Real was worth the bother. We drove inside the high, yellow concrete walls and left the outside world behind. When we stepped out of the car there was no real transition from the outside to the inside of the hotel. Outside there was a plush green carpet and overhead a concrete canopy held back the sun. Inside, the spaces were immense, areas of light and shade, and the carpet was brilliant red. After crossing a half an acre of it, we went down five steps to cross another half-acre to the reception desk.

There was a crowd of fans, tourists and sponsors checking in before a big race, and one group of business suits I recognised: the Falcon management from North America. They weren't the real biggies. They weren't the corporate men who controlled the whole complex of Falcon Aerospace, glass, cars, trucks, banks and real estate. They were the managers of Falcon's North American Car Division, in the $200,000 – 300,000 salary range, with a bonus that could double that in the good years. No doubt they were here to combine a series of meetings with a few hours off on Sunday for the Mexican Grand Prix.

I'd met them two years before when they were talking to Ken about supplying him with the new Formula One engines they were developing. Ken didn't get the engines, he didn't have the "track record", they said. But he was still hoping. I wanted the extra power, and the back up of their engineers and satellite-linked CAD-CAM computers to make us competitive with the teams on the front row.

They must have flown down on one of their corporate jets. They would have a marketing and sales meeting after checking in, a fast dinner, another meeting until midnight. Breakfast at seven, with meetings booked solid through to eight, when they would have drinks and dinner and talk informally about cars before the really important evening meeting. I couldn't help thinking that if they were smarter they wouldn't have to work so hard. I wondered when they found time to have children, walk to a store, experience thirty seconds of real life.

Sam Maddox recognized me and beckoned me over with what I thought was a welcoming wave. He was a biggie. A Corporate Vice President. As opposed to the other suits, who were just Division. He was short, overweight, balding, pockmarked and had a tangle of fine red veins on his nose. He looked nasty, but then you don't get to be a Corporate Vice President by making friends. You get to be a Corporate Vice President by making enemies.

"Forrest," he said with a big grin, "you going to treat us to another one of your spectacular crashes or are you just going to quit out there?" Then he looked at me with the corporate intensity that had earned him a seat in the boardroom. "If I were you, I'd think twice before I drove that car." Then he shifted back to his grin to say, "No offence."

I took offence. "Sam," I said, "you ever sit in a Formula One car?"

He gave his head a minimal shake. No.

"Well the day you can wedge your fat ass into a Formula One car and shift from first to second without doing serious damage, I'll listen to your advice about when and where I should drive."

His jaw stuck out. He liked to fight. "Son," he said, "I don't have to drive." Then he let just a touch of the man show through his corporate armour. "Forrest, you be careful out there. Don't take any chances you don't have to." He started to walk away, then he turned back. "We could still do an engine deal with you guys," he said. "But not this year. And not if you pull another one of your goddamn stunts."

I picked up our key, 263, and we went to our room to change for the pool. It was just five o'clock and the sun was still hot.

Beverly hooked her thumbs on the back of her jeans and slid

134

her jeans, white silk panties and Reeboks off in one move. She lifted her T-shirt over her head, unsnapped her bra and bent over to rummage in her suitcase for her bikini. Sunny California girl. Ready for the beach in ten seconds flat. A little white stripe for her bikini bottom; none for her top. Something made her look up and turn around. "Forrest. Staring like that is going to turn you into a dirty old man."

"I am a dirty old man."

"You're an oversexed middle-aged man. Put on your suit or we'll miss the sun."

"Thirty isn't middle-aged, it's mature youth. Beverly, why don't you go to the pool? I'll stay here, catch up on my paperwork. My bruises make me look like an escaped convict."

"So what? Tell people I beat you. You've got designer bruises, they're faded and besides, who cares?"

"I care," I said.

"Forrest, stop being a child. Your stomach's more like strawberry custard now. Just a few juicy purple bits, like plums. You could say you did it in your car. Drivers are always hurting themselves in their cars aren't they? Probably why you do it. Besides, unless you've got one of those dippy little jockstrap swimsuits the bruise on your tailbone won't show at all."

"You mean like this?" I showed her my blue jockstrap swimsuit dangling off the end of the hard on that had been launched from watching her.

"Looks like it won first prize. Come on, the sun will do you good, if you can squeeze your swimsuit over that obstacle."

"That's no obstacle, that's – " She shut my mouth with a kiss, grabbed a towel and walked out the door.

I stopped for a moment. What a relief to feel her sunshine melting my icy, cynical soul, to be buoyed up by Beverly's good sense. She had the gift of ease among strangers. Even Max liked her.

We fitted together; I felt as though I had known her for months, even years, rather than days. When I thought of Veronica it was as if the weight of her had been lifted from my chest. Although I would miss Veronica's wit. And her astonishing nipples.

I locked the door with the big key and went down the corridor to find Beverly. If the Aztecs had built hotels instead of temples and if they had put swimming pools in the middle of them, they'd probably look like the Camino Real: large trees, tangled gardens, a brilliant blue pool, enclosed by simple, massive, sloping walls. I stepped out onto the patio by the pool, momentarily dazzled by the brilliant blue of the pool and the sun. When my eyes adjusted I saw that she was alone, sitting upright on a chaise logue. Around the pool men were sneaking cautious looks at her. I could look all I wanted; lucky me. California girls are born with a tan and Beverly's was a honey. She'd swum a couple of laps to cool off, and was rubbing oil on her legs. I had the English skin disease, slug-white greyish skin that comes from a summer of heavy rain. Against the background of my skin the bruises looked like death.

"Rub oil on my back and I'll rub yours," she said rolling onto her tummy. I worked my way down Beverly's back, feeling the hot sun on my shoulders, massaging her long muscles, thinking she must work hard to keep in such good shape. And how good it must be to be twenty-four and not have any of those tight little knots that nerves tie into the backs of those who are so anxious to please. "If you ever want to stop driving," she said into her towel, "I'll hire you to be my personal masseur. *Ow!* That hurts. No, no, no, don't stop."

A shadow crept across her back. "What a surprise, I am not expecting to see you so soon again. No please, don't get up, I will sit down." It was Maurizio. In a swimsuit his body was much chunkier than you would expect. He sat down, heavy thighs splayed.

"Why don't you sit down?" I said.

"Sometimes, Forrest, I think you take the piss of me."

"True, Maurizio, of you, sometimes I do."

"It's OK. Sunday when I blow your doors off, I give you a little friendly wave." He made the Italian sign of the horns. "How come Beverly, so beautiful a lady hang out with such a terrible old man? Maybe he is your father."

Beverly raised herself on one elbow to look at him, squinting in the sun. "What's the matter Maurizio?"

"I am not so happy."

Beverly waited, shading her eyes. The shadows were getting long.

"These bastards, they are giving Cartablanca the better car. But I am ahead on points. I have the better chance of winning the Championship. I am the better driver."

"You couldn't find your way out of a parking lot, *paisano*." This was said with a cultured, drawling English accent from just behind me. "I don't believe we've met," he said to Beverly, elaborately ignoring me.

I stood up, blocking him off and leaving him staring into my shoulder blades. "Beverly, allow me to introduce Italy's leading English public school boy, Lucien Faenza." I turned to face him. "He's picked up all of the habits of the English, but none of the manners."

"Let's not be bitchy, Evers," he said. "There's so little left to the day, it would be a pity to spoil it."

Lucien came from a wealthy Italian family. As far as he was concerned, Maurizio was a peasant. It didn't matter that Maurizio had his own private jet, a small castle on the Costa Smeralda and a medium-sized palace in Tuscany. All the top drivers were multimillionaires. Lucien treated me better because he'd heard my ancestry went back to a medieval Norfolk bishop. Which, as far as I was concerned, carried the same weight as knowing somebody who'd once driven through Chillicothe, Ohio. After all, we all go back a long way.

We were interrupted by another driver. "Spoil what, old chap? You couldn't spoil 'it' whatever 'it' was. Nobody'd listen to you long enough." The mild Midlands voice behind Beverly belonged to Faenza's team-mate at Lotus, Michael Barret. I liked Michael. He was one of the drivers like Phillippe Cartablanca who made it look easy. He was very relaxed and very quick and looked like a smaller version of Graham Hill, without the mustache.

Normally, on the run up to a grand prix we would be kept busy with goofy PR stunts. Sailboat races on the Detroit River, for example, or shooting clay pigeons with the vice presidents of sales and marketing. Anything to amuse and entertain the corporations that sponsor Formula One. As well as giving interviews to eighteen separate French journalist who all wanted a different slant; and twenty-eight German journalists who all etc. etc. Normally the pressures of PR and the press are so great on the drivers that some of them make an audio cassette, have copies distributed to the press and retire to their motor home.

This time, the organizers had gone too far, and as a result we had the rare blessing of two hours with nothing to do. The Mexicans had scheduled a donkey race for the drivers and we had baulked. One of the journalists had suggested that it was because we were afraid the punters wouldn't be able to tell which ones were the drivers. But I agreed with Carringdon: riding donkeys was too much like a circus.

We were not clowns, we were athletes who could die on Sunday. So the event was called off at the last minute and we were free Thursday afternoon. Which is why, one by one, racing drivers kept showing up at the pool. We gravitated towards each other before a race, nervous as cats in a cage.

Lucien smiled warmly at Michael's insult, showing a row of perfect white teeth, and pushed Michael into the pool. As Michael flew by, he grabbed my wrist and pulled me in with him. Which left Lucien Faenza standing by the edge of the pool with his hands on his hips, congratulating himself, smirking. Maurizio pushed him in. "You are all very childish," Maurizio was saying when Beverly pushed him in.

As he was falling, he whirled round, grabbed both of Beverly's arms and pulled her in with him.

Beverly lost the top of her bikini, and there was an elaborate show of "having the honour" of returning it to her. Every time one of us tried to give it back to her the rest would jump on top of him and half drown him until he surrendered the top to somebody else, who would then get half-drowned. Beverly, laughing, a bit worried that her top might get torn or lost in the horseplay, tried to keep underwater from the neck down, but it wasn't always possible.

For a woman who has been sunning herself topless on the Los Angeles beaches since she was old enough to wear a top, it was mildly embarrassing. But *en la cuidad de Mexico, es un no no serioso.*

The pool attendant was horrified and started waving his arms and yelling at us in Spanish. Lucien sent a sheet of water over him with a swipe of his·forearm and the poor man ran off to fetch the hotel security. When three grim men in sports jackets ran into

138

the courtyard we were sitting around one of the round white tables quietly talking about the weather.

"Forgive me," said Lucien to one of the men who had been working himself up into a rage, "could you repeat that in English? Terribly sorry but I never could quite manage the ol' Español."

The three men left, muttering the Spanish equivalent of "assholes". Whereupon Lucien ordered, in perfect Spanish, a pitcher of iced tea brewed with Perrier.

"So, Forrest," said Michael, leaning back in his chair to catch the sun on his face, "what do you think of Max's automatic? From the way you were dawdling around the track this morning it doesn't look as if it's magic."

"Just running it in. Actually, once you stop trying to find the clutch, it's very nice to drive. It's that track that's the misery."

"For some maybe is a misery," said Maurizio, puffing himself up. "For me is a challenge."

Lucien ignored him. "Judging from those bruises, Evers, I thought Max had to beat you to get you to drive it. A bit like a Buick, I would have thought."

"In that case next year you'll be driving a Buick. In two years all the cars will have an automatic transmission."

"And the year after that they gonna have automatic drivers, then I don't have to put up with this shit." Maurizio was back into his gloomy mood.

"Really, Maurizio, do try to remember there is a lady present." Lucien smiled at Beverly. "I take it Maurizio is not happy with his car."

"Not happy is not the word. Fuckin' pissed off is the word if there was no lady present. Excuse me, Beverly, my bad language, but is very hard for me now."

Beverly gave him a look of motherly concern. "You were saying you felt your team-mate had a better car."

"Not saying; I know. I could win the Championship. I'm ahead of him on points."

"What's points?" asked Beverly.

"Ah yes, well, points," said Michael. "The almighty points. I take it, Beverly, you're not exactly a boffin."

"I've never seen a race."

"Well, let me explain." Michael spread his hands on the table just as the waiter was putting down the pitcher of iced tea and glasses. "There are sixteen grand prix in fifteen countries. If you win one, you get nine points. Come in second, you get six points. Four for third, three for fourth, two for fifth and one for sixth. Then at the end of the year they add up the total points for your best eleven races and the one with the most points is the World Champion."

"How many points do you have?" asked Beverly.

"Forty-six, which ties me for fourth place with Maurizio."

"But I thought Maurizio just said he could win?"

"He could if he won both here in Mexico and at the last race at Adelaide, and if Marcel Aral, who's leading at the moment with sixty-three points, finished out of the points in both races."

"So you could win too."

"I could indeed."

"But it's not very likely."

"Not *very* likely, but it's possible and it's worth thinking about. They say that Danielli and their sponsors are paying Phillippe Cartablanca six million this year. The World Championship is worth having.

Maurizio swore under his breath. He already knew how much Cartablanca was taking home, but as the second driver Maurizio was 'only' paid two and a half million and he felt he was seriously underpaid.

"What happens if you come in second?"

"You hope for better luck next year."

"Or change teams," said Maurizio.

"There are two championships," I said. "One for drivers, and one for the cars. For example, Lucien is second in the driver's championship, but his team – Lotus – is leading the constructor's championship."

"So there are two world champions, for a car and a driver?"

"Right. It gives twice as many sponsors twice the chance to say they are the world champion."

Beverly turned to Lucien Faenza, leaning towards him. "Forrest said you're second. Does that mean you could be the next world champion?"

"If sheer talent were the sole measure, I would be. But alas one also needs a bit of luck and a superior car. And both of those have been, shall we say, less than perfect this season."

"Faenza," I said, "if sheer talent were the only measure you'd be a bus driver."

"Keep your eyes on your rear view mirrors tomorrow, Evers. The bus will be passing you so many times you'll look like a turnstile."

Beverly put her hand on my arm to stop my telling Faenza where he could park his bus. "Lucien," she said, "I hope you won't think I'm rude, but I'm curious why you look so Italian and you act so English."

"What a delightful thought, your being rude. Although it does look as if you knock Forrest about a bit. But to answer your question, I am the quintessential Italian. Unfortunately I had the disadvantage of an English education. Slough Grammar."

"He means Eton," I explained.

"He means," said Michael Barret, picking up his team-mate's chair and dropping him, still sitting in the chair, into the pool, "that he is a shit in any language."

Late that night we were lying in bed, tucked in together like two spoons. My hand was on Beverly's soft tummy and her sea-taste was still fresh on my tongue. "Forrest," she said, "do you have any points? Could you be World Champion?"

"Two points for fifth in Monaco and three for fourth in the San Marino Grand Prix. But they won't count because I haven't competed in enough races this year."

"But Ken could still win the constructor's championship?"

"He's not even close."

"Then why are you racing?"

"Because I want to win. Because in this one little thing that I do, I'd like to show myself that I can do it better than any one of those other poor dumb bastards out there."

"Forrest, I thought they were rather sweet."

"It's better to dislike them. Then you don't mind so much when they get maimed or killed or some hotshot kid pushes them off the grid and into the home for the bewildered."

"You sound so bitter."

"I'm bitter because some bastard killed Michel and they are going to try to kill me."

"You're not exactly hunting them."

"I'm not hunting them at all. Hunting is when you go out and when you see what you're hunting, you blow its head off. I'm fishing. I want to stick a hook in the son of a bitch's mouth and yank him out of the water alive."

"What's the difference?"

"I want everyone to see him. And I want him to suffer."

"Oh Forrest, stop acting so tough. Revenge is a myth. I don't think there is any such thing. It's only something people want. What they get is a mess."

"I don't want revenge. I want him stopped and I want him punished."

Beverly rolled over to face me. I could just see her eyes and her mouth. She kissed me and asked me where all the drivers' wives were.

"They're home, in Monaco and Switzerland, tending their tax havens. They always get the runs when they come to Mexico and it's a long way to come so they stay away."

"But they go to other races?"

"Most of them do. Some don't. Until Michel's crash there hadn't been a death in a Formula One race for years. But the threat is always there and some wives meet it head on and some get as far away from it as possible."

"Ever read Unamuno and the grandeur of possibilities?"

"Not recently."

"When you're a kid, you think you could be a king or a queen. Then when you get a little older you realise you can't do that but you think maybe you could be a president or a rock star."

"Or both."

"Or both. But as you get older the possibilities aren't so grand any more and you find yourself hoping to be a something ordinary, like a driver or a teacher of philosophy. So you don't make any choices any more. You drift. When you are young there are millions of choices and when you are old there are none. So the fewer choices you make, the more you have left."

"I think you just don't want to grow up."

"Ok, I know it's childish, leaving it all to chance. But there is a kind of faith in that. I have the feeling that if we get through the next few weeks together, the choice will be made for us. And we'll be fine."

"You mean," I said, using her favourite phrase, "just 'go with the flow'?"

"Go with the flow. It's not all that difficult," she said.

We lay still for awhile and then she began to move. "I thought we just did that," I said.

"Not this way," she said.

"Oh," I said.

"It's time," she said, "that Mr Big-time Racing Driver learns how nice it is to go slow."

# CHAPTER THIRTEEN

On Friday afternoon I qualified eleventh on the grid. That night, Beverly disappeared.

We were in our room at around five-thirty. I would have preferred to have been at the pool, but the reporters from motoring magazines, newspapers and TV were making it increasingly difficult to appear in public. The combination of my two crashes, quitting, Michel's death, my blowing up on international TV, and Max's automatic transmission, made me a banquet of juicy stories. It was getting difficult to step out of my room without having a microphone and a notepad thrust in my face. "What did I feel about . . .?"

I didn't feel. I was trying to concentrate on the race. Qualifying eleventh was in the middle of the grid. Qualifying eleventh was nowhere.

Beverly was bored. She'd spent most of the day in the villa, and she'd heard everything I had to say about qualifying eleventh. She didn't want to go out to the pool alone, but she was a bright, healthy twenty-four year old who'd been in one room and then another all day long. So when she said she thought she'd go out to the lobby to get some magazines, I didn't even think about it.

By six-fifteen I started to get worried. Maybe she ran into Maurizio or one of the other drivers she'd met. But it was unlikely they would be prowling around the lobby. The top drivers had the added hassle of having to deal with the autograph hunters and the enthusiastic fans.

The fans from the Latin countries could be rough. They thought nothing of thrusting their faces into yours while you were trying to buy a pack of gum and telling you how great it was to see you. My fans tended to be British – more reserved and fewer and further between. I suspected that after I'd quit driving in Hungary both of the Forrest Evers Fan Club members had asked for their money back.

Maybe, I thought, she'd run into Ken or his wife, Ruth. I rang their room. No answer. Maybe she'd gotten lost in the maze of corridors, but that seemed far-fetched. Our room was easy to find.

At six-thirty I left the room to look for her. I'd taken six steps down the hall before a German reporter from *Automotor Und Sport* wanted to know "please, how was the driving of the automatic?" In three strides he was joined by another reporter who wanted to know if I was going to improve my time on Saturday. By the time I turned the corner towards the lobby, there were five reporters around me and it was difficult to see beyond them. I tried to wave them away, saying no comment and please go away, but the crowd of reporters drew more. And when I was able to get one out of the way another would take his place from behind.

They were bored, there wasn't much happening, their editors wanted copy; I didn't blame them. But I was finding it a hell of a nuisance that I couldn't walk into the little newsstand, and that to move down the corridor at all meant pushing three to five men and women backwards.

"Forrest, why did you lie about your crashes? Forrest, why did you blame it on the transmissions?" The voice, was unmistakably Janice Henrion. Sooner or later, I knew I'd run into her, but now was not the time. "Mr Evers, isn't it true that you lied about your crashes? Aren't you covering up your own incompetence? Or is there a dangerous fault in the Arundel cars?" Janice was right in front of me and she was not going to move back.

"Hello Janice," I said.

"Forrest," she said, loud enough for the other reporters to hear, "are you going to answer my question? Didn't you lie about your crashes when you blamed them on the transmission?"

"It's nice to see you, again, Janice," I said. "If you'll excuse me, I'm looking for a friend."

Other reporters were trying to get past her but she was standing her ground. I couldn't get past her either, not without shoving her aside. She was wearing a peacock-blue shirt, blue jeans and Doc Martins. I remembered her nipples like pink thimbles grazing the polished black granite table top at Olivier's and the old warm and protective feeling came over me.

She put down the little microphone she had pushed up at me and in the midst of the shouting of all the other reporters she spoke quietly to me. "Forrest, please. I'm not cut out for doing a hatchet job. But I will. Please won't you just talk to me?" she said. "Nobody wants to buy my article."

"Janice, I'm sorry; but right now I'm looking for someone and you will have to excuse me." I pushed past her.

It was slow going. Some of the reporters lost interest; but for every reporter that left, two or three tourists joined the group, curious to see what the crowd was about. Beverly wasn't in the coffee shop, and, moving slowly through the centre of a group of staring people, I found that she wasn't in the big bar off the entrance lobby where a trio was playing 'Bring on the Clowns'.

By the time I was back in the corridor, heading for my room, there were just three people left, tourists mildly expecting that something might happen. When we reached my room, I nodded to them, unlocked the door, went in, and shut the door behind me.

I'd been hoping that I'd find her lying on the bed, reading a magazine or slithering into a dress for dinner, wondering where I had been. But she wasn't there. It was 7.25. I'd been gone almost an hour. Beverly had been gone almost two hours. We were supposed to meet Ken and Ruth for dinner at 8.00 in the lobby. I rang their room again.

Ruth answered. "Hello Forrest, Ken's in the shower, do you want him to ring you back?"

"No," I said. "I'm just a little worried about Beverly. She went out for magazines two hours ago and hasn't come back. You haven't seen her, have you?"

"No, I'm sorry darling, we were out being lazy by the pool, and I'm sure if she'd been out there we would have seen her. She is such a striking-looking girl. She's probably just having a quiet little read and lost track of the time. She'll turn up shortly."

Ten minutes later Ken rang me. "What's up, old boy," he asked, sounding jovial.

I told him.

"I'm not sure I like the sound of this," he said. "I'll ring you back."

Fifteen minutes later, just before eight, my doorbell rang. Ken filled the frame for a moment then, ducking his head, came inside. He was dressed for our dinner together: navy blue double-breasted well-worn blazer, denim shirt, dark grey flannels. The gentleman at play.

"Still not back?"

I shook my head. "I'm going to call the police."

Ken sat down heavily on the bed. "I've rung the Minister of Sport and he has put the police at our disposal. A captain," Ken paused to consult a notebook he had in his jacket pocket, "Santacruz should be here shortly. I've arranged for him to meet with us in the assistant manager's office."

"The assistant manager's office? Where's the manager?"

"On holiday, apparently."

I wrote a note for Beverly and we left.

The assistant manager's office was one of several hidden behind the reception desk. There was a desk and two chairs, and a thin, unsmiling man behind the desk. The nameplate said Julio Ignacio Salazar. Plain walls, no pictures, no personal touches. It was a cube anybody could use, bring your own nameplate. When Ken and I went in, Julio Ignacio motioned for us to sit down.

Señor Salazar stood up behind his desk. He was five foot nine, slim, and the colour of an oak chest that has been in the family for generations. His big beak of a nose made him look, in profile, like one of the Aztec eagles they engraved on their ceremonial stones. Dark grey business suit, a white nylon shirt, intense, dark eyes. He held out his hand. "Sorry you are disturbed," he said. "She's probably just gone for a walk and gotten lost."

"That supposed to be reassuring?" I asked.

"Well, contrary to what most *gringos* expect," he said bristling a little, "the streets of Mexico are quite safe. She could be lost, but she wouldn't be in any danger. And if she gets worried, she could always find a cab. The Camino Real is the one address every cab driver in Mexico knows."

"Then why isn't she here? It's eight o'clock, two and a half hours since she left. We're supposed to meet Ken and Ruth for dinner."

"I suggest, Señor Evers, that when the lady returns you take all of your meals here in the hotel."

"I thought you just said the streets are safe."

"Yes, very safe. But in view of the threats Señor Arundel has told me you have received, I think you should stay here as much as possible. Our restaurants are very good." Then he turned to Ken. "I am sorry you have felt it necessary to call the police."

"I didn't call them. Alonzo de Parrago, your Minister of Sport, rang them. If you feel you can find the girl, then do so."

"Do not get angry, Señor Arundel. It is just that I am afraid that in Mexico the police are not always helpful."

"I've heard they're corrupt," I said.

There was a strong scent of aftershave and another voice behind me said, "Not corrupt, señor."

He looked as if he had just stepped out of the shower, his black hair sleek and combed back, greying at the temples. He wore a dark blue transparent shirt with white polka dots, with the three top buttons unbuttoned. A pair of aviator sunglasses stuck out of his brown rayon suit pocket.

"True, some of our traffic officers collect their own fines. But they are badly paid. Most of the corruption in Mexico, which it is my duty to fight, comes from other countries." He stopped addressing the room and looked at me. His eyes were small and black and bloodshot. "Who are you?"

I stood up. The room was so small we were very close, about six inches apart. I could smell his breath. I waved two fingers in front of his face. No, no, they said, naughty boy. It can be a useful device in Mexico, where nobody knows who you know, and where everybody is afraid of somebody.

"First," I said, "your name. We would like to be able to tell," I paused for a moment to remember the name, "Señor de Parrago, the Minister of Sport, what an excellent job you did for us."

The man in the brown suit pulled his wallet out of his jacket and held out a brass badge like a priest holds a cross in front of a congregation. "I am Alesandro Santacruz," he said, "Capitano de los Federales de Mexico" – he brought the badge around to my face – "and I do not give a fuck for your Señor de Parrago."

"I'll tell him that."

Julio Ignacio stood up, his hands making softly softly gestures. "Please, gentlemen, sit down. Let us discuss our problem."

A girl had brought a chair for Santacruz and he sat in it heavily, blocking the doorway. "Now," he said, "what is your name and what is your problem?"

I told him who I was and that Beverly was missing. He was impressed with my being a racing driver. But he wasn't interested in Beverly being missing.

"Perhaps you have a fight. She is your wife?"

"No there was no fight," I said. "And she is not my wife."

A little smile appeared on his face, then it left without a trace, like a stone falling into a pool and leaving no ripples. "She's not your sister or your daughter. No. Not your mother or your aunt. She is your girlfriend?"

I nodded yes.

"How long you know her?"

"Not long."

"A year, six months?"

"A few days."

"You bring a woman into our country for immoral purposes? And you expect me to look for her for you? You know that bringing a woman into our country for immoral purposes is a serious crime in Mexico. I have a duty to arrest you. It is a serious crime with a very serious fine."

"I will put it on your bill," said Julio Ignacio looking at me, putting his hands on the desk as if to say, calm down, don't make it worse.

I started to protest, but Ken spoke first, his voice smooth and reasonable. "We don't appear to be making progress. I'm sure if the officer realized there was a substantial reward for finding Miss Wyeth he would be willing to forego any fines."

"What reward?" asked Santacruz.

"£1,000," I said.

"You see, even if you don't tell me, I know she's not your wife." Santacruz tipped his chair back, enjoying himself. "If she was your wife you wouldn't offer a thousand, you'd offer £20, maybe £50." Then he leaned forward so the front legs of the chair were on the floor again. "I make a joke." He smiled broadly. Then his smile disappeared again without trace. "I'd like to help you, especially since the reward you offer. But there's not much for you I can do."

"You could check every room in the hotel," I said. "You could check the airport, the train station, the bus stations. You could ask the cops on the streets around the hotel, the hotel security – "

He put up a hand to stop me. "She's not in the hotel or she'd be back by now. If somebody abducted her, there are around 25,000 streets in Mexico City that aren't even on the map. You ever been to a Mexican bus station? You think they keep records? Either she's gonna walk back in here or you're going to hear from somebody."

"You're not even going to ask the cops outside on the street?"

"I will do that," he said, pushing his chair back and standing up. "But next time you come to Mexico, bring your wife."

He started to leave and I called him back. "Don't you want to know what she looks like?"

Julio Ignacio walked with us out to the lobby. People were bright and cheerful, dressed up, going out for the evening. Checking in, glad to be in the beautiful hotel after a long flight.

"I am so sorry," Julio Ignacio said. "This is a good country in many ways but the police are out of control and I am afraid no one can do anything about it."

"We've got to find Beverly," I said, watching three women in long ball gowns carefully mounting the stairs. "Could your maids check all the guest rooms?"

"There are nearly a thousand rooms here. Most of them have already been checked for the evening. And most of my staff has already gone home. I don't want to alarm the guests if I can possibly avoid it."

"Would a reward help?" asked Ken. "Say £200 for the assistant manager to distribute as he sees fit?"

"That would make it possible," said Julio Ignacio Salazar with a deferential nod. "But it will still take time. I can't check a thousand rooms in ten minutes."

"Could you also check the staff at the desk and the doors. A tall, young, beautiful American woman in a T-shirt and shorts would have to be noticed."

The assistant manager looked doubtful.

"For an additional small reward," Ken added.

Ken suggested that I join him and Ruth in their room for a quiet supper. "We can have your calls transferred, and you could leave another note for Beverly," he said.

"I'm too worried to eat."

"Good heavens, of course you're worried. But come watch us eat if you're off your feed. It's no good worrying on your own."

When I got back to my room there was another note alongside the one I'd left for Beverly. It was scrawled in pencil:

*A ver la gringa no sale*
*su cuarto domingo*

To see the girl, it said, don't leave your room on Sunday. Underneath it, in a shaky and childish hand there was another, even more disturbing message:

*zonko of a trip*
*go with the flow*
*it'll be all right*
*see you soon love Beverly*

I'd never noticed Beverly's handwriting so I couldn't be sure she'd written it. But nobody else would use that phrase, "go with the flow." It belonged to another time with phrases like "let it all hang out", "right on" and calling people "man". Either the phrase had taken twenty years to percolate down to the philosophy department of UCLA, or it was enshrined there among ageing philosophical hippies. Either way, the phrase was Beverly's.

I rang Ken and read him both notes.

"I don't think there's much point in bringing in the police again, do you?" he asked. "That chap couldn't find his backside with both hands. I'm afraid we'll just have to wait until we hear from them again."

"She's an innocent bystander."

"She could be an accomplice. That note makes her sound like one."

"Ken, it's one thing for you and I to play games and act as if we can catch these bastards. But it's getting out of control. They could kill Beverly."

"They won't kill her."

"It would keep her from telling who 'they' are. The one fact we know about 'them' is that they are willing to kill."

"I think you're overreacting. Why don't you bring the notes along and we can work out our next steps."

"You don't give a fuck about her do you?" I was furious, shouting. "Don't you know what those notes mean?"

"For heaven's sake calm down. Forrest, you're not going to get anywhere by shouting. Those notes mean we are dealing with kidnappers."

"They mean," I said, "that Beverly is still in the hotel."

"It's a possibility, but I don't see . . ."

I interrupted him. "I am going to talk to the maids, the doormen, the front desk, the lady in the magazine shop. I am going to do it personally because I don't trust Julio Ignacio. And I'll bet not one of them will have noticed a tall beautiful American brunette."

"They could have been bribed."

"They could be. But I am going to ask them, and if none of them have seen her then I'll know she's here. It would make sense. Beverly's tall, she stands out in a crowd; they couldn't walk her out without being seen."

"Are you sure? What about the parking garage? The loading docks, the laundry bays. There must be fifty entrances and exits to a hotel this size. What about the back doors of the shops?"

"I still think she's here."

"Maybe. But if I were a kidnapper, I'd want to get as far away as possible. There's too much risk of being caught in the hotel."

"Not if you bribed the right people," I said. "And there's something else. I was only out of my room for half an hour, so whoever left the note must have been watching me. They must have known I was out."

"Or they didn't care."

"Tell Ruth I'm sorry, but I can't have dinner with you. I can't sit and do nothing."

"What are you going to do?"

"Knock on doors."

"You know she could be up in the mountains thirty miles from here or on a plane back to California."

152

"I know."

The doormen, the ladies in the shops and the clerks behind the front desk all said no, they hadn't seen any lady like that. No, they were sure.

So I began by knocking on doors in our corridor. I knew it was a stupid thing to do, that the kidnappers wouldn't answer. That if they did answer, there was no way I could recognize them. That nobody was going to let me search their room. My only hope was that Beverly would hear me and answer me. If they didn't have her bound and gagged or sedated and unconscious or dead. It wasn't much of a chance, but it was better than sitting in my room staring at the phone.

Of course, most of the rooms were locked. It was dinnertime. People were out. But four of the rooms had men in their knickers, watching television, and several doors were opened with the safety chain on and a lady peering anxiously in the background while a man told me to go away. One overweight Spanish-looking lady in a red slip welcomed me inside, shut the door threw her arms around me and kissed me. I peeled her arms away and left her muttering a string of Spanish compliments.

I kept knocking. "Beverly," I said loudly each time. "Beverly, are you in there?" After half an hour I had covered more than half of our floor when three security men informed me that Senor Salazar, the assistant manager, would be grateful if I would be so kind as to visit him in his office.

Julio Ignacio's nameplate was on the other side of his desk. He didn't stand up when I came into his office. "I have had seven complaints about you. I cannot have you knocking on people's doors shouting 'Beverly'."

"That's her name. Her life is in danger." The three security men crowded behind me.

"Her life is not in danger in this hotel. I have spoken to my doormen, my security people, the maids, and the people in the shops and not one of them has seen your, ah, companion."

"That means they must have grabbed her right outside my door."

"That means she is not in the hotel. As you described her she could not have taken ten steps in the Camino Real without someone seeing her."

153

"Maybe they were bribed."

"Maybe. But she is not in this hotel and I cannot have you terrorizing my guests. They think you are a robber."

"I've got to find her."

"You will find her. Perhaps she went with some friends to dinner."

I showed him the notes. "I am very sorry," he said, sounding tired. "Very sorry. Unfortunately, this does not change very much. I still do not think she is in the hotel. And I still cannot allow you to go knocking on the doors. I will check the maids again and I will call you if I learn even a little thing.

"May I make a copy of the notes, please?" he asked. "I still do not believe it is a good idea to call the police again. Unless you continue to knock on doors."

I walked every corridor in the hotel, listening and calling Beverly from time to time. When people complained I said I'd lost my dog. Hearing my own voice calling her sounded like a bell tolling at sea for the drowned. Finally, at one a.m., I gave up and went back to my room. The hotel was a maze and she was there, somewhere. But I couldn't find her.

There was a note from Ken and Ruth asking me to ring them if there was any news and not to worry. Worry kept me alert until two when the phone rang. It was Veronica.

"Oh darling," she said, "I've got to talk to you."

"I can't talk to you," I said.

"You're not still in bed with that girl, are you? I wish that were my problem."

"I'm waiting for a phone call, an important phone call."

"What time is it there? Forrest, I'm sorry, I shouldn't have said those things to you on the phone. I think we were both a bit hasty. I really do love you darling and I have to see you. Have to."

"It's after two a.m., for chrissake. Hang up."

"Couldn't you just see me for lunch. Please, for me?"

"If you'll hang up."

"All right, all right. I just wanted to say how sorry I am I lied about Langford."

"The one you said was gay but you were sleeping with?"

"Him. Only now I think maybe he is."

"Veronica, I'll talk to you in New York. Goodbye."

She hung up.

I turned the TV on to an all-night movie. In the acid colours of a faded snapshot, Doris Day was a virgin on a farm.

I couldn't stand doing nothing, just waiting. I splashed some water on my face and went out into the maze of the halls again, calling "Beverly". Then I thought the doorman might have seen something. The doorman at the back entrance on Liebnitz was so sorry, but no, he had seen nothing unusual, señor.

The doorman at the front recognized me and shook his head before I could ask. I was turning to go back inside and I almost missed it. Behind a group of hearty, laughing American women in bright evening dresses and expensive hairdos, a flash of diamonds and gold. But there was a reflection somewhere. Somewhere in the back of my brain. Just a ring on a man's finger. Just a bad feeling. The man was gone, back into the labyrinth of the streets or into the hotel; I couldn't tell.

One of the Evers' rules of life: if you can't tell where a man is going, find out where he's coming from. His taxi was lumbering away from the curb and I ran after it. It didn't go far, just back out on the street to take its place at the end of the line of taxis waiting to take the guests of the Camino Real out into the real world.

The driver's face was flattened by fifty years on the streets. "*Que quiere, señor?*" he said, leaning out his window.

I said I wanted to go to the same place as *el ultimo hombre.*

"*Bueno. Una casa de putas,*" he said when I got in the back.

"*No, No una casa de putas. La* misma *casa.*"

"*Demasiado dinero. Son niñas,*" he said making a face. "*Yo conozco muchas casas mucho mejor.*"

I was sure he knew plenty of better whorehouses. I didn't want a better whorehouse, I wanted the same *casa de putas*. "*La misma casa,*" I insisted. "*El hombre dice que es fantastica.*"

He shrugged, resigned to the will of the crazy hombre with the hard grip on his shoulder.

It wasn't far. We crossed Reforma over to Hamburgo in the Zona Rosa, Mexico's shabby Fifth Avenue. The driver turned right and let me off in front of a doorway next to a restaurant that promised

155

the best shellfish in Mexico City in three languages. When I rang the bell the door was opened by a small dark man who looked at me with the insolence of someone who carries a switchblade in his pocket. I went up the narrow stairs, my feet making no noise on the thick new grey carpet, and opened the door of a room that looked like the lobby of a small, expensive hotel and smelled heavily of perfume and cigarettes. I stood in the doorway, looking at the little girls.

They were all teenagers. Small, dark, pretty girls in garter belts, stockings, high heels and silky undies. Dressing up in mummy's things and daddy's bad dreams. A girl who looked fourteen was tending a small mahogany bar. Three girls were playing cards. Two more were watching a Spanish video. A chubby blonde girl with big breasts was sprawled across an overstuffed chair, reading a comic book. One of the special features of Aids is that if you suffer repeated exposure, the incubation period shortens drastically. Some of these girls would be dead in a year.

"You may take any one of us, señor." A thin girl with sunken cheeks and a large voluptuous mouth was staring at her cards as she spoke to me.

"Or two of us, if you prefer." The girl sprawled on the chair gave me a professional smile and went back to her comic book.

"I'm looking for the girl who was with a man just a little while ago. A man wearing a gold ring with diamonds."

Three of the girls looked at each other, frowning, trying to remember. I assumed they were the ones who spoke English. Then one of them, the thin girl, put down her cards, stood up, crossed the room and took hold of my arm. She stood very close, engulfing me in perfume, squeezing my leg between hers, rubbing against my thigh. Her child's face had almost no make-up apart from the bright red lipstick. "I know who you mean," she said, "but she is finished for the night. I would be much better for you. Very good for you. What you like?"

"I'd just like to talk to her. My friend said she was fantastic. Changed his life."

She gave my thigh a hard push so I could feel her pubic bone. "I tell you she is finished for tonight. Maybe you like a rim job."

"I just want to talk to her. *Nada mas.*"

"It cost the same."

"Can you let me talk to her?"

She pulled back from me, doubt creasing her forehead. "You English? Must be English. Only an English man go to a whorehouse to talk. I'll see," she said, moving away. "You know, you pay the same."

I said I was willing to pay.

When she came back she said the girl would be willing to see me, but only for a short session, and only to talk. She was not feeling well, she said. Number 15, she said, pointing to the door beside the television. None of the girls watched me go. Just another faceless john.

Dark, narrow corridors with a multitude of doors, like a human filing cabinet. Behind some of the doors there was a line of light and the grunts of sex. "*Uh, uh, uh.*"

When I opened the door to number 15, she was standing in the narrow space beside the bed, just over five feet tall in her red high heels. A pretty little Mexican girl with short curly hair, bright eyes and a slightly frightened look. She was wearing a full, dark red peasant skirt and a peasant blouse embroidered with bright flowers. The blouse was seethrough.

She just stood there as if she expected me to do something. Her breasts were large and firm under the blouse, wide apart, standing straight out. I guessed she was sixteen or seventeen. Somebody's daughter. I told her my name.

"I am glad you like to look at me, Señor Evers. I am Perdita. Merida said you just want to talk. Which is OK with me, but first I have to ask you to pay."

I handed her the $100 she asked for. I guessed it would be $65 for the house, $35 for a family of fifteen in Sonora, and $5 for her. I asked her if she could tell me about a man with a gold and diamond ring.

"Please, may I sit down on the bed? I am very tired." Without waiting for an answer, she climbed on the bed, punched the pillows into a back rest, turned, sat down, drew her knees up and her skirt around her ankles, wrapped her arms around her legs and rested her chin on her knees. I sat down in a chair facing her. She looked like a pretty little child waiting for her daddy to tell her a bedtime story. She closed her eyes and for a moment I thought she was going to go to sleep.

She began talking while her eyes were still shut, some of the life, draining out of her. "In the house here where I work we were entertaining a group of businessmen tonight. They were all one group and they had a lot of money. Some of them were American, some Italian, and some a funny kind of French I think, and one of them was an Englishman. The Englishman like me because I speak English good and I went with him. But he had smoked a lot of marijuana and drunk too much so he was having trouble with his cock; it just wobble. I tried to help him, do some nice things for him, but nothing. So then I tried to make him laugh, so he can relax. But he mistakes me and thinks I am laughing at him and he hurt me with his ring."

"What did he look like?"

"I will tell you. What he does with his ring is very cruel and I cannot work for maybe days. It was a big jagged gold ring and he stick it up me and hurt me."

"I am very sorry."

"Yes. Thank you. I can't work any more tonight, so I hang around the bar and I hear him tell one of the Italian men that he was going to enjoy the race because he knows a racing driver is going to crash. He says he fix it."

"What exactly did he say, do you remember?"

"I'm not sure. I think he said pretty much what I just told you. I was a little drunk. I was trying to help the pain. It hurt a lot."

"Do you remember what he looked like?"

"Sure, pretty good. Lotta times I don't notice so much what a man look like. But after he hurt me, I look at him. I look at him good. He was shorter than you, a lot shorter. He had yellow hair, only not too much, and he was *rosa* in the face."

"You mean pink?"

"Sure, pink. Round. When I see his face I think of a doll's face, pink, you know? He looks like he drink too much and not take care of himself very good. He's not in good shape like you. He has one of those little bellies that stick out like a melon."

"Did you hear him say anything about Beverly?"

"Beverly? No. No Beverly."

"Anything about hiding, or kidnapping?"

"No, nothing like that." She shook her head, her eyes closed.

"Did he say where he was staying in Mexico City?"

"No, but I think he doesn't live here."

"Why's that?"

"He doesn't speak Español."

"Did he say anything about what country he was going to next or what airline he was flying?"

"No."

"Did he tell you his name, or did you hear anyone say his name?"

"No. I think he said his name is John. But then I always call gringos that. Except you, of course, Señor Evers."

"Perdita, is there anything you can think of that would help me recognize him?"

"He uses a lot of swear words. And his ring. His ring is a big gold ring and it has spikes with little diamonds on the spikes."

The glimmer in my memory. The man in the lobby of the Beverly Hills Hotel. "Anything else?"

"I hope you kill him."

I stood up to leave and she said, "It's too bad we just talk. I like to give you your money's worth. When I am better, I could do you for nothing. You only have to pay the house. Half-price. I would be very good for you."

"You are very beautiful, Perdita, and I would be very honoured. But I'm very fond of a lady."

"This Beverly?"

"This Beverly," I said, closing the door and returning to the dark perfumed halls.

When I got back to my room it was still empty, still a mess, still no messages.

A short, pink, blond, potbellied Englishman who swears a lot and wears a nasty gold ring and is maybe called John. That, at least, was something.

I turned off the blank, hissing TV and the lights and stretched out, waiting for morning.

# CHAPTER FOURTEEN

Nothing fit. Nothing made sense. I kept drifting off into half-sleep, reaching over for Beverly and hauling in an armful of air. I would jolt awake, and then my mind would treat me to movies of Beverly frightened and afraid, drugged, beaten. Raped.

I missed her and I wanted her back, and I could not understand why they had taken her instead of me. Of all the questions, that was the one that kept coming up again and again. Why Beverly? If they wanted to get at me, if they wanted to keep me from racing, why didn't they take me instead of her? I would have given anything for it to have been me instead of her.

Ken thought Beverly might have staged her own kidnapping. But I knew her well enough to know that that was not possible. It would explain why she had disappeared so quietly, and why they had taken her instead of me. It would explain her note. It sounded possible; but it wasn't.

The empty bedroom began to fill with light from the sunrise. Beverly was missing. And if I wanted to see her again I was supposed to stay in my room on Sunday. Was that too much to ask for Beverly, a day's confinement? Miss one race, save one life.

A little man with a pink face was looking forward to seeing me crash on Sunday. If he had kidnapped Beverly to keep me from racing why would he look forward to seeing me crash? And if he didn't speak Spanish, why was the note in Spanish? Why would anybody want me to crash? Why would anybody want me to stay out of the race? Eleventh on the grid was not exactly a major threat to the leaders. How had he fixed it? Or was he just another nasty drunk hoping for a racing driver to go smash?

Nightmares have a logic of their own. When you try to explain them they never make sense to anyone else. But when, in your dream, you are in a familiar room and the floor opens and you fall into the dark and quiet place where a bomb has just gone off, the silence before the screaming starts makes perfect sense. I could hear the silence. But nothing made any sense.

I felt as if Ken and I had been as naive as schoolboys playing with an unexploded bomb, thinking that a tap with a hammer would make it stop ticking. Why Beverly? Why not one of the cruel and selfish ones? Why not choose one of the mean-spirited? Beverly's instincts were kindness and forgiveness. Her soul was mild. She went with the flow, she said, like a leaf on a stream. I knew she was in the hotel, I could feel her, but I couldn't tell if she was alive.

At 7.15 there was a knock at the door. Wondering if it was Beverly or a message or Perdita, I opened the door to see Max, the fat rolls of his body encased in a T-shirt with giant red letters saying GIMME A QUICKEE. His belly hung over bright yellow cotton trousers, the elastic waistband stretched to breaking point, sprouting little rubber hairs.

"I'm sorry, Forrest," he said, surprising me. I hadn't expected sympathy from Max.

"May we come in?" The voice was Ken's, who was apparently behind Max's bulk.

I ushered them in and was aware of our clothes strewn all over the floor, the overflowing suitcases, the unmade bed and the stale air.

"I smell perfume," Ken said sniffing like an old, puzzled hound. "Not very good perfume."

"Perdita," I said. And explained about the pretty girl and the man with the pink face and the gold ring, thinking of the doomed child with the Mick Jagger lips who had rubbed against me.

"Doesn't sound like any Englishman I know," Ken said, "although I imagine there are hordes of them in the city nowadays. Do you recognize him, Max?" Max shook his head.

"Beverly was a very, very beautiful girl," Max said, looking at the carpet.

"It would help, Max," I said, "if you didn't speak of her in the past tense. It helps us pretend that she's still alive."

"Yes," he said, "I'm sorry. I didn't mean . . . She was a bloody fine lass, Evers."

"Thanks, Max," I said, "I knew you'd understand."

Ken walked over to the window to look out over the gardens and the pool. "I shall tell our Mr Salazar. The maids and doormen should have that description as soon as possible. And it is time, Forrest, that you went out to the track."

I looked at him, astonished. I hadn't thought about practice. I hadn't even thought about the race. The race which was the whole point of our being in Mexico in the first place.

"Think about it for a moment, Forrest," he said, his vast back encased in the Royal Navy blue of his favourite rumpled sports jacket. "There is nothing more you can do here or you would be doing it. We assume that Beverly will come back. But if she's not back by Sunday morning then of course we won't race. In the meantime, Forrest, there is nothing to prevent us from practising today. And every reason why we should. It's not just that our sponsors will feel cheated and start asking for their money back. Much more importantly, speculation about why we're not at the track will do Beverly no good at all. We don't want to make her kidnappers nervous."

He turned to face us, the old commander's smile widening his craggy face. "You and Max go to the track. I'll stay here and mind the ship."

I thought about it for a moment. There was nothing I could do in the hotel. And if I stayed there all day I wouldn't be in shape to drive on Sunday, whatever happened. "Let's go, Max," I said.

On the way out to the track, squeezed into the back seat of the chauffeur-driven Ford, Max tried to apologize. He really did feel bad about Beverly but he didn't know what to say except that it was "bloody awful".

"Max," I said, "just forget about it. The more people know about it the more Beverly is in danger. So stop talking about it; I don't want to hear about it. And I don't want to hear you telling anybody else about it."

At eight-thirty in the morning on the day before the race, the sun was beating down and the track was swarming with fans, officials, pretty girls and corporate men in a hurry. We drove through them slowly and cautiously, the car edging them aside. From the back

162

seat we saw a slowly passing parade of curious faces peering in our windows, wondering who we were.

The fans had always been a problem in Mexico. In 1970 they had swarmed out onto the track in the middle of a Formula One race. Miraculously no one was killed, but FISA suspended the track's Formula One licence for over a decade. Now there were guard dogs, police with sub-machine-guns and barbed wire on top of chain fences to keep *los aficionados* in check. The irony was that when I drove around the track, I felt as though I was trapped inside a maximum security prison. But then my mood wasn't what you would call cheerful. I looked out at the sea of faces with malice and impatience.

The last day of practice before a Formula One Grand Prix is a full dress rehearsal, a race before the race. 65,000 fans; 1,600 journalists, photographers, radio and TV reporters; 1,200 marshals, judges, scrutineers, timekeepers, observers, medical officers, first aiders, stewards; 1,278 mechanics, technicians and team managers; all had shown up so that thirty men in helmets could play musical chairs for twenty-six places on tomorrow's grid.

My spirits picked up when I saw our mechanics, Charles, Nigel, Bill and Dave, in their dark blue Arundel uniforms, waiting for me outside our little villa. Charles Laurence, our chassis specialist, came over to greet me as I got out of the car. "Where's your gorgeous new girlfriend?" he said, peering into the car and seeing only Max's unwholesome bulk.

"Dancing the Aztec two-step back at the hotel," I said with a phoney grin to cover the spike in my heart.

"I hope she doesn't have it as bad as Aral. I hear he hasn't stood up or laid down for two days. How are you, Forrest?"

"I'm eleventh, which means I'm angry, pissed off and dissatisfied. Let's get started."

We had an hour and a half untimed practice in the morning from 10.00 to 11.30. And an hour timed practice in the afternoon. We'd use the morning for getting the car set up for the timed session in the afternoon. That was the one that counted.

As soon as I got out on the track, I knew what was wrong. I hadn't been driving anywhere near hard enough. I'd been getting on the brakes too early and on the throttle too late. And the car was way down on power. I could stuff it right down Peralta's throat, roll on the power as soon as I got off the brakes and the car was still dawdling down the straight like an old bread van.

When I came back into the pits after four laps, the mechanics and Max were grinning like cats. Charles bent over the cockpit, his freckled boyish face beaming. "That's doing it Forrest. That's a second and a half quicker than yesterday."

I was furious. "Max," I shouted, "the thing is so goddamn weak I want to get out and push. What the hell is the matter with this thing? You sure it's running on all eight cylinders? And the front end is just washing out. It doesn't want to turn."

"I'm glad to see you pushing hard again, Forrest," Max said in a quiet voice. "Of course it's down on power. In this altitude the air is so thin we are 150 horsepower down. So is everybody else. We could stiffen the anti-roll bar in front. That might cure the understeer."

"Let's do that," I interrupted. "But you have to do something about the power. It couldn't pull the skin off a grape. I put my foot down and it just goes mush." I knew there was virtually nothing he could do now to the engine but I didn't care. The car didn't have enough power and I needed more. I turned to Nigel Weith, our fabricator. "If the air's too thin, can't you make up a scoop that'll force more air into the intake?"

"Sure, but you'll pay for it in drag. And they'll disqualify you."

"If the air's as thin as you say it is, then it won't drag much. See if you can make something up for this afternoon and we'll try it. Max, make sure the aerodynamics are right. It feels as if we could use more angle on the front wings." Max nodded meekly. He was having a hard time hiding his depression and he wanted to help.

I wanted revenge with the biggest possible weapon. And if I couldn't have that then I was going to beat that goddamn track into a straight line.

I was taking the car by the throat and hurling around the track, going deeper and deeper into the corners and coming out harder. I kept finding a tiny piece of a second here and another microdot of time there. After twenty more laps in the morning session, I needed a new set of tyres which meant I'd been sliding too much and braking too hard. Which was all right as far as I was concerned. You can always tidy up going fast. But you can't go faster when you're busy being perfect.

I felt that the faster I went, the quicker I'd find Beverly. I kept my foot down long after a sane man would have pushed the eject button.

When the car was rolled out for the afternoon session, the scoops that Nigel and Max had made for the car weren't scoops, they were slots. Max explained them. "From our work in the wind tunnel we know that the high pressure points are here and here," he said, pointing to the two slots they had cut into the cowling behind the rollbar. "We shaped them like this, like a funnel cut in half, because the wider leading edge creates a vacuum and draws the air down and accelerates it. It has the same effect as a scoop but almost none of the drag."

"Just like Concorde," added Charles, proud of his work.

"How much more power?" I asked.

"Two, maybe three per cent." Max was frowning, gingerly touching the new depressions in the dark metallic-blue Arundel body.

"That's not enough," I said, pulling on my Nomex balaclava. "What else can we do?"

"We could give you less wing angles and less drag." Max raised a sceptical eyebrow.

"No, it's still understeering as it is. I can't afford to lose more grip. Let's see what two to three per cent feels like."

Two per cent felt like nothing at all coming out of the slower turns. But I could see we were pulling an extra 350 rpm by the end of the main straight, enough for an extra three tenths of a second a lap. But not enough to keep from being passed by Aral and Faenza on the main straight.

Midway through the afternoon session I put together one lap that felt right. After the main straight there's a second gear chicane, another shorter straight, then a long twisty section of ten curves which gradually open up and get faster and faster before Peralta. And for once there wasn't a single back marker blocking the line and the rhythm from curve to curve all the way into Peralta felt exactly right. Except for the damn bumps. They seemed to be getting worse from all the traffic.

At the end of the final timed practice session the grid was: Marcel Aral in the number one McLaren on the pole; Lucien Faenza, Lotus, on the outside of the front line. Then Wilson Syfret, Williams, third; Michael Barret, Lotus, fourth; and Forrest Evers, Arundel, fifth, on the inside of the third row, with Maurizio Praiano alongside me in the Danielli, sixth. Prugno in the Ferrari was right behind me. Ian Norcross the young Australian driver in the other McLaren was on the outside of the fourth row.

The mechanics were slapping each other on the back, and were anxious to shake my hand and swap congratulations. It was the exact opposite of what I felt, but there was no point in letting the air out of their balloon. They had worked longer and harder than I had and their car was ahead of both Ferraris, and one each of the McLarens, Williams, and Danieles. Charles and Max's slot had given us three tenths of a second and moved us up an extra four places on the grid. Not bad for a little private outfit up against the big money. So what if nobody ever remembered who came in fifth. Let them have their taste of success, they'd had precious little of it.

I headed straight back for the hotel, dodging the reporters. ("How do you like driving an automatic, Evers?" "Great, great.") Beverly had to be there.

When I got back to the hotel it was that hollow time in the late afternoon when the clerks half-doze behind the reception desk and the sun streams in the windows at a slant. A pair of elderly ladies were waiting patiently in the lobby bar, staring into empty brandy snifters. A young American couple in Hawaiian shirts and jeans moved in slow motion across the acres of carpet, stunned by a day of sightseeing in the sun. "No, Mr Evers," said the pretty clerk with the long dark curly hair, "there were no messages."

I stopped to look out at the pool where we'd had our frolic. It seemed like years ago now, Beverly anxiously keeping her shoulders below the waterline, watching Maurizio waving her bikini top like a toy flag, bravely playing somebody else's game.

A mother with big gold earrings and a shimmering bronze tan pretended to read a paperback exposé of the movie business while her five-year-old daughter shrieked "Look at me" from the shallow end of the pool. When the mother looked up the daughter would put her head under water and stand on her hands with her feet in the air. But when the little girl came up for air her mother would be reading again so she couldn't tell if her mother had seen her stand on her hands. So she shrieked again. It was a game they played.

Nothing was happening. Maybe, I thought, a few laps in the cool water would help me think of something that might help Beverly. I headed back down the maze of corridors to change into my suit.

When I turned the corner for our room I heard a low growl At the other end of the hallway there was a large dog silhouetted against the light. The dog was moving slowly towards me

I moved closer and I saw it was too awkward for a dog. It was moving slowly, stiffly, making a low noise in the back of its throat. It moved into a pool of light from one of the overhead fixtures and I saw it was a woman on her hands and knees. I ran towards her and shouted, "Beverly." She was naked and her mouth was swollen and her lips were cracked. She smelt powerfully of urine.

"Beverly," I said, holding her head in my hands. The whites of her eyes were bloodshot and yellow. "Beverly," I kept repeating, kissing her dry, cracked mouth.

Her eyes half-focused on me and she looked puzzled, as if she couldn't quite remember me. "Uh uhscopped."

I picked her up as carefully as I could, her body limp and dangling, her head rolling. "Uhscopped," she said. "Uhscopped." Her breath had the sweet, sickening smell of decay. I carried her down the hall and as I unlocked our door I realised she was telling me that she had escaped.

I laid her down on the bed and rang Salazar. "I've found Beverly," I said. "She's very bad. I need a doctor here right now. I think she needs to be in a hospital. It looks like she's been drugged."

"I will send a doctor *inmediatamente*," he said and put down the phone.

I ran a warm bath, and lowered Beverly into it. She relaxed in the water as rubbery and helpless as a paraplegic. Five minutes later, when the doctor knocked on the door, Beverly was washed and dried and her hair was combed and she was lying on the bed in my bathrobe, screaming.

Before language, before the conscious mind catalogued the world into bits small enough to comprehend, there must have been screams like that in the dark forests and in the jungle. Screams in the face of the doom gods that made the earth quake and the skies go boom in the night. Screams without hope or thought, rattling with terror.

I held Beverly in my arms, rocking her the way mothers do with their crying infants, telling her that it was OK, she was all right, I was there, and everything was going to be fine. She made no sign that she heard me and the words sounded hollow to me. I didn't believe anything was going to be fine.

In between her screams and my reassurances, I tried to tell the doctor to come in, but of course he couldn't without a key. And when I tried to get up, Beverly clung to me and screamed harder, as if my getting up from the bed and leaving her even for a moment was unbearable. So I scooped her up, still screaming and, holding her in my arms like an overgrown, insane child, I carried her across the room to the door to let the doctor in.

He was a small man, no more than five foot one, with a neat dark suit, a yellow cotton shirt, no tie, and a mournful face. For a moment Beverly became agitated at the sight of him, as if he was a torturer returning, then she calmed, laid her head against my shoulder and fell silent.

"Does she have a history of psychosis?" he asked. "Are you aware of any psychiatric disorders she may have suffered?" He indicated that I was to lie Beverly down on the bed with a flip of his hand. The doctor in charge. He took some things out of a small black leather bag he was carrying while he kept up a stream of questions. The nameplate on the bag said Dr Luis Lopez. He had a habit of looking off into space while he asked his questions, as if maybe somebody in the audience might know the answers better than I did.

Was she taking any prescribed drugs? Was I aware of any ingestation of unusual substances in the past twenty-four hours?

I told him she had been kidnapped and that I had found her naked on her hands and knees in the hall and I had no idea what she'd been ingesting or where she'd been ingesting it. He didn't react to that but kept bent to his task, peering at her pupils, dilating a nostril and peering up. Was I aware of any unusual marks on her body, he wanted to know. How long had she been "agitated?" Was I related in any way?

All I could do was shake my head; no.

He felt her neck and under her chin with his doctor's touch. Still staring into space he gave me his diagnosis. "Her respiration and pulse rate are seriously depressed. Her temperature is slightly elevated and apparently she is in severe mental distress. I'd like to put her into hospital where I can keep an eye on her and run some tests in the morning." He started putting his things back into his bag. "In the meantime, it would be a good idea to have her stomach pumped. It may be too late to prevent more absorption into the blood stream, but if she's ingested any drugs orally there may still be some traces there, although naturally we'll also test her urine and her blood."

"I want you to help her, I don't want you to prosecute her."

He turned to me, bristling. "Until I know the cause there is nothing I can do for her. I can't even prescribe a mild tranquilizer until I know if there are any other drug or drugs it may react to. With that depressed pulse rate I wouldn't prescribe an aspirin without knowing what's behind it. Are you willing to act as her guardian?"

For the first time since he'd walked in I was able to say yes. Dr Lopez phoned the front desk for a car and then phoned a hospital while I packed Beverly's toothbrush and a few things into her overnight bag.

"Will she be all right?"

He shrugged his tired doctor's shrug and his face looked as if he hadn't had a full night's sleep in months. "Yes," he said, looking away from me. "She'll be fine."

I had carried her, still wrapped in my bathrobe, past the wide stares of the comfortably well-off guests in the lobby. For once the tourists and reporters had moved aside and turned away. Now, in the car, Beverly seemed more relaxed, her head against my shoulder. Little ladylike snorts of what sounded like indignant surprize came from her little ladylike nose.

We drove, as you always drive in Mexico City, straight into a traffic jam. I wanted to tell the driver to hurry up, that this was an emergency. But there was nothing he could do.

"Forrest," she said quietly and calmly into my ear, "I think they were Colombian." It was like hearing a voice in an empty room.

I turned slowly and carefully towards her. I didn't want to startle her. "Why?" I asked. But that was all she said. The little snores of surprize returned and I didn't think it was wise to wake her.

I had pictured the Mexican hospital as a jumble of cockroaches and chaos, with moaning teenagers in blood-soaked bandages sprawling in the lobby. I had pictured wrong.

Once we broke free of the traffic jam around the hotel, the Hospital Pablo Diaz was only fifteen minutes drive down Ejercito Nacional. It sits in spacious grounds, back from the street, a modern ten-storey tower with four wings radiating out like spokes from a hub of lifts and staircases. Inside the floors gleam and the nurses pass by with crisp efficiency. Apart from the dark eyes and broad faces, the only clue that the hospital is not the pride of downtown Minneapolis or LA is the Mexican boys in army fatigues carrying machine guns slung from their shoulders. They slip in and out of the doorways and stairwells like barracuda in a reef.

We checked Beverly in at the main desk while attendants lifted her onto a stretcher with wheels and rolled her away to have her stomach pumped. After Hospital Pablo Diaz was satisfied that the gringo had enough pesos to pay for the very best of modern medical treatment, I rang Ken.

"Good God," he said. "Ruth and I will be right there."

"There's no point in coming," I told him. "She's not conscious. She's having her stomach pumped now. After that she'll probably just sleep. You might have Salazar check the register for Colombians. She mentioned Colombians."

"I'll see what I can turn up."

Beverly was still unconscious when they wheeled her into her room on the seventh floor. Her face had gone white under the garish hospital light and I was struck with how young she looked, as if she were a schoolgirl tucked into bed after milk and cookies. I sat there, holding her hand for an hour before Dr Lopez came into the room.

"I've tried to get a lab technician to do some tests, but there is no one on night duty. She seems stable, but it would be a good idea if you could keep an eye on her."

I asked if he had any theories.

"Theories," he said, drawing a breath and looking out through the open door. "The slow pulse and breathing could indicate a large dose of barbiturates, and the paranoia might indicate a large dose of amphetamines; so it might be very large doses of both. Or it may be a purely mental reaction to severe stress. Or it may be a severe allergic reaction, a viral infection, or a combination of any of the above. On the other hand," he said, putting his hands in his pockets, "it might be something completely different. It might be a tropical disease that's found its way into the city. We'll start tracking it down in the morning," he said, resuming his confident bedside manner. He paused in the doorway on the way out to look at Beverly lying peacefully between the green sheets. "She's stable now; she should be fine."

After he left, I got up to stretch my legs, but as soon as I started to pull my hand away Beverly held it fiercely. "No," she said with her eyes closed. "No, no, no."

I tried to speak to her, but I don't think she heard me.

Close to midnight, Ken came into the room and sat down. They had found the room where they had kept Beverly. Salazar had alerted the Federales and they were on the case. Probably in pursuit of a payoff I thought, but I kept my thoughts to myself.

"There was a flight out of Mexico this evening and apparently they were on it. The Colombian police have agreed to meet the plane."

After an hour, Ken left. I stayed moored to the bed, Beverly making sharp cries of protest if I tried to leave. Once she started screaming again, bringing the night nurse running. And once she spoke in that eerily clear, calm voice. "I'm sorry," she said.

"For what?" I asked. "It's OK, you're going to be fine." But just as before, I doubted that she heard me.

Then at 4.19 a.m., Sunday morning, she gave out a little startled cry of surprise, the sort of sound she might have made if she'd had an Uncle Charlie whom she hadn't seen in years and who suddenly showed up on her doorstep. "Ah," she said, and she was gone.

I ran for the night nurse, but nothing she or the doctors could do had any effect whatsoever. I stopped them as they were about to pull the sheet over her head. I bent over her and kissed Beverly's open mouth. "Go with the flow," I whispered in her ear.

# CHAPTER FIFTEEN

There is a time, before a race, when I study faces in the crowd.

Waiting in the pits while Dave, Bill, Nigel and Charles polish the bodyshell for the fiftieth time, and check and check and recheck all the fastenings and circuits, pressures and temperatures, there is nothing to do but stare at the waves of faces that wash up against the edge of the cordon, the thin rope that separates us from 100,000 fans. It's a way of distancing myself from the rising tide of excitement, of letting the emotional distractions drain away. A way of becoming as cold and distant as a judge.

Some younger drivers revel in the excitement before a race. They like feeling their nerves rubbed raw, believing it gives them an edge. Until the day, just before the green light goes on, when their excitement accelerates out of control into panic.

I was watching the faces of some of the older Mexican marshals, the men in the white coveralls who wave the flags and push the stranded cars off the track. They looked at me leaning against the workbench in my dark blue Arundel driving suit, and at the car and the mechanics and the spare engines and tyres and tools. Their expression was set in a kind of I don't give a damn indifference, as if they had seen it all before. It was, I thought, the same expression they had worn centuries ago when they had drugged the most beautiful girl in the city, carried her to the top of the Aztec temple, disembowelled her, and offered her piece by piece to the gods.

I was watching for Beverly's face, hoping that the night before was only a nightmare, and that her face would appear in the crowd and smile at me, and I would wake up and none of it would have happened and the fury that was rising in me would evaporate like mist.

I was watching the face of a spoiled fat boy who probably had a Ferrari in the parking lot. He wore a soft chamois leather jacket over a designer T-shirt with a Ferrari logo. He had a small nose and pounds of baby fat on either side for cheeks. He was thinking that he could drive one of these machines if he had the chance. Thinking it would be like his Ferrari, only better. He was just a baby, no more than eighteen. Probably still threw temper tantrums to get his way.

He began snapping shots with his Nikon automatic. His girl-friend's eyes swept the Arundel garage for a point of interest, found none and went blank with boredom. He raised his lens to shoot me and a sparkle behind him caught my eye. Four or five rows behind him a man was shielding his eyes from the glare of the sun. His face was flushed in the sun and on the hand he held over his eyes like a frozen salute there was a fat gold ring with diamonds on little spikes.

Slowly, looking as natural as a crocodile sliding into the water, I shoved off from the workbench and walked over to the kid. I gave him my big crocodile trust-me-fella smile and took his camera as if I admired it, liked the way it was made. He was flattered that the big-time racing driver wanted to check out his equipment.

"Take your picture?" I asked. I was acting nonchalant, casual, but I was in a hell of a hurry.

His girlfriend's face lit up with interest again. She liked having her picture taken. I motioned for them to snuggle together for a cute shot of their day at the races. When I lifted the camera to include Pinkface he saw me. But I clicked the shutter before he had time to react. He ducked his head and disappeared into the crowd.

"Dave," I shouted, tossing him the camera, "keep this," and plunged after the man with the diamond ring.

Hands clutched my arms, an arm went around my shoulder, people moved in front of me to get a better look. I was the focal point in a sea of people and they weren't going to make way for me. They wanted to talk to me, ask me about the race, about the transmission, get my autograph. A teenager in a halter-top planted a kiss on my sweating neck. A hand was tearing at one of my Coleman badges, trying to rip it off my driving suit. A minute and forty-five seconds of violent effort had taken me less than four feet. He was gone, and I couldn't follow.

I smiled, I nodded, I turned, and saying thank you, pardon me, *perdóname*, and *gracias*, made my slow way back the four feet to the safety of the Arundel pit behind the cordon, detaching hands and fingers from my driving suit as I went.

Once inside, I was aware that the kid was leaning over the cordon, screaming for his camera back. Dave was ignoring him.

I picked up the kid's Nikon, rewound the film, snapped open the back, dropped the film into my palm, and gave the camera back to the kid. Apparently he wanted his film back too. I tossed the cartridge to Dave and told him to keep it in a safe place for me. "Guard it," I said, "as if it were your balls." Dave clutched himself in mock panic as I turned to the kid. "How much do you want for the film?"

He looked at me frowning, his thick black eyebrows knitted the way babies' do seconds before they cry. "*Que?*"

"*Cuantos pesos por la Kodak?*"

"*Son peliculas de mi padre y mi madre.*"

"*Bueno,*" I said, "good boy, taking pictures of mama and papa. *Cuanto?*"

"*Y mi coche, y mi casa.*"

"Look, Fats," I said, "don't jerk me around or I'll wrap that jacket around your neck and pull the arms until your eyes go pop."

He took my meaning. And 50,000 of Max's pesos.

The loudspeaker was calling the drivers to form up in pit lane for the warm-up lap. I had a hundred questions in my mind and I still could not believe that Beverly was dead. But there wasn't time for reflections. I put in my earplugs.

It was hot and humid; I was sweating heavily from wrestling with the crowd. So it was irritating to find my fireproof balaclava was already wet as I pulled it on over my head. Somebody must have spilled mineral water on it; empty bottles littered the benchtop. I zipped up my suit, pulled on helmet and my heavy fireproof gloves. With two layers of woolly flameproof Florelle balaclava under a five pound helmet, I was all set for a Sunday drive in the 95-degree heat.

Arms over my head, I slithered down into the car, and Ken knelt beside me as Nigel did up my safety harness, tightening the straps around my shoulders and my crotch until I was locked solid into the machine. My arms and legs could move, and I could turn my head, but my body was locked in, part of the unit. Ken connected the medical air and the radio to my helmet. He started to say something, then didn't. There wasn't anything to say. I felt the metallic clunk from the back of the car as Dave Spence pushed the socket of the starter motor onto the drive nut at the back of the transmission. There was the shriek of the starter motor, my engine rasped into life and I blipped the throttle, ready to roll.

Out into the blaring sunlight and heat and dust and noise, I accelerated up pit lane and onto the main straight. The fans were cheering as if the race had already started, waving the flags of their favourite teams. They rose in solid walls of grandstands on both sides of the track, their faces row upon row of streaks of flesh behind the chain fences and patrolling police.

Too bad, I thought, that they didn't have a Mexican driver to cheer, but they didn't seem to mind.

We were more or less in our starting order, a long colourful snake of Formula One cars winding around the track, making a wild and angry noise. Marcel Aral was in front and he would start from the pole. His McLaren had at least a seventy-five horsepower advantage over mine. Which meant they could set their wings for more downforce. So he was faster down the straights and through the corners. If he lasted the race, he was the favourite to win.

There were rumours that Montezuma's Revenge would force him to make at least half a dozen pit stops during the race. And it was a funny thought, Marcel leaping out of the car, undoing his zips and running for the loo. He'd been suffering the last few days, but it hadn't prevented him from setting the fastest lap in practice. And there was a big incentive for him to win. If he won the Mexican Grand Prix he was virtually certain to win the World Championship. I suspected the little Frenchman had started the pit stop rumours. It was his kind of humour.

Faenza in the Lotus would start alongside Aral's McLaren. Which was really a better position than on the pole. The inside of the track was filthy with chunks of rubber from the soft racing tyres, dirt, dust and paper. The outside row was on the racing line, so the cars had swept it free of debris. I would be starting two rows back on the inside, with Syfret in the Williams in front of me, and Michael Barret in the other Lotus alongside Syfret and just behind Faenza.

In other words the starting grid looked like this:

| | |
|:---:|:---:|
| Lucien Faenza<br>Lotus | Marcel Aral<br>McLaren |
| Michael Barret<br>Lotus | Wilson Syfret<br>Williams |
| Maurizio Praiano<br>Danielli | Forrest Evers<br>Arundel |
| Ian Norcross<br>McLaren | Alberto Prugno<br>Ferrari |

Max's automatic transmission gave me a good chance of getting ahead of everybody but Faenza at the start. And if Faenza blew his start I could jump him too.

Getting a Formula One car underway quickly and cleanly at the start of a race is like dancing on the deck of a sailboat in a hurricane. It takes practice. The clutch is either in or out; there is no in between. The power comes on between 6–9,000 rpm. Below that and the engine may stall or the car stagger before it runs cleanly. But hit it exactly right and you have to make the transition between zero and 700 horsepower at the rear wheels as gradually as possible, with the clutch either in or out. Too much power and the wheels will spin and make clouds of smoke while everybody else drives around you. Too little and you'll have somebody else's grand prix car up your backside.

Meanwhile, the maelstrom. When the starter's green light goes on, 18,000 horsepower breaks loose: the noise is stupefying; you can't see for all the dirt, smoke and rubber; and if you've done it right you've accelerated to over 100 miles an hour in under four seconds, while all around you cars are weaving, dodging, touching, and, if you are unlucky, stalling.

Men have died on the start line because they flubbed a start and somebody rammed them from behind, or because somebody else stalled and presented the driver of a rapidly accelerating ballistic missile with a partially obscured one-ton barrier of steel, carbon fibre and flesh.

Once, at the start of the Austrian Grand Prix, Nigel Mansell's clutch slipped and ten other cars crashed trying to avoid him.

But I didn't have to worry about a slipping clutch. I'd hold my left foot on the brake while I revved the engine up to 8,000 rpm, and when the green light went on, roll my foot off the brake and zoom past the men who had to worry about stalling and wheelspin. I'd practised starts with Max's automatic, and what was lost in power was more than gained in the smooth way it put the power on the tarmac.

We bumped our way around Peralta and up ahead, between us and the start/finish line, the gorgeous Marlboro girls in their white T-shirts and red miniskirts stood at the head of the grid positions holding the name and number of each driver. Beverly was holding my sign.

I pulled out of line and accelerated hard. You couldn't mistake her. The short black hair. That way she had of standing on one long leg, the other foot tucked behind, resting on the point of her sneaker. The high cheekbones; the full lower lip. I slid to a stop at her feet, causing her to jump back. I pulled off my helmet and started to pull at my safety harness when I looked up again and saw that she was blonde, she didn't have long legs or high cheekbones and she wasn't . . .

I felt a wind blowing through my mind, scattering my thoughts like litter through the city streets. The two Lotus cars in front of me, if I went up the middle. Max trundling across the tarmac looking like three triple shakes and a double whopper with cheese. Pinkface somewhere in the crowd, watching. My father in his Aston Martin out of control at ninety on the A30, my mother beside him, laughing. Nicole saying "If you are not afraid to drive, Michel he still would be here". The bumps in Peralta pounding my bruised coccyx. Susan's lawyer answering her phone. Veronica bending

178

forward, her long hair hiding her face, shoulders hunched, taking off her brassiere. Driving across Aral's line and straight off the track at Brands Hatch. Beverly holding my hand, saying she was sorry.

Ken was bending over the cockpit; Max was shouting at him from behind. Dave and Nigel were putting the car up on jacks so they could get the tyre warmers on. I put my head back, closed my eyes and drove all the thoughts from my mind. There was only room for one thought, the start.

"Brooms," I shouted. "Get some brooms." I wanted the track in front of me and to my left swept so that I could get maximum traction at the start. I had to get past Maurizio and Barret before I could get on the racing line and out of the debris.

The five-minute warning horn blew and the crowd began to leave the grid. Then the three minute warning and the tyre warmers were taken off and the mechanics left. The two-minute warning, one-minute, and we were off on the parade lap. As we came around again to the grid, marshals were pushing Esteban Ibarra's Scorese off to the pits. Just as well, I thought; that car was a moving hazard on the track.

When the twenty-five cars were in position, the red light went on: four to seven seconds to the start. I brought the revs up to 8,500, the green light went on as my foot was coming off the brake, and I was already past Barret on my left. Syfret had dropped behind me on my right, spinning his wheels; Faenza and Aral had gotten away and were ahead of me down the straight. I was third.

Under the second footbridge Maurizio in the Danielli pulled alongside me to pass on the inside, but I outbraked him by a foot and he had to lock up his brakes to keep me from driving over his nose as I turned right into the chicane. Maurizio must have been cursing: I'd forced him to brake too hard and slow down so much he was passed by both Ferraris on the exit of the chicane coming onto the back straight. Not that I had time to smile; the Ferraris were right behind me when I entered the first of the ten bends leading into Peralta. I found that by staying right on the limit, I could pull away from the Ferraris on the turns. But I realized that I would have to go flat out through Peralta if I was to work up enough lead to keep them from passing me on the main straight. Theoretically it is possible to drive flat out around Peralta, but no one has ever done it in a modern Formula One car. The speed of the turn and those damn bumps made it very hard not to lift off the throttle just before entering the turn and not put my foot down all the way until I was past the apex.

The bumps at the entrance of Peralta were so bad they bounced your foot off the throttle. Worse still, when the most important thing about entering a fast curve is to keep the car balanced and composed, the craters in the track at the entrance of Peralta were making the car bounce around like a ping pong ball.

There are times when you instinctively know what a car will do. Take the great Fangio, for example, driving a Maserati in the 1957 German Grand Prix at Nurburgring, chasing Peter Collins in a Ferrari. Fangio knew that if he went flat out through a certain curve that had a hump in the middle of it, his car would take off and land thirty yards away at the edge of the racetrack. He'd never done it before. Nobody had ever done it before. And when the spectators saw him do it the first time, they thought they were watching the beginning of a big and bad accident. But his car landed exactly where he thought it would, thirty yards away at the edge of the track and another second and a half closer to catching Peter Collins. He said later that he didn't know how he knew, he just knew that's how it would happen.

I knew that if I kept my foot down, I could take Peralta flat out. The bumps were rough all the way around, unsettling the car and sending it out to brush the curb on the exit. But I kept my foot down, and when I crossed the start/finish line I was thirty-five yards ahead of the Ferraris. By the end of the straight they had caught up with me again. I wasn't gaining any ground on Aral and Faenza, but by going flat out around Peralta, I was staying ahead of the Ferraris and Maurizio.

Which is how it went for the first six laps. I would pull out a little on the two Ferraris in the turns and take the car to the absolute limit on Peralta, and with their extra power they would catch up to me on the main straight. Aral and Faenza were having their own battle 150 yards ahead, the backs of their cars wavering like ghosts in the heat and smog.

Then, on lap seven, at the apex of Peralta, the car completely let go. One moment it was cornering at 170 like a ball on a string;

the next somebody had cut the string and the car launched up over the side and into the air, spinning.

The car landed in loose gravel going backwards, digging in and then, flipping and twisting so neatly that it landed the second time on all four wheels, plowing deep into the gravel, its nose submarining and sending a spray of stones up into the air like a speedboat. It came to a stop, half-submerged. Fantastic.

I felt terrific. I knew I was a little bruised, but I hadn't hit anything and I was alive. I released my safety harness, lifted myself out of the car before the marshals could reach me, took off my helmet and waved to the crowd. They cheered and I walked over to the fence, shrugging off the marshals who wanted me to sit down and wait for an ambulance. I flung my helmet over the fence to the crowd and they cheered again, standing on their feet, waving.

I realized what a beautiful afternoon it was, how pleasantly warm, how bright the colours. I had had a brush with death and I felt my heart pounding like a matador in the ring. I walked along the fence, waving to the crowd as I went, smiling and blowing kisses.

Then, towards the end of Peralta, I stepped back onto the track. The crowd went wild, screaming and cheering, waving their flags. I turned my back to the oncoming cars, daring them to hit me. The Mexicans love bullfights. They understand a brave man turning his back on the bulls in the afternoon.

Inches away, a car went past me at 170, at the limit of its control: the air that blasted by me was refreshing, invigorating. Two more cars passed, one on each side. I raised my hand to salute the crowd, then turned to face the cars as they came off the curb. The flag marshals were waving their yellow flags furiously. But that wouldn't do them any good, I thought, because once you enter Peralta you are committed, you can't brake, and you can't change your line. You can't even lift off without spinning.

But the cars were slowing down. The marshals must be waving the flags further down the track, I thought. If they were going to do that there wasn't any point, it was just traffic.

I shrugged to the crowd to let them know it wasn't me who had backed down and crossed the track, heading back to the pits. A crowd of marshals in white coveralls were running towards me, their Aztec faces set in stone.

# CHAPTER SIXTEEN

A broad fleshy pouch hung with smaller pouches and pockmarked from what must have been a world-class case of teenage acne. Purple pouches under the eyes, loose bluish pouches for cheeks, and a horizontal, split-open pouch for a mouth. His eyes were a filmy blue with yellowish whites, and his lower teeth were ground down to soft yellow stubs like kernels of corn. His thinning hair, combed flat over his wide forehead, was the telltale brass of hair dye. Maybe he wanted to have more fun as a blond.

There was nothing else to look at. There were other people in the room, Ken among them, but for the past quarter of an hour Alain Mafaison, Monsieur le Président de FISA, had been lecturing me from a distance of six inches.

FISA is the Fédération International de Sport Automobile, the body that makes and enforces the rules for Formula One, and virtually all other forms of international automotive sport. There were other directors of FISA, but Mafaison ruled them with the gentle touch of a Captain Hook. He made the rules, he was the judge and he was the jury. He was dogmatic, erratic and constantly contradicted himself. Think of a gorilla with the flight plan of a butterfly.

Aral had won the race hours ago and the crowd had disappeared back into the entropy of Mexico's traffic. Inside a conference room deep inside the race control tower, Alain Mafaison was delivering the prosecutor's opening charges along with the judge's opinion. If he ran true to form he'd give us the jury's verdict in about an hour and a half.

I didn't blame him. The crash may not have been my fault, but walking on the track was, and people could have been killed. Before I'd got back to the pits, Mafaison had been screaming that he wanted a press conference right after the race. He would show the world that "Formula One had no place for cowboys and clowns". Ken and I assumed that his "press conference" would be the public drawing and quartering of Forrest Evers.

So Ken had taken the old fraud aside and told him that bringing in the press would only make the incident seem more important than it was. Told him that the issues would be better resolved by him, Monsieur le Président, quietly and diplomatically, rather than by letting the journalists make a mess of it in the press and on TV. Somebody had to stand for dignity and restraint, he told Mafaison. Press conferences could be held later when he, Mafaison, could issue his own press release to his favourite journalists. Mafaison should be like de Gaulle, above the common everyday struggle. Almost, Ken told Mafaison with a straight face, like a God. Mafaison had agreed and for once the journalists had been kept outside. Or, at least, so the Président de FISA promised.

Inside the stuffy conference room, Mafaison was angry, sweating and, after a quarter of an hour, still warming up. "Let me tell you something," he said, the pouches of his face shaking, garlic breath spilling over me. "You have disgraced the sport. You have threatened the lives of the other drivers. If a car had hit you the driver would almost certainly have been killed. Maybe at that speed he might also have killed marshals, and maybe even gone into the crowd. The race was totally upset, and believe me the other drivers they are very much pissed off at you and I do not blame them. Some of them are very angry, I can tell you that. I do not blame them."

After the race, several drivers and mechanics from the other teams had come over to the Team Arundel pit to see if I was all right. They were more anxious than angry. Cartablanca and Aral thought I must have been suffering from shell shock after the crash. I doubted that Mafaison had ever asked a driver's opinion in his life. He'd certainly never asked mine.

I held up a palm to object, to get a word in, but he blew right past it. He'd been known to talk for two hours without allowing himself to be interrupted.

"Let me finish," he said. "You make a farce of this sport: you clown around and play with people's lives in front of 90 million people. Maybe you think this is funny. Maybe you don't care I have to pay the Mexican police £10,000 to keep you out of jail. £10,000," he repeated for emphasis. "Maybe, what the hell, I should turn you over to them, let them charge you with attempted murder, throw you in a Mexican jail. Maybe I am too soft-hearted. But this is a family affair and I will keep it in the family.

"I have to do my duty and I will do it. Never fear that Alain Mafaison does not do what is right, I have to protect this sport and its drivers and its spectators. You are a menace. Maybe you think this is not such a joke when I tell you you are fined £100,000 plus the £10,000 I pay to the Mexican police. Also I revoke your licence now. Effective immediately. Right now. You are finished as a driver."

He had been leaning forward, pushing his face into mine. I pushed my chair back and stood up facing him. "Then I will tell the reporters," I said.

"I don't give a shit about the reporters," he said, nearly shouting. Then, lowering his voice a few decibels, "Tell what to the reporters?"

"Tell them what happened."

"What 'what happened'? Everybody – the whole world – sees what happened: you can't keep the car on the road, you crash, and you act like a clown and almost kill some people. You think that's not what happened? You think anybody going to give a shit you tell a different story when they see it with their own eyes? Maybe you were drunk. Maybe you still are drunk."

"I was set up. My car was sabotaged and I was drugged."

I saw the dingy colours drain from his face. Suspicions of drugs in Formula One would do serious damage to the prestige and credibility of the sport. And suspicions of sabotaging the cars would certainly damage the drivers' confidence. Just the thought of a tyre deflating or a 50p bracket cracking is enough to keep a driver staring at the walls in the middle of the night. Even a hint of drugs would make the sponsors fly away like crows from a shotgun. They wanted their media squeaky clean or they didn't want it at all. And as far as they were concerned, racing cars were media.

Mafaison wrestled with the problem for a moment and came up with his answer. "It does not matter why you behave the way you do. The danger to the other drivers and the damage to sport is the same. Personally, I am not surprised you are on drugs."

It was time for me to stick my face into his. "I'll be generous with you Alain and I will pretend I didn't hear you say that. And if you ever say anything like that again, if you ever imply that I take drugs or have ever taken drugs, the next sound you will hear will be the sound of a swarm of lawyers carving my name all over your Swiss bank accounts."

"You listen – "

I cut him off. I had listened enough. "I was drugged and my car was sabotaged and I can prove it."

"How?" he said, a smirk of disbelief on his face. "How can you prove these wild claims?"

"I need two weeks."

"Two weeks he says." Mafaison turned to face the room, shrugging his shoulders and pursing his lips to show what insanity he had to deal with. "Fine, take two weeks." He turned to face me again. "In the meantime the suspension of your licence and the fine of £100,000 is in effect immediately. Plus the £10,000 I have to give to the Mexican police. Let me tell you, you will have to have very good proof, incontrovertible proof, to convince me; I can tell you that. Now," he said, his filmy eyes squinting, "I would like your cheque."

"The money's in the mail," I said.

"Forrest." The voice came from Arnold MacIntyre, head of the Formula One Constructor's Association, and a multimillionaire businessman. With his leathered face, T-shirt and designer jeans, he could have passed for any other businessman with a weekend interest in racing. But he had shaken the sport upside down and inside out. He dealt with all of the tracks and they paid him a flat million-pound-plus fee and he supplied the cars and the teams. He also paid the teams their prize money, represented them, and, theoretically, stood up for them. He was the most powerful man in Formula One and I always thought he was fair. He spoke for the first time since the meeting had started "Forrest," he repeated, waiting for everyone's attention, "those are serious charges you are making."

"What happened on the track this afternoon was serious, Arnold,"

185

I said reasonably. "But you can't believe I would have done that if I wasn't drugged?"

"Sure," he said, "I could believe it."

When I got up to leave I saw a small, blonde, spikey head ducking out. Mafaison had lied. He had let in a reporter. Somehow I doubted that Janice would slant the story my way.

Max and Ken and I were walking back from the control tower to our pit garage. The track had the look of an empty fairground, littered with tons of empty cigarette packs, food wrappers and half-chewed tortillas. The teams and the reporters had gone. They had planes to catch, places to go, deadlines to meet. Our plans were as vague as our shadows in the dim-watt late afternoon smog. As far as FISA were concerned, we didn't have a driver any more. I could see Ken was considering whether it was worth going on with Team Arundel. Maybe it wasn't. Maybe the stakes had gotten too high.

Max spoke first. "I'm sorry I have to tell you, Forrest," he said, not looking at me, "but your car wasn't tampered with."

"Then what the hell happened out there?" I exploded, the anger pouring out at Max. Then it disappeared as quickly as it had come as a wave of exhaustion swept over me and I realised I hadn't slept for two nights. "I'm sorry, Max," I said, "I didn't mean to blow up. What are you saying, that something broke? One moment the car was stuck in the groove and the next I was flying."

"It was my fault you went flying," Max said in a whispering voice I hadn't heard from him before. "I didn't allow enough for the lightness of the air. I calculated for the air pressure at 7,300 feet, but I didn't allow enough for the heat making the air so much lighter. With the heat today it was as if we were at 11,500 feet."

"Max, what the hell are you talking about?"

"I am talking about how the gearbox cracked because in this heat, with so little atmospheric pressure outside, the long chain polymers in my Formula One transmission fluid expanded. It expanded so much it created pressure inside the transmission case, cracked it and sprayed out on your rear tyre. That sticky stuff is adhesive, like Teflon, and very slippery. We found the crack and we found the fluid on your tyre. So all of a sudden you lose 100 per cent traction in your left rear tyre. Maybe on a smoother track the transmission case never would have cracked, but with these bumps and this heat . . ." His gruff voice trailed off. "I'm sorry," he said.

"You sure that's what happened? You sure somebody didn't crack the gearbox from outside?"

"Positive," he said. "The edges of the crack were pushed outward. The force came from inside."

"But Max, you dummy," I said, "that's good news. That means that only happens on hot days in Mexico and you can fix that. Strengthen the transmission case, shorten your polymer chains, do what you have to do. You can fix it. And look what we proved," I continued, giving him a pep talk. Max happy was ugly enough; Max depressed didn't bear thinking about. "Our automatic transmission is competitive. We were up there, in the front rows. We were third when I left the track." I slipped into my Marlon Brando voice, "We was a contenda."

"Well, I'm glad you feel it's a triumph," said Ken. "It's hardly going to boost your credibility with Alain. You told him you have proof that someone was tampering with the car."

"It proves the accident wasn't my fault so I don't have to prove anything about that. All I have to prove now is that I was drugged."

"And who did it and how," said Ken. He wasn't at all happy. "We should talk about the fine."

"Let me worry about the fine," I said, Beverly's face suddenly looming in my mind. The fine was unimportant compared to her. I'd pay it if I had to, but they could wait a couple of weeks. By then I knew I wouldn't have to. I would find the bastards or I would die trying. There wasn't any choice. "Two weeks has to be enough time. I left some urine samples in the pits and I think I've got a photograph of the man who may be able to help us with our inquiries."

Ken looked at me suspiciously. "You're always leaving urine samples in the pits." Then he started that terrible wheezing laugh of his until another thought stopped him in mid-wheeze. "I'm having dinner with Alistair Coleman this evening and I'd like you to come. I doubt that he will share your enthusiasm for today, but I think you better face him head on. If he withdraws his sponsorship I really don't think we can continue."

"Tell me where you're meeting him," I said, "and I'll join you. I have one or two errands."

When we got back to our pits the mechanics had gone with the Team Arundel cars to the airport, except for Dave who was sitting on the deserted pit wall. He was wearing his dark blue Team Arundel T-shirt and jeans, and his black hair was slicked back with hair gel; ready to travel. He was always immaculate, always tense, as if he might have forgotten something. He made lists and checked off the items one by one. Which was fine by me; my life depended on him. If he forgot to tighten just one nut I could find myself making a sudden, unexpected turn into a wall.

In the fading light Dave's face had an unhappy hound dog look, as if he'd buried a bone but he couldn't remember where. "How'd it go?" he said, sliding off the wall and looking at our faces. "You don't look like it was a party."

We stood there, the four of us, with the acres of deserted grandstands looking like the architecture of a lost religion. Steps leading up to nowhere in the darkening sky. Through the smog and the evening light we could barely see the ghosts of jumbo jets rising and landing behind the slats of the stands, but the thunder of their engines sounded as though they were ten yards away.

"It didn't go well," I said. "They've suspended my licence."

"Oh fuck. What about Adelaide? What the hell are we going to do for a driver for Adelaide? Why did you do it, Forrest?" Dave looked away from me as if something else had caught his attention. Then he looked back, angry. "For God's sake."

"Look, Dave," I said, "this is hard for all of us and it is going to get a lot harder. I told you why I walked on the track today and why I crashed at Brands and at Hungaroring."

"Sure. Right," he said, clenching and unclenching his fists. "You were drugged. How the hell would you know? Maybe you went a little nuts. You know, a bump on the head."

"I wasn't bumped on the head. And I've been in enough crashes to be an expert on how it feels. You feel lightweight, like you weigh about six ounces, like a little breeze would blow you away. You start checking around to make sure you're alive and see if you've lost any bits or if you're bleeding anywhere. And even when you've done that and nothing feels broken and you can't find any blood, your body is telling you to be very, very careful because you might be shattered inside in some way you don't know about yet.

"Maybe you force yourself to walk so the fans can admire how brave you are. Or maybe you sit still until your heart stops pounding and your muscles stop twitching. Either way, you start thinking maybe you could have kept it from happening. And even if you know that something broke in the car and that there was nothing you could have done to keep from crashing, you also know that somebody out there is going to think that it was your fault.

"But I didn't think any of that. And I didn't feel any of that. I felt great. Hey baby," I shouted out, remembering the feeling, "I felt like a god. I felt the way a junkie thinks he's going to feel when he gets his next good hit. You don't get high when you crash, Dave, you get low. Very low. And I was high. I know I was drugged."

"Sounds nuts to me," Dave said, looking at the ground.

"Did you keep that roll of film I gave you?"

He reached in his pocket and handed me the roll. "Who gets to give me a ride to the airport?" he said. "The plane's supposed to take off in an hour. And who knows, we might get lucky. It could be a first. The plane could be on time."

Max and Dave rode off to the airport in a taxi, their heads looking large in the rear window. We'd be in touch, I said, feeling for the first time since the accident the uncertainty that Ken must have felt ever since the car went over the edge of Peralta.

After they'd gone I found that the urine sample I'd so carefully let into an empty mineral bottle had disappeared with all the other bottles. With reporters following me, and the crews and drivers from the other teams stopping in to see what had happened, it hadn't been easy to unzip, reach through layers of driving suit and flameproof underwear and pee into an empty bottle without raising serious questions. But I'd done it, thinking someone like Cartablanca was going to shout out "Hey Forrest, what are you doing with your dick in your hand peeing into a bottle?"

I'd asked Nigel to save it because I wanted it analysed for drugs. And I wanted the drugs compared with the drugs I was sure the Mexican coroner would find in Beverly's system.

Somebody had known I wanted that bottle. Or didn't know. Or didn't give a damn. Or didn't want me to have it.

Evening softens Mexico City. Darkness hides the fractured buildings and the smog. Strings of coloured lights make dark alleys look like little fiestas. And on the streets the light is kinder to the faces of the begging children.

"She lives in Terre Haute, Indiana," I said. I was staring out of the car at the rows of nameless streets as we crept down the bruised elevated road.

"Who?" Ken was leaning back, his eyes closed.

"Beverly's Aunt Gretchen."

"How'd you find her?"

"I holed up in the villa with the telephone. UCLA had Aunt Gretchen listed as next of kin. She says she'd come to a funeral if there was one, but that there was no point shipping the body to her. She said Beverly had never been to Terre Haute."

"I thought you said Arthur Warren was arranging the funeral?"

"He is now. But I thought I'd ask a relative first."

"Is this Aunt Gretchen her only relative?"

"According to Aunt Gretchen she is. I didn't even know Beverly's parents were dead. She never talked about them."

"How long did you know her, Forrest?"

"Eight days."

"Poor girl. I was really quite fond of her. Will you go to the funeral?"

"I've already said goodbye," I said, remembering her little cry of surprise when she died.

Then I thought of what had been happening to Beverly since they pulled the green hospital sheet over her face. At the autopsy, under the bright lights, they would slice her scalp from the top of one ear to the other, and pull the skin forward over her face and back to her neck so they could cut a sunroof in her pink and white skull with an electric saw, the rubber gloves reaching in . . . I didn't need to say goodbye again. She wasn't there, in the coroner's plastic bags. She hadn't been there when I'd kissed her goodbye.

"Did you ring the coroner?" Ken asked.

"They're still doing tests, but it looks like she died from damage to her nervous system. They think she was injected with a cocktail of distilled cocaine, a barbiturate and a poison they can't pinpoint but they're saying resembles an alkaloid like the South American Indians use, like curare. They said they used so much of the stuff her nervous system had partially dissolved. It's also possible she was given different drugs at different times to keep her quiet."

I remembered Beverly's panic, her pounding heart, her skull beneath my kiss.

"What about the Colombians?" I asked Ken. "The ones who were in the hotel. The ones they were going to catch getting off the plane in Bogota. You were going to talk to Salazar."

"Another cockup, I'm afraid." Ken leaned back and pinched the bridge of his nose. It had been a ghastly twenty-four hours for him and it was beginning to show on his usually stoic face. "Salazar says the Colombian police were waiting inside the airport at customs. But unfortunately, as the passengers were climbing down the ramp, a military van pulled up on the tarmac and the military police grabbed our suspects, threw them into the back of the van and drove off."

"What military police?"

"Colombian. Or at least the markings on the van were Colombian. The Colombian army says it wasn't theirs. Do you want me to go on?"

"There's more?"

Ken turned to me. In the rise and fall of light and darkness from the passing lights I could see he was very shaken. His voice was husky, unsteady. "I mean do you want me to go on racing? I may well have to do it without you. I cannot stand another death."

"I'm sorry, Ken." I wanted to reach out to comfort him. I wanted to tell him it was OK. But it wasn't OK. Michel and Beverly were dead.

Two deaths in two races. We didn't know if we would be able to race again. If we did race again, it was entirely possible that the chances of another death were higher than they were before. I looked out of my window, he looked out of his, neither of us seeing anything. After a while, I said, "You have Ruth, a fortune and an immense reputation. I don't have any of that to lose, so I don't know that I should be giving you advice. But I know what I want," I said. "I want those bastards and I want them more than anything else. Give me two weeks. I need your help for just two more weeks."

191

"Why two weeks?"

"Because the Australian Grand Prix is in two weeks. And I swear to God I'm going to drive in Adelaide."

"Even if it costs me everything?" I looked over and saw that he had turned toward me and was smiling, his great spirit making a joke in spite of it all.

# CHAPTER SEVENTEEN

Later, in my room, I tried to remember Ken's smile. I needed cheering up. I'd found that all the one-hour photo processing shops in Mexico City were closed on Sunday night and wouldn't reopen until nine in the morning, an hour after my plane was due to take off for New York. Staying ten minutes longer than necessary in Mexico City wasn't worth thinking about. So Pinkface would have to wait for Broadway.

In the bathroom there was another specimen of my urine in the water glass. The sample was from several hours and several pees after the race. Even if there were traces of drugs, it would have to wait for New York, by which time the sample would be not hours but days old. A roll of film and a glass of old pee. I wasn't exactly holding all the aces. I dumped the urine in the toilet. To hell with it.

I changed into a light, rumpled linen sports jacket, a pale green Ralph Lauren shirt, baggy white trousers and Guccis. I looked like Miami Vice. Perfect for meeting a sponsor. They expect their drivers to look raffish and prosperous; it was the opposite of what I felt.

La Rubia is just off Liebnitz, which runs behind the Camino Real. An easy five minute walk from the back door of the hotel. On one side of Liebnitz there are the glossy jewellery, perfume, antique shops and travel agencies that attach themselves like molluscs to the sides of expensive international hotels. On the other side of the street Indian women squat over fires in the gutter and fry chillis and tortillas with mystery meat, their staring children clinging to their shawls and their skirts. Neither side of the street seems to notice the other; a miniature Mexico.

La Rubia means the blonde in Spanish, and she was just inside the door, a voluptuous sad-eyed girl wrapped in a black shawl, looking at me as if I were the most marvellous surprise in what had been, until I'd walked in the door, a boring evening. I told her Ken's name and her look changed to deep respect, as if I'd said I was having dinner with the Minister of Finance. As she looked down the guest list for Arundel, the façade fell from her face for just a moment to reveal that look of terminal boredom that hookers wear under their masks as they jiggle their way closer to death with each successive boring john.

She led me into a spacious indoor garden, flashing her eyes at me over her shoulder, turning demure as we approached Ken's table, holding my chair for me as I sat down. She managing to give me a secret quizzical look as she turned to leave as if she expected more, later.

Sex seemed to me something I used to do a long time ago, like riding a bicycle. When the blonde girl turned in the archway leading to the front of the restaurant and gave me a deep, soulful look, I didn't know whether to laugh or cry. I was having trouble in Mexico, telling the difference between tragedy and comedy.

Alistair Coleman half stood as I sat down, extending a soft white hand to shake hello. His smooth, round face looked as if nothing at all had happened that afternoon to worry him in the slightest, as if he was simply glad to see an old friend. I knew better. He was a salesman and a businessman and he knew he could handle you more easily if you liked him.

Alistair was medium size, medium age, medium weight, and despite the expensive cut of his suit and his hair, he could have passed for a medium man in the middle row of club class on the airplane. But of course, Alistair never flew club class, he always flew first. His bland and pleasant Charlie Brown face was known by the maître d' in the most expensive restaurants in Stockholm, Barcelona, Singapore and San Francisco. They knew him at Annabel's in London and Geoffrey's in New York.

Businessmen relaxed with Alistair because they trusted him. And because they thought they could outsmart him when the time came. But when the time came, the game was over and Alistair was holding the cards. He had a playful, jibing charm that kept you busy while he was working the angles. He'd been our major sponsor this season, one of the new breed of Britain's international businessmen. In two years, he'd cut his management sixty per cent, cut his board from twenty-four to six, sold subsidiaries, bought competitors, and extended Coleman's operations to America and Australia. He had also been the driving force behind Coleman's sponsorship of Team Arundel. But he wasn't afraid to admit a mistake. For all I knew, today's race could have been his last with Team Arundel.

"Good to see you, Forrest," he said. "For a moment there this afternoon I thought you were flying home without us."

"Ken told you what happened?" I said, making it a half-question and hoping to draw Ken in. Ken was more used to these verbal power plays than I was.

"Ken told me *why* it happened. I could see for myself *what* happened."

"We were leading most of the field at the time."

"Shame it was such a short time. But don't worry about it, Forrest, I'm not gonna pull your car out from under you. Ken, let's get this man a drink and bring him up to speed."

Alistair was drinking a gin martini in a cut-crystal glass the size of a small ice bucket. Ken held a goodly quantity of Highland Park, an Orkney whiskey that has made grown men weep for the years they've wasted drinking mere alcohol. I ordered a Perrier.

Ken put down his glass and leant on the table, his huge form dwarfing the crockery. "Alistair has been saying that his board is getting impatient with the investment he's been making in our team."

"That's right. So I'm thinking of getting a new board." Alistair leaned back, laughing at his own joke. "Seriously gentlemen, this year hasn't been our best. We've had to make a heavy investment in expanding our offshore sales force. And we've invested heavily in Team Arundel. Maybe that's been a mistake." Ken was about to protest, but Coleman held him back with a hand he barely lifted from the dark oak table.

"I've made Ken a proposition. I appreciate you have had an unfortunate year. I didn't expect you to win the World Championship. But I didn't expect you to drive off into the bushes every time the race gets started either." He picked up the big glass of gin and drank a tiny sip. Then he held it in front of his face and talked into the glass. "I'm repeating all this because I don't want you to hear it second-hand, I want you to hear it from me. I make

195

decisions based on people. I respect the numbers, but I believe in people. And I believe in you and in Ken and in that meatloaf you have for a designer. I think that automatic transmission of his is going to make you all famous and I'd like to go along for the ride."

He paused while he looked into the glass, then he put it down and looked at me. "On one condition," he said, leaning forward. "You change the team name to Coleman, and change the colours to our Coleman corporate green and yellow. Some people probably won't even notice the difference."

"I expect I'd notice," Ken said, looking up from his menu. "Of course, we have all the details to work out," he said with a thoughtful look at the backs of his hands. "The spelling of Coleman, for example. I'd like it spelled with an A.R.U.N.D.E.L."

"A few details to work out," said the soft-looking businessman with a pleasant smile. He was relaxed, taking his time, letting Ken make his weak joke to cover the hurt.

After a while, after the silence let it sink in that he felt he was the boss, Coleman continued. "There are one or two things we will need to decide." Coleman clinked his glass with mine in a mock toast. "Like who'll be the driver," he said. "Ken told me about your run in with old Frogface. I want you to know I'm behind you one hundred per cent, Forrest. I think you're a hell of a driver. If your car had as much power as Aral's you'd have blown his doors off. So you better get busy, mate, and get after whatever it is that's making you forget your car when you get on the track."

Ken picked up a parchment menu and we followed suit. But after a moment Alistair Coleman put his down. "How much do you have to go on? Do you have any idea who's behind it?"

I told him I thought it was probably drugs. And that there was a Colombian connection. "I've got a photograph of the man I think is behind it," I said.

"Let me see it," he said. "What's he look like?"

"I took the shot this afternoon, just before the race," I said. "He was in the crowd in the pits before the race. But with the labs shut I can't get it developed until I get to New York tomorrow."

"But you've seen him?"

"I've seen him twice. Once in the Beverly Hills Hotel and once this afternoon."

"Well come on, what's he look like? Maybe I can help you find him. Who knows, maybe he's a friend of mine."

"Well he's short, probably about thirty-five, got a little pot belly, combs his blond hair over the top of his bald spot."

"What's he look like up close?"

"Up close he doesn't look so good. He has a pink chubby face, yellowing at the edges, like he drinks too much, a pug nose and beady little blue eyes and wears a gold ring with diamonds on spikes."

"Kind of pork face?"

"Right, with little blue eyes. He's arrogant and nasty – "

"If he's arrogant and nasty . . ." Alistair interrupted and then paused for effect. "And if he wears a big chunky gold ring with diamonds mounted on spikes," he said, putting both hands behind his neck and leaning back, "you don't have to get that film developed, Forrest: I know him. He's no friend, but I know Miles Courtland." Alistair leaned forward again as if he was taking us into his confidence. "Known him for years."

A pretty blonde waitress had been waiting patiently beside Coleman. Apparently all the waitresses at La Rubia were blonde, although our waitress was sporting dark roots. He looked up at her, looked at his menu and ordered the fresh butterfly shrimp they flew in from the Gulf every morning. "What is this jabanero sauce?" he asked, saying the 'j' like the 'j' in Japan.

She rolled her eyes in mock terror. "The jabanero is a little chilli that comes from Yucatan," she said, pronouncing the 'j' like an 'h'. "We have a saying, 'The Yucatanos, they invented the jabanero chilli to show God the sun is not so hot.' It's hot, señor, *muy picante*."

"*Mucha salsa jabanero* for the big shrimps then," he said grandly. His grin showed white, even teeth. "And let me have another one of these straighteners." He looked at Ken confidentially. "Trouble with these damn martinis, the first one tastes terrible. Two is too many, and three," he said slurring his words for effect, "isn't nearly enough."

"The trouble with these," said Ken, holding up his nearly empty glass of Highland Park for a refill, "is the first one tastes wonderful."

197

I ordered another damn Perrier and ceviche for Ken and myself, which is raw scallops and fish marinated in lime juice and mixed with a bit of coriander, onions and hot peppers. If the fish is fresh, it's excellent. If it's not, it's lethal.

Coleman got his fresh drink, took a tiny sip, leaned back in his chair again and grinned at the story he was about to tell. The big money, talking.

"Coleman, Courtland and Arundel. Sounds like a damn advertising agency, Ken. One of us is going to have to change our name. The truth is Courtland's name is too much like mine. People are always confusing Coleman with Courtland. Miles Courtland inherited controlling interest in Courtland Mills about fifteen years ago when his father died. I think his great-great-grandfather founded it. Worsted, broadcloth, Oxford linen, same sort of thing we used to do; the upper end of the trade. But of course, by the time Miles inherited Courtland's, most of the mills had shut down and the bulk of their manufacturing came from outside Britain.

"I remember Miles' father. He had all the charm of a broken foot, but he was a force in the business. He was one of the first to expand his manufacturing base outside the Commonwealth, and to link up with the fashion houses. I gather one minute he was having dinner in São Paulo, and the next he was dead on the floor. I think he had meant to groom Miles to take over the company, but he never got around to it.

"Anyway, Miles had two problems. One, he was too young and inexperienced to run a big company properly. From the outside looking in, it looked to me as if he never really took it seriously. You can't run a big company part time, there's always some damn crisis you've got to face. Miles seemed to spend most of his time inspecting their holdings in the Far East.

"His board quit six months after Miles appointed himself chairman and CEO. Some of them came over to us. And I have to tell you, none of them had a good word to say about Miles, as a man or as a manager. In fact they said he was an absolute shit. And a lazy one at that. Maybe his father could have eased him into the business, gotten him to take more of an interest if he'd lived a few more years, but I always had the feeling that Miles liked the money but he didn't like the work.

"His other problem was us, Coleman's. We're the largest importers of textiles in Britain, supplying 143 clothing manufacturers in Britain, 270 – "

"We know, Alistair, we know," said Ken, his frown lines arched in gothic diplomacy, "but if I don't interrupt you we're in for your hour-long The Wonderful World of Coleman speech. And wonderful speech though it may be, and wonderful though Coleman's may be, I fear we are wandering from our point, which is those shrimp the young lady is placing in front of you. Not to mention my ceviche."

Midway through Ken's interruption, Coleman noticed the half-dozen immense pink and white shrimp on the dark plate. While the waitress was still putting the dish in front of him, the plate was still descending, he picked up a shrimp, stabbed it into a bowl of bright orange sauce and bit off the end with a chomp.

He smiled with satisfaction at the first taste of the crisp and cool shrimp flesh. Then the smile and the colour drained from him and his face took on a puzzled look as if he heard another note, from afar. The colour returned to his normally tanned face, but instead of the usual range of creams and yellows, tans and pinks, a bright hunting pink rose from his white collar.

Alistair Coleman was a confident man and he could be an impressive man, used to getting his way in running a complicated international company. He had charm, dignity, money and power. But he had not met the little jabanero chilli before. His jaw sagged open and from the back of his throat there was a hissing sound like a kettle before it boils. He grabbed his martini and drained the glass, swishing the icy alcohol around in his mouth before swallowing. Which made it worse. He opened his mouth again and made a small helpless cry of pain. I thrust my glass of Perrier into his outstretched hand and he gulped it down, his eyes squeezed shut, the tears running down his cheeks.

The waitress brought him another glass of Perrier, which he drank in a series of gulping swallows. After a time he opened his eyes, breathing heavily, and moaning every time he breathed out.

"How's the shrimp?" I asked.

He looked at me in disbelief, his mouth gaping. Then he saw Ken wheezing his ghastly laugh and, despite his pain, Coleman started laughing too. "How many of those little monsters did you put in there?" he asked the waitress between breaths. She had been watching impassively. She'd seen gringos blasted by jabaneros before.

"Just a couple of slivers, señor," she said. "It's hot, no?"

He jabbed another shrimp into the sauce and held it out to me. "Care for a shrimp, Evers?"

"You're too kind," I said, accepting the challenge and the shrimp.

"*Más agua*, señor?" The waitress poured me another glass of water. She knew the rules of the Mexican chilli showdown. Some players preferred a bite of bread to sooth their napalmed mouths, others preferred a sip of water. You were allowed just one bite or one sip, *nada más*. Neither one did much to cool the pain, but I preferred water.

"You were saying that Courtland is your competitor," I said. The end of the shrimp was dripping with incandescent orange jabanero sauce. I slid it whole into my mouth. Coleman and Ken watched me intently.

The secret of eating hot chillies is to never let the chillis touch your lips, and to slip them down as fast as possible. Practised regularly the technique will burn a hole in your stomach. But if you don't make a habit of it the only memory of the chillies will be their parting shot, a ring of fire as they make their dark exit on their way back to the cosmos. Mexico is the land of flaming sphincters.

I swallowed and made chewing motions with an empty mouth. The pain was horrendous. I smiled equitably, as if to say "not bad", took a large sip, held it for a moment, swallowed, and said, "Of course the really hot ones are in Merida on the north coast."

"Evers, you are a real prick. It's what I like about you; you're the most aggressive, mean-spirited, competitive son of a bitch I know." Coleman was English but he swore in American.

"It hasn't been a good week," I said, casually taking another swig of Perrier now that the contest was over. "And I get nasty when I don't drink."

"Well if the driving doesn't work out for you, you can always work for me."

"I'll remember that," I said, filing it in the discard file. "You were saying."

"I was saying – God that stuff burns," he said, his tongue feeling its way around his swollen lips. "I was saying Courtland's other problem was us, Coleman's. He doesn't need a bigger, stronger and smarter competitor, which is what we are. Especially since there is less business to go around. We've got a broader base than Courtland, and we work harder. But still, he doesn't seem to be hurting all that much. We're competing with him for the rights for this new Dumont fabric from America, Florelle. Of course you know all about that."

I knew about it. My racing suit was made out of it, and so were my flameproof racing knickers. Coleman had put together a catalogue with me on the cover.

As part of our contract with Coleman, I'd given speeches about it to their sales conferences. A racing driver talks about the wonders of Florelle. I could tell any salesman who could stand to listen that while Florelle was originally developed as a fireproof cloth, a competitor to Nomex, it was also lightweight, supple and repelled dirt as well as fire. It was too expensive to be a mass-market fibre, but they had hopes for upmarket, high fashion sports clothes, floppy trousers and shirts to wear on the deck of the rented yacht. Inside the catalogue you could see me posing in the stuff, with models looking as if they were bored with life and in love with me. "Forrest Evers Wears Florelle," the cover said.

Coleman pushed his shrimp away from his place setting. "Courtland has a year's trial contract for the European distribution rights – exactly the same contract that Dumont gave us. At the end of this year they'll award the rights either to Courtland or to us, based on how well we did."

"How are you doing?" Ken asked, his arms folded behind his head.

"Not bad. It's new, nobody knows it, and it's expensive. We thought by sponsoring you we'd get the product known a little better, especially among the major buyers who we take to the races. We're telling Dumont we're looking for the long-term, building the image. We're not getting rich on it but I know we're doing better than Miles Courtland."

"How important is the contract?" I asked.

"Maybe half a million the first year, ten million in ten years if everything goes well. But it could flop. It's not a live or die product for us."

"Do you think it's possible Miles Courtland would think it was worth having somebody killed to get the contract?"

"Not for a moment," he said. "He may be an unpleasant, nasty, selfish and vicious man. He may even be capable of killing someone. Or he may not; I wouldn't know. But the Florelle contract certainly isn't worth it."

Ken took a slow sip of his whiskey. "You said you thought the contract could be worth £10 million."

"Could be, could be." Coleman took another sip of water. You could still see the steam coming from his mouth. "That ten million is Dumont's figure and it assumes ten years of successfully developing the market with a lot of money behind it. Personally, I don't think Florelle is ever going to get beyond being a speciality item. We're willing to put the spend behind it and we've got the sales force. But it's a risk, and I doubt that Courtland has the money or the staff or the marketing savvy. So it's hardly a sure thing for him. It could lose him more than he'd make from it. In other words, he might fight for it, it might be important to him, but I can't believe he'd want to kill for it."

"You're sure it's him?" I asked, spearing my last piece of scallop.

"There's always the chance . . ." said Coleman, tentatively dabbing a shrimp on the surface of the sauce so there was just a faint tinge of orange on one corner. He looked at it, considered it, and put it back on his plate. "There's always a chance there is another loud and obnoxious pink-faced thirty-eight-year-old Englishman with blue eyes and a pot belly who combs his blond hair over his bald spot and wears a chunky gold ring with diamonds mounted on stalks."

"There's always that chance," I said.

# CHAPTER EIGHTEEN

It was after midnight when I got back to the hotel. I hadn't slept for two nights, my eyes felt like Brillo pads, and I had to pack and check out by six a.m. to catch my flight to New York. Which is to say I had been in better moods than when I unlocked the door to my room and saw the red eye on the telephone blinking in the dark. There were three messages. I called Julio Ignacio Salazar first.

"Senor Evers, I am sorry to disturb you so late. But we have you leaving early this morning when I will not be here and I have some news for you. May I buy you a drink in the bar?"

"Thanks," I said, "but it's late and I'm lousy company tonight Can I have my news straight up, on the phone?"

"They have found the men who have killed your friend. I think I would prefer the drink to tell you about it. Could you meet me in the Xochicalo Bar in, say, five minutes?"

The Xochicalo Bar is a dark, quiet room just behind the fluorescent glare of the 24-hour coffee shop. At one of the randomly scattered tables a middle-aged couple was trying to decide whether to go or stay, their heads bent towards each other. At another, three businessmen were quietly drunk, but not quite drunk enough to face the loneliness of the businessman's hotel room. The room smelt of strong cigarettes and of the scent of the women who were no longer there.

Salazar was sitting alone at the bar, his sloping forehead and hawk's beak of a nose outlined against a Mayan frieze behind the bar; a purple, orange and yellow plaster replica of "plumed serpents from the walls of the Temple of the Moon in Xochicalo", according to the plaque at the entrance. Salazar must have rung me from the bar because his drink was almost empty. Judging from the "plumed serpents" behind him, the Mayans wrestled with hangovers too. He held up his glass when he saw me. "You sure you won't have a mescal?" he said. "It tames the night dragons."

"I'll take my chances," I told him, pulling up a red leather stool to the ebony bar. I waved the bartender away, thinking of the clean cool sheets and soft pillow waiting for me in the darkness of my room. Julio Ignacio looked tired and rumpled, with dark circles under his eyes. What, I wondered, were the hidden stresses of an assistant night manager in a Mexican luxury hotel. Businessmen dying in their beds at night? Racing drivers losing their women? Keys broken in the lock?

The mescal he was sipping was gin clear and came with a little brown worm in the bottom of the bottle. Maybe one day, if the worm was good and drank all his mescal, he too would grow up to have feathers and teeth. You drink mescal like tequila if you want to be fancy. (In fact the whole lime and salt tequila ceremony was invented to kill the taste of mescal.) You drink it any damn way you like if you don't. It's made by fermenting and distilling the juice of the agave plant that grows wild in the Mexican desert, and it tastes like soda crackers and a nail file. Salazar was drinking his straight in little sips from a tall glass with ice and a slice of lime.

"I didn't know you were allowed to drink on the job," I said, wanting to get him started and to get to bed.

He drained the last of his glass and watched the bartender pour him another mescal without waiting to be asked. "Sometimes I make exceptions. I thought at first, perhaps I shouldn't tell you," he said, taking his first sip. "But it is not an easy story to forget, and after it had been in my mind for a while, I decided that I will tell you. It will save you the trouble of thinking of revenge."

"Know what?" I asked, impatient. "What should I know?"

"The two men, the men who kidnapped your Beverly," he said, pronouncing her name Bay-vay-lee, with care and caution.

"Bayvaylee". She was already changing identity. In Indiana, she said, they'd called the girl with the long knobbly legs and braces on her teeth, Bevvy. There were people in California who had only known her as Arthur's girl.

"These men are Colombian dealers but they are not part of an organization. They are small-time independent dealers, which for a dealer, is not a good thing to be. In the last two years, there has been much consolidation among the Colombian gangs. The American market has been very lucrative for them, especially for cocaine. But it is not a growing market so much any more, it is a saturated market. That was why crack was so good for them because it opened up a new market for children. But now the growth of that too is slowing down.

"The market is also very competitive, so the Colombians started cutting out the middle-man, the Mafia. They start in California, where there is a big Latino population, a lot of instant connections. Then they move into New York, Detroit, Chicago. This is now billions of dollars. Did you know the Spanish word for pain is *dolores*? Said a certain way it is sounding exactly like the Spanish word for dollars, *dolares*." He pronounced it slowly for me, as if he was revealing the truth. He must have been a while in the bar waiting for me, fighting off the feathered snakes.

"This is a long way from Beverly," I said.

"Yes, it is," he said solemnly. "My point is only that the big gangs like the Calitos are very rich now, very powerful, and they don't like competition. The men who kidnapped Beverly were two small-time dealers who wanted to join the Calitos, but there was a misunderstanding. They were accused, I don't know why, of informing on them, on the Calitos. Or on one of the members of the Calitos, I don't know the story. So they have to leave Colombia, and they come to Mexico City to hide and they think if they do something very big for the Calitos, maybe they have a chance to survive. Maybe even the Calitos will reward them.

"They come here to Mexico City two weeks ago and they see in the papers the Grand Premio is coming here. And they see a picture of your car with the name of your sponsor, the textile importer, on the side. Their English is not good. They are small time, but in the drug trade even the little ones can be very rich and have good connections. They know from their business, from their connections, the Mafia has a good outlet in Britain, a textile importer. This is a dream for the Calitos, to have a reliable and respectable pipeline into a country like Britain. Private planes and couriers and offshore drops from freighters are expensive and risky. Britain, they know, is an underdeveloped market. Europe, they think, could benefit with a much better

Colombian distribution. So the cover of a major importer is of great value."

"You can't tell me Alistair Coleman is connected to the Mafia."

"Listen," he said, "I will tell you. Their idea is they will kidnap the girl of the driver of the Coleman's racing car, and they will hold her before the race. And then, as they know the sponsor is coming to Mexico himself, they think they can then exchange the girl for him or maybe trap him – either way they give him to the Calitos. At the least, it is bound to complicate the Mafia distribution of cocaine into Britain. At the best they get to force Coleman to open up the whole British Isles for the Calitos. They think the Calitos will be grateful and forget about this informing."

"But why her? Why not me? Why not kidnap Alistair himself? He didn't even know Beverly. He never met her. He'd never trade his life for a stranger. He wouldn't even do it to save his mother."

"I don't know. They are not smart. They don't know him, this Alistair. They don't know he wouldn't save his mother. I don't know what they think."

"What do you think?"

"I don't think, I just guess. You want a guess?" he said, looking at me over the top of his glass, "I can give you plenty of guesses, no charge. Maybe they don't take you because they think the girl is easier to handle. Maybe they think you are too strong for them in the hallway of the hotel. Maybe they are worried for themselves because Coleman does not arrive until Saturday evening and they think the Calitos will find them before then. Maybe they are worried this Coleman is so important, he's going to be surrounded by security, and they think it will cause less fuss if they steal a girl nobody knows instead of the head of a big company of some big-time racing driver."

"They were right about that. You weren't even going to ask the maids to check the rooms."

"It's true, I was not so worried at first about some girl. The two little dealers think it is wise to protect themselves, to contact the Calitos, to tell them they are cooking up a big surprise for them. They call them from a public phone. They say they have a big gift coming, the head of the Mafia importing company into Britain. They will deliver to them Alistair Coleman. And the Calitos say that yes indeed that is a very big surprise because Coleman is not the Mafia importing company in Britain. The two little dealers didn't read English too good. They got the wrong name."

"You have to be connected to the Calitos to know this."

He looked at me levelly across the top of his glass. "You have been in Mexico less than a week, but even in that short time I would expect you to know there are questions you do not ask. I am trying to do you a favour."

"Fine, I won't ask. I don't have to."

He smiled, relaxing. "What will you do, report me to the police?"

"You deserve each other. What is it you want me to know?"

"When the two little dealers learn they have made a mistake they panic, because they know the Calitos will find them wherever they go. So they try to be clever; they think no one will expect them to go back to Colombia. So they give Beverly an injection to kill her and they go to the airport. The Calitos may be in Bogota, they think, but they are also everywhere else, and at least in Bogota the two dealers have friends. They are so frightened when they leave their room, they don't even lock the door."

"You said they found these two guys. I thought they flew to Bogota and the Colombian military police picked them up?"

"The Colombian military police did pick them up – and delivered them to the Calitos. The next day the two little dealers were found in a little village, sitting against a church wall in a small and peaceful square, necktied. Do you know what this is, necktied?" Salazar put his empty glass down and the bartender brought over the bottle with the pickled worm and filled up Salazar's glass. Salazar did not look at the bartender, but picked up the glass the moment it was full and took another sip.

"The necktie," he said, "is now common in New York City where you are going. Maybe you will see it there. It is what the Calitos do to informers. After they slit the man's throat, they reach inside and pull down his tongue so it hangs out the slit in his throat and over his shirt."

# PART THREE

# CHAPTER NINETEEN

Life at 165 miles an hour through a carwash.

The spray is intense, microfine, high-pressure, and comes from all directions. My front wheels fling it out in pinwheels, a mist travelling at tremendous speed. The spray is impossible to see through, but it swirls to reveal flashes of shining black grooved tyre making channels through the water down to the track surface, rows of miniature black Moses parting the sea for an instant so that my car can pass through one more moment in time unharmed.

The spray also comes from the three cars in front of me, swirling, shifting clouds that hold at their furious centre a red aerofoil or a glowing red light or a flash of flame from an exhaust. And it comes from the car alongside me, Maurizio Praiano in the dark wine-red and silver Danielli. He thinks if he can get his nose in front of me before we brake for Ste Devote, he can pass me and take fourth. He is wrong.

In my tiny, vibrating, rain-speckled mirrors, I can see the dim buzz of a swarm of aquatic bees behind me: the other twenty cars flat out in sixth as we pass the start/finish line at Monaco. I can't see the lap board through the spray and the rain, but it doesn't matter. There is almost the whole race to go. It doesn't matter, counting laps, now.

The rain falls on the spectators in a moderate shower, a refreshing break in the heat of Monte Carlo in the middle of May. For me it is like sitting ten feet in front of the nozzle of a firehose. It is powerful and horizontal, every drop exploding to bits when it hits my visor.

The mist and spray are everywhere, come from everywhere, covering the instruments, my mirrors and my facemask with microdots of fog. The rain comes straight at me. The harder I drive, the more it raises the pressure of resistance. It is like driving straight up Niagara Falls.

I've turned up the medical air to try and keep the inside of my visor clear, but the corners steam with fog.

Like the rain, the noise is a consistent scream with only minor variations in intensity. After years of expecting to hear the rise and fall of the engine note as I play up and down the gears, the single, mad, screaming note seems wrong. Max's automatic keeps the engine operating at it's peak power, between 10,750 and 11,500 rpm. There is no let-up.

I start braking early for St Devote and Praiano's Danielli starts to nose ahead of my car. St Devote is a classic right-hander, almost 90 degrees, and the approach to it is one of the few places at Monaco where it is possible to pass. So Praiano is throwing everything he has into getting inside me, taking the inside line. I'm braking early, but lightly, gradually increasing the pressure all the way up to and into the turn.

Driving in the wet means driving on tiptoe, making all your transitions super-smooth because you have so much less adhesion. It's like driving on ice – turn suddenly and you don't change direction, you just slide. But if you make the turn gentle and smooth so the force of your momentum is fed gradually into the transition, by the time you reach the limit of adhesion just before the apex of the corner you will have eased off the brake and started rolling onto the throttle.

Praiano has to shift down to second while braking on the absolute limit, and at the same time keep his car absolutely settled and relaxed, rolling the weight onto his two left tyres and suspension as gradually and as evenly as possible. His nose drops back as he has to stand on his brakes and I turn into the corner going six or seven miles an hour faster than he is. I have the advantage of the outside line which means I can use more of the road. I am still lightly on the brakes as I turn in to the corner, and I can imagine the trace of panic and frustration that Praiano must feel as I close the door on him and force him to brake even harder to avoid my back wheels driving over his front wing. Fuck him.

As I clip the inside of the corner at around 90 miles an hour I've already let up on the brakes and am squeezing the accelerator gradually to the floor, feeding the power to the rear wheels until the engine is screaming at its limit. I head up the hill towards Casino, the back of the car fishtailing as the tyres fight for grip.

Praiano is of the old school, doing all his braking and shifting in a straight line before turning into the corner and accelerating gradually through. In slow, out fast. In the rain, I brake all the way through the turn-in and up to the apex. But I brake earlier and more lightly. In fast, out faster. Praiano has lost fifteen yards behind me and I forget about him, concentrating on the three mad swirls of fog in front of me.

In any race there is only one place to be: in front. In the rain it is doubly, triply important. Because in front you don't have to drive through the fog screen of another car in front and guess about where you are on the track.

I am not in front, I am fourth. But I know I could be and will be first. As I leave St Devote the car launches up the hill like a jet fighter from the deck of an aircraft carrier. I can almost relax here and enjoy the feeling of power when you stomp on the accelerator of a Formula One car: the feeling of immense, infinite grandeur, of 700 horsepower launching you forward at a rate of acceleration that dazzles the mind with the clarity of detail it brings as you approach the next second in time. You accelerate so fast that the future and the present are brought together, side by side, and you see the grain of paint on a lamppost yards away, see the glint of gold from an earring behind a screen of blonde hair. At the same time you are intensely conscious of the car, the track, and the race. It takes you into two times at once, both of them demanding and both of them getting all of your attention. I feel twice as alive as a normal human being who has never strapped this 700 horsepower vibrator on his back.

As I accelerate up the hill, up the Montée du Beau Rivage, up to Virage Massenet to turn into Casino Square, I see a patch of blue in the dark sky and feel like heading straight up into that. The wild blue yonder. Braking, turning into Massenet, into Casino Square, I see the face of a woman with dark eyebrows, green eyes, and dark blonde hair bound up in a green scarf. Her sunglasses are pushed up on top of her head, a second pair of insect eyes staring at the sky, pebbled with rain. Her face is calm and beautiful with a fine straight nose and almost no make-up.

I can smell her perfume, from that distance, the crowd shoulder to shoulder, the car screaming in my ears. Her scent, a buttery, sweet spice with a musk of peach and sex, perfumes the inside of my helmet as I flow left and right and left again through Casino Square and downhill, accelerating into the streaming rain towards Mirabeau.

During a race, the heartbeat of a Formula One driver ranges up from 140 beats per minute (which is the normal heartbeat of a normal man after running for 100 yards), on up to 200 beats per minute. Which is what the human heart does when stirred by terror. Except that you are not terrorized, you are not even afraid. You are simply taking in an immense amount of sensation and information at a very high rate of speed, enjoying it and acting upon it. Braking, sliding, accelerating, I inhaled her perfume and tried to hold on to it even as it slipped away.

Coming out of Casino and plunging downhill, I closed up on the other three cars. Bunched like this, the lead car, which I could not see except as a cloud of spray and mist, must be holding up the other two.

I am closing up on a yellow Lotus – Lucien Faenza's car. Inside the shroud of spray thrown up by the cars in front of me, I can barely see the track. Mirabeau is a sharp right downhill corner, the Hotel Mirabeau towering like a stone cliff above it. Once you are through Mirabeau you are into the tightest and slowest part of the track. The track keeps on going sharply downhill, with a kink right and left, and then comes a very tight downhill left through Station hairpin, two sharp rights, and then stand on it through the tunnel, which bends slightly right, before you emerge again out into the rain at 175 and start braking for a left/right chicane.

I was going through my mental map of the course because, apart from Faenza's little round red taillight in front of me and an occasional glimpse here and there, I can't see the track. Which, as long as nobody is parked on it, doesn't matter that much. There is virtually no chance of passing until we go around the harbour to St Devote again. I stayed glued to Faenza's taillight.

Four Formula One cars in the tunnel at Monaco at speed on a rainy day make a godawful racket. Dense fog, dim light, and noise. The surface of the track streams in places and is almost dry in others, giving you wildly different limits of adhesion within a few yards.

But it is the noise of four Formula One engines at once – three V8s and one V12: £258,000 of delicate, highly-stressed high-tech titanium alloy machinery pumping out 2,800 horsepower: 36 pistons, 16 camshafts, 152 valves, 4 crankshafts, and 137 gears all spinning, rising and falling, opening and closing, sliding against each other 13,000 times a minute, along with the preposterous BANG BANG BANG of 3,900 petrol bombs exploding every second, reporting out of the exhaust pipe trumpets and ricocheting off the tunnel tiles – it is this noise that sends the rats swimming for Sicily and vibrates in the vault of the skull for days. If Hell has bells, this is how they ring.

Coming out of the tunnel with the sudden whoosh of decompression, I catch a flash of red turning left at the chicane and guess it's Prugno's Ferrari which is holding us up like a Sunday driver hogging the passing lane. I follow Faenza left, right through the chicane, left at the harbour, left, and right at the harbour kink. Suddenly, out of the fog, like a ghost ship suddenly looming large, Aral's McLaren takes up half the track, sliding sideways. I flash by him just as the back of his car touches the Armco barrier, sending up a flash of sparks, and brake for La Rascasse, the right-hand hairpin that sets you up for Virage Anthony Noghes, then on up the main straight past the pits and the grandstands before St Devote.

I gain a little bit through the corner and run wide alongside Faenza coming out of La Rascasse, forcing him to stay inside and setting myself up for a better line through St Devote. If I could stay alongside him all the way up the straight I could pass him at St Devote just like I'd passed Praiano. Then I could take Prugno, if not at Mirabeau then again at St Devote. I will lead this goddamn race.

Faenza and I accelerate flat out through Noghes, side by side up the main straight. I had expected cheering but there is silence. The crowd isn't looking at us. I can't see the pink of their faces, they are turned away, looking ahead at something else.

Up ahead, in slow motion, appearing out of the mist and fog, the red rear wing of Prugno's Ferrari floats gently towards us like a scythe. I sense Faenza standing on his brakes, but I see no need. There is plenty of time.

The red airfoil is turning lazily in the air, curving away from me, and there is time to duck and let it float by overhead. Except that I am strapped in tight and I can't slide down in my seat. It is also time to start braking for St Devote. The wing, still tipping away from me, suddenly accelerates as if it were in a zoom lens, presents its leading edge to my face and slices my throat beneath my chin.

I felt no pain, but I know I am behind time now on what I should be doing with the car. I should be braking now, I think. I try to scream but I make no sound: there's only air coming out of my severed windpipe. I feel a shawl of blood flowing down the front of my blue driving suit and the car shaking as it leaves the surface of the road. And I smell the peach-and-sex perfume of the blonde woman with the green scarf in the crowd in Casino Square.

"Mr Evers? Are you all right? Mr Evers, we're almost in New York. We'll be landing in twenty minutes." She was shaking my shoulder. I looked up into the green eyes of the stewardess, inhaling her sexy, peachy perfume, still not sure. "You were making quite a noise, Mr Evers. Would you like brandy before we land? Coffee? Tea?"

"No, nothing," I said. "I'm fine."

I'd slept since Dallas, my mind bruised and sore, trying to find the nights of sleep I'd lost. I looked out the window at the vague green landscape stained with the brown of towns. A warm evening with the sun throwing long shadows pointing east.

Pennsylvania, Delaware, New Jersey? I didn't know if Salazar's story of the two bumbling coke dealers was true or not. I suspected it was but, apart from the random violence of Beverly's death, it explained nothing. Unless I was prepared to believe that two semi-literate Colombian dope dealers were behind Michel's death in Japan and my crashes in England and Austria. Tired as I was, there were gaps over which the imagination would not leap. Courtland had killed Michel and he had tried to kill me, and he would try to kill me again, in the largest, most public way he could. But of course I couldn't race until I found him and held him up for everybody to see with one hand and held the proof in the other.

The brown towns blended together like a mudslide that ended

in the Hudson River. We flew low over the Statue of Liberty and up the East River, joining the procession of planes coming in to land every twenty-two seconds at La Guardia. The sun had just set, leaving a pink sky to outline the tall buildings at the end of Manhattan. From the air the city seemed to rise out of the water, with the end of the island looking like the bow of a great stone ship pointing out to sea. All around the water glittered pink and blue and gold, crisscrossed on the East Side with the trailing ropes of bridges. The lights were on in the steel towers, glowing with energy, money and power.

Down on the ground it was the end of a freakishly hot October afternoon, a rerun of a day in July, a double 98: 98 degrees Fahrenheit and 98 per cent humidity. Carrying my battered leather suitcase, I joined the shuffling queue of tired businessmen on their way home from day trips to Detroit, Washington, Chicago and Pittsburg, their sleeves rolled up, jackets over their shoulders, their minds on mortgages, the Mets dropping both ends of a twilight double header, the frosty six-pack of Rolling Rock in the fridge, and the little phial of crystals Patsy found in Tommy's jeans.

My luck was changing. As the herd of battered yellow cabs eased cautiously forward like embarrassed rejects from the old taxi's home, mine was the rarest of all.

It wasn't just new and shining and undecorated with garbage truck stripes down the side.

It wasn't just the heavy Chevy, the big full-size Caprice with heavy-duty suspension.

Its windows were shut.

It had air.

# CHAPTER TWENTY

I shut the taxi door, breathed refrigerated air and cannons boomed in the distance.

"Fuckin' thunda," the driver said, as he pulled out into the world's largest non-stop dodgem rink. New York City traffic. "It's not enough we gotta have a fuckin' steambath like it was August, we gotta have the fuckin' flood to go with it. You know what this fuckin' traffic's like inna rush hour inna fuckin' rain?"

I leaned back into the soft upholstery and tuned him out, cushioned by two tons of V8, Hydramatic, foam rubber, squishy tyres and air conditioning on 'Hi'.

The six-lane highway to the Tri-boro bridge looked like it had been blasted by a meteor shower, but the big Chevrolet floated over the craters like an ocean liner. As we crossed the East River, black storm clouds the size of Ohio were cruising in over the sky scrapers. By the time we turned off the East Side Drive onto 66th, New York City was at the bottom of a waterfall, a sluice of rain washing away the noise, the dust and the heat of the day.

The driver was right, the traffic was "a fuckin' mess". But I didn't care. Tom Castleman's house was only five blocks away and he wasn't expecting me for another twenty minutes. Plenty of time. The driver droned on like a chicken with a deep voice, "Fuck-fuck bawwk, fuck-fuck bawwk." We crept along the streaming street, a log in a log jam of taxis, trucks and Cadillacs.

Sir Thomas Castleman bought international corporations, broke them into little pieces and sold the parts. I thought of him as a corporate scrap dealer. According to *Fortune* he was a "Venetian pirate" raiding sleepy corporations. *Forbes* called him a "modern Medici" for his life style.

The stories about Castleman kept getting better and better. Like the one in *Fortune* claiming that when he was mounting a hostile bid for Texon Oil, he took over the Texon board meeting in Dallas via satellite. Sir Thomas was yachting off the coast of Melides, his island in the Aegean, and beamed himself into Midland, Texas, like a pirate from outer space. "That's totally exaggerated," he told me. "I didn't take over their meeting. I just gave them something to think about."

He had a wife in Paris and mistresses in London and New York. Houses in Maiori, Melides, and LA as well as in London, New York and Paris. And he had enemies everywhere. He said Onassis "was a poor little fisherman" and ran an annual budget twice the size of Canada's. I was looking forward to seeing him. We were old friends. Or enemies. He lived in a perpetual combat zone.

His town house was one of a row of high-window, high-ceiling, high-security brownstones on 63rd near Central Park. It looked average New York rich from the outside, nothing special. A small brass plate by the door said "CFC" – Castleman Finance Corp. The rain had stopped and the steps up to Castleman's door were already drying, steaming from the heat of the stone. I rang the bell, there was a ten-second pause and a woman's voice seemed to whisper in my ear, "Come in Mr Evers, we've been expecting you."

The door swung open, I stepped forward and it shut behind me. I was standing in a circle of light, just inside the door, so it took my eyes a moment to adjust to the gloom. I was in a wide walnut-panelled entrance hall and a woman in white was walking towards me. Along the sides of the hall, in individual pools of light, were marble columns with marble heads of Greek and Roman senators, poets, teachers, generals and dictators: Caesar, Demosthenes, Socrates, and for all I knew, Caligula. Maybe it was intended to make me feel as if I were among the gods of Western culture. But it looked like the entrance to a provincial museum. The woman's little white Reeboks went chirp, chirp, chirp.

"Hi. Forrest? Is it OK to call you Forrest? I feel funny saying Mr Evers when I'm wearing a tennis dress. I'm Jean."

Jean held out a tanned hand. Her other hand held a tennis racquet. She had short brown hair, wore a white headband, a white halter top that wobbled in calypso time, and a tennis dress that flounced when she walked. She bounced and jiggled like she was in her early twenties, but judging by the crowsfeet that radiated like lines of intelligence from her brown eyes, I guessed she was about thirty-five. On her left breast there was a small green lion's head – Castleman's logo.

"Forrest is fine, Jean," I said, shaking her hand, wondering where the tennis court was.

"Tom's up in the games room. He asked me to bring you right up." She smiled and turned, leading me down the hall, going chirp, chirp to the flounce of her little white skirt. She looked like she played quite a lot of tennis.

The lift was grey inside with grey office carpet and the size and speed you expect to find in an office building. No expense spared, but no excess either. Jean smelled of hot girl and perfume and covered the awkwardness of strangers in a lift with polite questions about my flight. The doors slid open with a whoosh before I had a chance to answer.

". . . leverage their debentures with a buyback guarantee – *hooo* – linked to Hofax plus three, see if that'll – *hooo* – make them hold still, hello Forrest – *hooo* – while we find a key to unlock that trust fund – *hooo*." Castleman's deliberate voice, punctuated with the effort of making a Nautilus weight go up and down, dominated the room, sounding more like a First Sea Lord than a moneyman spinning deals.

Jean spread her arms to include the vast space: "Behold the games room. Where the great one plays his games." She gave me a nice tidy smile, turned back into the lift and with a whoosh of doors was gone.

"Two nine would save us twelve," said a voice, on my left.

"Three sounds better – *hooo* – and we're not going to get stuck on any guarantees – *hooo* – we are going to make this turkey fly – *hooo* – Jesus, that's enough. We're not going to end up with an empty paper bag to pop. This one we want to keep the whole deli, leverage it, and use that to wrap Universal around the core."

Castleman was unstrapping himself from the machine. The room looked like a French château caught in a time warp. French tapestries hung alongside the great empty stone fireplace. The cathedral beams high overhead and the panelling on the walls were polished oak.

Into that vast, antique box Castleman had seemingly lowered

three sections. A light and airy exercise room at one end, with a scattering of Nautilus machines, a steam room, an open shower lined with polished green granite and a deep pool set in the same green stone. In the middle, there was an island of bland American beige upholstery floating on the minestrone of an oriental carpet. And at the other end, where I'd just stepped out of the lift, the room was a high-tech office with pale blue-green carpet and two tense men in their shirtsleeves staring into banks of computer terminals.

One of the men was short, fat and spoke with a harsh Brooklyn accent. He punched out numbers in columns and stared into his green screen before answering Tom, his face computer-screen green. He said "dey" for "they" and "dem" for "them". "You could offa two nine and go ta tree if dey squawked. Y'know, be reasonable. Or offer dem tree with a sixty-five per cent buyback guarantee based on a market plus, say plus ten per cent. Let dem squabble about it while you jimmy da trust fund."

"It has to be simple," Castleman said, walking towards me. "If it isn't simple they won't buy it. How good to see you, Forrest. How's real life? What do you think of my new security system?"

"I didn't see it."

"That's the point. I always thought a security system is a contradiction in terms. All those cameras and winking red lights and buzzers. Makes everybody nervous. Makes you feel insecure all the time. But the insurance company insists, so I got Jean. By the time she meets you, you've been screened, checked and rechecked. If she doesn't have a complete profile on you and if you don't have an appointment, you don't get in. She has a good deal of technical backup, naturally, but happily one never sees it. Unless one tried to force a way in, then you would see rather a lot of it."

"And it's not really a tennis racquet?"

"It's not really a tennis racquet. Drink?"

He threw a towel over his shoulders, rubbing the white terrycloth into his face. His face emerged fresh and dry, almost seamless, sleek as a seal, with girlish long lashes and large brown eyes that had the depth of optical instruments. He was bald except for a carefully tended silver fringe. Evenly tanned and softly formed he looked pliable, as if his bones would bend. In his clean white T-shirt and white shorts he looked like a vulnerable and wide-eyed schoolboy who didn't quite understand what was going on. It was a look he cultivated and it often meant he was about to strike.

He turned his head to the second man who sat at a computer terminal, a thin brooding Kafka lookalike with sucked-in cheeks and red rims around his eyes. "Take a look again at that trust fund and see if you can find a weak sister in their holdings. Something tidy that we could buy short, run down and rub their nose in without taking a shower."

He turned to me again, giving me his appraisal while he talked. "Energy's like money, Forrest. The best way to get it is to spend it. You told me that. Trouble is I can't afford to let a fortune slide by while I do sit-ups. So I do both at once. Some of my best ideas come to me on an exercycle. Which is just as well because otherwise I'd die of boredom on the damn thing."

Castleman looked around the room and dismissed the stone fireplace, oak panelling and cathedral ceiling with a sweep of his arm. "It's all fake," he said. "Made in Brooklyn in 1936. It was built by one of the Studebakers whose idea of Europe apparently came from watching Hollywood musicals. I keep thinking I'll change it, but I don't know where I'd begin." He smiled disarmingly, sitting down on a beige sofa and stretching out his legs while he kept up his friendly, inconsequential disclosures.

Most people feel a warm glow in the presence of the very rich, a kind of welcome aboard, hey, they're just folks like us. It is exactly the opposite of what the rich feel, and what I felt now. I felt he owed me a favour and I'd come to collect.

"Trouble with owning all these damn houses," he said, "you never get them the way you want to. And if you do they end up looking all alike inside so you might as well stay home."

"You're too much of a pirate to stay home," I said. "It bugs you that you only own six houses and a hundred corporations when you want to own the world."

"Just building a business, Forrest," he said comfortably. "And to tell you the truth, ownership has nothing to do with it. I don't even do it for the money, if you can believe that, anymore than you do. That's why I so rarely lose. What can I do for you?"

He looked at me and gave me a self-satisfied nod as if he read my mind. "I know," he said, spreading his hands in a gesture of openness, "I owe you a favour." He closed his hands into fists, smiling vaguely. "But then I owe a great many people favours and I'm afraid I don't have the time to pay them all."

"There's a company called Courtland International in Britain. I need to know everything there is to know about them."

"I don't think I know them offhand, but I expect we could find out if we wanted to."

"It's probably beneath your notice, but it's important to me."

"Nothing, Forrest, is beneath my notice. A pound interests me if it's profit. Tell me what you know about Courtland and what you need to know."

"It's an old firm that imports fabrics into Europe. They used to manufacture, now they just import. I think it's privately held, respectable, and importing cocaine under cover." Castleman's face registered no surprise, the smooth face of the professional poker player. "I want to dig up the sewer pipe that brings in the drugs," I said. "I want to turn it upside down and shake out the rats."

Castleman caught the rising note in my voice and held up a soft hand to stop me. "Castleman's law. Never fuck up thine own pure judgement with emotion. You're not personally involved are you?"

"Of course I am personally involved."

"And if there are drugs, surely you should be talking to the police. Or," he said, crossing his legs and looking up at the ceiling, "are you telling me that you are involved with drugs as well?"

"I am being drugged, and I think it's Miles Courtland who's doing it. Or having somebody do it for him. I also think he drugged Michel Fabrot and caused his death."

"Fabrot?"

"My co-driver. He died in the Japanese Grand Prix. There was also a young woman who died in Mexico. Courtland wasn't directly responsible for that. But I blame him." (And me, I thought to myself.)

"Do you have any proof of any of this?"

"No, I don't have any proof. If I had any proof I'd go to the police. Let me make it as simple as I can."

"Good," he said smiling a quick, automatic smile. "I like things simple."

"I think he killed my co-driver and I think he's trying to kill me."

"Think? You must have some reasons."

"Several. Something is altering my state of mind when I'm driving in a Formula One race. Not when I'm practising, not when I'm warming up, just in the race. The road divides in two; I want to put my foot to the floor and leave it there; accelerate forever. I saw the same symptoms in Michel Fabrot's driving when he crashed at Suzuka. It may sound strange to you, but you can tell a man's personality by the way he drives, and Michel's personality was radically changed in his last race."

"Just from the way he drove. Anything else?"

"I was warned off driving by the Mafia in California. And I was told by a Colombian drug gang that Courtland Mills is the Mafia's conduit for importing cocaine into the UK."

"Even if it wasn't from the mouths of thieves that would still be hearsay," he said.

"Hearsay," I agreed.

"Forgive my innocence in all this, Forrest, but you are straining my sense of reality here. Why should the Mafia give a damn if you drove or not? Or, indeed, why should Courtland? I don't follow racing but I don't see you bruited about as the next World Champion. At least not this year. And I've always thought of motor racing as a lot of advertisements going by too fast to read. I never thought of them as drug runners," he said, smiling at his little joke.

"It's nothing to do with the cars, it's the sponsors. My car is sponsored by Coleman, and Coleman is a competitor of Courtland's. By sponsoring us, Coleman's made our team the focus of marketing a new Dumont fibre called Florelle. My driving suit is made out of the stuff. Both Coleman and Courtland want the rights to distribute Florelle in Europe, and my guess is that Courtland thinks if he makes the team crash every time we go racing he'll screw up Coleman's marketing effort."

"And Courtland will take away the Florelle contract from Coleman," Castleman said, looking at me as if I were a bad investment. "Doesn't sound like enough of a motive to me. I can imagine there are an almost infinite number of reasons for wanting to kill somebody. But I can't imagine a successful businessman trying to kill you for a textile contract. Surely it'd be simpler to hire a few more salesmen, fire the advertising agency and take Dumont to lunch on a yacht on the Potomac."

"Maybe he's not successful."

"Maybe. But I think you're paranoid. You have any ideas about how I'm supposed to pick up this sewer pipe and shake out the rats?"

"No. Except it has to be quick; I've got a week."

"Forrest," he got up, smiling his "how absurd" smile, "really. I am not a magician. You can't pressure a company in a week."

"You can if they are weak and you know where their soft spots are. And who knows, Tom, you might pick up a nice European textile company to add to your collection. The last time I put you onto a company they gave you $85 million just to go away."

He bent over the coffee table and picked up a newspaper. "Texon wasn't that simple. And it wasn't greenmail. But I'll see what we can find. Give me a few minutes and I'll get my people started on it. In the meantime you might like to read about yourself in today's *Daily Mail*," he said, tossing me the newspaper.

It wasn't on the front page, it was buried in the sports section.

## CRASH DANCING AT MEXICAN GRAND PRIX

*Mexico City. The score after yesterday's Mexican Grand Prix was Marcel Aral won, Grand Prix racing minus ten.*

*Three-times crash artist Forrest Evers lent weight to Formula One critics who say the noisy spectacle is not a sport and should be banned. Not content with crashing yet again while trailing the leaders, Evers ran back onto the track to pose for the Mexican crowd of 125,000 and for the 110 million fans worldwide who watched the race on television.*

*While the more responsible drivers swerved to avoid him at speeds of up to 170 mph, Evers pranced and waved like a clown at a circus.*

*Faced with a fine and suspension in a hastily convened hearing after the race, Evers claimed he had been high on drugs and therefore not responsible for his behaviour.*

*In an effort to repair the sport's damaged reputation, FISA chairman Alain Mafaison banned Evers from racing indefinitely. Motor racing experts (and fellow drivers!) heaved a sigh of relief at Evers' departure.*

*But one question remains unanswered. Why, ask the experts, was the ever-dangerous Evers allowed to race in the first place?*

I folded the paper and put it back down on the coffee table. Dear Janice.

It was distorted, inaccurate and unfair. And worse, it had a ring of truth. I suppose I should be grateful it wasn't headlined "Formula One Drug Addict Banned." Janice hadn't been explicit, there was nothing you could pin a libel suit on. But the implication was unmistakable. The implication was that I was on drugs. And of course, I was. Except I didn't know what I was taking, or how, or when.

I pictured Janice lying on her back in bed, her legs apart, snoring lightly. Poor sad scrawny little thing, scavenging among the leavings of disaster, tragedy, death and corruption, the stuff of everyday news. She had a sharp bite, but she didn't kill. She'd probably go to dinner with me if I asked. And bounce into bed if I asked nicely. No hard feelings. Just doing her job.

I paced for an hour and a half listening to the clickety clack of the computers until Castleman came bustling back into the room, barking instructions at his computer operators, his hands full of papers.

"You're right, unfortunately," he said. "It is a private company, so a fair amount of the information about Courtland's is out of our reach, but not all of it. Thank God for the fax." He dumped the papers on the coffee table. "While London sleeps, Castleman's raiders feed the fax. Look at this."

I took the sheaf of papers he held out to me. Faxes from last year's newspapers.

"Read them later, if you want. The story is that he tried to take his company public last year, and the financial press ripped him apart. One of them made a list of eleven contracts he'd lost in the first six months of the year. There was some speculation that he didn't have any business left, that all he had left was the buildings. Anyway, what's obvious is that his capital was strangled with debt. I don't know why he'd try to go public under those conditions unless he was desperate – and misinformed. Now look at this."

Castleman held out what looked like a draft for a company

226

prospectus dated last year. "There's something very interesting in there: see if you can find it. Apparently when he had thoughts of taking the company public he had this drawn up."

I started reading it and Castleman impatiently grabbed it from me. "No, no, forget the front pages. That's all bullshit, what the company likes to hear. Company history, wonderful employees, caring responsible management, wonderful year, where the past and future meet. If you want to find anything out from a company prospectus, treat it like it's Japanese. Read it from the back."

I looked at the back page. Footnotes on loans, special disbursements, directors' stock holdings, pension plans. "Look at footnote 16," he said.

Footnote 16 was two pages from the back. "Debt retirement," I read aloud. I looked up and Castleman signalled me to keep reading. I read that the company had paid £750,000 to retire the debt on their research building in Aintree.

"Doesn't that strike you as interesting?" Castleman's large, optical instrument eyes were glittering. I paused and Castleman leapt into the gap. "Three things," he said holding up three fingers in case I misunderstood. "First, don't you think it's odd they have a research facility?"

No, I didn't find it odd. It was something companies had, like houses have bedrooms.

"It's odd," he said, retiring one finger, "because you told me they import everything. Why would they need a research facility if they don't make anything? It's also odd," he said, retiring a second finger, "that at the same time he's announcing this in a prospectus, he withdraws his company from sale. My guys can find *no* mention in any of the financial press of any new contracts or white knights propping him up. Nevertheless, all of a sudden he's so flush with cash he pays off a mortgage early."

"You mean he suddenly found a way to save his company?"

"The money had to come from somewhere. It's entirely possible that once the press started writing that his company was in trouble he got a visit from some men who said they could solve all his problems. Did you notice where this research centre is? Aintree. You know where Aintree is?" He didn't give me time to answer. "Aintree," he said, retiring his last finger so his hand made a fist,

227

"is four miles from the north Liverpool docks. If you're looking for a conduit, that's the place to look.

"There's another thing," he said. "The date of this draft prospectus is just a week after the last newspaper article. He must still have thought he could go public. And he must have been in a hell of a state: his company is collapsing, he's about to go bankrupt, and he is afraid he is going to lose his family, his house, his cars and his reputation. I've put men, very successful men, in that position and let me tell you it can make a man do the dumbest things . . . things he wouldn't have dreamt of doing the day before.

"If he has a wife, she won't talk to him because they won't let her charge her drinks at the golf club anymore and the kiddies are on their way home from their expensive schools because he can't pay their expensive fees. His friends call him up and ask if they can help. So he swallows his pride and asks for help and they won't answer his phone calls. His girlfriend loses interest in him and the credit card companies cancel his credit cards. The mortgage is due and he can't pay it. He can't meet his payroll and the unions accuse him of fiddling their pension fund contributions. His suppliers cut off his supplies. Along with the bills that keep arriving in the morning, he starts getting threats of legal action. He could face a jail sentence.

"So he has his problems. And he's probably a lousy businessman or he wouldn't be in such a mess in the first place. He can't think of a way out. He can't even think of a way forward. All he can think of is what his life used to be like. He may even consider suicide.

"Then the dark men in dark suits fly in on their jet plane and tell him he can save his company. He can keep his house and his family. He can be seriously rich, richer than he ever would have been before. He can command respect again. Run for public office. All he has to do is keep the corporate shell shiny and make the world think that his business is still legitimate. He knows he's making a rotten deal but he probably tells himself that he's doing it for his wife and kids. Although I have to say, Forrest, that even if his business is a Mafia front that still doesn't give him enough motive to go around killing racing drivers."

"It might." Castleman looked at me, doubting. "It might if Florelle was the only business he had left. If it was his last piece of business he'd *have* to keep it, because if he lost it then your men in the dark suits wouldn't have any legitimate cover anymore and Courtland would go from being an asset to a liability. They might be putting pressure on him as well as giving him a helping hand. No front, no Courtland. Does this 'research facility' have an address?"

"No, but it shouldn't be hard to find. Are you sure you have to do this in a week? I have to admit, I find the prospect of an import company in Britain could be quite useful to me now. But I don't want to go charging into the bushes just to see the quail fly. I want to do it right, leave them no options, no back doors."

"It has to be in a week. I have a week to get him out in the open."

"You know, Forrest, living in America has taught me something. The Americans are very different from the British. They know the meaning of words like paracetamol, advil and imbutan."

"Those are painkillers."

"That's right. And when they have a pain they kill it."

"I don't want to kill him, I just want to prove he's guilty. Unless I can prove he caused my crashes I can't race again. Unless I can prove he killed Michel, Michel's going to be just another dead and forgotten sloppy racing driver."

"Forrest, be realistic. After that article I don't think they'll let you drive down Chiswick High Street, let alone race. And really who the hell cares about how people might think about the way a dead racing driver drove?"

"Goddamnit, I care. And I care because unless I can find proof that Courtland's importing drugs, a lot of kids are going to be junkies, puking their brains out and robbing your six houses."

"Let me make a suggestion. It looks to me from what my guys could get hold of that he's got more cash than he can use and I can't see where it's coming from – but there's nothing we can prove there. Let me do two things. With all that cash I think it's time he had his books reviewed by the special branch of Her Majesty's Inland Revenue tax collectors. That should keep him busy and scare the hell out of him."

"You can do that?" I asked.

"I can probably do that. Lord knows I've come to know Her Majesty's Special Branch tax collectors well enough. Their chief,

Nigel Strickland, is almost a personal friend. I'm sure he'd appreciate a tip. I also think that you need somebody inside the company to keep you in touch with what he's up to, where he is, where he's been and where he's going." He tossed a fax of the *Manchester Guardian* at me. "Look in the back," he said.

I was about to say something about his habit of always starting at the back end when I saw his researchers had circled an ad under the "Appointments" section. Courtland International were looking for a receptionist. "There's a woman in our office," I said. "Can I use your phone?"

He gestured to a row of phones on the fat one's desk. "Second from the left is a priority line to Britain. You do realise it's after midnight there?" He handed me a slip of paper. "Before you call, my secretary gave me this for you: a message I think."

Veronica had rung to say she couldn't make dinner tonight but if I'd go to her apartment at 444 East 79th the doorman would give me the key. She signed it *Can't wait, Veronica.*

I rang Marrianne in Hendon. Her husband the policeman answered.

"You woke me up," he said gloomily.

"I have to talk to Marrianne."

"What for? It's after midnight. She's asleep."

"I want to triple her salary for a week."

"I'll go get her."

There was a fumbling with the phone and a thud as it was dropped. More fumbling and Marrianne was on the phone. I pictured her in a white nightie, her long blonde hair streaming down over her face, a ski jump holding the nightie out a foot from her tummy. "Wha issit?" she said, her voice husky with sleep.

The only thing New York and London have in common is that you can't get a cab between the hours of seven and eight in the evening. All the cabs in the city are crammed into Broadway and Covent Garden, stacked up ten deep and ten wide in front of the theatres, disgorging tourists, suburbanites, businessmen on expense accounts and honeymooners. Castleman had lent me his driver and car. "Take it," he said. "Costs me $350 a night whether they sit in the garage or take you to the airport. They need the exercise."

As we crawled slowly across Manhattan towards JFK, the evening had turned from Summer to October. I dialled the number Veronica had given me.

"Hi," said her answering machine, "I'd love to talk to you but I can't come to the phone right now. Could you call back later or leave a message. Bye."

"Veronica," I said into the phone, "I'm sorry you can't come to your phone right now. Call me in London. Bye."

# CHAPTER TWENTY-ONE

*Squawk, bleep.*

"Oh God, I loathe these machines. Like talking to a drain. Alicia here – in case you mistake my voice for one of your little frolics. Ken used to say I sound like twenty-nine trombones. You just rang an hour ago to ask me to lunch and if I don't remind you, I know you, you'll forget. Don't forget, will you darling? Or I'll pull your eyelashes out one by one. Shall I book? For Thursday? Piero's? Because if I leave it to you, you won't and we'll end up in some dreary place with the waiters thrusting their peppermills at us. Look I can't think Ken has mortal enemies, apart from me. And I don't want to talk about me. So we'll talk about the weather, condoms, the price of fish, or the way they do it in Bangkok. God, I'll even talk about motor racing if that's what you want to talk about. I find I'm quite looking forward to seeing you. You haven't run into a wall and shortened yourself have you, darling? I'll ring back when I've fixed a place. Bye."

*Squawk, brrrrrp, bleep.*

"I've booked Piero's, Thursday at one. See you there. Bye."

*Bleep.*

"Forrest, when are you coming back? I don't think it's good for either of us to drag this out a moment longer than we have to, do you? Frank has drawn up a list of what's mine and I must say, I think it's really quite fair. After all it is my house, you were hardly ever there. And from what I gather you won't even miss the money. I posted the list over two weeks ago and I think we deserve the courtesy of a response.

"And don't go sulking over the Aston. You said you gave it to me and that was before you even started mucking about with it.

232

It's my car. Are you sure you don't want Frank to come to lunch with us? I'd feel better if he were there. You know how I hate scenes, and Frank is a very skilled arbitrator. Ring me will you darling, let me know when and where? I'll wear the little black dress you used to like, the stretchy one with the scoop neck. You have our number but you've probably lost it. 927 9489."

*Bleep.*
"'Allo, Forray. Maybe you call me soon. Please. It's Nicole. Nicky. Maybe you forget. Oh, I forget. Probably you are not home yet. Goodbye."

*Brrrrrp, bleep.*
"It is 4.37 p.m. Friday the 16th of September. This is Martin Pimmons, Inland Revenue. Mr Evers, you will by now have received our third and final request for an interview regarding your year ending April 1987 return. This was mailed to you on the morning of the 9th of September, and even given the leisurely pace of Her Majesty's postal service, I feel it is safe to assume that you shall have received the final notice. I am also sure you are aware that the penalties accruing to nonpayment of the substantial sums assessed as owed by you to the Inland Revenue, that those penalties are, as marked on your notice, quite steep even by your measure. I am ringing to see if we could possibly meet to discuss these sums outstanding. And I would suggest you bring along your accountant and your lawyer. If we do not hear from you within the next week, that is by end of business day, Friday the 23rd, then we shall undertake legal proceedings. To repeat, my name is Martin Pimmons and you can reach me during normal offices hours at 01 605 9800, extension 36. I am out to lunch between the hours of 12.45 and 1.30. Good day, Mr Evers."

*Bleeep.*
"Allo Forray. It's Sunday. I hope you are OK and maybe you can call me when you come home. It's Nicky. OK? Goodbye."

*Bleep.*
"Forrest, you shit, you absolute shit. I come into my apartment,

I was running for blocks down 79th, couldn't wait to see you, out of my mind. All week I was expecting to see you and hold you again and fuck your brains out and all there is is this shitty message on my answering machine. No explanation, no apology, no nothing. Christ, I could scream. How could you be such a bastard? (eight-second pause) Oh sweetheart. Sometimes I get so depressed. Forrest, what is going to happen to us?"

*Bleep, burrrrrrrp, bleep.*

"Hello, Mr Evers. I did what you said and it was easy-peasy, really. I was in Manchester by nine-thirty and I was talking to Miss Wiggins who runs the office by ten. Told her about my poor mum in Manchester 'n' all. And here I am at Courtland ringing you. Are you sure? It's ever so boring. The pay is terrible, but I can keep it, right? And you're sure Mr Arundel won't mind my being away for a week and paying me triple? Plus expenses. Promise? Being receptionist, I can't talk for long, doesn't look right. Anyway, the Courtland gent you mentioned, Mr Courtland, he's definitely the gov here, but he isn't here. They expect him in tomorrow or the next day. So there's nothing to listen to. But even when he's here it'll be a bit iffy. I can pick up on his incoming 'cause they come through me, but his secretary makes his outgoing. And if I pick up on 'em he'll know 'cause he'll hear this bleeping sound. So I'll only pick up on about half and I won't know who he calls. Uh oh, gotta go. Bye byeee."

My house in Edwardes Square felt hollow, like an empty, drifting ship. Just the answering machine, a cascade of bills flowing out of the letter box, and me. The rooms were orderly, all the furniture was in its place. The chairs around the dining table were lined up for inspection. Zilna, the Cypriot fascist, had faithfully cleaned and dusted and the kitchen floor gleamed.

But the life had gone out of the house like a TV studio set after a series has had its run, the walls and the sofas and the coffee tables waiting in the dark for the joking stage hands to knock it all down to make way for a game show.

Dylan's kitty litter box was empty. The wardrobe in the bedroom had my clothes in my side, nothing in the other. The fridge had a carton of milk and a wedge of cheese that had turned into a biological farm. The loo off the bedroom smelt of disinfectant and mould. The chrome arms on the black leather sofa that Susan and I had bought at Conran when we were first married were peeling with rust and there was a tuft of stuffing coming out of the middle cushion. I picked up the phone and dialled.

"Now what?"

"Hello, Bill."

"Marrianne's not here. She's in Manchester. All week. Thanks to you."

"Bill, I want to talk to you."

"What for?"

"I need your help. You know Marrianne's up at Courtland International to listen in on Miles Courtland's phone?"

"You didn't say that. If you said that, it'd be my duty . . ."

"Right, I didn't say that. I am also not going to say I've heard you've done some undercover work in the course of your duties, and I would guess that you have made acquaintance with one or more gentlemen skilled in the art of phone tapping. I need Marrianne to monitor Courtland's outgoing calls. I need to know who he's calling and where he's going. And I need it on tape."

"You must be joking. Look, Mr Evers, I don't want to get unduly agitated over this, but you have already put Marrianne at risk and if she'd listen to me she wouldn't even be there. She'd be here cooking my dinner. Even if you do pick up something with an unauthorized tap, you can't use it in court. Get serious, Mr Evers. You're asking a police officer to do a tap and I'm thinking it must be true what they said in the papers, you got hooked on some kind of drug thing. You can't be serious?"

"The drug thing I got hooked on is this: Courtland is using his company as a front to ship drugs from South America into this country by the ton."

"You got a story, Mr Evers, talk to Special Branch."

"I'll pay you two thousand."

"Three."

"Done."

"Plus the equipment."

"Three-five if it's in by tomorrow morning."

"Done. And you never rang."

"No I never."

"You really think there are drugs?"

"I'm betting £3,500 on it, Bill."

"If there are drugs, Mr Evers, you'll let me know?"

"You'll be the first."

I rang Susan next and Frank answered the phone. "Good afternoon, Forrest," he said, professional warmth and sincerity ringing in his high tenor. "I imagine you're ringing about lunch and Susan's list."

"You have a limited imagination," I said. "Let me talk to Susan."

There was the sound of the phone being dropped onto the desk and Frank's distant voice calling to Susan to pick up. Frank went off the line with a little click.

"There's no need to be rude, Forrest," she said. I always liked her best when she started to get angry.

"None at all," I agreed. "Why don't you come over to the house for a drink?"

"I thought we were going to have lunch. Besides, I can't. We have a dinner engagement."

"Susan, you're not going out to dinner now, it's three in the afternoon. I'm only in London for a day and I haven't got time for lunch. Come on over, there's still a bottle of that Chambertin in the cellar. I'm off to Australia in a couple of days and if we don't get together now it'll be another month or two. If you want to talk."

"All right, I'll bring Frank."

"Fine, and I'll get my lawyer and maybe I can find a judge who does house calls and we'll make it a party. Look, Susan, it's our marriage and our house and you and I have to settle it. I'll see you at five."

Next I rang my accountant.

"Hello, Climpson here."

"Mervyn, it's Forrest Evers."

"Oh yes, Mr Evers. And how may I help you? Have you completed those forms I sent you?"

"There's a Martin Pimmons at the Inland Revenue: 605 9800, extension 36."

"Yes, Mr Evers?"

"See what he wants."

"Yes Mr Evers."

"And don't give it to him."

"Indeed Mr Evers."

Next Alicia, who answered after the seventh ring. "Nobody rings at three in the afternoon," she said irritably. "Who is this?"

I told her and she brightened. "Sorry to be such a grouch," she said, "but I had a bite of cheese and a glass of water for lunch and it makes me mean as a snake. You are coming to Piero's, Thursday at one? I'm sorry I haven't been able to dig up any deadly enemies of Ken's. There must be some lurking in the bushes, but I don't seem to be able to turn up a single one. You do still want to have lunch?"

"Thursday at one, Alicia. Have you ever run across a Miles Courtland?"

"Not that I've noticed. Who is he?"

"He's about thirty-eight, has a textile company up north called Courtland International which he inherited from his father. Possibly you could beat the bushes and see what you can find about him."

"And that's what you want to talk about?"

"Anything you can find about him."

"As long as we don't talk about motor racing. Spoils the wine."

Finally I rang Paris.

"Forray, I am so glad you have called. I am very glad to hear your voice. It has been terrible to lose you too, besides Michel. You are like a big brother, you know. But a bad one because you have not called me for a long time."

"I know."

"Forray, the service for Michel is at eleven on Saturday morning at Ste Chappelle. You know Ste Chappelle? It's OK?"

"Sure." Ste Chappelle is on the Ile de la Cité near Notre Dame, a fragile gothic frame for the most beautiful stained-glass windows in Europe. At eleven in the morning the interior would be glowing with cathedral reds and blues. "It's perfect."

"You know, Forray, that they say nasty, awful things about you. Especially after Mexico, it is much worse. Maybe you can come the night before, Friday night, take me away to dinner or something. I cannot bear my family now and Michel's family is horrible."

"I'll ring you Friday morning, Nicky. I'll try to come early, but it's hard to tell. I have to do one or two things here."

"I hope you catch them and fix them. Whoever do these things to you and Michel."

"You know about that?"

"I just know Michel would never drive so stupidly, and you would never act so stupid. It is not you. It was not Michel. Somebody is causing that."

"I will find him, Nicky."

"I hope you bring me his head on a platter."

Later, when I heard the doorbell ring I thought it was the phone in the other room and I put off answering it. But of course it was Susan with wet hair and her face fresh with raindrops.

"For God's sake, Forrest, at least you can open the door and let me in to my own house."

I let her in, she flung her wet raincoat on the couch and disappeared down the hall to the loo to dry her hair. She was wearing a white linen jacket and skirt, very crisp and formal, the modern businesswoman. Except that she wore no shirt or bra under the jacket. She had a Coppertone tan and her feet were bare in her mahogany loafers. She was twenty-nine and looked nineteen, with a sly little body full of curves and soft places. She came back into the front room rubbing her head with a white towel, talking. "Look, Forrest, I haven't got much time and I appreciate this must be as hard for you as it is for me," she said tossing the towel on top of her wet rain coat.

"Is Frank waiting for you in the car?"

She shook her head. "You worried he might come in?"

That made me smile. "No, I'm not worried. I wondered why you are in such a rush. You have time to listen?"

"I can listen."

"Fine, then listen. I am going to put on your old Dire Straits track, open a bottle of that Chambertin from the case that Freddie gave us, and then we are going to see if, instead of behaving like a couple of vultures fighting over a carcase, we can talk like two people who used to love each other."

She had always seemed so indifferent to money, taking it for granted but never really thinking about it. Now she wanted it all, the house, the money and the Aston Martin. I wondered how much of that was her lawyer with the tenor voice and how much of it was a woman I used to know.

By the time I'd opened the second bottle we had both relaxed enough to remember why we'd gotten married in the first place. We remembered the night we got our car stuck on the beach in a thunderstorm on Cape Cod, a can of beer between us, and the big warm tub we shared when we got back to our hotel in the morning. And Dylan, the cat Susan trained to fetch sticks (he never brought them back).

We sat side by side on the black leather sofa, an old married couple breaking in two.

Susan remembered the summer night we drank Pimms and painted the ceiling in the loo. In the morning I couldn't work out how we had missed the stripe down the middle until Susan came in and saw the wide stripe of white paint on my head from dragging it across the ceiling.

"It's worth about a million two now," I said.

Her mouth opened in surprise. Little pink tongue in a round pink O. "We only paid three hundred and twenty thousand. Are you sure?"

"One four doors down the terrace sold for that two months ago."

"Forrest, I had no idea." She was frowning, working out in her mind a whole new, much bigger set of figures.

"You can have it if you want it."

"Forrest," she said in a soft voice, "I love this house."

"To tell you the truth, Susan, it doesn't mean anything to me without you in it." She shook her head to object but I cut her off. "Let me finish. There are a couple of ways we can handle this. You can have the house. From what I see, Frank has plenty of money, probably more than I have. So there's no need for support. And I'll keep the Aston. Another way to do it is sell it off, all of it, and split what's left fifty/fifty, after the appraisers, auctioneers and lawyers take their bites. Another way is for me to prove adultery and leave you with fuck all."

She stiffened and started to get angry. "Frank says – "

239

"Fuck Frank. What do you say?"

By the time we got to the end of the second bottle, we agreed she would get the house, I would take the car, and she'd forget about alimony. It wasn't exactly fair, but then what is.

She looked at her watch and stood up. "I've got to go."

I stood up with her and she put her arms round my neck. "I'm sorry, Forrest."

We kissed and it lasted. Just one of those kisses that felt right. I put my hand on her bottom the way she liked and pulled her to me for another kiss. That went on for a while too and it felt even better. I pulled Susan down to the sofa again, her arms around me.

"Forrest, this is a terrible idea."

Her white linen jacket gaped open and her breast looked soft and trembling. "A terrible idea," I said, kissing her behind her ears where she wore her perfume.

Susan stood up, shook her long, fine brown hair and unbuttoned her jacket and flung it carelessly behind her. "We're still married."

I stayed sitting on the couch, unzipping her skirt. Underneath her panties were a light blue and I pulled then down and nuzzled her with my nose. "I don't think we should let that get in the way of anything." I looked up and Susan was smiling her old sly smile.

We did all the things we used to do with the slow ease of a thousand hours of practice together. She was the same silky girl and when she came she still held my hands, our fingers laced together and she still made little muffled cries as if she were afraid someone else would hear.

We lay still for a moment on the sofa and then Susan leaned over to look at her watch on the floor. "Oh shit! I'm late. We'll never make it. Can I use the phone?"

"It's your phone," I said.

Outside Edwardes Square was losing light. The trees were blending into the grey background and across the square the roofs made a jagged line against the city sky. It was still raining when I went to bed and I could hear the sound of the water dripping off the roof onto the flagstones in the garden. The bed was damp and when I turned off the light I thought of the five years I had lain with Susan in the same bed and I fell asleep in an instant.

*Squawk, bleep.*

"Hello Mr Evers, I'm ever so sorry for ringing you so late. I didn't want to disturb you or anything. And I have to talk soft so's I don't wake Bill. But I did want to thank you for the lovely dinner. It was such a lovely surprise to see Bill and by the time I got packed up and out of my little room and we were settling into the suite, it was already almost nine. Is that all right, the suite? Bill says not to worry but I do. We had a lovely dinner and Bill says it's all down to you and it was such a posh place I'm really grateful. You sure it's all right with the triple pay and the suite 'n'all? Anyway we didn't get back until almost midnight and I have lots to tell you. First, Bill says not to worry as far as the equipment is concerned. It's all set up and it's the best.

"You said to keep a look out for anything to do with the research facility. Well this morning I typed out a release-through form for the Liverpool Freeport for a container of cotton to be picked up tomorrow, I mean this afternoon, for the research facility in Aintree. This bloke here, Danny, is going down to pick it up. He's in and out all day, sort of odd jobs, like, and I let him take me for a drink. Oh I know, I am wicked. He couldn't believe his luck. What I put on the form – do you have a pen? – was that there is a shipment of containers of cotton cloth from the *Atlantic Star*, port of origin Cartagena, Colombia, off-loaded last night and held in bond. And that we were taking manifest number 33432MXCZ – bulk grey cotton cloth, container 338/LA, duty paid for sampling and quality control – from interchange pad 19 at 1.30 pm after the dockers come back from lunch. Got that?

"Anyway, this Danny says it's quite simple, really. They've got it all down on computer. He says you drive through the Freeport police gate on the outside, then through the Freeport security gate where they check your papers and make sure the container is on the interchange pad. You drive in, back up, and this straddle thingy drops the container onto your lorry and you're off, checking through the two gates. Anyway, he says he's taking the lorry from here at noon to give himself a little extra time, so I guess if you want to meet him and talk to him you should get here before then. He's dead easy to recognize. He's big as houses and wears a really nice chamois leather jacket. But his face is all scrunched up with

241

bushy eyebrows and he looks like a toad, warts 'n' all. And he's dead cheap. He wanted me to buy the second round. Crikey, can you imagine?

"Mr Courtland is supposed to be in this morning, I think just for the day. Could you ring me when you have a chance? I'm ever so worried about this. Bill says you're crazy. He's talking about bringing in Special Branch."

# CHAPTER TWENTY-TWO

Beverly woke me up.

I was dreaming I was in the corridor of the hospital in Mexico City and the attendants were wheeling a body past me with a sheet draped over it and I knew it was Beverly. I ran after them but I couldn't catch them as they went down to the end of the corridor and disappeared. I ran, but they were always just turning around the far corner. Then, at the end of a long corridor, I saw they were wheeling her through wide swinging doors, but when I got to the doors they were too heavy to push. I put my shoulder into it and the doors began to give, creaking open just enough to let me through into an enormous room. The room smelled of formaldehyde and meat and there were rows of bodies on tables covered with green sheets.

I turned down a sheet, and it wasn't Beverly, it was a skeleton.

So I turned down another sheet and another, and it was another skeleton, the skull grinning. And another skeleton, different, missing teeth, smaller. I knew Beverly was there in the room, but I couldn't find her. I didn't know if I had already found her, if one of the skeletons I had exposed to the damp air was her.

I ran down the rows of the bodies pulling the sheets off the skeletons as I went. I started to panic, getting out of breath and realizing the rows were endless, stretching into the distance and the dark. Then I heard her voice behind me, saying, "Forrest, relax. Stop running. I'm here." And I turned around and she was standing behind me in a hospital nightgown, smiling. She put her arms around my neck and kissed me and her breath was warm and she felt soft and sweet.

Beverly pulled back a little and said "I'm sorry". She kissed me again, then she stopped smiling and her face twisted into an ugly knot and she screamed that scream I'd heard in Mexico City when

I first found her in the hotel. The scream that had been echoing in the back of my mind ever since. I woke up, still hearing her scream.

It was 4.30 a.m. Wednesday. I got up and walked downstairs into the front room, the stairs feeling familiar but unreal, as if I had been here a thousand times before, but I wasn't quite there now. As if I was transparent, weightless and the world ended behind me.

I switched on the light, and the two empty bottles of Chambertin were on the coffee table, the two wine glasses each holding a small cone of red wine and dregs. One with lipstick on the rim. Susan, too, had put her arms around my neck and said, "I'm sorry."

The black leather couch was crossed with fresh creases; one of the back cushions was still at the end, lying against the arm where I had placed it under Susan's head. Next to it, on the glass table, the answering machine was winking with Marrianne's message.

I rang Ken in his flat in Fulham.

"Forrest, for God's sake. What time is it? Goddamn it, man, it's four-thirty in the morning. I can't sleep as it is. What is it you want?"

I played the answering machine with Marriane's voice sounding like an old radio recording over the phone.

"What the hell is Marrianne Plummer doing in Manchester, for God's sake? And goddamn you; I thought she was out ill. I had a hell of a time getting a girl to replace her this morning. What's all this about triple pay and suites?"

"How long will you be in London?"

"Through Friday. I've booked an early flight to Paris on Saturday for Michel's service. Look Forrest, I've been talking to other drivers. Alfonso tells me he is available for Adelaide. I think you should know that. I don't see any other alternative."

"Talk to them, but don't make any promises. Not before Thursday night."

"Thursday is tomorrow."

I told him my plan.

"Forrest, that is ridiculous; much too dangerous. Go to Scotland Yard and let them sort it out properly. If you'll hang on a moment I'll give you a name to ring."

"If I go to Scotland Yard with what I have now it will take three weeks to get search warrants, find the evidence, make arrests and even begin to clear me. If there is any evidence left by then. I doubt they let it just sit there and wait for the police to do their paperwork. In the meantime whoever your driver is in Adelaide, he is going to drive into a wall and that will be the end of him and the end of Team Arundel."

"I wasn't thinking of that. I was thinking of you."

"Then think of me for a moment. What have I got to lose? I'll ring you tomorrow."

Upstairs in the medicine chest there was an unused package of Loving Care Natural Black Semi-permanent Hair Colour Lotion with Creme Rinse. Susan had bought it a year ago when she had discovered a grey hair. I'd recommend that you use it when you're not expecting visitors because you have to sit still for half an hour with a plastic bag on your head and black soapy dye on your eyebrows. The effect surprised me.

Instead of the seamed and friendly face I'd grown accustomed to seeing framed with chestnut, I looked paler, older, harder, and bogus. The face that looked back at me had the pinched and resentful look of a man who has seen pieces of his soul eaten alive inside a prison. A man you wouldn't trust inside your house without an armed guard. Maybe it was just the fluorescent light, but I looked at my new black hair and my criminal self and I thought I looked just fine.

I put on an old faded work shirt, jeans, a dirty pair of training shoes and a worn leather jacket I hadn't had on since I was hauling my Formula Three car across Europe in a trailer. Maybe I didn't look like an average trucker, but I could pass.

Walking through the streets I felt lighter, freer. The unbearable lightness of lost responsibilities. The pain was still there; my debt to Beverly that I could never repay. But the freedom was an unexpected surprise, like a cheque that slides through the letter box in the morning. I wouldn't come back to the house except to pack. And I doubted that I would see Susan again. And Beverly and Michel were dead. And Veronica was better off without me. I was a dangerous man to be around, I joked bitterly to myself. I made all my friends and lovers disappear. The extra space was intoxicating.

I kept the Aston in Pembroke Mews, behind the pub. When I

unlocked the garage door and slid behind the seat, the car had that unused car smell of leather, mould, oil solidifying on the crankcase, and a faint whiff of battery acid for tang. Time for a run, old girl, I thought. Time for a change.

At 5.30 am the rush hour on the M1 heading north had already begun. Truckers getting an early start to get to the factory in Ayr before opening time, delivering the lumber to make the end tables for the day. The accountants have figured out that having thirty days' inventory on hand is dead money, so what used to lie quietly in the warehouse is now careening up and down the motorways at eighty-five.

Dodging in and out of the behemoths, the reps in Sierras and Cavaliers were racing to meetings in Glasgow to see if they could get a few more orders for end tables. To make up their quotas to qualify for the trip to Madeira, all expenses paid.

I wasn't in a rush. The old rag-top Aston needed time to warm up and unwind. Driving fast on a motorway bears as much resemblance to racing on a racetrack as running in a closet bears to the Olympic 100 metres. So I dawdled along in 5th at eighty-five along with the big artics, up the M1 to the M6, around Birmingham and Wolverhampton before the rush of the car and tyre workers on their way to the first shift, and turned off for Liverpool on the M62, driving into the St George's car park in the heart of the city by 8.30, in time for breakfast.

Downtown Liverpool and downtown New York reflect each other 3,000 miles across the Atlantic. Both Water Street and Wall Street are lined with dignified granite financial buildings looming over the docks. Both cities grew rich in the nineteenth century trading with each other. But now New York has the money and Liverpool wants it back. I wondered how many tons of drugs were leaking through the nets of harbour security, the police and Her Majesty's Customs and Excise. Maybe none. Maybe this was a wild goose chase.

Along Lime Street the breeze smelt of the fresh sea and the sun was cracking the flags topping Lime Street station and St George's Hall. A sharp, clear day.

I prowled the streets, getting the feel of Liverpool, easing myself in slowly. On the streets, the prices were scrawled large in the shop windows. Life closer to the bone; every penny counts. In the café,

246

as I had my cup of coffee, the clerks and the shopgirls, on their way to mind the counters in the big stores, ended their sentences on a rising note, questioning. Hopeful for the future; cynical for now.

After breakfast I went back to Lime Street. I looked rough for a tourist, but the grey ladies behind the Tourist Information counter didn't mind. If I wanted to see about a job on the docks, they said, go down to Pierhead to the Liver Building with the big Liver birds on top and turn right. The working docks were just north along the river.

Liver Birds?

"Well, they truly were mythical," she said, pushing her bifocals down her nose, "in the sense that they never existed. They were originally intended to be the eagles of St John the Evangelist, but there were still rather a lot of Cromwellians about in 1668 who felt it was rather sectarian for the city crest to have a Catholic bird on it, so they named the birds after the city. The Livers," she said, pronouncing it lie-vers. "No other city has them. Truly mythical."

She took a fresh look at me, pushing her glasses back on. "As mythical as your chances of getting a job on the docks. Do you not know Liverpool then?"

"Only what I've heard."

"Well the city is much maligned. Like the cod. But while they were saying it was dead and finished they built the biggest, and the best, Freeport in Europe. Never mind the Albert Docks with the museums and shops and restaurants, that's all for the tourists and the yuppies. You go north up to the Freeport, that's the real port of Liverpool now."

Her little chest was filled with pride and she tilted her head back as she ticked off the features one by one. "Six hundred acres. Multinational trade exchange. Freedom from customs import duty, Value Added Tax, EEC levies and quotas. Motorway and railway networks from the gates. Four-hour access to goods in storage. And when you take it out, the customs and paperwork are all done by computer."

She handed me a brochure. The new Liverpool Freeport: it sounded like a drug smuggler's dream. It was a fortress, patrolled by security, harbour police and customs, but if you had the key, if you were a paid-up member of the international business community,

247

you were safe. You wouldn't have to strap it a kilo at a time to junkies' bodies in plastic bags and pay their airfare, or off-load offshore in high seas or run the risk and expense of shipping by air. The Freeport was a legitimate, protected pipeline designed to speed bulk raw material into Europe by the thousands of tons. All you needed was an established business so no questions were asked, and no containers inspected at random.

"But you see what I mean," she said, 'about your chances. It's all done by machines now. Unless your dad was a docker and your brother's the head of the union I don't think you'll get a job today."

I drove down to the Mersey, turned right at the mythical birds and drove fifteen minutes north to the Liverpool Freeport gate at Boodle. In the distance, through the chain-link fence, I could see the *Atlantic Star*. A big blue crane was picking up containers from the dockside, lifting them up and turning them to stack sideways, athwartships. It looked like they were nearly finished loading. Twenty-four hour turnaround for the largest RO-RO (roll on roll off) in the world, the PR brochure boasted.

Courtland's cargo must be among the thousands of identical containers stacked in rows over 200 acres. I watched the trucks pausing at the gate, driving in and driving out. I tried to see the second gate inside, but it was hidden out of sight.

I'd be back.

It was only twenty minutes from the gates to the address at the Aintree Industrial Estate. The Courtland Building was larger than most, but it had no markings, not even a number. I drove past it twice and had to check the numbers on both sides to make sure I had it right. Behind a high chain-link fence the building was brick with a large roller door and no windows, about fifty yards by twenty. Two nondescript Montegos were parked outside; there was no sign of life. But of course it was early. Danny wasn't due for hours.

I drove the Aston over to the Aintree racetrack, parked it near the clubhouse where it wouldn't look out of place, and rang for a minicab to Urmston.

Urmstom, the International Headquarters of Courtland Mills at the edge of Manchester, had two main features: the Manchester Ship Canal and the River Mersey. Courtland Mills lay between the two, a sleek, manicured corporate park, with carefully tended shrubbery and lush green rolling lawns. A corporate vision of the perfect suburbia; no loitering, keep off the grass. A polished black granite stone set in the lawn said COURTLAND INTER-NATIONAL in gold letters. Est. 1868.

The driver let me out by the gate and I walked up the wide, curving drive. The Courtland building, as I rounded the corner, seemed odd, out of proportion, a high rectangle of stainless steel and dark glass. When I got close to it, I could see brick beneath the reflecting glass. It was a reskin. They had covered over the Victorian Brick of the old mill with a twentieth-century wrapping.

Except for a few Metros, Cavaliers and Sierras, and a couple of dog-eared Minis thrown in for spice, the parking lot was as empty as a racetrack parking lot the day after a race. The only truck was around to the side, a new big Mercedes cab-over. I walked over to it and waited, leaning against the grill.

Danny, when he showed up at a quarter to one, was bigger than I expected. He had the thick neck and heavy slabs of muscle of a man who has picked up weight and carried it and put it down again for a living.

"Get off the fuckin' cab," he said.

"Danny," I said loudly, pushing off the cab, grinning the big confident Evers grin and holding out my left hand to shake hands.

He didn't believe me, he knew it was a trick. But at the same time he took a half-step towards me, studying my face to see if maybe he could place it, and half-holding out his left hand.

I swung from a long way back and landed a hard right on the corner of his jaw. He staggered and fell to his knees, pitched forward towards me and I caught him in my arms. He was asleep, dreaming like he had when his mother had wheeled him in his pram. Another free ride for Danny.

He must have weighed seventeen stone, so dragging him to the far side of the cab out of the sightlines of Courtland windows was hard work. Hauling him up into the passenger's seat was even harder, but I managed it by opening the door, slinging him over my shoulder and charging like an American football lineman. I strapped Danny into his seat belt and pulled the across-the-shoulder belt tight, forcing him to sit upright. Then I got in on the driver's side and, squeezing my thumb and forefinger on the hinge of his jaw, forced his mouth open and jammed six of Veronica's sleeping tablets down his throat. One was enough to make Veronica go to sleep. Two and she'd sleep for twenty-four hours. Danny was going to sit still for a while.

He looked about thirty-five and as peaceful as a vicar. He'd probably never heard of Michel. He probably didn't know any of the kids with the greedy eyes who were hooked on crack in Manchester, London, Glasgow, Nottingham and Liverpool. He was just doing his job, getting extra pay for dirty work. I pushed his jaw shut and he started to snore.

I took the keys and the computer printout out of his fancy chamois leather jacket and walked around to the front of the building and into the front entrance of Courtland's Mills.

They had clad a two-storey-high reception area in art deco marble in the style of the 1920s. Potted palms, and no visitors. Alternating black and white marble slabs.

Marrianne sat behind a kind of marble pulpet with a computer screen and a telephone console. Behind her on the wall there was a radiating fan of black and white marble. With her fine long blonde hair and high cheekbones, she looked as if she were a high priestess in a forgotten corner of the corporate kingdom. She gave a start when I walked in the front door, but then she gave me her impersonal, professional receptionist smile.

"How can I help you, sir?"

"There's an error in the printout. There should be two drivers." I handed her the paperwork.

"No problem," she said, rolling it into her machine. She punched a few buttons, the computer screeched, and she handed the paper back to me, leaning forwards and whispering under her breath. "Crikey, what happened to you? You look horrible." She pronounced it 'orrible. "What are you doing with Danny?" Her grey eyes were bright with worry.

"Danny's fine. He's having a nap and he's going with me."

"He's a nasty piece of work, I can tell you. Don't let him out of your sight."

Through the closed door at the back of the room we could hear the sounds of an office. "Is Mr Courtland in?" I said loudly.

"Mr Courtland is expected in this afternoon," Marrianne said, back to her professional persona. "Do you have an appointment?" Then she leaned forward, whispering again. "Dave rang this morning – your mechanic. He said he had to talk to Mr Courtland. He left a number in London."

I leaned forward again as she wrote down Dave's number. "Marrianne, you are fantastic. Where can I reach Bill this afternoon?"

She wrote another number on a yellow memo pad, tore it off and gave it to me. I put it in my shirt pocket without looking at it. "Bill stayed over in Liverpool," she said, "with Special Branch. You be careful. I hope you know what you're doing."

"Just going for a drive," I said.

# CHAPTER TWENTY-THREE

The road below and the cars on it shrank to miniature from the high cab of the big Mercedes. The empty flatbed trailer behind me rattled and bounced and I had to be careful to swing wide going around corners to keep it from crunching one of the hatchbacks that darted in and out, looking for an opening. I looked down on people's heads in the street and from a room over a newsagents two girls with bright red hair who should have been in school waved.

Danny's head lolled with the turns, but the strap across his chest kept him upright and his breathing was as steady as a grandfather clock. His jaw was bruised and swollen and his mouth was open, snoring loudly. Just another drunk, along for the ride. The police at the Liverpool Freeport main gate waved us through and I drove around a long bend and pulled up at the second gate. A man in a crisp white shirt and strands of thin black hair combed over his bald spot came out of the gatehouse and took my paper and went back inside. Just routine. When he came out again he waved me through and pointed to the scales. I drove over the platform sunk into the tarmac and stopped.

He read the electronic read out, went back to the gatehouse, and a minute later was standing on the step of the cab handing me the form, stamped and completed by computer. So now the largest port computer in Europe had a record of a Courtland Mills lorry, registration number CX 9876 WAG, entering the Freeport, towing a flatbed trailer weighing 2,786 pounds. The lorry collected container number 338/LA, off-loaded 21st Sept. *Atlantic Star*; manifest number 33432 MXCZ; grey cotton cloth, grade E-76, weight 12,430 kilos; port of origin Cartagena, Colombia; duty paid. When I left the computer would verify the total weight on the scales and the fact that I left with container number etc.

"Interchange pad number 19," he said looking sideways at

Danny. Danny's head was on his shoulder and he was making wet, slobbering sounds.

"First trip in," I said. "Where's 19?"

"It's just behind that second shed. It'll be a few minutes because your container is still on the mafi and we're down a straddle crane. Ten minutes at the most. 19 is on the near end. What's with him?"

"He was still in the pub when they opened up this morning. He's a mate and I couldn't see him get canned, so I'm helping out, like. He'll be OK in a couple of hours."

"That's Danny, isn't it?"

"That's our Danny boy," I said, smiling as if it was a joke. The balding man gave me a that's-not-funny look and waved me through.

The interchange pad was just wide enough to back the trailer in and it took me three passes to back it in straight. Ten minutes later, a 46-foot-high straddle crane, looking like a giant yellow Meccano spider with four legs and a rust-coloured, 30-foot-long container swinging high up against its belly came roaring around the corner of the shed. The crane eased up over the flatbed bellowing smoke and noise, let the container gently down onto the flatbed, backed off, and roared away in search of another container.

I drove back to the scales, the container and the flatbed were weighed and entered on the computer, and the security man came back to give me the receipt. He stuck his head in the cab again looking at Danny. "Jesus. He's even uglier when he's asleep."

I handed in my receipt at the outer police gate and I was out on the open road, headed for Aintree. A fool rushing in.

Years ago, when I was racing in Formula Three, I took tremendous risks to gain a hundredth of a second, or another six inches of track. I never thought about the risks: I knew nothing could happen to me. I was twenty-three and I was immortal; nothing could touch me. I was going to be the world champion. Towards the end of my second season in Formula Three, Lotus offered me a test drive in one of their Formula One cars. Every young hotshoe's dream: a test drive with one of the leading Formula One teams. But I blew it. I never even got to sit in their car.

The week before I was scheduled to drive the Lotus, at Clermont-Ferrand, I was battling for fifth with another driver who probably thought he was going to live forever too. It was towards the end of the race when we went side by side into a blind uphill corner. He was on the racing line and I was on the outside, but I didn't back off. The turn crested at the apex and my car went light for just a moment, as if it was about to go off. I kept very still and the car settled, digging in, just inches ahead of the other car. I thought I'd gotten away with it and mashed my foot down to accelerate downhill.

Maybe if I'd fed the power in gradually, smoothly, feeling my way into the power curve of the engine, I might have gotten away with it. But I didn't. I mashed the pedal to the floor and the car spun instantly, the laws of physics taking control from the young man who was in too much of a hurry and smashing him into the trees.

I had two fractures in my right thighbone, a fractured pelvis, a broken collarbone, and plenty of time to find an excuse. There was no excuse. It was my mistake.

The doctors said I was lucky, and they were right. I was lucky to be alive and lucky to have a bright shiny new lesson to carry with me. You need finesse to translate power into speed. Fools in a rush don't go fast, they go smash. I wasn't going to live forever. But with a little caution, a little more delicacy of touch, I might live a little longer.

Driving into Courtland's "research facility" did not come under the delicacy of touch column. There would be more of them and they would be on their home track. But I didn't need to take them, I just needed to fool them. Back in, let them off-load, drive out to a telephone. Tell Bill to come and collect the bastards.

Only that wouldn't help me. It wouldn't make a connection between Courtland and Michel or between Courtland and me. I had to get next to Courtland and bring him out with me. I needed a few minutes uninterrupted conversation with him. Alone.

When I pulled up to the fence outside Courtland's research facility the gate was still locked, but the two Montegos had been joined by a blue and white Rolls Royce with gold-plated trim, registration number MC1. Evidently Courtland didn't believe in a low profile. I leaned on the horn and the Mercedes blasted like a locomotive.

The door in the building started to roll up and two men in work shirts came out to open the gate. I pulled the lorry out into the middle of the road and with one man in each of the wing mirrors signalling, I backed through the gate, through the door and into the building. Inside there was a loading dock and I gently backed the container against the rubber fenders. The two men were both in their twenties. One was short and stocky and the other had the build of an athlete, wide at the shoulders and trim at the hips. They had the bored look of working men facing a day's hard work. The stocky one pressed the button by the door and it cranked down slowly off its roller and shut with the bang of steel hitting concrete.

From the cab I could see the interior of the building in the wing mirrors. It looked like any one of a thousand warehouses, with stacks of cartons on pallets, a fork-lift, fluorescent lights overhead. Except that one of the rows of pallets was 100-pound sacks of baking soda. The home remedy for indigestion. And the purifying ingredient in the manufacture of crack.

I climbed out of the cab and a man I hadn't seen before walked out of the shadows to greet me. He was wearing a tailor-made glen plaid suit and polished black loafers with little black tassels. He had blond hair cut short on the sides, long at the back and standing up high on top. He walked about fifteen yards across the concrete floor to stand six inches from me. He was about twenty-eight, had intense blue eyes and his face was red with anger.

"Who the fuck are you?"

"I'm a mate of Danny's," I said. "He's sick and I'm giving him a hand."

"Bullshit," he started to say, but before he finished the word he was swinging for my face. I had plenty of time to block the swing and hit him, but my arms were grabbed from behind so all I could do was pull my head back. His fist cut a glancing blow across my cheek. At the same time I kicked him hard in the crotch and he went down.

Whoever was holding my right arm must have been surprized because he relaxed his grip just enough for me to duck my right shoulder and roll the other man over my back. As he flew overhead I saw it was the athletic one. He landed hard on his back on the concrete and lay still. I tried hitting back behind me with my left fist where I thought the stocky one's face would be, but he was too quick, pulling back just enough to kick me in my side, knocking the wind out of me. I turned to face him and he was picking up an iron bar.

I couldn't breathe and I was in no shape to take him on but he looked far enough away to give me time to get up onto the dock. I forced myself to run the thirty-five feet to the dock, feeling I was in slow motion, and vaulted up, still not getting my breath. I got my leg up and I was on my stomach on the edge of the dock, aware of the dirt and cigarette butts on the floor and rolling out of the way, when he hit me across the back with the iron bar. I slid back off the edge of the dock like water, four feet down onto the concrete floor, landing so softly it didn't hurt at all. I remember pointed, polished black shoes with tassels kicking me, but I didn't feel them.

When I woke it was slowly, as if layers of gauze were being pulled away. There were voices – men's voices – at first in the distance and then nearby. My first impression when I opened my eyes was that I was lying in a pool of blood. An immense pool of dark blood. It was deep and soft; blood-red carpet.

I started to push myself up and a black tassled shoe came into my range of vision, moving rapidly, kicking my stomach. I went back down, the pain of the kick giving way to the slow blooming of a hundred other kicks I must have gotten on my stomach, chest and back and legs and side. My face felt like layers of sponge.

"Leave it off, Jeremy; he's not going anywhere. Let him sit up if he wants to. Do you want to sit up, Evers, or are you going to continue staining my carpet with your face?"

I went out again, and when I came back my mind was sharper but my hearing seemed out of focus. I heard voices, but I couldn't take them in. I sat up, propping myself against a wall which seemed to be covered in the same carpet. Courtland was seated in an oversize black leather executive chair at a big chrome and walnut desk. He was making a phone call. Tassel shoes was leaning against the desk, looking at me. His suit had grease stains on his knees from falling on the concrete.

The athletic one and the stocky one with the iron bar weren't in my range of vision. I turned my head, ignoring the pain, to take in the room. It was large, carpeted completely in a bright red carpet which ran halfway up the walls. Above that, the walls and the ceiling were painted in black. Across the room, on a raised platform, there was a jacuzzi, a vast circular bed with a fur cover, and a mirror over the bed. Behind the jacuzzi, an open door led into a bath panelled with mirrors.

Beyond Courtland, there was a long sofa covered in zebraskin and a chrome and glass liquor cabinet with rows of bottles and crystal glasses. Alongside it, an identical cabinet held a rack of expensive-looking stereo equipment. The ceiling concealed miniature spotlights which threw pools of light on the sofa, the desk and the bed, leaving the rest of the room in the half-light of a nightclub. I guessed I was in the secret playpen, done to the taste of a man who would wear a gold ring with diamonds on gold spikes.

He put down the phone and my hearing started to come back. He waved his ring hand with a mild, deprecating gesture, including and dismissing the room. "What do you think of it? A bit garish, I know, but one's fantasies tend to be garish, I find, Evers." He stood up, his little potbelly emphasized by the bulging stripes of his shirt. "Some of the finest slags in England have been in here, I'm happy to say. Sit still, I'm just going to have a piss. And leave him alone, Jeremy. I don't want any more mess in here than necessary."

He mounted the steps up to the platform and disappeared into the loo, leaving the door open. I could see him reflected in the mirrors, unzipping; hear the falling water and the flush. Jeremy stayed put. I tried to get up, but I don't think he noticed. I didn't have the strength to close a fist.

Courtland came back, zipping up his fly, his hard pink rubber face relaxed and smiling, little jovial laugh lines crinkling the yellow flesh around his eyes. "I don't suppose you can talk; doesn't matter." He reached into a drawer in his desk and put a small medical phial and hypodermic needle on his desk. Then he sat down again and leaned towards me like an insurance salesman about to close a deal, all smiles and confidence.

"I'm surprised you got this far. Or, rather, this deep. Fortunately you came here in disguise and you weren't followed; we've checked that. But I am curious about how you got to Danny. Not that it matters; I'm sure he'll tell us all about it when he wakes up.

"I don't suppose you have any idea of the size of what you've stumbled into. One container in a shipment of fifty containers might contain two tons of cocaine – or it might not. Even if customs did a random check, they'd never find it. The street value of two tons of cocaine – any idea how much that is? Take a guess. Say £100 million and you won't be far off. Say £200 million and you'll be nearer. And that's just one shipment. Our forecasts show Europe taking fifty-two shipments a year.

"Of course, we're only wholesalers, but those kind of figures rather put your life into perspective, don't they, Evers? I mean personally I really don't care what happens to you; never did. But now that you've put your foot in it there are other lives at stake, including mine. And the money naturally." He laughed. "God, and I used to think I was rich."

He went back to his desk, picked up the hypodermic needle, and stuck it into the small clear phial. He kept talking as he filled the needle. "We'll let the professionals do you. If you want a job done well, don't do it yourself, I always say, give it to a professional. Unfortunately they've got to come up from London. But in the meantime, as far as I'm concerned you might as well enjoy your stay."

He withdrew the needle, and, like a doctor, tipped it up, pushing the plunger to get rid of any trapped air. A little stream of clear white liquid dribbled from the needle.

"Meperidine hydrochloride. Demerol, as I believe it's called in the medical profession. One of the more useful cocaine derivatives. It will help your pain and you will ease away on a nice little pink cloud. Jeremy here will be your babysitter." He handed the hypodermic to Jeremy. "You inject him, Jeremy. I don't want to touch him."

I tried to rise, but nothing seemed to work. There was a hot wire of pain up my spine that branched out into thousands of throbbing cells behind my forehead. After what seemed like several minutes of effort while Jeremy was crossing the room, I had pushed myself up several inches. Jeremy's free hand slammed against my throat and my head cracked against the wall just above the carpet. I slid back down.

"Goddamnit, Jeremy, I don't want any more of that," Miles said, in a quiet voice, running his hand over his pink scalp. "You kill him before they get here and I'll have your kneecaps nailed to a brick wall. I don't want any connection between him and us. You know as well as I do that if he's dead our friends from London won't take him. Then you'll have to get rid of him, and I'll still have to pay the fee. So relax; be a good boy."

Jeremy relaxed his grip on my throat about five per cent. He stepped on my left hand and brought the needle to the crook of my arm. My right arm was bent behind me and seemed detached, uninvolved, unwilling to come forward and rip Jeremy away. His eyes were bloodshot and his pupils seemed unusually large. Anger came off him like heat.

"Just a moment, Jeremy, before you stick him." Courtland had stood up again and was putting on his suit jacket. "I suppose you'd like to know how we got to you on the track? Why you had those funny feelings and drove into the wall?"

He walked to the door and turned back to face me, straightening his tie with the little d for Dunhill. "I'm sure you'd love to know. Well, fuck you. Sorry Mick and Rainer aren't here to say goodbye to you; I know they'd like to after your fracas this afternoon. But they're working lads with work to do. It doesn't pay to hang about." He gave me a little wave, shut the door and he was gone, leaving a heavy scent of aftershave in his wake.

Jeremy stuck the needle in my arm. I watched his thumb push the plunger down and stop. He withdrew the needle with two thirds of the Demerol still in the syringe. "Don't want you sleeping all the way through, sunshine," he whispered. "I've got some lovely fun and games lined up for you."

I felt better almost immediately, warmth spreading all through my body and the pain flowing away like fragments of ice turning to water. Looking around the room I could see why Miles had done it the way he had. All that red was sexy really, although there again he was right. It was turning pink.

This time I woke up to the sound of the loo flushing, then water running in the sink. Jeremy came out holding an empty glass. He was one up on his boss. He washed his hands.

I felt better and quietly tested my muscles and bones. I didn't feel up to launching an all-out attack just yet. Sitting up seemed to be my limit. And Jeremy was busy at the desk. I watched through nearly shut eyes so if he looked my way he'd think I was still out.

He placed the empty water glass in front of him, drew a small sheet of aluminium foil from his breast pocket and carefully folded it over the rim of the glass. Then he pushed the foil down to make a small pocket. Taking a small folding knife, he pulled an ivory toothpick from its side and carefully punched a series of pin holes in the bowl he'd made from the aluminium. He put the toothpick away, pulled out the knife blade and cut a slit in the aluminium along the rim of the glass.

He worked with the singleminded care of a child using crayons. His forehead wrinkled with the task, knotting his eyebrows together at the bridge of his nose. He looked at his work for a moment, grunted satisfaction and drew out a small plastic phial from his breast pocket. He put it on the desk alongside the glass. Then he pulled out the desk drawer and took out a small blue-framed mirror like the ones women carry in their handbags. The surface was blurred and streaked.

He lay the mirror down flat on the table, flipped the plastic top off the phial and sprinkled white crystals onto the glass. He rummaged in the desk drawer, found a razor blade and began to chop the rocks into a powder. Then he lit a cigarette and leant back in his chair. After two deep puffs, he leaned forward again and, tapping the cigarette with a finger, carefully deposited the ash into the bowl of aluminium foil. Carefully scraping up the white powder with his razor blade, he dumped it on top of the cigarette ash.

He picked up the glass with his left hand, studied it, reached into his right pocket and came up with a miniature blow torch that erupted with a bright blue flame with the touch of a button. He held the glass with the slit in the aluminium foil up to his lips, and lit the bowl with the blue flame. When it was lit, he inhaled deeply and held his breath. After a time he exhaled and, with his eyes shut and his head thrown back, he said "Good ol' ready-wash." He stayed like that for maybe thirty seconds before he took another drag from the glass, draining the last of the smoke. He sat back again, his eyes shut, satisfied.

I could feel my strength coming back to me. The longer I waited, the better my chances. On the other hand, the gentlemen from London were coming to take me away and I didn't have forever to make a move.

As it went down, I didn't have long to wait, and Jeremy made the first move.

After he had been sitting in Mr Big's chair for about ten minutes his eyes snapped open and he looked nervous, edgy. He turned to look at me propped up against the wall and I could see the rage making red and white blotches on his face. He stood up suddenly, sending his chair skidding back on its wheels, and walked over towards me, his bright blue eyes on my face. I was expecting a kick – it was his style – and it came from a long way off, aimed at my crotch. He was putting everything he had into it.

I caught his foot with both hands and rolled, twisting his leg suddenly and sharply, feeling the ligaments tear in his knee. He screamed, out of control and twisting in midair, and landed hard on his stomach. I drove off the wall, still holding his foot, wrenching his leg sideways behind him and feeling it give as if I had pulled it out of its socket. He passed out from the crack or the pain. Or both. I stood up slowly to catch my breath, but standing up was a mistake. I sat down, dizzy, waiting for my mind to clear.

I crawled over to him and took off his jacket, shirt and tie. Then I found the hypodermic needle in the desk and emptied the rest of the Demerol into his arm. At least his leg wouldn't hurt so bad. I pulled off his shirt, shoes, socks and trousers. His knickers were powder-blue nylon bikinis with a monogrammed J in fancy script. I let him keep those. Then, working slowly, I dragged him into the loo, found I could stand without too much pain, and left him with his head draped over the toilet bowl to look for a razor. There was the razor he'd used to cut up the crack, but that wasn't going to be much use. I found a fresh pack of blades in the medicine chest, but the nail scissors that were in there worked much better.

After I'd cut his hair and taken his gold earring off I found some black shoe polish. After fifteen minutes of rubbing, washing and rubbing again he'd changed from a golden blond to a shiny brunette. I dragged him back out and laid him out on the floor. His knee was swelling badly and his lower right leg went off at an angle.

261

I stripped and put my clothes on him. They were about one size too large, but being work clothes it didn't matter. I went into the loo and shampooed six times until the colour of my hair came back. My face wasn't too bad. One ear was swollen, there was a cut above my eye that kept bleeding when I touched it, and one cheek was bruised and swollen so that my eye squinted behind it. But the face looking back at me was mine.

His trousers weren't a bad fit, although tighter around the ankle than I would have preferred, and his black tassled shoes were tight but I could get them on. Once I'd squeezed into them I had an urge to kick him, but it passed. His shirt was too tight and I couldn't button the collar, so I draped his tie around my neck and left the collar open. The jacket was two inches too short in the arms so I left it hanging on a hanger on the loo door.

I propped him up against the wall where I'd been, and sat down in the big leather chair and waited.

I didn't look like Jeremy and he didn't look like me. I didn't think it would matter. I was betting that the gentlemen from London didn't know either of us, and didn't want to know. I was betting that they were expecting to be passed a package. Courtland might have given them a description of what I was wearing, but now that the shoes were on the other feet, I doubted that they could tell that Evers wasn't Evers any more. It was a risk, taking the time to change suits, but it was important that they thought they had me so they wouldn't come looking for me again.

Then I realized I didn't know where I was.

# CHAPTER TWENTY-FOUR

The centre of evil is so often like this. As dull and repetitious as a warehouse, with a sordid room like Courtland's playpen in the middle, like a sore.

I had opened the door of Courtland's red-carpeted hideaway and found I was still inside the warehouse. The Mercedes lorry, along with Mick, Rainer and Danny were all gone. But the rows of boxes on pallets and the sacks of baking soda were there on the dock. Further back, there were rows of fifty-gallon drums cased in foam. Behind them, along the windowless back wall, was the factory. It looked like a commercial soup plant, and I suspected that Courtland had bought his equipment second-hand from Heinz or Campbell's. There were 200-gallon stainless steel cauldrons, with self-contained gas rings vented to the roof. All you need to make crack is cocaine, water, baking soda and plenty of heat. The cauldrons were mounted on swivels to make them easy to empty. Only one of the five cauldrons showed signs of recent use. The factory was just starting up, planning on a big future. The unused cauldrons were a capital investment in market growth. Boom times ahead for crack.

I looked back at Courtland's room, a large, blank box in the middle of a warehouse. Children would eat garbage, steal, pimp and suck on the cocks of strangers. They would kill and be killed so Courtland could indulge his fantasies. When you got to the centre of evil, there wasn't any centre, no grand plan. Just small men with no imagination who could not conceive what suffering meant outside their own skin.

A car horn blew.

I walked up to the front of the warehouse, found the steps down off the dock (the thought of jumping down hurt) and pushed the up button for the roller door. Outside the gate, there was an industrial-blue two-door Sierra 1.6L. The kind of car you wouldn't notice if it drove through a cricket match. I waved the car in and shut the door when it was inside.

A paunchy, middle-aged man got out and slammed the door shut, looking around as if he'd seen it all before and he didn't like any of it. He had deep blue and purple bags under his eyes and looked as if he hadn't slept in a year. He wore a dirty brown cotton pullover and Big Boy denim trousers with an elastic waistband.

"I thought there was going to be two of you," I said.

"Oh Christ, we're so fuckin' busy this time of year you wouldn't believe it. They said they can't spare two guys so I gotta make the trip alone. It's all screwed up, innit? They talk about new management, new procedures, and it's all bullshit, it's all worse. I mean I shouldn't be driving all the way up from London. They should handle this outa Birmingham or Leeds, much closer. Or Manchester – there's a couple a geezers in Manchester sitting on their hands bitching they got nothing to do. So I gotta drive all the way up from London, don't I? And alone."

"I thought the organization was better organized."

"Look, mate, the hours stink, you never know when they're gonna call. I haven't had a weekend off or a holiday yet this year and they just keep piling it on. It's stupid. And everybody thinks the pay's gotta be terrific. Well it sucks, it really sucks. I gotta find another line of work. Where is he?"

I told him he was inside and nodded towards the "office". We started walking. He looked at me for the first time. "Oy, you're a mess, boyo. What'd you do, fall under a train?"

"I had a little trouble getting him to relax."

"He's not dead, is he? I won't take him dead; I'm not a fucking dustman."

I opened the door and Jeremy was sleeping peacefully, propped up against the wall, his leg bent sideways at the knee. The man from London ignored Jeremy and let out a low whistle, impressed with the layout. He'd probably looked at the same men's magazines as Courtland had looked at when he was a boy. He probably still looked at them.

"Gimme a hand will you, son?"

We toppled Jeremy onto his stomach and the man pulled a roll of glass-fibre reinforced packing tape out of his trouser pocket. Jeremy's knees were touching but his ankles were four feet apart so he had to force Jeremy's ankles together. He grunted with the effort and there was a wet grinding sound like the ripping of cartilage and tendon from Jeremy's knee. The man didn't seem to notice the sound. He could have been tying up a supermarket chicken. He ran the tape around Jeremy's ankles, up to his wrists behind his back, and on up around his neck. Then he wrapped the tape twice around Jeremy's mouth. When he had finished Jeremy was trussed in a U-shaped, his back arched, his head back, his feet almost touching his head. The man gave Jeremy a nudge and the body rolled on its side.

"Whattaya got him on?"

"Demerol."

"How much?"

"About 45–50 ccs."

He nodded, then looked up at the ceiling at the hidden spotlights. "You got a hand-truck, a dolly or summit?"

"A dolly?"

"Yeah, right. A dolly. You got a warehouse, you got a buncha fuckin' dollies. Or you wanna carry him out yourself? 'Cause I ain't lifting the bugger, am I."

We found a dolly, tipped Jeremy onto it, and shoving it with his foot, the man wheeled Jeremy, arched like a driver sideways, out to the dock. He backed his car up, opened the boot and we more or less rolled Jeremy in. The man shut the boot, got in the car and drove away without looking back.

I shut the gate and the door, went back to the desk in the office and dialled Marrianne. My watch said five. "Is he there?"

"Oh, Forrest, hello. No, he's not. He came in, in a terrible rush around two-thirty. He ordered an air ticket to Paris and he was out again in about fifteen minutes."

"Marrianne, listen carefully. I want you to get up, walk out the door and get out of there. Right now. You could be in danger. And don't come back. Go back to London. I'm sure Ken will be grateful if you came back to him in the morning."

"All right, if you say so, but I haven't been paid and I – "

"Just do it," I said, interrupting.

"All right, all right, don't get your knickers in a twist. Two things, then I'll go. Bill called; I think you should ring him. He's still at the same number I gave you. I don't think he's too happy with you."

"Let me have the number again. What's the other thing?"

"201 2121. Dave rang three times and he sounded upset. But he missed Mr Courtland."

"Tomorrow, when you're in London – "

"I already have," she said. "I knew you were very interested in Dave's calling 'n' all, so I rang my friend Pauline at directory inquiry and she gave me the address of the London number. Would you like it?"

"In the morning. I'll ring you at Hemel Hempstead. Now go."

"I'm going, I'm going."

I rang Bill and asked him to meet me by the clubhouse at Aintree in half an hour. "Bring your friend from Special Branch," I said. "I'll be there," a second voice on the line told me.

"While I've got you on the phone, you might alert the motorway police to a blue Sierra 1.6L, two-door, registration D 544 YAH. There's a man bound and gagged in the boot requiring medical attention. He's a crack addict and he's dangerous. The driver is a hitman you may be looking for."

"We've got them," said the second voice.

I rang for a minicab, turned out the lights, locked up and waited by the gate. Ten minutes later, when I got out of the minicab alongside my Aston Martin, I staggered and almost fell on my face. The Demerol was still very much with me. I realized that under its pleasant disguise, it hurt to breathe, that my body was thick with bruises that went down to the bone, and that I was exhausted. The minicab driver thought I was drunk. Wearing Jeremy's ill-fitting clothes didn't help either. I fished in his trouser pockets and came up with a £10 note. Keep the change, I told the driver. No doubt Jeremy was a big tipper. Easy come, easy go.

My car was covered with dust from sitting in the lot for seven hours. I wondered why a £125,000 automobile gets dirty five times as fast as a £100 banger. Maybe dirt likes money. I unlocked the compartment in the door panel and pulled out my wallet, feeling reassured to get my identity back. Forrest Evers, former racing driver, former motor racing announcer. Former husband, lover and former gangster. Presently unemployed.

Bill made a great show of driving a new Jaguar saloon into the lot, siren screaming as he bounded across the pockmarked tarmac at seventy-five, slid to a stop alongside me, and kicked up a shower of stones and a cloud of more dust. He rolled down his window and leaned out. "It's fun to be a copper," he said with a straight face. "Care to join us?"

I got in the back of their car, shut the door and the man in the front seat turned to face me. "You've had a colourful day, Mr Evers." With sandy hair, short back and sides, small, close-cropped military moustache, and the mild eyes of a disappointed schoolmaster, he looked like an average undercover cop.

Some of the bruises were beginning to make their claim for my attention. My neck was stiffening and I had to turn my whole upper body to turn my head. The leather in the Jaguar seat felt as comfortable as a bed and I was tempted to close my eyes and sleep. "What do you know about it?"

"You committed an unaggravated grievous bodily assault, a kidnapping, and the theft of a vehicle with an insured value of £45,000. You were guilty of trespassing, as well as transportation and possession of a large but unknown quantity of narcotics. You then committed a second assault and you were an accessory to an attempted murder. Quite a colourful day Mr Evers."

"Bullshit. If you knew what was going on, why the hell didn't you come in and get me? They tried to kill me."

"That's not bullshit," he said turning around in his seat and looking out the front windscreen. "Those are my personal observations and they are on the records of the Freeport of Liverpool. As far as coming in and getting you, if that is the way you wish to operate – on your own – you can stay that way: on your own. I am not going to put myself or my men at risk for a man who does not seem to recognize that the police and the laws of this country exist."

The pain was intensifying and I had the feeling he could be a worse enemy than Courtland. Beware of the generation of men in Britain who sound like nannies. Bill shifted sideways in his seat and gave me a big wink. I think he meant to be reassuring, but it had the opposite effect.

"Are you trying to tell me that you know all about Courtland, and the way they smuggled cocaine, and the crack factory?"

"Not at all. If it wasn't for PC Plummer, I doubt that we'd have picked it up for some time. Although I assume that in telling him, you intended him to tell us." He looked at me through the rear-view mirror, a little self-satisfied smile on his face.

"If you were really smart," I said, "you'd let the factory sit and follow the crack through the whole distribution network and trace the shipment back to Colombia. Then you might do some real good."

"I doubt we're that smart. I'll write a report, and it will be out of my hands."

Which reminded me. "But you've got Courtland."

The man from Special Branch continued looking out of the front windscreen. In the distance a flock of white pigeons were taking off from the lush green grass at the centre of the racetrack. Bill turned around to tell me. "We don't have him. We lost him."

"Lost him? You can't 'lose' a two-tone, gold-plated Rolls Royce. He was going to the airport, flying to Paris."

"The Roller is still in his parking lot at the Mill. He never showed at the airport."

Special Branch turned in his seat so that the two heads were side by side, facing me. Bill had a big, handsome, boyish face, heavy in the cheeks, narrow in the chin. Special Branch wore a pleading look. "There were just the two of us," he said. "We're quite short of men, and I had no idea but that this was some wild goose chase. Bill stayed on to keep an eye on you at Aintree and I followed Courtland to his office. He never came out. He must have another car and a back entrance. I posted a man at the airport. Marrianne, Mrs Plummer rather, said she'd booked a flight for him out of Manchester. But he didn't appear."

I laughed. "Now I understand. Now I see why you don't introduce yourself and then come on with a bunch of threats. You fucked up. You lost the big one. So the only entry you have to that cocaine is to claim Jeremy told you; say it was just a lucky catch. You stopped the Sierra for speeding and the gent with the bent knee trussed up in the boot is delirious and tells you all about a cocaine factory. You tell some story like that. But if you link me to it, you have to wind the clock back to when Courtland is still around. And all the noise about kidnapping and assault and transporting illegal substances is to keep me quiet."

"Got it in one," he said. "But those are not idle threats, Mr Evers. You were observed. And if you continue to interfere with our work in any way, I promise you I will see that you are prosecuted. Leave it to the professionals in future."

His voice lowered to a whisper. "You don't appear to be taking this seriously. Let me give you a few facts. There are about ten tons of cocaine a year coming into Europe from South America now. We know that they are planning to ship more, and that they are depending on crack to expand their market. They're withholding the supply of marijuana and hashish and discounting crack. Crack is selling for as little as £10 a phial on the street now and we estimate that one out of two or two out of three who try it are addicted to it with their first hit. We're not just talking about our children. We're also talking about their children, the next generation." He fished in his pocket for a cigarette, found a crumpled one, put it in his mouth, looked at me, took it out of his mouth and telescoped it into the ashtray. Then he turned around again, looking out at the Grand National racecourse.

"Cocaine is fat soluble. When a pregnant woman uses cocaine, it penetrates the placenta. Once inside the placenta, in the amniotic fluid, it changes to norocaine, which is not only stronger than cocaine, it's water soluble. So, this norocaine is trapped inside the placenta. The fetus sucks it in, excretes it, sucks it in and excretes it, and sucks it in. Over and over for days."

"So the fetus gets addicted before it's born," I said.

"It's worse than that," he said. "If it gets born, it will probably be born prematurely and be abnormally small. There's a good chance it will be brain damaged and have an abnormally small head. Some of them will have deformed genitals and some of them will be missing their lower intestine. The worst effects happen before a mother even knows she's pregnant, in the first three months of her pregnancy when the baby's organs are forming."

He paused for a moment, then turned around to look at me again. "I'd like to be hard and cynical about it but I'm not. Last year we seized 406 kilos of cocaine and we are just scratching the surface. How much cocaine do you reckon is in that warehouse?"

"Courtland said there were two tons."

The two men looked at each other. They had had no idea there was that much.

The tiredness was coming back in waves, my muscles were twitching and throbbing. "Look, I don't want to play detective. I want to drive racing cars; period. I need proof that I was drugged and without Courtland, I haven't got it. Bill, I still need your help. Can you be in Buckingham late tomorrow evening? I'll give you the address." Bill and Special Branch looked at each other and shrugged. I looked at Special Branch in the mirror. "It's a simple job. One man is plenty."

I had planned to drive to London, but I woke up with a jolt when the tyres changed pitch and the car started to veer off the M6. So I turned off at exit 19 and the first bed I came to was a twee little art nouveau restaurant with rooms at Knutsford. A girl with long dark hair and beautiful long hands showed me to a room with cutsey prints on the wall and different cutsey prints on the bedspread. As soon as she left the room I fell face forward onto the bed and played dead.

# CHAPTER TWENTY-FIVE

"You gave that lovely house on Edwardes Square to that NINNY?"

Alicia's trombone voice punched a hole in the roar of Piero's at lunch, and for a moment forks paused. (One of the jokes about Piero's is that the reason why the plants are so lush and green is that each one conceals a gossip columnist.) Then the noise closed over us again and we were below the surface of clattering cutlery, rumours, deals and promises.

"I don't want it and I don't blame her. I was never a model of fidelity."

"Oh bosh. Fidelity is a trick on husbands. God knows, I was faithful to Ken, but I think I was just dumb, darling. If I hadn't been maybe I wouldn't have been so hard on him. But look, I am sorry, we didn't come here to talk about my dreary life. You look like you've been sliding down the motorway on your face. Do tell me what you've been doing."

Alicia rested her chin on a triangle of freckled hands and forearms, trying her best to look wicked. She had translucent porcelain skin with a barely visible blue willow pattern of veins like the china they keep locked in museums. She had a fine long nose that wrinkled with distaste at snobbery. Her father had been Master of Clare and had a title he never used. But a grand country house and estate went with the title and that was where Alicia was born.

When she married Ken, she wore her grandmother's cream silk wedding dress and a Victorian rope of peals. The effect with her long flowing red hair was recorded in most of the glamour magazines, and for a short time, young women in London were dyeing their hair red.

Now, ten years later, at forty, she was easily the most beautiful woman in a room full of beautiful women. When you were with Alicia you were the centre of attention whether you wanted to be or not. She had learned to be outrageous; it kept the attention focused on her, off-balance. She speared a mushroom and raised an eyebrow, waiting for an answer.

"I've been in Liverpool, looking for the 'gent' I asked you about."

"Ah, yes, Miles Courtland. He's only a little thing, I gather. I can't imagine he did that to you. Anyway I did find out a bit."

I waved the waiter over for another bottle of Falchini Vernaccia di San Gimignano. Alicia had insisted on ordering just half a bottle ("If I'm going to drink alone, I'm not going to get caught downing a whole bottle") and had then poured half of it into my glass. "Well just let it sit if you don't want it; it's so pretty to look at. Makes me think of all those lovely vineyards below San Gimignano. Ken used to know the Falchinis. I suppose he still does," she said, remembering, looking out across the room.

The waiter poured, I took a sip of the delicious dry wine, nodded, and Alicia continued her "little bit about Miles".

"Well, by all accounts he's a disgusting toad; I can't imagine why you want to know him. Anyway, I had a ring round the old girl network and my cousin Cecily knows the poor girl who married him. Anne, I think her name was, or is, rather. Life goes on. They separated five years ago. Anyway, she thought he had 'loadsa money' and found out after the honeymoon that he was as poor as a parson. Big house, big debts, no cash. Cecily said he kept selling things. Mrs Courtland would come home and the dining room furniture would be gone. Not that he ever stinted on himself; always had some vulgar Rolls. You probably know, yes of course you know, that he inherited that weaving company or whatever on its uppers. He's seems to have kept it afloat, so some credit there, but I expect he's hocked it to the hilt."

"Any idea where he'd go if he wanted to hide?"

"Bangkok, Manila, Djakarta," she said without hesitating. "One of those sad cities where they drag peasant girls off the farms and paint them up for businessmen. He likes wallowing in fleshpots; brags about it. Apparently he gave his wife some vile version of a – " she paused to emphasize the current phrase " – 'sexually transmitted disease' he brought back from one of his annual trips to Bangkok. And that's when she left him. She told Cecily it was the only lasting thing he ever gave her."

Bangkok, Manila and Djakarta. They were all on the way to Adelaide. Courtland would still want to make his rival, Coleman, go smash in public. And when he found out I was still alive, he would come after me.

"Let's see, what else? He read chemistry at Reading and was sent down for cheating. No brothers or sisters. His parents were probably horrified at what they'd brought forth, and quit. And he was in a psychiatric hospital for a bit after his wife left him. Apparently that hit him quite hard."

"Alicia, I'd like to ask you a favour."

"You're asking rather a lot of favours. Don't I get any?"

"The farmhouse up in Bucks. If you're not going up there this evening, I'd like the use of it tonight."

"And I'm not to know why?"

"I can't tell you why."

She reached down under the table for her pocketbook. "Shall I tell you what I've been thinking lately?" She came up with a key and laid it down softly in front of my plate.

"I seem to be running into rather a lot of men these days who seem to have chosen parts for themselves, rather like choosing suits off a rack or characters from a play. Businessmen; lawyers; politicians. And they play their parts rather well. So well that they and hardly anybody notices, apart from their wives, what a jagged mess they make of their lives. They don't even notice themselves how angry they are.

"And what is especially cruel is that they can't talk about it. I mean they must have some curiosity about how other men are doing, if other men feel as false underneath it all as they do. But they don't know how to ask themselves, let alone each other. They don't have the words.

"They can talk about their cars, their sports, their companies and their holidays. But they can't talk about themselves really. Partly because if they do, if they say what they really think, people dive for cover or hurl rocks at them. So it's too dangerous. They might lose their precious part in the play. So they end up talking about themselves the only way they can; indirectly, in jokes, as if they are impersonating themselves. Which makes me think the world is full of imposters. And I've been wondering, Forrest, where are the men? Where did they go?"

She took a long sip of her wine and put the glass down, staring into it. "I was looking forward to seeing you, Forrest, because you aren't separate from what you do, you just are. Look out everybody, here comes Forrest. Whoosh, and you're gone, like a force of nature. You've always been perfectly straight and decent to me, heaven knows. And despite that, I've always rather fancied you, even though I know I could never hold you down. You'd always be buggering off to some bloody motor race on the other side of the world, just like Ken. But you have to admit, that it is a joke. That the only decent man I know, wants my house but he doesn't want me in it."

Then she laughed loud enough for the forks to pause again. "And you only want it for the night." Then she started to cry.

I took her hand across the table. "How long has it been since you and Ken broke up?"

"Two years and eleven months, but who's counting?" she said sniffing, gaining control. She reached down into her handbag again and brought up a tiny mirror in her palm. No damage.

"Look, I'm sorry. I've just had an unpleasant end to what I thought was quite a happy affair until he ran off with some brainless twenty-three-year-old clothes rack. Now I worry that the whole thing between us was a fraud, and I tend to burst into tears in public. But I'm all right, really. I'll be fine." She squeezed my hand, reminding me of my bruised knuckles. "Anyway, take my house. I'm staying on in the flat in London anyway. As long, Forrest, as you promise you'll tell me what this is about, and why you want my house for a night and why your face is in such a shocking state. You do look as if you've been brawling."

"It takes a long time to tell."

Alicia arched an eyebrow.

"But I will," I said, "when I come back from Australia."

"You'd better," she said with mock anger. "And if it turns out it has just been to get some bimbo to lie down for you, I'll have your eyes for breakfast."

I spent the rest of the afternoon organizing the evening. Ken called it a "harebrained scheme". But when I worked it out so that he wouldn't have to leave his dinner party, he started to come round.

The address Marrianne gave me was a little mews off Holland Park. I waited outside until I saw the light in the bedroom switch off. I waited a few minutes, then rang the bell. It was just before midnight. After five rings Dave answered the door, a purple silk dressing gown wrapped around him. He wore a thin gold watch I hadn't seen before and he was perspiring lightly, his black hair damp against his skull. He smelt of perfume and the musky scent of sex.

"Forrest, what in hell! How'd you find – "

I pushed my way past him, sounding urgent. "Look I'm sorry to get you out this time of night, but Ken just rang me. Max has made some changes to the transmission and we need an adapter plate. They're up at Hemel Hempstead and they need you to help Max make one up. Ken says if we can do a blank by morning, he can get a machine shop to make up a batch to take to Adelaide."

"For fuck's sake, I'm a mechanic, not a machinist. Why don't you get Kenny – "

"Davieee, what's going on?"

She had come halfway down the stairs, her voice sounding husky and sleepy, her little blue nightie barely covering her hips. She was honey and cream, about twenty-six I guessed, and her breasts swung heavily as she leant on the bannister. She pushed her long blonde hair out of her eyes and waited for an answer.

I knew Midge, Dave's wife; a short, tough, funny, curly-haired girl from his village in Yorkshire. They had two sons about five and ten years old. Dave looked at me in panic and confusion and then back to the girl on the stairs. I filled the pause that threatened to stretch out long enough for Dave to get his bearings and start wondering how I'd found him. "If we leave now, you can be back here for breakfast."

Dave's shoulders sagged, giving in. "I've got to go," he said to the girl. "I'll be back in the morning, first thing. Go back to bed."

She looked at me resentfully and turned and did what she was told, changing our view from the V of downy blonde to the wobbling

275

ample bottom of a naughty girl sent back to bed. Dave followed her upstairs.

Twenty minutes later we were heading North up the M1. Dave had been silent since he'd gotten in the car, not knowing where to begin. He jerked in his seat when the phone I'd had installed that afternoon, rang. I let it ring twice and picked it up. Ken said hello and I said loudly, "Hello, Ken, don't tell me Max has changed his mind."

"Is Dave with you? Good, good. Let me talk to him." I switched the phone onto the speaker and handed the receiver to Dave. "Dave, look, sorry for rousing you in the middle of the night, but I think we're onto something. Max and I have packed it in at the shop and we're up at the farm in Whitefield. Do you mind coming up? It's not that much farther and we really would appreciate your advice. Forrest knows the way."

When Ken and Alicia bought the farm at Whitefield after they were married, it was a derelict sixteenth century farmhouse with holes in the thatch and two feet of water on the stone floors. Now it was every young stockbroker's dream, with fresh thatch, an Aga in the kitchen, polished stone floors, exposed beams, a new dampcourse, a heated swimming pool out back, and stone fireplaces big enough to roast an ox in. They had restored it with the money and the care they would have lavished on a child if they'd had one. It was only twenty-five minutes north of the Arundel workshop at Hemel Hempstead and forty-five minutes from Heathrow. They had planned to live there until Ken retired, but they'd only lived in it for a year before they split up.

Dave was full of questions which I dodged irritably, feigning ignorance and letting the ragged edge of fatigue show. He started, haltingly, to explain about the girl and the mews house and why he wasn't with Midge in Rugby. I told him I didn't want to hear about it. The longer I could keep him on the defensive, the better.

My life had depended on him. You have to trust your mechanic or you can't drive. You can't force a car to its limit if you're worried that it's not put together exactly right. We'd been friends. I was his youngest son's godfather. Looking at him I felt as if I had drawn the short straw and I was to be his executioner. It was not a good feeling. And what I had to do would make me feel even worse.

I pulled up outside the unmarked gate, opened it, drove through and shut it behind us. There was a full moon and when we drove through the open fields, the medieval ridges in the land looked like the rolling waves of the sea. We drove over a ridge and the old house came rising out of the landscape to greet us, backlit by the moon. The thatch roof fell steeply down from the crest three-storeys high almost to the ground. A "catslide", Alicia had called it. I drove through the gates, over the cattle grid and parked in a courtyard of farm buildings.

"No lights. Doesn't look like anybody's here."

"They're probably in the front room," I said, as if that explained the darkened house. Dave followed me to the kitchen door. I knocked once, and turned to face Dave. He started to say something, but I hit him hard on the jaw before he said whatever it was he had on his mind. My right hand screamed with pain. I was going to have to learn to hit with my left. I unlocked the door, turned on the lights, dragged him inside and shut the door.

The kitchen smelt of beeswax from the freshly polished oak cabinets and the big kitchen table. There were rows of glass jars with dried beans and pasta on the shelves. The big green Aga filled the kitchen fireplace and rows of expensive wine lay in racks by the fridge. I dragged Dave across the polished stones, down the hall and into the front room.

After they had broken up Alicia had chucked out all their old furniture and sparsely decorated the big front room with high-tech modern leather, glass and chrome. It had a spare, cold look that looked even colder with the empty stone fireplace. Alicia had said it matched her mood. In front of a long, low butter-soft grey leather sofa there was a low coffee table; a thick plate of glass suspended on four stout chrome legs.

I swept the magazines and ashtrays off the coffee table and then took off all of Dave's clothes. I dragged him on the coffee table naked on his back, and lashed his ankles and his wrists to the chrome legs with the copper wire I'd brought with me. His head hung over one end and his legs were spread wide at the other. I went back into the kitchen to find a hammer, found it in a bottom drawer, and then came back to sit down on the sofa, facing his crotch and waiting for him to wake up. Legs splayed, he was not a pretty sight.

When he woke it took him a little while to realize where he was. He tried raising his head to look around the room, but it was tiring to hold his head up and look down his stomach to see me sitting on the sofa. After ten seconds his head dropped back down, staring into the empty stone fireplace behind him.

"Forrest, *Jesus*, what's going on? Where are we?"

"We're two miles from the nearest house, so you can scream if you like." I wanted him to feel as frightened and as exposed as possible. From the tremor in his voice, I was succeeding. The sooner this was over, the better. I stood up. "I want to know why and how you did it." I rapped the plate glass between his legs with the hammer for emphasis. It made a dead, brittle sound.

"You're crazy. You're fucking out of your mind. Jesus Christ, Forrest, this is no joke. What the fuck are you talking about?" He struggled, but bent over backwards, he couldn't exert much force and the wire cut into his wrists and ankles.

I went over to the stereo in the niche by the fireplace, switched it on and pushed in Bill's audio tape. I turned the sound up full. There was the mechanical flutter of a phone ringing on the end of the line then Marrianne's voice, "Courtland Mills."

Then Dave's voice. "Hello, is Mr Courtland in?"

"Whom shall I say is calling?"

"Dave. Just tell him it's Dave."

"I'm sorry, but Mr Courtland isn't in just now. We do expect him later. Would you like to ring back after lunch?" The line went dead and then there was the fluttering sound again.

"Courtland Mills."

"Is Mr Courtland in?"

"I'm sorry, Mr Courtland hasn't come in yet. Shall I tell him you rang?"

"Yeah, look it's Dave. I rang before. I have to talk to him. Tell him it's urgent. When do you expect him?"

"We are expecting him this morning. I expect he'll be in any time now. Would you like to leave a number where he can reach you?"

"It's a London number: 629 9496. Look, is there a number where I can reach him?"

"I'm sorry, but Mr Courtland didn't leave a number."

"Fu – " Again the line went dead and again there was the sound of a line ringing. This time it was a different voice.

"Did you intercept any calls for me this morning, Mrs Plummer?"

Marrianne gave him messages from a salesman and two creditors. Then she said, "Some Dave rang twice. He seemed quite anxious to talk to you."

"Marrianne, I don't want him calling here and he knows that. If he rings again tell him I've left the country." Then there was a chuckle. "At least that will be true enough. And ask after young David. He'll appreciate that."

At the mention of Marrianne's name Dave's head had jerked up and looked at me. He started to say something and thought better of it and his head sank down again. The sound from the stereo was unbearably loud.

"Courtland Mills."

"Hello, this is Dave again. Is he there?"

"I'm sorry, but Mr Courtland has left. I gave him your message and he asked me to tell you that he would prefer it if you didn't ring him here. I believe he has left the country."

"*That bastard!* Goddamnit, he owes me a fortune. I did exactly what we agreed and he owes me. You tell him, sweetheart, that if he doesn't pay me within a week I'm coming up there and collecting it myself with interest."

"I'll see that Mr Courtland gets your message, but I don't honestly know when to expect him. He didn't leave his itinerary."

"*Bastard!*"

I rewound the tape and let it play again, leaving the volume up.

"Courtland Mills."

Dave shouted over the tape. "Turn that goddamn thing off. That doesn't prove a fucking thing. Courtland owes me money. So what? He's a gambler. He probably owes a lot of people money."

I stood over him, looking down at his splayed body over the glass table, holding the hammer over his cock and balls. "What was your agreement with Courtland?" I said softly, under the din of Dave's voice on the stereo.

"It was just a bet on a horserace, you fucking idiot."

I smashed the hammer down on the thick plate glass between his legs and it shattered. Dave's body fell heavily in the broken glass. He looked up at me, afraid to move for fear of slicing himself.

"Listen to me," I said. "You killed Michel and you tried to kill me and you are going to tell me about it or I am going to smash you into pieces."

It is a terrible thing to see a man break. He holds himself bravely, day after day, keeping all of his terrible secrets hidden from his daily friends and his wife, thinking it will all turn out fine in the end. But it doesn't turn out fine and it is much worse than he could have imagined it. And no one cares.

Lying carefully among the spears of glass, Dave opened his mouth wide and nothing came out. He opened it again and bellowed as if all the demons of guilt that had been torturing him came roaring out of hell and into the night. He had seemed strong to other men, admired by women, loved by his wife, trusted by his children. Liked and trusted and admired by Ken and me. And he knew he would never be any of those things ever again. Tears ran down his cheeks.

I turned off the stereo and sat down on the sofa. Bill came into the room, followed by the man from Special Branch. I don't think Dave was aware of them. "Tell me about it," I said to Dave.

"I didn't kill Michel," he said. "I didn't have anything to do with that. Courtland had his ties with the Yakuza, not directly, but he had them. He bragged about all the Japanese bint they fixed him up with. He said he had a new formula he wanted to try and I didn't need to bother."

"Formula?"

"He fancies himself a chemist. His Mafia gave him some LSD to play with. He had some transdermal stuff I think he called it." Then Dave started to cry again. "He threatened my kids. He was gonna make Davie an addict. Davie's just started at this school. Courtland could do it, I know he could. You don't have kids, Evers, you don't know what it's like." Dave was staring at the ceiling, his eyes wild.

"No," I said, "I don't know what it's like."

"Perhaps I should ask the questions," the man from Special Branch said in his quiet Scots burr.

Dave didn't pay any attention to him. "Please, Forrest, get me off this glass. I'm cut." Blood was leaking out from underneath him.

We unwrapped the wire and lifted him up carefully. There were several splinters glinting in his back and a nasty gash in his bottom that would need stitches. Bill went out to his car at the back to get his first-aid kit and the man from Special Branch drew me into the hall. We left Dave lying on his side on the carpet.

The man drew out a cigarette, started to light it and then changed his mind and put it back into the pack. "You realise we have no real jurisdiction here. There may be something in his connection with Courtland, but crimes committed in Mexico and Hungary are slightly outside our bailiwick."

"What about Brands Hatch?"

"Well, if he wants to confess to that. But I'd guess that in the morning he's going to think anything he said here tonight was under duress. He's certainly going to think that if he gets a lawyer. And I'm not particularly keen about explaining PC Plummer's and my presence here tonight."

"I don't care about prosecuting him. I don't know what good it would do to put him in prison. But I do want to know exactly how it was done."

"I think I can find that out for you."

"There's one other thing."

He wrinkled his brow, dubious.

"Are you free this afternoon?" I asked.

# CHAPTER TWENTY-SIX

Arnold MacIntyre, President of the Formula One Constructors Organization and the most powerful man in racing, leant back in the Recaro racing seat he used as office chair and surveyed the four of us. The window behind him was a sheet of glass that reached from the floor to the ceiling. From where Ken and I were sitting, it looked as if Arnold and his aluminium desk were floating over Hyde Park. The blue-green of the carpet matching the hazy blue-green of the park, the light blue of the walls matching the light blue of the afternoon sky.

"I don't think I can help you," he said. "I would if I could, but I'm afraid I can't."

Ken stood up and walked slowly over to the window, staring out at the park, the tower of the London Hilton ghostly in the distance. "Arnie," he said, "in all the years I've known you, this is the first time I've ever heard you use that word, 'can't'. I never imagined it had a place in your vocabulary."

"The impossible I can do. Miracles, I can't."

"In that case I would seriously have to consider taking legal action for 'unfair prohibition', or whatever the damn legal phrase is. There is no reason for not allowing Forrest to drive in Adelaide."

"If you want to sue Alain, be my guest. I keep telling you, talk to him; I didn't bar Forrest, he did. Although I have to tell you I agreed with his decision at the time."

Ken went over to Arnold's desk, his great bulk looming over Arnold and his great sack of a face red with frustration. "Alain won't even answer my phone calls. And you are supposed to represent the constructors. Meaning me. Goddamnit, if you don't represent me, who the hell do you represent?"

"Let me go through it again," I said.

"You don't have to explain things twice to me. This, what's

your name, Dave? This Dave, your mechanic, drugged you and that's why you crashed and why you acted like a clown out on the circuit. And Dave here says he's not going to do that anymore and this gent from Scotland Yard says he's not going to do it anymore, so there's no reason to ban you. Right?"

"That's right," said Dave, standing beside me. "Forrest didn't have anything to do with any of it."

MacIntyre looked at Dave, who had put on a suit and tie for the occasion. "Why don't you sit down, Dave? Relax. Nobody's on trial here."

"If it's all the same to you, Mr MacIntyre, I'd prefer to stand."

I had another idea. "Arnie, you have a contract with the track owners and with television and radio companies around the world?" I said.

"That's correct."

"You provide all the teams, pay all their transportation and all the prize money, and the track owners pay you a flat fee?"

He nodded.

"Plus a percentage of the gate? And your TV and radio contracts are based on the size of the audience? Arnold, wouldn't you say that with all the publicity I've had – the coverage of the crashes, the clowning and my being banned, not to mention our automatic transmission – wouldn't you say that if I did race in Adelaide, the gate, and the TV audience, would go up twenty per cent?"

Arnold wrote some numbers down on a pad. "Five, ten per cent at the most, not twenty."

"It's worth thinking about."

"I'm not that cynical, Forrest. I'm not in this for the money. You know Alain; you know what it's like trying to deal with him."

"You could ring him."

Arnold stood up. He was a tall, thin, handsome man, greying at the temples. He dressed like a successful movie actor: baggy white cotton trousers, a soft yellow pullover, gleaming mahogany loafers to match his suntan and his aviator sunglasses. He'd come a long way since his scrap metal days. "One thing I'm not clear about is why Dave did it – what his motive was? You keep telling me that's part of a larger investigation which, I have to tell you, doesn't make me feel relaxed. But the thing that puzzles me is how it worked. You didn't really explain that."

The man from Special Branch who had sprawled lazily on the oatmeal sofa fished a phial of clear liquid from his jacket pocket. He got up and put in on MacIntyre's desk. "We ran a quick analysis on it this morning. It's mostly a transdermal medium, over ninety-nine per cent polyethlybiphemerol, which means that it is thin enough to penetrate the skin. The drug, as Dave told you, is LSD or lysergic acid diethylamide, to give it its clinical name. We're seeing it in the streets now in the form of a drug the kids call Ecstasy.

"As you may know, LSD is odourless, tasteless, colourless, and a single dose is so small it's almost invisible. A million 250-microgram doses would only weigh nine ounces. The liquid – of which this is a sample – that Dave used contained a very small dose, less than 100 micrograms. It wasn't enough to cause serious psychological trauma, but it was enough to affect Evers' perception.

"What makes this formula unusual is a small amount of a soluble polymer which I'm afraid we haven't yet been able to identify precisely. In any case, the polymer acts as a kind of thermostat. At skin temperature, the soluble polymer makes the formula too thick to penetrate the skin and the LSD has no effect. But raise the temperature 15–20 degrees Fahrenheit to the 120 degrees Fahrenheit or 48 degrees Celsius that a driver normally experiences inside his helmet, then the polymer expands sufficiently for the formula to penetrate the skin.

"Dave simply splashed some of the formula on Forrest's balaclava before a race, and since the LSD would take a little over thirty minutes to take effect, after the temperature inside Forrest's helmet had risen enough with the warm-up laps and the wait for the start, that puts us some five or six laps into the race before Forrest suffered mild hallucinations and impairment of his judgement. One other clever feature about this formula. After the race it would be virtually impossible to detect, even if you knew what you were looking for and where to look for it."

"This LSD is addictive, right?" Arnie had sat back down and was looking at the figures he'd written on his notepad.

"Not really. It's possible that for some people there could be some psychological dependence with heavy usage, but there is no evidence of that. In Forrest's case there is no possibility of addiction.''

"What did you say your name was?"

"I didn't."

Arnold picked up his phone and started to punch buttons on the built-in console. While he waited for the call to go through, an idea struck him. "Tell me, Dave, what made you change your mind? I'm just curious, but what makes you so co-operative all of a sudden? You in a rush to go to jail?"

The man from Special Branch answered for Dave. "Mr Spence is helping us with our inquiries and he is here on the understanding that Mr Evers will not prosecute."

"It's Arnie, is Alain in?" There was a pause. "Alain . . . Listen, I have some very good news for you . . . Alain. Listen . . . Yes, yes . . . I know, Alain . . . Listen . . . Listen . . . I want you to reinstate Forrest Evers." He held the phone back from his ear and winced for our benefit. We could hear Mafaison yelling in French on the other end.

"No, Alain; listen . . . I have proof . . . Absolutely . . . No, Evers was the victim . . . Victim, Alain. V.I.C.T.I.M. . . . It means someone was doing it to him . . . To him . . . Yes he's here in my office . . . And the police . . . No question . . ." Then he paused, looked down at the figures he'd written on his notepad and looked back at me and made a fist with his thumb sticking up. "Yes, I personally guarantee it. My personal guarantee, Alain . . . Yes, Alain, I know . . . Yes . . . Yes . . . Ste Chappelle at eleven o'clock . . . Fine, right after the service . . . No, no. Sure I'm free for lunch but it's your turn, I got the last one."

When he put the phone down he said there was an informal FISA meeting after the service for Michel on Saturday in Paris, and perhaps Ken would like to come with him. "What he wants is a statement that he can send privately to the team owners on why he's reinstating Forrest. Why don't you bring that with you, Ken? You heard I gave my personal guarantee. So if you crash again Evers, you're taking me with you."

"Don't tempt me," I said, grinning and shaking his hand.

I also thanked the man from Special Branch. "If you hadn't been here, I'd be watching the race on television."

"Well," he said, "it isn't everyday that someone leads you to two tons of cocaine. I felt I owed you something."

"What's happening with that? You making any progress?"

"You'll read about it in the papers I'm sure. Keeping that much cocaine under wraps is like trying to hide an elephant on a skating rink. Every policeman in Britain is claiming credit. But our little branch of Special Branch is up for a budget review, so who knows, I might even get a rise."

"What about Courtland? Is he still out there?"

"He's still out there. We did trace him to Paris. He took a train down to London and flew out from Heathrow to Charles de Gaulle. Then we lost him. Fifty-thousand passengers a day pass through there. So he may be headed for the Far East or New York or Chichicastinango for all we know.

"He obviously has financial resources and underground connections, so it wouldn't be difficult for him to get a false passport, credit cards, a beach house in Taiwan, whatever he wants. We alerted Australian immigration. But if he's travelling on another name you might just bump into him in Adelaide. And if you do, for God's sake, don't try to handle him on your own. He's not going to be best pleased he didn't kill you the first time. And now that you've tipped over his train set . . ." He let the sentence hang.

"I keep thinking you're going to tell me your name."

"It varies. Changes week to week, so I don't bother. What I can do, though, is give you this." He handed me a card with a telephone number. No name or address, just a number. "You can ring that anytime," he said. "Ask for Bob. Give us a buzz the next time you run into a couple of tons of the white stuff."

I drove the Aston back to the garage in Pembroke Mews and parked it outside. It was filthy and those godawful wire wheels that flex every time you go around a corner would take hours to clean.

I cleaned them.

I washed the whole car with cold water, no detergent, and wiped it dry with a chamois. I rubbed Classic wax into the finish and rubbed it off until the car glowed in the afternoon sun. I rubbed the leather inside with saddle soap. Vacuumed the carpets. Cleaned over, under and around every one of the seventy-two spokes in each wheel. I checked the oil and the tyre pressures. Then I backed it into the garage, took out the spark plugs and squirted upper-cylinder lubricant into the cylinders, replaced the plugs without their leads, spun the engine once and replaced the leads. I smeared the battery terminals with Vaseline, and put the jar in my pocket. Then I removed the high-tension lead from the coil and hid it on a shelf at the back of the garage so it wouldn't start even if a thief did break in. I set the alarm, then I stood outside and admired the car, its dark green colour and fared-in headlamps, its soft shapes and aggressive stance. Then I closed the doors and locked them. My father's car.

When I got back to the house Alicia was on the answering machine.

"Sorry you missed me when you rang, Forrest. I was on my way up to see if you wanted a home-cooked breakfast in my kitchen. Probably drove right past you on the A41. You're a pig of a housekeeper but I will not hear of you paying for it. Anyway, that room looked like a penal colony before you had your little party. It's the perfect excuse for Alicia to get busy and redecorate it with something a little more interesting. Like nude frescos on the plaster, Greek boys waving their willies; I'll think of something cheery. So look after yourself, darling, and if you see the old fart, kick him in the shins for me. You must tell me one day about what you do in my house while I'm away. You could invite me, you know. Byeeee."

I rang Nicky in Paris to tell her I'd arrive at Charles de Gaulle at nine.

"Oh, I am so happy you are coming. I will come and meet you and we can go to dinner, and maybe if we are late, you won't have to meet my horrible parents."

I packed a dark suit for Michel's memorial service, the one necktie I could find without stains, a pair of jeans, a pair of baggy trousers and a handful of socks and knickers out of a drawer. I added a pair of loafers, a toothbrush and my shaving kit. Then I stood in our old bedroom and took a last look around. My suits and sports jackets hung in a neat queue in my wardrobe, followed by a row of trousers hanging down. Pictures of Susan and myself on holidays and weekends lay unseen in the dresser drawer. My trophies were downstairs along with my books. Zilna could pack them sometime. And send them somewhere.

When the taxi arrived, I locked the front door and dropped the key into an envelope with Susan's "other" address. Then I walked to the red letter box on the corner and dropped it in. Goodbye. All the best.

Parisians named their main airport Charles de Gaulle, but they never call it that. They call it Roissy, after a village of 1,500 deafened souls crosshatched by the shadows of jumbos roaring in and roaring out. No doubt they call it Roissy out of respect for the Grand Old Nose who never would have allowed that confusion of concrete doughnut and plastic tubes to sully La Gloire de la France. I'd been going to Charles de Gaulle since it opened in 1974 and it never failed to impress me with its complication and irritate me with its confusion.

Riding up on an escalator inside one of the dozen clear plastic tubes suspended in the interior of the doughnut, it was easy to imagine there was a balding, pink-faced, British psychopath somewhere up above. Watching.

Miraculously my beat-up leather suitcase popped up on the right conveyor belt like an old friend and Nicky was waiting outside the opaque sliding glass door.

She'd lost weight and there were dark circles under her eyes, but she ran up to me and gave me a big hug and a smacker of a kiss and I realized how glad I was to see her. Her hair was cut short, shorter in the back than in the front, framing her huge blue eyes and her wide mouth like an ivory cameo in a black oval frame. She was wearing a black stretchy minidress that emphasised her long legs. And her flat chest, I thought to my discredit. I gave her a big hug, picked her up and swirled her around. "For a lady in mourning," I said when I put her down, "you look pretty good."

"It is almost over, the mourning, Forray. But please don't make a joke of me." She awkwardly tried to pick up my bag, but I shooed her away and she led us outside where her little black Renault 5 was being glared at by a gendarme. There was a sharp exchange of French too fast for me to understand and the gendarme went away grinning and muttering under his breath.

We were away with a chirp of tyres, swooped down the off ramps and onto the expressway into Paris. She drove with confidence and speed, slipping up and down the gears with the smoothness of a professional driver. Something Michel taught her, I thought. Then, as she passed a trio of slow-moving cars by driving at twice their speed on the verge, I thought maybe she taught Michel.

The car's interior was surprisingly plush: grey velour, thick carpets and a telephone. Among the extra dials there was a turbo boost gauge. "It's the only car for Paris," she said, shifting down for the off-ramp onto the Péripherique. "Yves St Laurent has the same. The suspension is very supple for the big bumps and it is very small so you can park. Also you don't mind when somebody mash it like they always do in Paris." We crawled along the never-ending jam on the Péripherique. "Listen, Forray, is it OK if I pick the restaurant? It is a special night for me."

The restaurant Nicole chose was L'Etoile du Bois, on a little street off St Germain. It was mirrors and mahogany and curving brass, with Edwardian paintings in art nouveau frames of busty ladies in seethrough gauzy gowns. All of it had that honey-glow which comes from a century of polishing.

"Belle Epoque," Nicky chirped over her shoulder as a waiter in a dinner jacket, black bow tie and long crisp white apron led us up the staircase that curved over the bar. The maître d' knew Nicky and greeted her with a kind of sad reverence ("Ah, Mademoiselle Marichal, I am so very glad you have come this evening," he said in courtly French. "We have your table"). And as he led us through the crowded dining room under the great stained-glass dome, and heads turned to watch, I realised that as Michel's lover she must have been in the newspapers and in the magazines, that she must have had to endure a grisly kind of celebrity for the past three weeks.

I had thought that she would be withdrawn and sad, but when she sat down on the tufted black leather banquette facing me, she gave me a dazzling smile. "I am so glad to be here with you. The first night Michel had enough money for a restaurant in Paris, he took me here. And always when we had a special occasion we came here.

"No. No, don't frown, Forray. We were very happy here and I want to remember the happy times with Michel before we say goodbye to him tomorrow. For me it's a kind of way of saying goodbye without sadness. We were like two children together. I knew him since I was fourteen in the convent. His mother was the chef and I seduced him when I was fifteen. We had wonderful times together; we shared everything, you know?"

I knew.

The waiter brought a silver ice bucket with a bottle of 1980 Möet et Chandon Dom Perignon. "Monsieur Dombravaulle, the manager, sends his compliments, Mademoiselle Marichal. And he hopes he is not intruding and that also he hope you will accept this tribute to yourself and Monsieur Fabrot and the very happy times we have had when you are here. If this is acceptable to Monsieur, that is," he added, directing a small bow of his head in my direction.

Nicky thanked him and he opened the champagne with a muffled pop. "You see? Michel was a happy time for me and I cannot spend my life under a cloud because we were together. Probably no one will understand why I want to be here, drinking champagne with you, but Michel would know. I was a child with him and that was my gift to him. After tonight I am not a child anymore."

So I broke all my rules and I sipped the finest champagne in the world with the smiling, laughing, beautiful girl with the dark circles under her eyes. She told me her Michel stories, how he was so solemn and had to win, and how she made him laugh. And I told her my Susan and Veronica stories, and the stories of the girls I knew when I was a boy.

We looked up from our coffee when we heard our laughter echoing and were surprised to see the restaurant was almost empty. It was just past one-thirty in the morning. "Good," Nicky said. "My parents will be asleep and we will not have to talk to them."

When Nicky pulled up in the forecourt in front of the stone mansion on the Rue Filles du Calvaire I assumed her parents had a flat in the building. But they didn't; it was their house. And of course they hadn't gone to bed; they had waited for their daughter to come home.

Her mother opened the cast-iron and glass door as we were mounting the steps. "Paul has gone to bed," she said in mild rebuke to her daughter, speaking English for my benefit. "So I am afraid," she said, breaking into a charming smile, "that I must open our door myself to welcome you, Monsieur Evers. Please do come in, we are quite honoured to have you as our guest," she said, holding out her hand. "Nicole has told us a great deal about you, but you neglected to say, Nicky, that he is quite so handsome." She had kept hold of my hand and inspected my craggy face at close range. "But you must let me put a compress on your cheek, Forrest. May I call you Forrest? It looks quite painful."

Nicky kissed her mother formally. "Mother," she said, "you are an outrageous flirt."

Nicky's mother was small and pretty, and her thin wrists and hands made her look frail. But she also had the original of Nicky's wide mouth and enormous eyes. Her light silky dress with its old-fashioned skirt swished as she led us down the hall to meet Monsieur Marichal. Obviously frailty had nothing to do with her being small or thin.

Nicky's father was in the corner of a dark room panelled with books up to the ceiling, staring into a green computer screen flickering with numbers. He rose to greet us and there was another formal exchange of kisses, one on each cheek, between father and daughter. He had a large head on a small body, his eyes sunk deep into his skull, and he stood back, inspecting me.

Nicky introduced us. "Father, may I present Mr Forrest Evers. Forrest, my father, Charles Chardenoux de Marichal."

"Charles, please," he said, with a surprisingly deep and resonant accent that was as much British as French. "Call me Charles. Actually call me anything you like, except Charley. They called me Charley at Oxford and I loathed the place for it. Now you ladies run on to bed, it's way past your bedtime, while I see if I can persuade Mr Evers to share a cognac with an old man." He had already taken hold of my elbow and was steering me towards a shelf with brandy snifters and a cut-crystal decanter glowing in the light. Brandy was the last thing I needed, but it was a night for breaking rules.

He poured two glasses, handed me mine then went over to switch off his computer. "Games I play on the Bourse," he said dismissing the machine with a wave of his hand. "Something to keep an old man occupied." He came back across the room to me, the parquet floor creaking as he walked and we touched glasses in a silent toast,

Following with the ceremony of swirling, sniffing and sipping. It was a very old, very beautiful champagne cognac that had the deep glow of dying fire.

"Nicole speaks very highly of you, so if you'll forgive me I feel I can be quite direct."

"She has not had an easy time."

"Exactly. Naturally I was quite desolated – I am quite desolated at Michel's death. I understand you were there and that he was a friend of yours as well, so I don't have to tell you how terrible his death was. But I would be less than honest if I did not confess that I also felt a sense of, what is the word, relief."

I nodded. It was a speech he had rehearsed. A speech, not a conversation. No comment required.

"It was not that his family is beneath ours. We are not so old-fashioned as that. But I think you must have been aware that he was not in any way her intellectual equal. I do not wish to interfere with my daughter's life. I doubt that I could if I tried. But she has a first-rate mind that may make her seem older and more sophisticated than she really is. She is nineteen, Mr Evers, and I hope you would agree that it is quite important that she attend university. It would be terrible to see her waste her intellectual gifts."

"Is that what she wants to do, go to university?"

"She has been accepted at the Polytechnique, which as you know is quite an honour. But no, at the moment her wish is to go with you to Australia."

"And you don't want her to go?"

"I passionately do not want her to go. And I particularly do not want her to go with another racing driver. You are married, I understand."

"Separated, but I don't see what that has to do with Nicole." I had been through too much to be patronised like a schoolboy.

He held up his hand, sensing my anger rising. "Please don't misunderstand me. I don't want her to go but, rationally, I must accept that it would be very good for her to be out of Paris for a while. The point I wish to make to you is that we value her very highly, more than anything. And I would ask you to please do the same. As a gentleman."

"She'll be in very good hands."

If he noticed the awful gaffe, he was too much of a gentleman to let it show.

He led me up the wide stairs, down a corridor and around a corner to a small room filled by a four-poster bed with the covers turned down. He wished me good night and disappeared down the shadowy corridor, his duty done. No doubt Nicky's room was in another wing on another floor, as far away as geographically possible.

I fell asleep naked between crisp linen sheets and slept until a small girl in a maid's uniform woke me with a cup of tea, the sun streaming in the window behind her, illuminating her like an angel.

# CHAPTER TWENTY-SEVEN

My spirit soars when I walk into a Gothic cathedral. They were built in a time when there was no question of the existence of God, a time when heretics were men who disputed the number of angels on the head of a pin. If it occurred to a man that there was no supreme being, he probably kept his mouth shut, fearing for his sanity and his head.

Pilgrims walked for days, even weeks, until the spires rose out of the landscape. Then, as they approached slowly on foot and on horseback, the whole impossible structure of the cathedral rose higher than any other building on earth. Higher than the new castles of the kings, or the towers of the warlords. Looming over the puny fortunes of men. Inside there would be an immense, soaring, gloomy space; the arches, like the spires, pointing up. Inside there would be incense, choirs singing, and the brilliant colours of the cathedral windows pulsing with the force of the living God.

Ste Chappelle is not a cathedral, it is a Gothic chapel. Still large, but smaller and easier to take in. It was a bright sunshiny day and the light inside Ste Chappelle pulsed with the colours from fifteen of the finest stained-glass windows in Europe.

In the front, bathed in the shafts of green and red and blue and gold, there was a group of small, broad-shouldered people, Michel's family; his mother and father, his little sister and two older brothers, cousins, aunts and uncles, and two ancient souls who must have been grandparents. They had dressed in their best suits and dresses before dawn and driven up from the Midi.

I was in the middle of the chapel, standing next to Ken. Nicky was three rows up, a head taller than her mother and father who stood on either side. Looking around I could see that the chapel was packed with people who had come to pay homage to a national hero – along with the tourists and the merely curious who had seen the crowd, heard the music and wandered in. Most of the teams had flown straight from Mexico from Adelaide, but here and there I saw the diminutive figure of a racing driver.

Marcel Aral, almost certainly the next World Champion, had flown his wife and two small children from their home in the French Alps. Carringdon, the drivers' spokesman, was standing next to Arnold MacIntyre and Alain Mafaison. Maurizio Praiano had flown up from his home in Almalfi. Luigi Prugno and Lucien Faenza had flown in Lucien's jet from Monte Carlo. Michael Barret and Allan Proffit had flown in from London. Huybrechts, still recovering from his accident at Spa, was leaning on crutches two rows behind me.

It was a simple, dignified ceremony. There had been a private, family funeral three weeks before in Michel's home village. This wasn't a funeral, it was a memorial, a ceremony for the family, friends and the public to celebrate a brave man as much as to share their loss.

The Archbishop of Paris was meant to have conducted the service, but he'd had an asthma attack, and his place in the pulpet was taken by a priest from Michel's village. He spoke softly, in an antique, courtly French. He had a round face and close-set eyes behind large round glasses that made him look like an owl.

"It is so easy to fail. Failure holds the hand of success. We reach for one and are embraced by the other," he said, his voice filling the chapel through loudspeakers mounted high on the Gothic columns. "Every achievement has its risks. But the worst failure is to do nothing, to let life pass by as if it were something else, apart from you. To be a spectator.

"Michel Fabrot did not fail. Like Icarus whose father made him wings, he soared over the heads of the rest of us at speeds we can imagine but cannot feel. Icarus flew too high, too close to the sun. The heat melted his wings and he fell back to earth, and died.

"But who of us can say how high is too high, too fast, too far? There are limits: God has limits we transgress at our peril. But if there are not men who test them, how will the rest of us mortals know where those limits are. How will we know where are the limits of life?"

After the ceremony the crowd milled around outside in the

courtyard, warmed by the sun. I said hello to the other drivers, feeling the relief we all felt that the ceremony was over and that it had not been for us. Feeling sad for Michel, and proud to have known him.

Mafaison came over to me and shook my hand, saying, "I am very glad Forrest, you are coming back to drive. Personally I never believed you would be so stupid as to take drugs, but of course it is my duty to protect the sport. So sometimes I must do things that are very unpleasant for me to do."

I had a hard time keeping a straight face because Arnold MacIntyre was behind Mafaison, making a face.

Gradually, Nicky and I moved towards each other through the crowd. She said goodbye to her parents, and her father and I shook hands.

"I have your word you will be a gentleman," he said, "and look after our little Nicole."

"You have my word."

Nicky was dressed in a long black dress and looked very tired and very pale. She slipped her hand in mine. "Let's go now, Forray, straight to the airport. As soon as possible."

As we were leaving, Ken's tall figure intercepted us. "I have a present for you, Forrest, to celebrate your return to racing." He paused, drawing himself up.

"Carbon brakes," he said.

# CHAPTER TWENTY-EIGHT

I couldn't catch her. I ran hard, my feet sinking into the soft white sand, but she easily kept her distance, her big feet flying, her long arms and hands flailing.

I fell face forward, exhausted, sweat pouring off me, and she turned around and came jogging back to me where I lay face down, the sun burning on my back. She made a noise of dismissal and contempt, like the French do, blowing air out of her pursed lips. "*Phhhhh*. What a poofter. You have your little run and when you come back you cannot even catch a little French schoolgirl." Behind her there was the roar, crash and hiss of the waves rolling in from Antarctica.

"I ran five miles." I said, gasping for air, feeling the dampness and the salt of the sea air in my throat. "It's not fair, you have feet like flippers and they don't sink into the sand. From now on I'm calling you Frog."

"Oohh, you are disgusting. From now on I'm calling you Cod, because you are such a cold fish." She kicked sand at me and ran off to dive into one of the big rolling waves, her diving silent in the roar of the waves falling onto the white sand. A schoolgirl disappearing. I rolled over on my back. Overhead the sky was a deep and perfect blue. I closed my eyes, feeling the warmth of the sun on my chest and the warm sand on my back. Monday, Tuesday, Wednesday, Thursday, Thursday afternoon. I should be at the track.

We'd left Paris late afternoon Saturday, stopped at Bahrain, changed planes in Singapore, and arrived in Adelaide on Monday morning. We'd sat side by side in the cushy first class seats like tired strangers, making meaningless small talk, asking unimportant questions, Michel and Beverly's deaths following us like our own shadows.

When we got through customs in Adelaide, I hired a car and

drove fifteen minutes out to Glenelg, on the beach. An hour later we were in our own beach house with twenty miles of white sand beach outside our deck. And separate bedrooms inside. We were in the sea before we unpacked, the icy shock of it washing away the film of grime from nonstop travelling, Paris to Adelaide. Then we'd gone inside and slept until sunset in our separate rooms. Just good friends. We both needed time to recover from our losses and our bruises.

Nicky was painfully thin, so I'd fed her a diet of big breakfasts, long lunches, steaks and wine, swimming and running, walking on the beach and sleeping in the sun. By Wednesday the dark circles were gone and she was tanned and lazy and you could no longer count the cords in her neck one by one. Apart from the food and the wine, I had the same diet, supplemented by a healthy dose of Dieter Kuebel's Swiss commando training regime. Run run, stretch stretch, run run, stretch stretch, run run run.

Nicole learned that the Petaluma and the Penfold's Chardonnay and Cabernet Sauvignon from the Barossa valley above Adelaide could be as fine as any wine she'd had in France. And I learned that you could get used to the local water.

Tuesday noon, we drove over to the Murray River and rented a houseboat. With a big steak, a sackful of fresh Aussie veggies, two bottles of Penfold's Grange Hermitage '76, we drifted down the clear cool river, swimming when we felt like it, sunning and snoozing when we didn't. In the evening after dinner she asked what had happened in Mexico and for the first time, I talked about it.

I told her how Beverly and I had felt so at ease and relaxed with each other, as if we'd known each other for years instead of days. About the day she lost the top to her bikini in the swimming pool, and about the night she disappeared. And I told her how Beverly died. I also told Nicole how, even though he had no connection, I blamed Courtland as much for Beverly's death as I did for Michel's.

"You are sure he killed Michel?"

"Certain. I'm sure he put a concentrated dose of the formula into Michel's aftershave, and from the way the accident happened I think Michel must have felt the effects all at once. He may have even been unconscious."

"And you think he will come after you here, at the race?"

"I know he will; I can feel it. There is something in the mind of a man like Courtland that makes him feel cheated, that makes him want revenge. Maybe it was his father bullying him, or his wife leaving him. Maybe he was weak in the first place. Maybe something else. I really don't care why.

"Whatever the reason why, that feeling of getting the short end of the stick is magnified a hundred times. It makes him feel that whatever he does, however monstrous, is justified. He has no sense of guilt. The joke is that whatever he does, it won't satisfy him. Nothing can satisfy him. He'll always feel cheated. However much money or power he has, it will never be enough. But, take it away from him like I've done, take away his money and his place in the world, and he will feel a thousand times worse. He'll be a real monster, head down, charging."

"Yes, well, revenge. I want it for Michel, I suppose, because I am still very angry. I remember I asked you for his head on a platter. But if I ever have it I am sure I will hate it and hate myself for wanting it."

"Beverly used to say that there is no such thing as revenge. That it's just a word we've invented for something we think we want. Anyway, whether you and I want it or not, he's coming. I've stolen his toy box of drugs and money and he's going to charge after me like a bull towards a red flag."

"But how will you be safe, Forray, from this formula he has? You know, a few drops on the skin. And this time I think he raise the dose very high."

I told her how and she laughed. "Oh that. I see that slippery stuff in the loo. I thought you have that for some sexual thing, maybe. I should have known better, you disgusting cold fish."

Sex had been coming up more often. Bumping into a beautiful sleepy girl in the kitchen in the morning, having coffee together, lazing on the beach, rubbing suntan oil on her long sinuous back, having long lunches and dinners and long walks on the beach in the moonlight. Cruising down the lazy river. The days had all the ingredients for a love affair but our souls were still too bruised to handle it. So we did what all wise and mature people do when something awkward shows up. We made it into a joke. We pretended that we found each other ugly, unattractive, repulsive.

"Nicky, you ever think of auditioning for a Popeye movie? If you tied your hair in a bun you could pass for Olive Oyl."

"Forrest, I used to think you were handsome. But now that the swelling in your cheek has gone down, you look like a goat. A hairy old goat."

At night we went to our separate beds.

"Good night Forray."

"Good night, Nicole." *Bonsoir*, Charles Chardenoux de Marichal. She was the ungainly and ugly French girl, I was the cold and ugly Englishman. And the more I saw of her and the more time I spent with her, the lovelier she became. That night on the Murray River I moored in a silent cove, out of sight. We stayed in our separate beds anchored to the past. The next morning, when we took the houseboat back, there had been a lot of accidental bumping and touching. A couple of extra microseconds of lingering, her hand on my neck, my hand on her hand.

I opened my eyes, lying with my back on the white sand, staring at the blue sky and thinking of the lovely curve of tummy sloping down . . . when she came back from her swim and startled me out of my reverie by shaking cold water all over me. I jumped up. "You see, you old cod, you are so cold, the water from the sea warms you up, brings you back to life."

It was our last carefree afternoon on the beach. "I've got to go to the track, Nicky. They need me to set up the car. And I want to see it and talk to Ken and Max and the crew."

"It's OK, codfish. Leave a lonely girl alone in a strange country with nothing but a bikini." Then she laughed. "Go. Honestly, I don't want to go. I don't want to see Ken and the crew. I don't want to see a racing car. And I don't want to see you driving one. The beach is very good, and I have a lot of work to do on my tan. When will you be back? For dinner, I hope?"

"For dinner, I hope."

Adelaide looked like the dream city of the 1950s, orderly and safe, laid out on a grid, wide streets. All of the front gardens in front of the tidy houses were absolutely perfect, the colours as bright as they are in childhood, every petal and every leaf standing out as if this was the day they were going to have their photographs taken.

All it needed to make Adelaide come alive was people. Where were they? It was as if they had built this wonderful city of parks on the river between the mountains and the sea and then they'd all gone home to Manchester or Tokyo to watch telly. The streets weren't absolutely empty. Over there, at the crossing, a lady and a dog were waiting. On the other side there was a man, walking, his long bent shadow following him against the buildings. But this was a city of a million people. Where were they? Then I realised it was only four o'clock in the afternoon. They were inside the buildings working, you lazy beach bum, Evers. Working for a living, you whinging, pommy dill.

Seen from the air, the track at Adelaide looks like a knuckled fist with the index finger pointing down towards the sea. The finger could also be described as sticking into a green pie since the finger is the part of the Formula One track that runs through Victoria Park racecourse where, normally, one horsepower thoroughbred horses canter round. Come Sunday our more noble, 700 horsepower thoroughbreds would reach 190 mph on Dequetteville Terrace. Where the city speed limit is 38.

There is a special feeling about the Australian Grand Prix. It's the last race of the year, the end of term, so it's a party to celebrate the year and to say goodbye. The old days of the mechanics getting drunk and chasing squealing girls down the streets are gone, but the spirits are definitely up. The Formula One rumour mills churn flat out with stories of drivers, mechanics and designers changing teams, with stories of next year's new superengines putting out double the horsepower, and superchassis made of superstrong and superlight materials that nobody's heard of yet.

As I drove across the track and into the pits, the teams seemed more colourful, busier and happier than at any other track all year long. Then, too, the Ozzies can be bonzer. Even if they do speak Strine. If they do something, they have a go. There's no hanging about, they do it headfirst. The track was a case in point. From the day it had opened in 1985, it was the best-organized track in Formula One. The only trouble is, you needed an extra set of brakes.

I drove around to the back of the pits, parked in the shade, and went in the back door of the Team Arundel pit garage. I was blinded for a moment because the late afternoon sun was streaming into the open garage from behind the pits straight stands. Then a tremendous bulk blocked the sun. When it said, "Hello, Forrest", and "Where the hell have you been, Evers?" I realised it was Ken and Max standing alongside each other.

I shook hands with Ken, and told Max I'd been swimming. Then I said hello to Bill Williams, as relaxed and confident in his new role as head mechanic as he had been as number two to Dave. I looked over Nigel Weith and Charles Laurence's shoulders, not wanting to interrupt their work, but glad to see them. We talked about Dave, and how sorry we were. "He must have been under terrible pressure," Bill offered and we were all glad to let it go at that. They seemed as glad to see me as I was to see them.

I congratulated Bill on being made head mechanic. "I hope you'll try to keep me on the track. I need all the help I can get."

"You'll get all the help you need," he said, grinning and relaxed. They'd been working flat out since dawn getting the car set up, but to look at their grinning faces you'd never know it. Bill told me Mexican customs had delayed all the cars almost a week, so all of the teams were in the same boat, a week behind schedule.

Then, before I climbed into the cockpit, he led me to the front of the car, saying loudly, "Hey Forrest, let me introduce you to our new mechanic, Larry Hutchins."

A pair of feet slid out from under the car followed by a dishevelled but compact and powerful man who had a habit of brushing his hair back with the back of his hand. "G'day. Pleased to shake hands with you, mate. Always admired your driving."

"Ken told me you used to work for Brabham."

"Yeah, right. When Jack and Ron had the team. I did the brakes and the donks."

"He means the engines," Bill translated.

"Glad to have you with us, Larry."

"We'll give it a go," he said.

"We're going to do better than that," I said. "We're going to be the best team in Formula One."

Ken grinned and gave Larry an affirmative nod of his massive

302

head. It was exactly what he felt too. To an outsider, looking at our tiny team, with just one car and no money, up against the big and powerful factory teams, that may have seemed like a dangerously romantic notion. We were outdated, outpowered and underfinanced.

But there is only one reason to race and that is to win. We weren't going to win that year and we knew it. But we also knew we had the technology to attract the kind of money that could make us competitive. I had almost blown it in Mexico, but if we could finish in the points on Sunday we could get the sponsorship we needed to win the world championship in two years. One year to build; the next to win.

From the end of the pit lane, in amongst the back markers and the also-rans, we were a sparrow shaking his claw at the eagles.

But there was no doubt in my mind, or in Ken's, that we could do it. And if Larry was going to come along with us, he would have to become one of the four best mechanics in racing, the other three being Bill, Nigel and Charles. Ken was the best team manager, Max was the best designer, and I was as quick as anyone.

Max took my arm. "Let me show you what we've been doing while you've been swanning around with the ladies in London." He led me over to the car. It was on set-up wheels which look like the wheels from Ben Hur's chariot. Set-up wheels make the car easy to roll around the shop and easy to work on; you can get to the brakes and the suspension. But they look antique on a sleek, high-tech Formula One car, as if the wheels hadn't been changed since they fed Christians to the lions.

Max bent over and pointed to the brake discs. "Here, you see? Carbon. You know about carbon-carbon discs?"

I knew about carbon fibre. Carbon fibre is to Formula One in the eighties what aluminium was in the sixties and titanium was in the seventies. The immensely strong tub which holds the driver and supports the engine and suspension is made from carbon fibre. Carbon-carbon is the same stuff, but tougher. Most of the Formula One clutches are now made of carbon, and most of the other teams had had carbon disc brakes for years. They were first developed for Concorde. Then Brabham introduced them to

Formula One in 1984. Max was going to tell me all about them anyway.

"They save us twenty kilos in unsprung weight," he said, trying to draw his stomach in, "and the coefficient of friction is much higher, so you'll notice a much easier and more sensitive pedal."

We would need the extra braking power. Adelaide chews brakes for breakfast. It's the toughest course on the circuit on brakes and on the closing laps its not unusual for half the cars to be limping around with almost no brakes at all. With Max's automatic transmission, I couldn't use the engine for braking, there was no shifting down, so more than any other car on the track, I'd need good brakes. But I couldn't resist teasing Max.

If anything he'd gotten even fatter. His T-shirt said WHY NOT TAKE ALL OF ME? and his yellow trousers were beginning to split their seam in the back.

"I don't know if I'll need them, Max, that engine has so little power, there's not much need to slow down."

"You drive so slowly it's hard to tell whether you're braking or accelerating," he snapped back, half-grinning.

Larry slid out from the car again. "It's an interesting process, how they make the little buggers," he said, standing up and wiping his hands. "Basically its a sandwich of carbon graphite cloth and carbon graphite structural fibres. They take a web of carbonized rayon and stick it in a methane gas furnace, and with carbon vapour deposition it gets covered with carbon atoms. Then they turn up the wick a bit and make it denser by impregnating the fibres with the carbon. It's all a bit secret and the whole thing takes weeks."

"Which is why it costs me slightly more than the Kohinoor diamond to equip us with a set," Ken said. "So try not to bash them first time round."

"You don't mean to tell me we've only got the four discs?" Carbon brakes were good, but they weren't perfect. I'd seen them explode.

"No, no, no" said Ken. "Certainly not. We have another set." One more set.

"'Allo, anybody home?" Marcel Aral, his small figure casting a long shadow stood in the doorway. "Forrest, I want to say to you personally, I am very glad you are back on the track again."

"Spoken like a World Champion," I said. "You have to finish, what, fourth to win the championship on Sunday?" I hoped he would be the next Champion. Out of all the drivers, I felt he was the most professional. And although I liked to feel that there was no one in Formula One faster than myself given equal cars, I had to admit that I had my doubts about keeping up with Marcel.

"Even better," he answered. "Just sixth. Even if I don't finish, Faenza would have to win to beat me, so I think I am OK; but naturally I would prefer to win the race. Tell me, I saw Nicole with you in Paris at Ste Chappelle and I hear she is with you. Is she OK?"

"She's getting better all the time. But she doesn't want to come to the track. Maybe you and Hélène would like to have dinner with us tonight?"

He shrugged the Gallic shrug. Atlas with the world on his shoulders. "No, we would love to. But you know, they don't let me alone." He pulled a little card out of his pocket. "I am leaving now to tape a TV talk show. Then, at six-fifteen, there is a radio programme with the mayor of Adelaide; at seven-thirty we have to be at some house for drinks with all the Renault car dealers in Australia; then there is a Goodway dinner where I am supposed to make a little speech. Tomorrow morning at eight there is another TV show. I think it is American, but I am not sure. I tell you, Forrest, when I sit in the car on the grid, I feel relieved. All I have to do is drive. I don't have to smile." He mimed an immense smile. "Give my love to Nicky. Maybe we will see her at one of these parties. Tell her I hope so." And he was off, a tiny, immaculate figure, his shadow trailing behind him, putting him on a pedestal.

When I got back to the beach house, Nicky was sprawled on a chair on the deck, reading a novel and watching the sunset at the same time.

"Oh, Forray, you are back so soon; I hardly notice you are gone four hours."

"I know. I was gone so long I almost forgot how ugly you are, Frogface."

She stretched and smiled, stood up and gave me a sisterly kiss. "Let's go someplace nice tonight, by the sea."

When we got back, the moon was beating a path to our door. Nicky put her arms around my neck and kissed me, her mouth still fresh with the wine.

I pushed her away gently. "Goodnight, Frogface."

"Good night, you hairy Cod." She pronounced it airy.

From my bedroom through the open door, I could hear the rise and fall of her breathing and, in between, the waves on the shore.

# CHAPTER TWENTY-NINE

Friday morning's untimed practice was a shambles.

Larry Hutchins told me seven times that the brakes should be warmed up before standing on them.

Max fussed over his automatic transmission, making last-minute adjustments, checking his computer read-outs, making clucking sounds like a bulbous mother hen. "Make sure it's warmed up plenty before you start driving it hard. You could do a lot of damage if you drive it quick right away."

And Ken told me what I already knew, that the surface was tricky and could change from lap to lap. "So take it easy at first."

I accelerated out of the pits and onto the track at 10 a.m. sharp, right at the beginning of the hour and a half untimed session. I wasn't in a hurry, but I knew I needed as much time as possible out on the track.

Adelaide is the best of the street circuits, but it is also the toughest. Much more difficult, I think, than Monaco. Monaco demands total attention for the whole circuit. There are no straights to speak of where you can relax for a moment and take a breather, and there is only one knife-line through the corners. The track is so narrow that if you stray off the line a few inches you can tear off a wheel, so you put yourself into a mindset and stay there.

But Adelaide is physically more demanding. It's hotter, the speeds are higher through the fast corners, and it's the longest race, lasting nearly two hours to do the eighty-two laps. The better I could learn the track, the smoother I could be and the quicker those eighty-two laps would pass on Sunday.

The pit straight leads into a chicane out of the horseracing track and onto Wakefield Road. Then it's right, left, right, left, right, through a series of open, 90-degree turns, which you have got to get just right at the entry to the first corner, get the car balanced or you're off-line and off the pace for the whole series. Most of the drivers stay in second gear for most of the switchbacks, alternatively standing on the accelerator and standing on the brakes. It was going to take me a few laps to get the entry speed exactly right because I didn't have the rise and fall of the engine to judge my speed. With Max's automatic, the engine speed stayed within a narrow range, however fast I was going.

After the last 90-degree right-hander, you get to open up a bit to around 165 on the Jones straight, brake hard down to around 120 mph for a sweeping turn into Brabham straight (Dequetteville Terrace in everyday Adelaide life), where you put your foot to the floor and see how fast it will go. Then it's stand on the brakes for a hairpin right, accelerate through a long looping left, through a couple of kinks and stand on the brakes again for the hairpin right leading back onto the pit straight.

Those two hairpins are the easiest corners on the track. Normally you'd get into first gear to go around them, and there is only so much trouble you can get into in them. Anybody can drive around a slow corner; it's the 150 mile an hour corners that separate the men from the boys. But those two corners are hell on brakes, and the brakes don't really have a chance to cool down before you're standing on them again and again through the switchbacks.

I did a cautious lap, feeling my way around, checking the gauges, letting the tyres, the transmission and the brakes warm up. The second time around I started to lean into it a little bit and the car wouldn't turn in. It just wanted to plough straight ahead and washed out in the corners. I thought at first it might be the tyres, that I hadn't heated them up enough.

Theoretically, with the carbon brakes giving us so much less weight out on the wheels, the car should have been more sensitive and give me more grip, not less. But the steering was mushy, and at speed it was like driving on ice.

There's always the temptation to try and overcome a handling fault by driving around it. Turning in earlier when you've got too much understeer, standing on the brakes harder and getting onto the accelerator earlier, driving over your head. But then the tyres overheat and lose their grip. No matter what you do you can only make a car go so fast before you bend it. By the time I'd finished my second lap I pulled into the pits.

I switched the engine off and climbed out of the car. "It's a mess," I told Ken and Max. "It's understeering like mad, and I have to be late getting back on the accelerator or it swings wide at the exit. It just doesn't have any grip at all. It just doesn't feel like the same car."

"It's not the same car," Max shouted over the screams of the other cars accelerating up through the gears out of the hairpin and up the pits straight. "We redid the whole suspension for the new brakes. There wasn't any time for testing. We'll reset it."

Nigel, Larry, Bill and Charles swarmed over the car with Max supervising. Normally it would have taken them less than five minutes to reset the front and rear wings, adjust the front and rear anti-roll bars, and install soft springs at the front, but a nut got cross-threaded on the anti-roll bar and they had to replace the whole unit. It shouldn't have happened, not at the end of the season. But the mechanics were as nervous as I was and I spent the first half hour of the session in the pits.

By the time I got back on the track the car was cold again and I needed another lap and a half to warm up. And another lap to tell me the car was better, but it was still a mess, loose on the turn-in, its rear end wanting to slide wide.

So the morning went like that: two laps out on the track, and fifteen laps in the pits. I got in two good hard laps in the last five minutes of practice, but the sequence through the switchbacks wasn't as smooth as it should be. It was me as much as the car. I missed the rhythm of shifting the gears, and the car was rolling much too much.

We weren't the only team having trouble getting started. Maurizio Praiano blew an engine on the Danielli. Lotus were having electrical problems, and Prugno's Ferrari was locking its right front wheel. Alberto Brava spun off at the top of the Jones straight and mashed in the front of his Scorese. Allan Proffit had a sticking throttle and grabbing brakes on his March. And Cavelli got on the throttle too soon coming out of the pit hairpin and spun his Ferrari in front of the pits, flat-spotting all four tyres.

I thought the roll and mushy feeling could be a duff front shock absorber so, in the hour and a half we had before the timed session in the afternoon, the crew changed the front shocks.

Qualifying is more dangerous than the race itself. There's a big spread between the fastest drivers and machines and the slowest, as always. The situation is exaggerated by having drivers on the track who are doing a warming up lap, drivers doing a flying lap and driving at the absolute limit of their machine and their ability, and drivers on a cooling down lap after their fast laps.

In the middle of this warming up, cooling down and kamikaze do-or-dying, there is another flock of drivers testing suspension settings, brakes or trying a few laps with an airfoil turned up or down a notch. It's like standing on the stage of a movie theatre, shouting "fire" and then trying to get out the door first.

In America, in their Indycar series, only one car at a time is allowed on the track during qualifying. It drags out the qualifying sessions, but it's so much safer it makes the Formula One system look like dodgem cars at a fairground.

The green light went on for the Friday afternoon session on the dot of one o'clock and I followed Aral out of the pits to do a warm-up lap. We went around together, nose to tail, and then, coming out of the pits hairpin and onto the straight we both booted our cars for a quick flying lap before the course got crowded. Aral took off like a scalded cat in the McLaren. My engine made a sound like chinese firecrackers, but I'd already passed the entrance to the pits so I cruised around, keeping out of the way of the field as they went charging by, my engine popping and spluttering.

When I pulled into the pits, Aral's time was posted on the electronic board: 1m 18.347s; close to the qualifying lap record. The best I'd done in the morning was 1m 25s. If we didn't do better than that, we wouldn't even be at the back of the grid. We wouldn't even qualify.

Bill changed the black box, the electronic computer that does everything but pat the driver on the back. It's the most complicated bit of electrics on the car, the easiest to replace, and it's usually what's wrong when there's an electrical fault. Having lost ten minutes, I pulled back on the track, did a warm-up lap, came into the pit straight, trod on the loud pedal and the engine went *thwawp pop bang*. Another lap, and this time Bill traced the fault to a partially clogged fuel injector and a loose spark plug lead.

Out once again. The car felt better, much more neutral and taut in its handling. When I came onto the pit straight I thought this time it has got to work, and it did, accelerating cleanly and then braking hard for the chicane. Once they'd warmed up, the carbon brakes felt good. They really were an improvement; much lighter and more sensitive and they had tremendous power. It was going to take me a few laps to get the most out of them.

Margoles held me up coming out of the east terrace, the last left-hander of the switchbacks, and I felt there was plenty of time to come, plenty of places in the switchbacks where I could find a tenth of a second here, a half-second there. Once I got the feel of the new brakes, that should be worth a couple of seconds. There was plenty of time that I could take off my lap times.

In the middle of the Jones straight I moved over to the left to pass two slower cars, Barret in front in the Lotus and Jose Montalvo in the pretty little Camilla.

All drivers in Formula One racing hold a Super Licence issued by FISA. Which means that the governing body of Formula One thinks that all of the drivers out on the track are sufficiently skilled and experienced to be out there in the middle of thirty 700-horsepower machines trying to get to the finish line first. Which means that Montalvo should know enough to look in his mirrors before pulling out to pass. But he didn't and I had to go off the track to keep from running up his backside.

I thought it was going to be all right. I had two wheels on the track and two off but I knew if I kept my foot down I had enough speed to get past Montalvo and back onto the track before the fast right turn onto the back straight. I had to get back on the track, because having your two outside wheels on the outside curb is no way to go around a 160-mile-an-hour curve.

It would be close, but I had time to make it. Apparently, when Montalvo finally noticed me alongside him, going past, it startled him and he lurched toward me. Anything is better than touching wheels at that speed, so I twitched left and went completely off the track.

When things go wrong at high speed, the world goes very quiet.

I kept my foot down. The surface was too loose for braking and I didn't want to upset the delicate balance of the car. Turning gradually, I managed to get the car back on the track. Unfortunately, as soon as the right wheels got back onto the hard surface the car started to spin and there was nothing I could do but go along for the ride. The car spun twice, went off the track again, and tore off the left front corner on the Armco in front of Brabham grandstand.

I wasn't hurt but I was mad. Montalvo had let his mind wander for a fraction of a second, so my car was wrecked. And so were my chances of qualifying this afternoon. If we didn't qualify for the race, the chances of our keeping our current sponsors, let alone pick up new ones, for next year were sweet fuck all. Later a journalist told me I shook a fist at Montalvo when he drove past on the next lap. Montalvo probably didn't see that either.

The long walk back to the pits settled me down. I needed another crash like I needed another ex-wife. Fortunately it had happened in front of a few thousand spectators, so there wouldn't be any question of its being my fault. Except. Except maybe I shouldn't have been so close to Montalvo. He was inexperienced. Maybe I should have expected him to do something stupid. Maybe Formula One cars should be equipped with turn signals.

When I got back to the pits Ken asked what had happened and I told him.

"Doesn't sound too bad. As long as the tub isn't damaged we should be able to rebuild it. Throw on a new front suspension and a new set of discs, and we'll be set for tomorrow morning."

"A new set of discs? Does that mean we'll have to qualify and race on the same set?" I asked.

"Well, they're all different. Fronts are different from the rears, right side different from the left. And like Ken said, we've only got the one extra set." Larry had joined Ken and me at the pit wall, watching the cars go by.

"Ken, you can't be serious. I can't qualify and race on one set of discs. You can't use the engine for braking with the automatic. One set of discs may not last the race as it is."

"Well, I'm afraid – "

"Afraid, bullshit. What kind of word is that? Larry, who makes our discs? Girling, CI, AP?"

"AP. But I don't know if they'll have the .9 inch discs Max specified."

"Look, Larry," I said. "Go down the pit lane and find the AP rep. If he doesn't have a spare set in his back pocket, have them sent from London. Hire Concorde. And if you can't do that, scrounge a set off one of the other teams. One of them is bound to have an extra set that we can use. It's all right, Ken, I'll pay for them," I said. "You can pay me back later," I said under my breath. It was one thing running a team on a shoestring. But there were some things you couldn't do without. Like shoestring.

Larry was back in fifteen minutes with the AP rep. He had black wavy hair, a Manchester accent, and a bulldog face that looked like it had been run into a wall. His T-shirt said STOP THE WORLD.

"Right. I can't match the compound, but we've got a newer one that Ferrari and McLaren are using. Lasts better in this heat. 'Course you'll have to change all four to get them to balance. And I expect your front caliper's a mess. I can let you have one of the titanium piston ones for uh . . ." He looked off into space, then opened his briefcase and showed us some numbers that looked like the price of a new house in Adelaide.

"How extraordinary," Ken said. "That's precisely the cost of a decal on the front of the car."

"I'd have to check with London. How big a decal? Where? And does that include a badge on Evers' driving suit? 'Course any deal would be linked to how you qualify and how you finish, and I'd still need cash up front."

I left them to do their deal, wondering how Montalvo would feel if he had had to pick up the tab.

Just before the end of the practice session, Aral had qualified first, with Faenza and Cartablanca just behind. Then, with just a minute and a half left, Lucien Faenza went out in the Lotus and put in a brilliant 1m 17.994s for a new qualifying lap record. Team Arundel hadn't qualified at all.

When they brought the car back to the pits, swinging from a tow truck crane, the damage was worse than I'd thought. The front wheel had crushed the side pod, mashing the fibreglass body and crushing the radiators. It could be fixed, but the mechanics would be up most of the night.

At nine, when I was leaving the garage, Bill called out to me. "Hey Forrest, did you see this?" He brought my helmet over to me and showed me a faint tread mark on the top. When the wheel was torn off it must have passed over my head, touching just enough to leave a print. I'd never felt it, but if it had been just a little lower, say an inch, I might never have ever felt anything again. "Drive on the track, not on your head," Bill said cheerfully.

When I got back to our beach house, the lights were all on and Nicky was out on the deck, blazing. It was a warm evening and the breeze was puffing out her loose silk shirt.

"Damn you, it's not fair. When you don't come back I don't know what happen. Maybe something terrible, maybe you are in hospital. Why don't you call, say something? You know how to make a telephone call, you pick up the receiver, punch the buttons. It's not so much trouble."

We went to a restaurant we'd found where the fish was fresh and the waves rolled silently beneath the dining room window. Nicky was right; it was thoughtless not to ring her. The sport makes so many demands on you that you forget that there are other people out there.

I told her about my accident and wished I hadn't. It had been a light and easy evening until then. Nicky had cheered up and was planning places we might go after the race, "If of course, you old cod, you think maybe a little holiday with Nicky would not be too terrible." After I told her she seemed to lose her spirit and her appetite, leaving a big swordfish steak almost untouched. "No, no coffee," she said. "Maybe we could just go back."

When we got back she took my hand and led me through the house, out onto the deck. The moon was up, full and low on the horizon. I went to the railing and turned, and Nicky put her arms around me and clung to me. Her oval face turned up to me, her large eyes shining in the light.

"Forrest, I want us to make love tonight."

I started to push her away. "Nicky, this isn't a good idea."

She refused to be pushed away and moved against me. "You are so stupid." Then she did move away and stood beside me leaning over the rail, staring out at the dark sea and the dancing gold coins spilling from the moon.

"Your father – " I started, but she cut me off.

"My father is a liar," she said with a ferocity I didn't expect. "I know him. He give you some noble reason never to touch me, make you think you must protect me. But you don't know what a terrible snob he is. He thinks you are not good enough to kiss his daughter. He hated Michel for the same reason."

"Not that it makes any difference, but my family – "

"He doesn't give a shit about your family. You are not French. End of story."

"Look, Nicole, you are only nineteen."

"Did he tell you that? I am twenty. My father tells everyone I am younger than I am so he can hang on to his little girl." She turned and stood up to face me.

"What about university? Your father seemed very anxious that you should go."

"What about it? I have been three years at the Polytechnique; I left to be with Michel. I will go back in January. That is what I want to do. It's all arranged. Don't worry about me, I could not stand to hang around outside these stupid racetracks and wait for the phone to ring."

"I think you may be overreacting a little, Nicky. You've had a rough time."

"Oh you mean I am vulnerable now. You think I still grieve, maybe. You think the patient fall in love with her doctor?" she said, angry. "Sometimes you are so patronizing. And so stupid. Do you really think I am such a little girl? Well, maybe I am, a little. So what? Everyone has a child who lives inside. But I know what I lost when Michel died, and I know that you could, maybe tomorrow or maybe the next day, not come back."

"Nicky, the risk really isn't that great. The chances – "

"Don't tell me what the chances are; I know what the chances are. And don't tell me it can't happen. I saw it happen, to Michel." Then she softened and moved close to me again. "I know what I feel for you, it is very strong, and I am very much frightened I could lose you. But, even if something terrible did happen, I would feel glad that we had made love, that we were together."

"Nicky you are very beautiful and I am very fond of you. And

315

God knows, I am powerfully attracted to you. But I did tell your father . . ."

"What did you tell my father?" she whispered in my ear. "That you would not make love with me?"

"I told him," I said with some seriousness, "that I would be a gentleman."

She giggled. "You English are incredible. Doesn't a gentleman make love with a lady who is in love with him?"

A gentleman does.

We went into her room, with its big open window looking out over the beach and the moonlight making us look ghostly. We spent a long time kissing, and enjoying the wonderful release from the strain of not kissing and not touching. I took off her blouse and she unbuttoned the buttons on my shirt one by one.

Her breasts were a delicious surprise, pink in the light. She was terribly sensitive and soft, shuddering at the slightest touch. But she was not shy and she made a great fuss about "ripping my trousers off".

"Buttons?" she said. "What kind of English school boy wears trousers with buttons? I am not so sure now, Forray. Maybe you are too young for me."

"Those are the trendiest trousers in Paris. I know because that's what they said where I bought them."

"Well it's very difficult. I think you buy the wrong size; your cock make them too tight for you. Nicky the jungle woman rip them off." And she did.

Her loose black silky trousers came off easily. And when I took her little white panties off I kissed her ankles and her strong calves, the inside of her knees, and the inside of her thighs.

In that light her eyes seemed even larger. She drew me to her with surprizing strength, her long legs and arms holding me so tight I wondered for a moment if she were frightened. Her soft mouth was delicious, and sweet, kissing me again and again. She kissed my mouth, my chest, my stomach and my cock. I drew her face back up to me, and kissed her again and we lay still, kissing for a long time; listening to the sea.

After a while she began to move to the slow time of the surf, a deep and slow rhythm that, once she started, she could not stop. I

316

rolled over her, and Nicole's long slender fingers went around my cock and she guided me in a little at a time, pulling back, pushing deeper, pulling almost all the way back, the tip just touching, then back in again. We moved with the sea, wave after slow wave, and we had all the time in the world.

We slept and when I woke up Nicky was lying against me with her face snuggled into my shoulder and her arm and leg lying across me. I took her face in my hands and kissed her mouth, waking her. She smiled, kissed me and I rolled her over onto her stomach, massaging the cords of her neck, her long back and soft bottom. I bent to my task, kissing her as I went, taking the big muscles of her legs in my hands, kneading them until she was as soft as butter. Then I ran my hands and tongue lightly over her, brushing and kissing until her breathing deepened and she turned over, pulling me to her. I teased her, massaging, brushing and kissing her breasts, following the soft rise and fall of her stomach down to her thighs, the way I had kissed her back, taking a long time, until she began to move, lifting herself to me.

"Forray," she said in a hoarse little voice, "you are horrible to me. If you do not stop this and come inside me now I will scream."

I took her bottom in my hands and lifted her pussy to my mouth and gave Nicole a long, slow, circular lick and she screamed and laughed at the same time.

When I was on my hands and knees over her, I put my right hand under her bottom and pulled her up to me, slipping inside her with astonishing ease. Nicky's long, supple and strong legs wrapped around my back and her arms held tight around my neck so she was completely off the bed. Then she began to buck like wild.

"Wait," I said, kissing her just behind her ear. "Wait." With me deep inside her and her arms and legs around me clinging tight I rose up from the bed and carried Nicole out of the bedroom and out onto the deck. Over her shoulder the moon was gone and on the edge of the black sea there was a rim of light from the dawn. And we began to move again like dancers to the roar of the sea.

# CHAPTER THIRTY

Some automotive journalists (who should know better) and even a few drivers (who should know) have advanced the theory that fast cars, and especially Formula One racing cars, are a substitute for sex.

If there is any coincidence between racing cars and sex, it isn't just coincidental, it's hilarious. To those poor shrivelled souls who believe there is a substitute for sex, I offer my condolences. The sun had come up bright and full and Nicky was in the kitchen squeezing oranges and making coffee. I was standing on the deck smelling the calm sea air and the coffee, and thinking how good it felt to be alive. Nicky came out bearing a tray clattering with breakfast.

Saturday's qualifying went far better than Friday's. My reflexes felt sharper and I felt I could see with greater clarity at speed, picking out the markers in the distance and reading them at 165 mph.

We spent the morning session, tuning the chassis, balancing more downforce against the loss of speed on the straights. As the chassis got better, I began to use the brakes more, going deeper into the corners and braking harder. I also found that I could get on the throttle sooner. Max's automatic laid down the power so smoothly that I was using the overlapping technique I'd used in Mexico, rolling on the accelerator while I was rolling off the brakes. Making the transition from braking to accelerating fluid and easy within a tiny frame of time.

In the afternoon I qualified twelfth, in the middle of the grid, with a time that was just about average for the field. Average in Formula One stinks.

But I hadn't had a clear run in my qualifying laps; there was always someone in the way. It was frustrating being in the middle of the field. I knew that with a clear track I could have taken at least two seconds off my time. I was fast enough to have been on the second row. All I had to do was prove it.

I had dinner with Ken and Ruth and Coleman's Australian sales force of six. "Sell English wool in Oz, mate, and you could sell condoms to the Pope."

"Ho, ho."

I excused myself and left before coffee, saying I had to rest up for the race. They politely said they understood. Ken glared. I was going to have to work on my public relations.

When I came back to the beach house, Nicole couldn't wait to show me the Adelaide newspaper. The local coverage of the Grand Prix had been so heavy I worried that people might be sick of the race before it started. I was certainly sick of reading about myself.

"Can't it wait?"

"No. No, it can't wait."

There were two news items: In the business section there was a short piece about the international businessman Sir Thomas Castleman rescuing Courtland Mills, UK, from bankruptcy. Castleman was assuming total control of the assets for a nominal sum, undisclosed. And in the international news there was a small item about the record seizure of two tons of cocaine in Liverpool. The largest ever in Europe. Police were pursuing their enquiries.

I felt like the matador holding the red cape. Waiting for the bastard to make his charge.


Race day was sunny clear and hot.

"You will call me right after the race? As soon as you can get to a phone?"

"As soon as I can get to a phone."

"Promise?"

There were 127,000 people in the stands and lining the fences to see the half-hour warm-up from 10 to 10.30. Every one of them held a ticket stamped, along with the price, "Motor Racing is Dangerous. It is a condition of admission that all persons attending the event do so entirely at their own risk."

Around the world, ninety six million, three hundred thousand people would watch the race on television. Whatever numbers

Arnold had written down in his office, I was willing to bet they were too small.

But I wasn't worried about money or spectators, I was worried about brakes. I did ten good laps with full tanks and when I came back into the pits, the brakes were blazing hot.

"Ken, we've got to change them."

"We did just change them. We changed them Friday night for Saturday's qualifying and we changed them again last night for the race. That's three sets, do you have any idea what that costs?"

"Ken, you can see the wear, and that's just ten laps at nine tenths. The race is eighty-two laps. I don't want to start with a ten-lap handicap."

Poor Ken. He knew and I knew that it was entirely possible that somebody could drive into me at the start. That the engine could die on the first lap. That a hundred things could go wrong and we would never be in contention anyway. And he really didn't have another £10,000, let alone £10,000 to spend on my brake discs. He spent it anyway.

There were hours to kill between the end of the warm-up and the beginning of the race. I killed them by going to the mobile home behind our pit, shutting the door, pulling down the shades and lying down. Outside I could hear the PA system blaring, the roaring of racing engines as the supporting races came out of the pits and onto the track and back in again. I could hear the air show, with low-flying jets and the whirr and whine of acrobatic flying. And yet it all became farther away, less important and less real. I was emptying my mind of all thoughts, even of Nicky and the little man with the pink rubber ball for a head.

When Ken knocked on the door to say it was time to get into the car I was as relaxed and as at ease as I had ever been. I went into the loo and rubbed my face and hands with cool clear jelly that Nicole had thought was for sex. I put on my flameproof Florelle underwear and socks and zipped myself into my driving suit, put on my earplugs, stuffed my Florelle balaclava and my driving gloves into my helmet and went out into the blazing sunshine. There was a huge crush and I had to push my way through. People were reaching out to touch me, wishing me luck, but they appeared to me almost as through a screen door, on the other side.

320

The car looked gorgeous, gleaming blue and white with silver Coleman Florelle decals along the side. I pulled on my balaclava, helmet and gloves, they shoved the starter into the back of the transmission, the engine came alive with a scream and I was off, twelfth in the procession motoring around the track to take our place on the grid.

Ten minutes later I had my helmet and balaclava off and Larry was holding an umbrella over me to keep the sun off. The tyre warmers were on and Ken was bending over the car talking to me but I wasn't taking it in. There were eighty-two laps to pass eleven cars in front of me. Plenty of time. You can't win a race on the first lap, the great Jackie Stewart says, but you can lose it. My strategy was simple. Move up. Keep out of trouble. Finish in the points.

I was taking nothing in. I needed nothing and wanted nothing. Not even the wonderful three-dimensional wobbling in red shorts and no knickers that floated by could engage my interest. So I didn't see the flash of gold so much as sense it. I thought of the black mamba snake that hides in trees in Africa, the one whose fangs squirt a powerful gush of poison into its victim's eyes, blinding him.

What I saw was a glint, an open sleeve, and on its way, in midair, a stream. I was too late to move; I just had time to close my eyes. The stream splashed on my face, feeling cool in the sun. When I opened my eyes a fraction of a second later, he was gone.

I closed my eyes again and went back to the last frame – the glint from the gold spikes on his ring, the spurt of colourless liquid in the air – and concentrated on what I'd seen. In the background, lying inside the circle of his gaping sleeve, a small circle of light. A tube? A clear plastic tube? Did he have a rubber bulb hidden out of sight, under his arm I wondered? Or a plastic bladder in his pocket to squeeze? It didn't matter.

Ken stood up. "Good lord, what the hell was that? Did somebody spit? Spit on you? Who, in God's name? Here let me wipe you off." He started dabbing at my face with his handkerchief. Only Ken, I thought, would have a linen handkerchief.

"Don't worry about it," I said pulling my face away. I didn't want him dabbing at it. "It doesn't matter. It'll dry in a minute."

The five-minute horn sounded and I pulled on my balaclava,

helmet and gloves. Then three minutes and every one except the team members holding the starting motors and the race officials left the grid. At one minute the engines were started again. Then thirty seconds, then the green flag and we went around one last time, in starting order, no passing allowed, following Marcel Aral on the pole.

We formed on the grid again, the red light went on, and twenty-six engines were brought up to a screaming rage; 18,000 horsepower starting to overheat and ready to explode, all of the drivers knowing that once the red light went on there would be at least four but no more than seven seconds before the green light came on and all hell broke loose. I felt relaxed, feeling easy. The green light came on, and the world exploded in a roar of heat and light. Rather than try to fight my way up the middle, I shot outside on the pit side, the automatic transmission feeding the power so smoothly I passed four cars before the first chicane. A puff of smoke in my mirror told me that someone behind me had gone into the pit wall in the mêlée of the start. Couldn't tell who; it didn't matter.

Being on the outside, away from the pits gave me the inside position going into the first corner, so even though I was way off the line and had to creep around it, I held my position going into the switchbacks. Eighth. Up ahead the leaders were screaming down Jones straight. We went single file through the switchback, one by one, holding each other up. Good little boys. Well, there is only one line through, no point getting pushy. Relax, enjoy the ride.

With Jones straight came an awful truth. The car was simply too slow. I was able to catch up on the corners but the other cars walked away from me on the straights. They could easily pass me on the straights but it was almost impossible for me to pass on the corners. Halfway down Brabham, Margoles and Proffit went by me. Tenth.

Fuck.

They both held me up in the hairpin at the end of the straight. I got alongside Margoles on the exit into the long left that curves around the back of the pits, and squeezed by him and held the lead around Foster's, the slightly more open hairpin leading into the pit straight and the start/finish line. Again my exit was faster and I crossed the start/finish line a length ahead of him. Nineth. Not too bad. Eighty-one laps to go.

The chicane on the end of the pit straight is sharper than it looks. I once described what it feels like when somebody asked the old chestnut at a dinner party.

"Forget speed," I said. "As long as you are in control you are far too busy and concentrating too hard to feel much speed. But you do feel G-forces."

"G-forces?"

"Lie down on your left side on top of a cliff with your head hanging over the edge of the cliff. Tie a rope around your head, and hang a bowling ball from the end of the rope. Now get a ten-year-old child to hang onto the bowling ball and bounce. That's what it's like going through a fast right-hand corner.

"If the fast right turn is followed by a fast left, cut the rope, switch over to your right side in a half or quarter of a second, with your head again hanging over the side, tie another rope around your head with another bowling ball and bouncing child on the end of it and you have some idea of a fast switchback."

Rational decisions under these circumstances are not always possible. But they are necessary, because along with the stereo bowling balls and the vibration and the noise and the vague little signals that tell you how much adhesion you have left and whether you are about to go flying off the track, you may have an angry Venezuelan alongside you who thinks you are blocking his entrance into the corner. He thinks that because you are. Even though Margoles was faster down the straight, I wasn't going to let him get by me and hold me up through the switchbacks. So I shut the door on him. And Proffit held me up going through the switchbacks.

They both passed me on Brabham straight again and I realised my problem was twofold. I was at least half a second a lap faster than they were, maybe more. But unless I got past both of them and stayed there I was going to be forever in nowhere land.

Questions nobody ever asked dept. "Who came in nineth in the Australian Grand Prix?"

My other problem was that I wasn't driving my race. I was using up my brakes and my tyres and going too slow. Either I had to get around both of them and stay there, or ease up and wait for some of the cars ahead of me to fall off and hope to get in the points through attrition. I put my foot down and urged the old slug forward.

When Margoles went by I nipped in behind him and caught a tow, slipstreaming, letting his car punch a hole in the air and letting mine get sucked along in the vacuum behind. Slipstreaming is fine for straights, but it can be very tricky in fast corners because the car behind loses downforce. A corner you were able to take almost flat out on the last lap will feel like its coated with ice when you're slipstreaming.

When Margoles started to brake, I pulled out and went past him into the hairpin. Then I hounded Proffit through the long sweeping left, staying behind him even though I could have passed him. As we entered the pit straight, I slipstreamed Proffit, catching the free ride, outbraked him into the chicane and went into the switchbacks. Eighth. Eighty to go.

Now it was my race again. Over the next few laps I pulled away from Proffit and Margoles a half-second to a second a lap. I was also able to go easier on my brakes, braking earlier and lighter, braking all the way into the apex of the turns and putting my foot down on the throttle before my foot was off the brake. Just like they tell you not to do at all the racing driver schools.

On lap eight I saw Ian Norcross getting out of his McLaren parked up against the fencing on Wakefield Road. Seventh. Seventy-four laps to go.

Prugno's Ferrari was about 100 yards ahead, the last of a group of three cars but I couldn't tell what the others were. I judged I was gaining around ten yards a lap. What they took away on the straights, I more than took back on the turns.

By lap fifteen Faenza had dropped out with a blown engine. This meant I was now sixth and in the points, and that whatever Aral did he was the new World Champion. It also meant that up front, where I couldn't see, the pace might ease up a bit.

Two more laps and I was right behind Prugno. It was Cavelli in the other Ferrari who was just ahead of him, with Cartablanca in the Danielli leading the trio. I waited behind them for two laps, planning my move. I didn't want to wait too long. Prugno had been dropped by Ferrari for next season and he would be anxious to prove that he was quicker than Cavelli. I wanted to get past both of them before Prugno did anything crazy.

On lap nineteen I slipstreamed Prugno down the long Brabham straight, a little over 190 mph, and when Prugno started to brake, I went out alongside both the Ferraris and into the hairpin first. I stayed close to Cartablanca, and tried to slingshot past him at the end of the pits straight but he cut me off. Fourth. Fantastic. I felt terrific.

Lap twenty-one: I started to move left at the end of the pit straight, then moved left, passing Cartablanca and shutting the door on him. Into the land of the bowling balls, the switchbacks. Third. Where I should be, go for second. Go go go.

The car felt better and better as it shed weight, burning fuel. I really had the switchbacks down now and I flowed through them like a river. Passing the pits on lap forty-four Ken's board showed I was twenty-five seconds behind Praiano and thirty-five seconds behind Aral. Aral was probably just cruising, keeping ten seconds up on Praiano. I had almost half the race to catch Praiano in the Danielli. I would need some luck to catch Aral.

On lap sixty-three I got some luck. I had been pulling in on Praiano about half a second a lap, so I was about fifteen seconds behind him when his gear linkage baulked, he missed a shift at the end of Brabham, stood on his brakes and his carbon disc exploded, sending him spinning off the track and out of the race. Second. Twenty-five seconds behind Marcel; nineteen laps to go.

On the next lap Aral pulled into the pits for fresh tyres. I think they thought they had plenty of time to change rubber and get back out on the course before I came around. And they did. But when Marcel pulled out of his pits, one of the mechanics from the next pit tripped and stumbled into his path. Marcel stopped the car dead and it stalled. By the time they got it started again, I was fifteen seconds in the lead and disappearing into the sunset, with eighteen laps to go.

Not that I felt confident. Marcel was a great driver and his car was on fresh tyres and fully capable of hauling me in at a second a lap. But I did feel like the king of the world. Going down Brabham straight at 185, leading the Australian Grand Prix, I let out a yell they probably heard in Melbourne.

The trouble with being the king of the world was that I only got to rule for six minutes. Five laps later I could see Aral in my mirrors on Brabham straight. He was gaining two to three seconds a lap. I went flat out and I put in a real scorcher, and he gained a second on me, setting a new lap record.

I put in another lap at the limit and Aral gained another two seconds. Ten laps to go, three seconds lead. I could see his little red helmet in the cockpit of his red and white car. I also noticed that I was having to brake sooner and harder, and I was still arriving at the corners too fast. Then I remembered Larry Hutchins telling me that if the pedal pressures rose and the brakes got weak, it meant that the discs were overheating, and they would oxidise and wear out completely in a couple of laps. So I had to ease off.

With eight laps to go I let Marcel by on Jones straight, giving him a wave. The new World Champion. Well, I thought to myself, if you have to be second.

But I wasn't second. The brakes didn't get better, they got worse. I let Praiano go by on lap eighty. And on the last lap, Phillippe Cartablanca went by easily on Brabham straight. So I was fourth.

I cruised around for the cooling down lap, and at the end of Brabham straight eased right into the pit entry road which curved around inside the finger tip of the racecourse. On the other side of the track behind fences, the grandstands held three or four thousand people. As I drove down the pit road, a pit marshal stepped onto the pit road and motioned for me to stop, holding up his left hand.

I had the same feeling as I have when my car is out of control. Total attention, and the world goes silent. He was wearing a blue hat with a long beak to keep out the sun. Yellow curly hair sprang out of the sides and hung long down the back. He was tanned, and the yellow around his eyes was less intense. But his little potbelly still stuck out and his eyes were glittering as they fixed on me and his head shook with a high frequency vibration.

He had tried to kill me at Brands Hatch, at Hockenheim and in Hungary. He had been certain I would be destroyed when he left me in his playpen in Liverpool. Little flakes of crusted white stuck in the corners of his mouth. I didn't know what he had sprayed on me that afternoon, but it was bound to have been stronger than tranquilizer. It must have given his sanity a kick in the teeth to see that it had no effect on me.

No doubt it happened quickly, all over in, say, two seconds. But I saw it in slow motion. He was drawing a gun out of his pocket. It was a short-barrel Baretta, silver-plated, with pearl grips. A playboy's pistol. But when a gun is pointed at you in menace, the barrel grows in size until it seems as big as your head. Behind the barrel his eyes were fixed on me and I could see his trigger finger turning white at the knuckle as he squeezed the trigger.

I stomped on the accelerator and the car leapt forward with a roar. I didn't want to kill him, but I didn't want to wait around for him to kill me either. My left-front tyre went over his pointed right shoe, hitting him in the shin and throwing him backwards hard against the pavement. The shot, which I did not hear, went over my head. I kept my foot down, accelerating hard.

The front tyre rode up over his pelvis, over his rib cage and over his shoulder. Still hot from racing and coated with stone chips, broken bits of metal and glass, the rear tyre was as encrusted as one of Simon Rodea's towers. Spinning wildly, the tyre began at his toes and drew him in with tremendous force, grinding through his clothes in an instant, peeling off the skin and grinding the bones of his foot and shin, tossing his kneecap out behind him, smashing his pelvis, cracking and grinding his ribs one by one, and smashing his collarbone before spitting him out in a bloody, crumpled ball.

I spun the car around 180 degrees and stopped. I turned off the ignition, undid my seat harness and climbed out. I took off my gloves and my helmet and my balaclava and tossed them in the car. Miles Courtland was ten feet away. His eyes still glittered. He tried to push himself up and fell the few inches back onto the pavement.

From across the track a wall of people were running towards us. I turned around and headed for the pits, wiping the Vaseline from my face.

# CHAPTER THIRTY-ONE

Little riverwaves were lap lap lapping against the hull.

Lap lap lap.

A white sun twenty yards overhead made the surface of the river look like liquid heat. From time to time the air carried the whine of a mosquito or the buzz of a fly.

Nicky was stretched out on a towel on the rear deck, eyes shut, trailing her feet in the water and wearing only her mahogany tan. I was standing nude in the wheelhouse, toying with the wheel. Thinking it had been hours since I had been in the water. My watch said it had been six minutes. And thirty seconds. Nine forty-seven a.m.

Courtland was in a hospital in Melbourne that specialized in skin and bone grafts. In nine or ten months, they predicted, he would be well enough to be flown back to Britain to stand trial, although "stand" would be an exaggeration of the amount of mobility he would have by then. It would be at least a year, the doctors said, before he would be able to use crutches. So much bone, they said, had been ground away.

The Australian authorities had deferred their charges of assault with a deadly weapon, possession of same, and illegal entry into Australia so the British could prosecute him for racketeering, drug trafficking and income tax evasion. Plus any other charges their "inquiries" might turn up. Scotland Yard had sent a man to Melbourne to interview Courtland, and he had come away with pages of names, dates and places. Courtland, he said, was holding nothing back.

In the meantime Nicky and I had hired another houseboat farther up the Murray River and were drifting slowly downstream, taking two weeks to reach the sea. We would be, we thought, our own island, away from the rest of the world.

328

We were relaxed and easy with each other, old friends and new lovers. Getting up at dawn, swimming and loving. Playing and eating Nicky's fractured French–Australian cuisine. Swimming nude under the moon. But after a few lazy days Nicky started turning the radio on in the morning "to find out what's happening", she said, and the world started it's tidal pull.

As the days went by, our silences lengthened like shadows and London and Paris came up more often in our conversation. We'd done all of the things that lovers do for one another. It wasn't enough; and it was too much.

Maybe, I decided sitting in the wheelhouse, it was enough. I turned the key in the ignition and started the engine.

"Forray, what are you doing?" she called, sitting up.

"Turning around. Taking us back."

She lay back down as I wheeled the boat around, trailing her long legs in our wake.

When we had gone about an hour upriver, I heard her behind me, felt her breath on my neck. She put her hands on my chest and pulled herself tight against me, her soft body, hot from the sun, against my back. "You know, Forray," she whispered in my ear, "I am going to miss you, you horrible slippery old cod."

I called Ken from Paris, having delivered Nicky to her parents, tanned and tired from the flight, crying a little, and obviously glad to be home. No, I'd said, they were very kind, but I could not possibly stay the night.

"Where the hell have you been?" Ken's voice boomed in my ear.

"Swimming."

"I thought you'd drowned. Do you want the good news or the bad news first, old boy?"

"What news?"

"Coleman's pulled out. Alistair said no hard feelings, but now that Courtland is out of the picture his Florelle contract is all sewn up. Doesn't really need us. 'Too much money', he said."

"I hope that's the bad news."

"How clever you are. We have a new major sponsor. Major meaning some £15 million."

"At last you can afford a haircut. Who are they?"

"Now Girls. Or at least they were. Ever hear of them?"

"The multinational employment agency. Office temps."

"Absolutely. Twelve thousand million worldwide. Only no one calls them that anymore."

"Calls who what?"

"Women girls. They don't call women girls anymore. Evidently they don't like it. Besides, Now Girls doesn't fit the women executives and board members they're placing nowadays. So they're changing their name. They want us to spearhead their new corporate image. Establish the new name."

"You spearhead," I said, "I'll drive. What's their new name?"

"Women Unlimited."